AN ACCIDENTAL KISS

Quinn and Heather stood facing each other near the door. Quinn found himself looking into the softest, warmest brown eyes imaginable. They were clear, so unguarded, so beautiful. Slowly, he extended his hand. "Heather, thanks . . ."

"No thanks necessary." She smiled, drawing his gaze to her soft generous lips.

There was no mistaking what she requested from him. Friendship. And Heather would make the ideal friend. She was a warm, generous person. But she was also a very attractive woman. The male part of him wasn't about to let him forget that, either.

Quinn cradled her jawline, caressing it before tilting her face up toward his. He paused, his heart pounding like a jackhammer in his chest. He gave her time to withdraw if she wished. Yet when her lovely lips parted in surprise, desire blazed like a forest fire as he covered her mouth with his.

"Quinn," she moaned as she pulled away. What was she doing?

"I'm sorry," he said, his voice heavy with surprise and desire. "I didn't mean for that to happen," he finished, but deep in his heart, he knew he was very glad it did.

SENSUAL AND HEARTWARMING
ARABESQUE ROMANCES FEATURE
AFRICAN-AMERICAN CHARACTERS!

BEGUILED (0046, $4.99)
by Eboni Snoe
After Raquel agrees to impersonate a missing heiress for just one night, a daring abduction makes her the captive of seductive Nate Bowman. Across the exotic Caribbean seas to the perilous wilds of Central America . . . and into the savage heart of desire, Nate and Raquel play a dangerous game. But soon the masquerade will be over. And will they then lose the one thing that matters most . . . their love?

WHISPERS OF LOVE (0055, $4.99)
by Shirley Hailstock
Robyn Richards had to fake her own death, change her identity, and forever forsake her husband Grant, after testifying against a crime syndicate. But, five years later, the daughter born after her disappearance is in need of help only Grant can give. Can Robyn maintain her disguise from the ever present threat of the syndicate—and can she keep herself from falling in love all over again?

HAPPILY EVER AFTER (0064, $4.99)
In a week's time, Lauren Taylor fell madly in love with famed author Cal Samuels and impulsively agreed to be his wife. But when she abruptly left him, it was for reasons she dared not express. Five years later, Cal is back, and the flames of desire are as hot as ever, but, can they start over again and make it work this time?

Available wherever paperbacks are sold, or order direct from the Publisher. Send cover price plus 50¢ per copy for mailing and handling to Penguin USA, P.O. Box 999, c/o Dept. 17109, Bergenfield, NJ 07621. Residents of New York and Tennessee must include sales tax. DO NOT SEND CASH.

For Always

Bette Ford

PINNACLE BOOKS
WINDSOR PUBLISHING CORP.

PINNACLE BOOKS are published by

Windsor Publishing Corp.
850 Third Avenue
New York, NY 10022

The P logo Reg U.S. Pat. & TM Off. Pinnacle is a trademark of Windsor Publishing Corp.

Third Printing: April 1996

Printed in the United States of America

Dedication:
In loving memory of my dearest sister,
Mary Alice Beverly

Acknowledgments to:
My loving parents;
James and Rosena Ford
and
My special friend
Bill Demps

One

"Quinn Montgomery," the deep, masculine voice answered on the first ring.

Heather Gregory couldn't decide if she should jump for joy or scream her frustration into the telephone.

"Hello?"

It took her a full five seconds to recover enough to respond. "Good morning, Mr. Montgomery. This is Heather Gregory, your daughter's counselor at Lawrence High. I've tried to reach you for over a week. I need to see you about Cynthia. Can you come in today?"

Ever cool and efficient, Heather effectively disguised her impatience since learning of Cynthia's problem. A problem for which Heather held Mr. Montgomery almost singularly responsible. If he had just taken a little time with the troubled teenager, Heather was certain Cynthia wouldn't be in this mess.

"Today? That's impossible. What's Cynthia done now?"

"Mr. Montgomery, you don't seem to understand." Despite the abrupt nature of his speech, Heather found herself distracted by his voice. It was deep and so utterly male.

"No, Ms. Gregory, *you* don't understand. I'm extremely busy at this time, and my schedule doesn't allow any flexibility. What's the problem? I had breakfast with Cindy not an hour ago, and she didn't mention any difficulties in school."

"I'm sorry, but I can't go into the details over the phone. But I assure you, it's important."

"It will just have to wait, Ms. Gregory."

"Mr. Montgomery, I don't think you understand the urgency."

"I don't have time to argue. In fact, you're lucky to have caught me here at the office this early. I only stopped to pick up some documents."

"Mr. Montgomery—"

"I've a meeting in Southfield within the hour and appointments all afternoon. Tomorrow I'm back in court. What is it?" There was no mistaking his annoyance and impatience.

Heather was livid. Although she detested his arrogant male attitude, a feminine part of her was thoroughly aware of the sensuality in the man's voice. And that awareness annoyed the hell out of her.

"Mr. Montgomery, this is your child we're discussing. Cynthia is in trouble. I must talk with you today. Once we've talked, I'm certain you'll see why a face-to-face meeting is necessary." Heather congratulated herself for not shouting into the phone. She took a deep breath and forced herself to listen with professional calm.

"Cindy has been in and out of trouble ever since her mother died. And I might add, she has been thrown out of at least six schools during those five years. Whatever she has done now is hardly news."

"I realize Cynthia has had her share of problems. You're her parent, and I think you'll agree it's your—"

"I'll have my secretary call you and arrange an appointment. Perhaps next week?"

The line went dead and Heather stared at the phone as if it had suddenly grown arms and legs. Finally she recovered enough to replace the receiver. She couldn't remember the last time someone had made her so downright angry!

Heather pushed her shoulder-length black hair away from her face. It was styled in a profusion of very thin individual braids. Her hair was center-parted and curled around her slender shoulders. The black braids complemented her flawless, molten-gold, light brown skin and caramel-colored eyes.

She'd spent six years working in Chicago's inner-city schools. When she was ready to relocate, she'd been lucky enough to land this job back home. Although small, Lawrence was a private prestigious high school that drew a major portion of its students from the wealthy sector of the Detroit community.

Heather headed the counseling department and worked with a staff of four other counselors. The job had been a challenge since day one, and she was quite pleased with the programs she'd helped develop in her two years at Lawrence. Her pet project was expanding their scholarship program in order to increase the enrollment of minority children at Lawrence. They started with a core group of twenty students. Heather had hopes of doubling that number in the next school year.

No wonder Cynthia was in such a mess, Heather decided, tucking a stray braid behind her ear. The girl had an excellent reason to feel as if she had nowhere to turn. With a father like Quinn Montgomery, she was lucky not to be in jail or strung out on drugs, rather than being pregnant at fifteen.

According to Cynthia, after her mother's death, her father was too busy to care what happened to her. Yet in spite of her conversation with that horrid man, Heather couldn't make herself believe he didn't love his own daughter. Quinn Montgomery seemed to have been caught up in making it. He was extremely successful. He'd gotten over the death and left his daughter behind.

Heather had been working with Cynthia since she'd been admitted this past fall. Cynthia had some real problems adjusting to the new school. She was a loner. She didn't seem to want any friends and was constantly in trouble—from cheating on tests to skipping classes and disrupting classes.

"Morning, beautiful. You're early, aren't you?"

Heather turned, a welcoming smile replacing the scowl. "Hi, Charles." She greeted the extremely tall, black slender man leaning against the open door. "I had a call to make. I could ask you that same question."

Charles Randol, the basketball and tennis coach, was considered to be quite a catch. And he knew it. Yet Heather only thought of him as a good friend. They'd gone out a few times, but it was something neither of them took seriously.

"I called last night," he said, dropping into the chair in front of her desk. "Who were you with? Another date with one of those musclebound freaks your brother's forever fixing you up with?" Charles let his curious gaze run over her, his eyes finally resting on her sparkling light brown eyes.

Heather laughed. "Was it anything important?" She refused to tell him she had eaten dinner with her older sister Gwen and her husband and their two daughters. Charles was a big tease and had a memory like an elephant. She'd once foolishly admitted that she believed in love and a lifetime commitment to one special man. A dumb mistake. Charles was a skeptic by nature and cynic by design.

"Just wondering if you'd have dinner with me before the panel discussion on Friday evening?" Charles eyed her roguishly. "A little candlelight and wine. Then later—"

"Charles, please. I'm not interested and neither are you. Will you quit! It's not even eight o'clock in the morning!"

"A table for two?" he persisted.

"Thanks, but no. Why spoil a perfectly wonderful friendship?"

"Girl, your problem is you've got too much romance in your soul. Face it, doll-face, ain't no such animal as Mr. Right! You should be jumping at anything over thirty with all his own teeth. I would hate to see a foxy little number like you end up an old prune."

Heather laughed merrily. "Charles, you're growing peach fuzz between the ears. Must be old age."

"Old age! When did thirty-two become old?"

"On you, it's ancient," she teased.

"I'm serious. Sex is sex, why give it a fancy name like love? That sweet little word means s-e-x."

"We, my friend, are discussing two different topics. Sex is marvelous, perfect in fact, with the one you are in love with. Love is the key ingredient. I won't sleep with a man just because I think he's nice. Feelings are what it's about, Mr. Randol. Don't you think it's time you stopped changing women like your socks?" She wiggled her finger at him. "Afraid of commitment, aren't you, bro?"

"And you, doll-face, are too romantic for your own good!"

The bell sounded, breaking into their laughter.

"Got to run. We still on for dinner Friday night?" he asked, getting to his feet.

She rolled her eyes. "Sure. Want me to drive?"

"Nope, it's my turn. See ya." With a wave he was gone.

Charles got a kick out of teasing her about her old-fashioned ways. A smile lingered as her thoughts moved to her family. She wanted what her parents had shared for almost forty-five years. And her older sister and all four brothers had all been lucky enough to have loving relationships. Heather didn't expect a relationship to be without problems, but she knew for a fact that love was the glue that kept two people together. And she wouldn't accept less for herself. Why should she? She'd seen first-hand how long-lasting and satisfying love could be.

"Miss Gregory?" The slender black teenager tapped lightly on the open door. "You busy?" At five-seven she topped Heather by a good five inches. The lovely brown-skinned girl was extremely slender, almost to the point of appearing frail. Her black hair had been cut into a short bob.

"Morning, Cynthia. How are you?"

"I know I don't have an appointment, but it's kind of important."

"Come in, I'm free. Close the door so we can talk," Heather said, noticing the girl's unhappiness despite the bright makeup streaked flamboyantly across her delicate face. "How have you been?" Heather came around the desk, indicating the tweed settee beneath the window.

"Have you talked to Daddy? He hasn't said anything to me." She held her books tightly to her small breasts, her fingers moving nervously over the bindings. She wore an overly short denim skirt and tight yellow sweater. She had such beautiful dark gray eyes. "Maybe I've been right all along . . . he just doesn't care." A single tear slid down the soft brown cheek.

Heather sympathized with her. Even with Cynthia's defensive attitude, Heather liked her. She reminded Heather a bit of her own two nieces, who were about the same age.

"I haven't contacted you sooner because I haven't met with your father. We did talk briefly on the phone this morning. From what I gather, he's been involved in an important trial."

Cynthia rolled her eyes. "Tell me something new. It's either a new case or some trial. Look, Miss Gregory, don't sweat it. I shouldn't have bugged you about this. I'm the one who got myself into this, so I'll get myself out of it."

Heather imagined how Cynthia would handle her pregnancy, and she wasn't prepared to leave the matter up to her. If she could get the parent involved—and Heather fully intended to try—she would do so. Heather suspected it was what Cynthia really wanted. Why else would she have come to her counselor with this?

"If you're thinking about an abortion clinic, remember you've got to have a parental consent in Michigan—which is where I come into this, remember. I'll tell him for you—but you have to let him help you."

"There are places beside Michigan, Miss Gregory,"

"I know that. But it was my understanding that you wanted your father to help you decide."

"Yes," the girl said, hanging her head.

Heather let out a slow breath before she said, "Cynthia, the baby's father also has rights. You haven't told me anything about him."

"Yeah, I know."

"Does he go to school? I would be glad to talk to both of you together."

"No!" Cynthia shouted quickly. "He's not the problem. Daddy is. I already told you why I can't tell him. Daddy won't understand. He'll probably send me off to live with my mother's sister in New York. And I'll just die! I can't stand her! Aunt Joan's a fashion editor. Living with her would be worse than being sent away to boarding school again. Daddy might not want me around, but he's all the family I have! I love him!" Tears blurred her vision.

"It's going to be alright," Heather said squeezing her hand. "Let me speak to your father—then it'll be your turn to talk to him. Alright?"

"Yeah," she sniffed.

Heather handed her a tissue. "Good. Just remember, be honest with your father. Let that be your first step toward solving this problem." Heather gave her a quick hug. "Now let's talk about the baby's father?"

"We broke up." She answered sullenly. "There's nothing more to say."

"Cynthia, you're not alone," Heather said, her heart going out to the troubled girl.

"You're wrong, Miss Gregory. I've been alone since the day they put my mother in the ground."

"No, I don't believe that. And what's more I don't think you do either."

The girl sighed heavily. "I like you, Miss Gregory. I like you a lot. Not because of the usual stuff, but you listen to me and take time to talk to me. No one else even bothers to ask about what I think. If only . . ." Her voice trailed away as she brushed a tear away and dropped her chin.

Heather put her arm around Cynthia's small shoulders and held her for a time. "Better?"

"Uh-huh." Cynthia nodded.

"After I've seen your father, we'll talk again."

"Wait!" Cynthia jumped to her feet. "I think maybe we should just forget about telling him."

"Why?"

"I'm telling you to forget it. Daddy doesn't have time for me. All that matters to him is work. If I went out and killed someone, then he might notice."

Heather shook her head. "You asked me to talk to him for you. That was my promise to you. Talking is only the first step. Promise me that you won't do anything about your pregnancy until I've seen your father."

Cynthia hesitated for a moment before saying doubtfully, "I promise. Look, I'm late for class. Can I have an excuse?" Cynthia didn't seem pleased as she stood up to leave. In fact, she looked plain scared.

"Sure, whose class is it?" Heather reached for a pad and pen on the desk.

"Mr. Thomas."

Heather quickly jotted down the explanation. "Here." She tore off the top sheet. "I'll try and reach your father again a little later. If I can't get through today, give me a few more days. Alright?"

"Sure. But it won't matter to him," Cynthia said, her shoulders slumping, dejectedly.

"Adults don't always take the time to show their feelings, but that doesn't mean they don't have them." Heather walked her to the door.

Even though there were two students waiting to see her and several reports to get through, Heather telephoned Quinn Montgomery's office. His last appointment was at seven, and Heather intended to be in his office no later than seven-o-two. He would see her today or she would pitch a tent on his doorstep. The jerk!

Two

"Well, Quinn, I think that about does it," Darnell Hunter said as he brushed sandy brown hair off his forehead. Looking up from the documents they'd been reviewing, he glanced at his watch, frowning. "I've got to get out of here. I promised Elaine I would be home no later than eight thirty. It's after eight now. If I intend to stay married, I'd better get the hell out of here."

Quinn Montgomery stretched his stiff shoulders and neck, then leaned back in his chair. "Sorry it went so long. But I think both our clients will appreciate the effort, especially if we can settle out of court. Tell Elaine it's my fault."

Darnell, who'd began collecting his things, smiled easily at his longtime friend and business associate. He and Quinn were also seasonal neighbors with lakefront properties in the Traverse Bay area. "Let me get back to you in a few days with McDonnel's response. I'll be relieved if we can come to satisfactory agreement out of court. Save a lot of time and energy."

"Not getting soft are you, Darnell? It's been years since we've had an opportunity to square off opposite each other in the ultimate arena," Quinn said.

"Not since you began limiting yourself to criminal cases. Why did you take Gordon on? There's nothing challenging about this liability case, not compared to someone's life hanging in the balance."

Quinn shrugged. "No special reason. Maybe I need a change. How are the twins?"

"Great! Michigan State agrees with the boys. It's been good for my marriage, too, if you know what I mean." He raised his eyebrows. "We're able to spend quite a few uninterrupted hours together. How's Cynthia?"

Quinn's brow creased as the conversation with Heather Gregory flashed uneasily through his mind. "Between this case and the Jameison murder trial, I'm ashamed to say my daughter hasn't seen much of me. In fact, I can't remember the last time I made it home before midnight. I've got to start making time for her. She's growing up too fast."

"Things have been hard since her mother's death. For her and you. Hey, how about a game of racquetball sometime soon? It's been a while." Darnell grinned boyishly, snapping his briefcase shut. "That may not be such a great idea considering you spent two weeks in Hawaii last month. I probably don't stand a chance against you."

"My time was spent in the courtroom, Darnell, not the handball court—and I could really use a game," Quinn said as he flexed his tight muscles before pushing away from the conference table. "Time's the issue. There's never enough."

"You seeing anyone special these days?" Getting a blank look from the other man, Darnell added, "Of the long-legged variety."

Quinn poured himself a drink from the bar housed in the armoire against the far wall. It held a small refrigerator and stereo equipment and was adjacent to a gray leather sofa and matching wingback armchairs. His office was home rather than the dream home he'd purchased for Peggy ten years earlier.

He eyed the scotch in front of him with little interest. "No time, my friend. The only thing I've seen intimately is a pile of legal briefs."

"Man, you need more than that," Darnell said, tightening his tie.

Quinn shrugged but said nothing. The comment required no response. No woman could replace his wife. He'd loved Peggy with all his heart. Those feelings just didn't disappear. He still dreamt about . . . still recalled the softness of her skin, the welcoming warmth of her smile.

"Go home, Darnell. Give Elaine a kiss for me."

"Right. Call me when you can squeeze in a game," Darnell called, crossing the room.

Quinn waved briefly, moving to stand in front of the floor-to-ceiling window behind his massive desk.

Detroit's Riverfront and Windsor's twinkling lights stretched out before him—a breathtaking view, but one that didn't hold his interest. There was no point in going home now, he decided. He couldn't relax—not with several more hours of work ahead of him.

How he longed to lose himself within the warmth of a woman's soft body. There were any number of women he could call. Women always seemed to be around him. But that wouldn't be enough. The temporary physical release he found in sex would hold no true satisfaction, and emotionally he would remain unaffected. He focused on work rather than women. Quinn absently wondered when he'd lost the ability to feel and to give love.

It was during the endless twilight hours of the night that the force of his emptiness would seem to seep beneath his skin, settle in his pores until it twisted itself deep into his gut.

"Mr. Montgomery?" The silky intonation of the speaker, rather than the sharp tap on the open door, caused him to jerk toward the sound.

At thirty, Heather felt confident enough to handle just about any situation. She viewed facing Quinn Montgomery on his own turf as a necessary inconvenience.

With her professional demeanor firmly in place, Heather was nevertheless intensely aware of the man following her progress as she crossed the book-lined masculine room.

His eyes weren't black but a charcoal-gray, and they were moving leisurely over the lush curves of her petite frame. They didn't stop until he reached her high-heeled pumps. Her clothes, although feminine, tended to be well tailored and simply designed. She had worn a cream jacquard silk dress softly gathered and cinched in at her small waist with a wide cream and black woven belt. It was teamed with a black wool jacket. Her shoes and shoulder bag were black leather. Large onyx earrings trimmed with a metallic gold braid glimmered in her ears.

Heather tried to force herself not to react to the handsome man. It shouldn't matter that his deep chocolate-brown skin showed vitality despite the lateness of the hour. Nor was it of any consequence that his strong well-defined features could only be enhanced by that thick black mustache above his mouth. Heather checked her thoughts sharply—this was no blind date, this was Cynthia's father.

"Mr. Montgomery?" she repeated.

"Yes, I'm Quinn Montgomery," he said around the lump in his throat as he looked down into the most beautiful brown eyes he'd ever seen. They were the color of rich sweet caramel. They were framed by thick black lashes and complemented skin the color of molten gold. He waited expectantly for her name.

"Heather Gregory, Cynthia's high school counselor." She extended her hand.

Although he was an expert at disguising his emotions, Quinn lifted a brow in surprise and his eyes shone with admiration. The woman had guts, that was for sure—not just any woman would have the courage to show up in his office without an appointment.

His rush of concern and worry for his child wasn't evident in his face or his posture as he engulfed Heather's small fine-boned hand in a large yet surprisingly gentle masculine grip. The ache churning in his stomach had started the instant he recognized the name. For the life of him he couldn't recall the last time he had eaten. A serious mistake for a man with a temperamental ulcer.

Quickly releasing the hand of the most fascinating-looking man she'd ever laid eyes on, Heather was astonished by her profound reaction. She seemed unable to look away from his deep-set eyes. She'd never been so quickly drawn to any man—nothing like this had ever happened to her before . . . and she was at a loss to explain it. What difference did it make if his black, closely cut natural, strong, square jawline, and strong six-two frame only added to his devastating appeal?

"I realize I don't have an appointment. But as I told you on the telephone this morning, it's important that we speak as soon as possible. Can you spare me a half hour?"

"Please, sit down." He gestured toward the black leather armchairs in front of his desk.

As Heather dropped gracefully into one of them and crossed shapely legs, Quinn watched, thinking that what she lacked in height she certainly made up for in looks. This small bundle of correct professionalism possessed an earthiness, a womanliness that he found frankly appealing.

Busily trying to reclaim her equilibrium, Heather folded her trembling hands in her lap. Enough of this silliness. Quinn Montgomery might be fine, but he certainly didn't possess the qualities that she admired in a man. She detested the way he neglected his child.

"May I get you something, a drink, coffee?" he asked, while marveling at the absurdity of his position. The only female who'd engaged his interest in quite some time was broadcasting volumes of disapproval his way.

"No, thank you. I realize you're very busy, Mr. Montgomery. But Cynthia's problems can't wait for a more opportune time. She's in trouble now and needs your support."

"I deal in facts, Miss Gregory. It is Miss, isn't it?" He focused on her small ringless left hand as he waited for her response with more interest than was circumspect.

Her caramel-colored eyes mirrored her surprise, yet

her reply was immediate. "My situation has no bearing on this discussion, Mr. Montgomery—but to expedite matters the answer is yes, I'm not married. Now shall we discuss Cynthia?"

"By all means."

Amusement lit his eyes so fleetingly that Heather almost doubted what she'd seen. As he made himself comfortable behind the desk, Heather tried not to take note of the way his white shirt followed the wide planes of his deep chest, wide shoulders, and trim midsection or speculate on how nicely his navy dress slacks molded the contours of his hips and thighs.

"You've been deliberately vague about the entire situation, Miss Gregory," Quinn said. "I fail to understand the need for urgency. Nor do I understand why you couldn't go into this on the phone."

Not for a second did Heather underestimate this man's keen intelligence or his ability to assess a situation in an amazingly short period of time. He was a trained observer. There was also no question of his acclaim in his chosen career. He was a partner in one of the *most* successful law firms in the country.

No matter how direct he expected her to be, Heather wouldn't dare spring this on him. A certain degree of preparation was essential, regardless of how much she personally disagreed with his method of parenting.

"I don't know if you're aware of it, Mr. Montgomery, but I've been counseling Cynthia since she enrolled at Lawrence. She's been involved in a few minor infractions, nothing serious. Cynthia is a loner. She doesn't have any friends. When she came to me, it was because she didn't know what else to do."

Quinn's forehead was creased in a frown, but he remained silent.

"I understand both your parents and your late wife's parents are dead. And Cynthia's only female relative lives in another state, is that correct?"

"Yes, and my brother is currently serving time in Jackson State Prison. Now that we've summarized my family history, you can tell me why you're here."

Although momentarily lost for words, Heather recovered quickly. "Mr. Montgomery, I'm here on Cynthia's behalf and with her consent."

"Miss Gregory, had you considered going into law? You would make an excellent district attorney. Shall we jump to the heart of the matter. What's so important that it couldn't wait another week?" He paused, tugging at his mustache. "You see, Cynthia's not above using others to get what she wants from me. You're obviously a compassionate person. She's probably using that fact to her advantage."

"Mr. Montgomery—" Heather started.

"I don't know what terrible secret she has entrusted to you. But I do know my child."

Despite her attempts to cushion the news, Heather could see that he was losing patience, but she couldn't just dump her news in his lap.

"Cynthia's no angel. Sometimes I think she does things solely to antagonize me. She begged me not to send her away to boarding school this year. She promised faithfully that she would settle down to her studies and stay out of trouble."

Fed up with waiting, Quinn's nerves were taut with tension and his stomach ulcer felt as if it were on fire.

He forced himself to ignore the distress signals his body was sending out.

"Mr. Montgomery—"

He interrupted, his tone deliberately casual. "There's nothing, you see, that she hasn't already done to thumb her nose at my beliefs. She has already been arrested for shoplifting at the tender age of thirteen. I wouldn't be surprised if you came here to tell me she has stolen a car. So what is it now? Has she been caught drinking?"

"Cynthia is pregnant."

His facial muscles hadn't altered with the announcement. Only his grip on the arms of his chair indicated that he'd even heard what she said. The distant sound of a car horn blaring was the only distraction in the too-silent office. Quinn pushed back his chair and went over to the window. With his back to her, he stared down at the Jefferson Avenue traffic.

Heather had read Cynthia's case history and was familiar with the teenager's past exploits. But she wasn't ready for Quinn Montgomery's cool demeanor. She waited for an explosion or an oath, something to signal he loved Cynthia. But he said nothing. Not one blasted thing.

"I'm sorry. I didn't mean to just blurt it out," Heather said, hoping to spur conversation. "I'd hoped that my coming here would make it easier. But I can see now that there's no easy way."

As the minutes continued to tick away, the tiny bit of optimism Heather held inside dwindled. Heather likened him to a perfectly tuned machine which showed no emotions whatsoever.

Eventually he turned, then said coolly, "Thank you for coming, Miss Gregory. I appreciate your interest in my daughter. Cynthia's my problem, and I'll be the one to handle it."

Heather's anger was as inevitable as gasoline trailing toward a flickering flame. "What kind of father are you?" she burst out. "You spend your time locked away among these law books while your daughter's life is in shambles. And that elderly housekeeper you employ as watchdog for Cynthia is a joke. That poor woman hasn't a prayer of keeping up with a teenager. Have you tried it yourself lately? Don't bother answering. I know the answer. You can't pay somebody to love your child, Mr. Montgomery. That's *your* job."

Heather rushed on with all the finesse of a sledgehammer crashing into a brick wall. "Cynthia isn't your *problem*, she's your *daughter*. And she's carrying your first grandchild. What are you planning to do about it, Counselor?"

"I believe you've said quite enough." His voice was laced with steel as he glared at her from penetrating dark gray eyes. But Quinn wasn't really seeing Heather. He was locked in the grips of disbelief and despair. *No! Not his Cynthia, not his baby.*

By this time Heather was functioning on sheer emotion. Cynthia was her only concern. Somebody had to care, and it looked as if she was elected. As far as Quinn Montgomery was concerned—that heartless jerk—he could go jump . . .

"Do you know that she doesn't think you love her?" Heather continued. "That was why she was afraid to come to you with this. She doesn't think you care about her! I worked in the Chicago public schools for a number of years. Many of the parents I worked with were struggling each and every day just to survive. Many were substance abusers. But that didn't stop them from caring about their kids." She paused for breath, then fueled with anger, rushed on.

"I bet you don't know anything about your own child. What are her hobbies, her favorite movies, food, music? Where does she spend her time? Cynthia didn't ask to come into this world. But she's here now—so when are you going to start acting like her father?"

"My personal life is none of your business. You've done your job. Now get the hell out of here," Quinn said with icy disdain while his eyes shimmered like molten lava. Unwittingly he massaged his midsection.

Heather was thrilled by his outburst, not the least bit taken back. Instead she was flooded with an overwhelming sense of relief. Maybe she'd been wrong about him. Something in his tone told her he was experiencing emotion . . . raw, unvarnished emotions.

Quinn Montgomery must be a master at concealing his true feelings, Heather surmised. His eyes told her what he hadn't said: he genuinely cared about his daughter. Heather was just beginning to recognize that his neglect of Cynthia didn't mean he didn't love her—and that sudden awareness forced Heather to face the truth about her own high-voltage behavior.

She mentally kicked herself. She had lost it! Her carefully tendered objectivity had blown up in her face. She had done more than step over the professional line. She had torn it into little pieces and practically tried to shove it down Quinn Montgomery's arrogant throat.

Never in her career had she lost control of herself as she had done here. She had tossed away years of training and hard work in a moment of blind outrage. But why? Was it him? Was Quinn Montgomery the reason? Heather swallowed a groan of dismay. That made even less sense.

There was no valid excuse for her unprofessional behavior. And now she was going to have to admit her error and hope she hadn't completely antagonized Cynthia's father. She didn't have the luxury of pride. She had come to help Cynthia. The girl's future was at stake.

"Mr. Montgomery, I apologize. I lost my temper. I had no right to assume anything about you or your relationship with Cynthia. That's not why I came." Heather paused before saying, "I'd like to help. I have a few suggestions that may be useful. Naturally the final decision as to whether or not she keeps her baby is Cynthia's, with your input of course."

"Good night, Miss Gregory." His brow was damp with perspiration and pleated into a heavy scowl.

Heather bit her lower lip, deciding a woman would have no easy job trying to understand and care about Quinn Montgomery. He was too blasted self-contained. Where did that thought come from? Hadn't her wandering thoughts and emotions caused enough trouble for one evening?

"Are you alright? You look like you're in pain," Heather said softly.

His frown deepened as he seemed to realize he had given himself away. He shoved his hands deep into the pockets of his slacks. "My ulcer isn't your problem.

I'm lucky you haven't got me up on child neglect charges. I'll deal with my daughter, Miss Gregory. Goodbye."

Heather wasn't given a choice. But before she left she reached into her bag and extracted a business card. On the back she jotted down her home address and telephone number.

"If I can be of service, please contact me."

The front of the house was dark, only the light shining in the foyer was visible from the circular drive.

Quinn had worked hard to be able to own this particular house, on this specific street, on this block, and in this neighborhood. Indian Village—with its lavish brick homes, some of which dated back to and were even built by Detroit's elite auto barons. Indian Village represented success with a capital "S."

Quinn was that. He had made enough, invested enough, to afford the best car, the home, clothes, and acceptance. His kid had every advantage he could give her. Evidently there were some advantages he couldn't provide. He couldn't bring her mother back, that was for damn sure.

He had grown up under the care of an older brother. Their parents had been killed in a car accident when Quinn was twelve, his brother Chad, seventeen. To support himself and Quinn, Chad had taken a job in the auto factory, but soon grew bored with the work. His interest in fast cars and beautiful women led him into the drug scene. He was smart enough not to use but became deeply involved in the buying and selling of narcotics.

It wasn't until the day of Quinn's high school graduation that he'd learned how Chad had managed to keep him in school and supported them both. It was a day embedded deep inside of him—for on that very day his brother had been arrested for murder in a drug-related incident. Chad had a lot to do with Quinn's diligent pursuit of a career in criminal law.

Quinn knew what it was to be a black and male. Hell yeah, he had made it, but he hadn't done it alone. There were those who believed in him. First there'd been his parents, then he'd had Chad's help, and later Peggy. Their belief in him and unwavering love over the years had been a source of strength.

Quinn and Peggy had met at college. He'd been struggling to stay in school, working three part-time jobs while going to class full-time. She was a secretary at the financial aid office. They'd fallen in love and never looked back.

They married right after he started law school. He would have preferred to wait to marry until he was able to provide for them. Peggy argued that since she was now working as a legal secretary, there was no reason to wait. It was rough going for a while, but they had each other. Together they made their dreams come true.

As he unlocked the front door, Quinn wondered how he was going to save their baby girl. He'd tried, God only knew how he'd tried to connect with Cynthia after her mother died. Quinn himself had been hurting so bad at that time, he still wasn't sure if he would have been able to make it if he hadn't had his work. It had given him a reason to get up in the mornings. It had provided substance, something to focus on outside of the pain and emptiness. And somehow he'd lost their daughter.

"Dear God please don't let it be too late," he prayed as he walked past the neat pile of mail waiting for him on the side table in the foyer. He followed the sound of the music pulsating from the family room at the rear of the house. Quinn wasn't sure why they called it a family room. It was much too hi-tech for that label. The latest in electronic and video equipment was housed there.

A rap group flashed and danced on the huge television screen. Quinn—like most parents of teenagers—had no idea who the group was or even what they were saying, on the off chance that it was something that needed to be censored. That counselor was right. He really had no idea what was really going on with his child. He didn't even know if she was seeing a special boy.

"Daddy!" Cynthia gasped, whirling around as her father tapped her on the shoulder. "When did you get home?" She had to shout in order to be heard over the music. Her nervous glance darted to the wall clock. Nine thirty.

Quinn's patience was dangerously low. It wouldn't take much to send him over the edge. Rather than engage in a shouting match to be heard over the racket, he motioned with his hand for her to turn it down.

"You're kind of early tonight, aren't you, Daddy? I'll call Mrs. Thornton. I'm sure she has something she can make for you. Are you hungry?" Cynthia asked with a bit too much eagerness.

"Don't bother. Let Mrs. Thornton enjoy what is left of her evening. Cut that off, Cynthia. We need to talk."

He waited until the television was turned off, then pointed at the blue suede sofa behind them. "Sit."

"Is something wrong, Daddy?" Cynthia asked, smoothing the hem of her miniskirt, her eyes on her clothes and not on him.

Quinn took his time answering, loosening his tie and releasing the button at his throat. His briefcase and jacket went onto the matching suede lounger. Finally he said, "Yes . . . if what Miss Gregory told me is true, something is very wrong."

He watched a collage of emotions tremble across his daughter's lovely face, a face so like her mother's. "Oh," she said softly.

"Oh? Oh! Is that all you have to say to me? I want to hear this from your mouth. Are you pregnant?"

"Daddy, I'm not on the witness stand," she said, jutting her lower lip in much the same manner as she'd done when she was a child.

"Don't mess with me, little girl! I want an answer and I want it pretty damn quick. Did you or did you not allow some low-life asshole under your dress!"

Even though Cynthia knew it was coming, had planned it, in fact, she was terrified by the bitter disappointment she saw in her father's face. It was too late to back down now. Her affirmative response was barely audible, yet Quinn heard it.

As he looked down at his daughter, Quinn was filled with rage. His hands curled into fists, twisted tight balls of fury. He'd never struck a female in his life. Yet as he looked at the child that he and Peggy had created out of their love—and pinned so many hopes on—Quinn was frightened. He was afraid of himself and of what he might do.

"Go to your room."

Cynthia didn't argue. She didn't dare.

Three

In spite of the intense debate whirling around her, Heather found it impossible to concentrate. She and her staff had worked for months to turn this series of panel discussions on substance abuse into reality. This last one in the series was on alcoholism.

Time and time again her thoughts traveled back to the meeting she'd had with Quinn Montgomery. The conversation had been very unsettling. And now Cynthia hadn't come to school for three days. Heather was told the girl was out ill, and Heather was worried. Should she wait until after the weekend to find out what had happened? If she didn't hear from Cynthia by Tuesday, Heather wouldn't have a choice—she'd have to contact Quinn Montgomery again.

If only she could stop thinking about him. Recalling her strong reaction to the man, she was amazed at the way he had managed to throw her completely off balance. She had known him only since Tuesday, and already she thought of him as Quinn. She couldn't seem to get him out of her thoughts. She recalled little things—things she hadn't been aware of memorizing were lingering in her mind.

At the most inopportune moments, she'd remember the graceful movements of his long-fingered hands or the tilt of his head when he concentrated. His eyes had smoldered like charcoal as he watched her cross his office to introduce herself. Yet later they had glinted like metal on a frosty December morning, when she'd lost her temper and told him what she thought of him.

Never, not ever before had she lost her professionalism. Why did she let her emotions take control of the situation? It made no sense, she argued with a shake of her head.

What was it about Quinn? In the past few days she'd asked herself that question at least a thousand times. And she still didn't know the answer.

Heather had grown up in a male-dominated household. Being the youngest, she found the male of the species held little mystery. For as long as she could remember, she'd been teased, taunted, and protected. It had been exasperating at times, yet there had always been love.

Quinn wasn't like any of her brothers or her father. Nor was he like Charles or any of the men she dated. He was too self-contained. He seemed to make an art form out of guarding his innermost thoughts and feelings—which he treated as if they were live ammunition that could someday be used against him. He was an enigma. He had concealed his emotions so successfully that even his only child didn't believe he loved her.

Despite it all, Heather found him attractive . . . dangerously so. She had lain awake on more than one occasion thinking about him. He was hardly a dashing romantic figure. He was, in a nutshell, a highly paid, extremely successful, unemotional workaholic. No clear-thinking woman would become involved with such a man!

Yet Heather couldn't forget the look in his dark eyes when they met. It had sent her blood pressure soaring toward the heavens, and just for a fleeting moment, she wondered what he'd thought of her. Did he find her the least bit attractive? How could he after what she'd said to him? Frowning, Heather stared down at the tape recorder in her lap.

Why was she tormenting herself this way? Even if he wasn't off limits to her because he was Cynthia's father, she wasn't actively looking for a man. Her family, her friends, her career—plus the volunteer hours she spent working at the Crisis Prevention Center with teens who had attempted suicide, as well as being close to completing a doctorate in clinical psychology—didn't leave her much free time to worry about not having one special man in her life.

Like so many single, successful men, Quinn probably had women falling over themselves to get next to him. He was so eligible that Heather was surprised he didn't have the initials "S.B.M." (single black male) stamped on his forehead. Hard as she tried, she couldn't think of one girlfriend who'd doubt the man's eligibility.

Could that be the problem? Was a woman the reason he spent so much time away from his daughter? One special woman who insisted he spend his nights with her?

Her heart raced when she wondered if Quinn was a skilled lover? Yes, she decided instantly. He was so utterly male, it was impossible for her to believe he was anything less than a talented lover—but that didn't mean he was capable of giving of himself. Could a woman ever hope to know the inner man, the one he kept under lock and key?

Enthusiastic clapping abruptly brought Heather back to the conference on alcholism. As the clapping ended, it galled her that she had spent so much of this special session focused on Quinn. He was not her problem, Cynthia was.

Heather threaded her way through the crowd in the school gymnasium in order to offer her personal thanks to the distinguished panelists. They included two of her father's colleagues from Wayne State University and several well-known community leaders. She congratulated her counseling staff as well.

A local disc jockey was setting up his turntables, speakers, and lighting on the rear platform. A school dance had been planned immediately following the discussion.

"Ready?" Charles asked, just as the pulsating beat of a hard rock tune poured out of the loudspeakers. Teenagers far outnumbered the adults. A handful of the teaching staff remained to act as chaperones.

"Don't you want to stay and get it on?" Heather teased.

Charles scowled. "This isn't my scene. Mrs. Silvers seems to have everything under control." Taking her arm, he led her toward the exit. "Besides—" he smiled, his first to Heather's recollection for the evening, "—our leaving will give the crowd something to talk about. The entire school thinks we're lovers."

Heather shrugged, glad to see his sense of humor

emerging. The air outside was heavy with the scent of lush blooms, but it was still a bit cool for the middle of May.

"Not shocked or horrified?" Charles teased.

"Nope. Why can't men and women be friends? There isn't a law against it, is there?"

He chuckled, unlocking the passenger door. He had given her a ride into work that morning and then shared a meal before the panel discussion.

Charles had been unusually self-absorbed all day. Heather hadn't a clue as to what had him so preoccupied. Yet she knew something definitely was bothering him.

"Heard from the garage?" he asked, after sliding behind the wheel.

Heather's ancient Firebird had refused to start that morning.

"Carburetor. It won't be ready until tomorrow. I hope that means morning. I don't want to be without a car the entire weekend."

"Tough luck," Charles whistled, putting on the headlights. "A new carburetor can be pricey."

"Don't I know it."

"What do you have on for tomorrow?"

"I'd planned on taking my nieces to the Hispanic ethnic festival at Hart Plaza and shopping for summer clothes. Oh, turn that up! I love that old song."

Charles complied.

"To be young, gifted and black," Heather sang loudly, clapping in time to the music.

Charles laughed, raising the volume higher on the car radio. "What do you know about Nina Simone? That song was way before your time."

Heather stopped singing long enough to say "Uh-uh. You forget I have four older brothers and a sister. Mark, the oldest boy, used to eat and sleep with his guitar. To be . . ."

The lively music had served to lighten the mood some-what, even though Charles still seemed to be brooding after the song ended.

"No date?" he asked.

"Yeah, with Max."

"That football bean-head your brother introduced you to? Come on, Heather. His brains are in his biceps. Admit it, the only reason you're going out with him is because you feel sorry for the guy. Who ever heard of a million-aire who can't get a date?"

Heather giggled in spite of herself. "You've got some nerve! Did I mention where I thought your Beverly's brains are located? Tell you what, I won't critique your dates if you extend me the same courtesy."

"Very funny. Tell me this, smart mouth, how long are you going to save it for Mr. Right? You've been going out with yo-yos like Max for years. I know and you know, the dude is safe and b-o-r-i-n-g. I said it before and I'll say it again—you, my friend, wouldn't know Mr. Right if he ran you over with a truck."

Heather knew Charles was deliberately trying to get a rise out of her and had nearly managed it. No matter how dear he was, she wasn't about to get into an ar-gument with him just to make him feel better. Then she blinked as Quinn's image appeared in her mind and faded just as quickly. Disturbed, she decided to change the subject. "I'm so glad the panel discussions worked out so well. But I swear—it seems as if I've been working on this project half my life. Do you think they went well?"

"Absolutely. Great job, kiddo." Charles was silent for some time, eventually saying, "I'm sorry to be so hard on you. You know I love you, don't you, sweet pea?"

Heather grimaced at the endearment, one of his favorites. "The feeling is mutual. So tell me, what's the matter, hmmm?"

"Nothing. Everything is great—couldn't be better. I think I'll call brainy Beverly for a late supper tonight. Does that sound like I have a problem?"

Heather swallowed her laughter. She didn't dare say what she was thinking.

"Have you spoken to Diane?" Charles asked.

"No, why do you ask?"

"Curious that's all," he said, concentrating on the road for a time. Then he asked tightly, "Why didn't she show tonight? You would think the little flirt could postpone one of her endless string of dates for the sake of old Lawrence High. I know she's your best friend. But even you have to admit, Heather, she thinks she's God's gift to mankind. Black men beware, Queen Diane is on the prowl! Only problem is she has absolutely no interest in marriage. How can you two be friends? You're as much alike as a dolphin and a shark."

"So that's what's bothering you," Heather said as he turned right onto her tree-lined street.

"She was supposed to be there! She's part of the faculty." Having come to a stop along the circular drive in front of her condominium, he glared at Heather. His black brows were drawn harshly together. It was a dark, cloudy night. Neither noticed the sleek black Mercedes parked a few yards away or the man at the wheel.

Heather couldn't remember seeing Charles so upset. She lifted her hand to soothingly stroke his cheek. "Don't do this to yourself. I'm certain there's a simple explanation as to why Diane couldn't be there tonight. She's a responsible person. She takes her career seriously."

Diane Rivers, a tall, vivacious beauty, taught business and computer classes at the high school. She and Heather were roommates at Central State and had been good friends ever since.

The two career-minded women were alike in many ways, except for one major difference. Heather dated just as often as Diane, but Heather didn't sleep around. She hoped to find a lasting relationship while Diane cherished her freedom and refused to even consider becoming emotionally dependent on a man.

"She's a man-hungry piranha!" Charles said tightly, infuriated by his lack of control. Heather's concern was evident. He leaned forward and kissed her. "You're my best buddy."

Heather sighed. She was beginning to feel like the cream in a sandwich cookie, smack in the middle of their problems. Diane and Charles had dated for a while. And then they stopped abruptly with no explanation from either of them. Lately they spent their time sparring like two prizefighters. And Heather was getting tired of it, especially since they complained about each other to her.

"Chuck, isn't it time you told her you want more from her than a casual relationship?" Heather—privy to both their secrets—found it frustrating not to be able to offer an explanation. Diane didn't want to end up like her mother, divorced four times and looking for husband number five. But Heather knew Diane cared for Charles.

"Do I look like a fool to you? She isn't about to add my name to her extremely long list of conquests. When I found myself becoming too involved, I chose to bow out."

"Sweetheart, you both have lists. And if we were to be so indelicate as to place them end to end, they would no doubt reach Montreal." Heather laughed, saying, "Thanks for the ride. I'll see you Monday. Cheer up Sugar dumplin', and have a good weekend. Oh, give Beverly my love."

She walked gracefully up the walk. She'd chosen her two bedroom condominium with care and was especially pleased with it. It was in the Lafayette Park area, close to her job and easily accessible to Greektown and Renaissance Center shopping areas.

Heather had just hung her jacket in the hall closet when the doorbell chimed. She opened the door without hesitation. "What did you forget?"

But it wasn't Charles on the other side. Her eyes widened at the sight of Quinn Montgomery standing beneath the glow of the outside lamp. The business suit had been replaced by a snug-fitting black knit shirt and slim black jeans. A black leather jacket was thrown over one broad shoulder. He exuded a raw masculinity.

"Do you always open your door without checking?"

"Criminals don't generally ring the bell, do they, Counselor?"

An appreciative gleam filled Quinn's charcoal-gray eyes as he silently acknowledged her answer. His eyes took in the way her silk jersey dress hugged the fullness of her breasts, smoothed over her tiny waist and settled sweetly around her shapely hips and thighs. She was every bit as lovely as he remembered.

"I know it's late, but may I come in?" Quinn asked. "I need your help." It was difficult for him to make that admission, and he knew he would be lucky if she didn't turn him down flat.

She stepped back, allowing him to enter. Her curled braids swung around her shoulders as she led the way down a short entrance hall, past the archway into the living room, carpeted in a sky-blue shag. Heather switched on cream porcelain table lamps.

Quinn's gaze traveled along the L-shaped room done in shades of vibrant blues, peach, and touches of ivory. Floor-to-ceiling shelves filled with books lined the short wall beside the archway, a Queen Anne desk, brass floor lamp, and oak rocker filled the cozy corner. Her home generated warmth and comfort.

Quinn tossed his coat over the back of the rocker.

"What's happened?" Heather asked.

"Nothing. That's the problem." His lips thinned beneath the veil of his thick moustache.

Quinn was a man who knew his own strengths. It took skill to sway reluctant judges or undecided jurors into accepting his view as sound. He knew he had a lot going for himself. He was both well read and able to intellectually discuss a wide range of topics. But when it came to expressing what was going on inside of himself, he was hopelessly inept.

It had taken him a while to cool down. By then, when he'd tried to talk to his daughter, he'd failed. Each new attempt left him feeling even more helpless, impatient, and frustrated. They'd also left Cynthia in tears, stubbornly insisting that he didn't love her. Cynthia refused to discuss her condition with him. Now what was he supposed to do?

Cynthia was a part of him. He loved her. She meant the world to him. But somehow he'd failed her. When it came down to expressing his innermost feelings, the words never came. Cynthia was his daughter—why did he have to explain himself to her? He had done his best for her, given her everything she wanted in order to show her how he felt. He wanted to make her happy, but something had gone very wrong. Cynthia was why he'd come tonight. How in the world was he going to explain all that to this beautiful woman?

Did nerves account for the way his heart was pounding, beating erratically in his chest? Who was he trying to fool? He was sexually attracted to Heather. In his opinion, Heather was exceptionally easy on the eyes. Did she have to be so pretty? Just looking at the rich creamy texture of her golden-colored skin and the generous curves of her raspberry-tinted lips with that tantalizing mole in the corner of her mouth made him want to taste her lips. But it was more than her beauty that sparked his interest. She was a highly intelligent, gutsy lady. She wasn't easily intimidated.

Heather was busily trying to settle her own nerves. She motioned with her hand, "Sit down, won't you," indicating the bright, robin-blue circular sofa accented with peach throw pillows. She sat on one end of the three-piece sectional, automatically kicking off her high-heeled black pumps and curling her legs beneath her.

Quinn remained standing, his face grim. "I owe you

an apology. I was wrong the other day. Logically I recognized you were attempting to explain a difficult situation. It's time I set the record straight. I do appreciate your interest in my daughter."

Heather looked into his deep-set eyes and was touched by the sincerity she saw there.

"Apology accepted. Please, call me Heather, and won't you sit down?"

If he noticed the unsteady tremor in her voice, he ignored it as he settled himself on the far edge of the sofa.

"I called before showing up on your doorstep. You weren't home, so I decided to come by and wait."

"Wait? Then you saw—"

"You kissing your friend good night. I thought for a moment I might have to wait until morning. Poor guy, or are you expecting him later?" Quinn found himself asking, knowing doggone well he was out of line.

"I'm sure you aren't really interested in my love life, so shall we limit ourselves to Cynthia?" Her eyes sparkled like caramel-colored diamonds.

"I wouldn't want my being here to become a problem for you." Quinn could see that he had angered her. But why? There was nothing unusual about the question, even if it was a bit personal. After all, they were both adults.

"Are you always so blunt?" Her delicately shaped brows came together in a frown at the same time a blush of color heated her cheeks.

"Yes, I find it saves time." Quinn smiled for the first time.

His lower lip was slightly fuller than the top. How had she failed to notice? Warning signs flew inside her head.

Look out, the man could be charming. It meant he was
especially dangerous for this woman's peace of mind.

Heather inhaled sharply, answering in spite of her better judgment. "Charles is my friend, not my lover. And
no, I'm not expecting anyone."

He nodded, shocked by his own keen interest.

Taking a deep breath, she said, "Now tell me about
Cynthia."

Four

"She won't talk to me," he said gruffly.

"I don't understand."

"What's there to understand? My daughter refuses to discuss her pregnancy with me."

"But that doesn't make sense. When I spoke to Cynthia the other day she wanted you to know about her condition. And now you tell me she won't talk to you?"

Getting to his feet, he said, "Are you deliberately trying to provoke me? If you are, you have my congratulations, for you've done a remarkable job." Quinn shoved his hands into his jeans pockets, unwittingly drawing her eyes to the well-defined muscles of his thighs. He felt so blasted powerless . . . frustrated.

"I'm trying to figure out what brought about this sudden change in Cynthia," Heather said softly.

The problem wasn't Heather. It was him. He was the one on edge. He didn't have the vaguest idea how to help his daughter.

Quinn went over to the redbrick fireplace. He stood with his back to her, staring at the landscape hanging above the mantel. Mist rolling in against a backdrop of a pine forest, very earthy, sensual.

He glanced at Heather from over the width of a shoulder. "Can I have a drink? Scotch if you have it." The liquor would probably upset his stomach, making his ulcer wake up and take notice.

"Don't you mean milk?" Heather said lightly.

Quinn was so startled that he turned back into the room. He laughed outright, responding to her playfulness. He couldn't remember the last time he'd felt lighthearted enough to laugh at anything, especially himself.

"You have a beautiful smile," he said grinning boyishly. His dark eyes lingered on the seductive curve of her mouth, the enticing mole near the corner. As Heather's lashes flickered down, Quinn followed the journey, marveling at the delicacy of the movement.

"Thank you. Shall we compromise with herbal tea?" She swung her legs down but didn't bother with shoes. Her toes sank into the carpet.

The dining area was at the base of the L-shaped room and extended into the kitchen. The glass rear wall opened onto a small patio.

Heather worked quickly and efficiently in the small bright room. The walls were papered in a cheery peach print. Warmth was reflected everywhere he looked. A half-wall topped by a gleaming Formica counter served as a breakfast bar.

"You're well organized," Quinn noted.

"It's not unusual for a woman to manage both a career and home successfully, Mr. Montgomery," Heather said while preparing a tray, adding servings of deep-dish peach cobbler.

"Call me Quinn," he urged, then smiled at her nod of agreement.

"So many women I know professionally would be insulted if asked to make a cup of coffee, while some of the wives of my colleagues could prepare a ten-course banquet for the city council without batting an eyelash," Quinn remarked. "I've met only one woman who could shine in both areas."

"What about your wife? In which category did you place her, Counselor?"

"Peggy stopped working as a legal secretary once I graduated from law school and could support us. Yes, she was that single exception. She would have had a marvelous meal waiting after typing briefs and answering the phone all day. She was one of a kind." He stopped, amazed by his candor. He never talked about Peggy, not ever. His thoughts of her usually came at night. The memories often kept him awake. Would he ever stop missing her . . . ever stop wondering if he had done right by her?

Heather watched pain dart across his features.

"Did you make that delicious looking cobbler?" he asked.

"Tell me, Mr. Mont—I mean Quinn—can you prepare a sweet potato pie, a pound cake?" Heather returned.

"Me?" His eyebrows shot up as if she'd asked him for a detailed report on the secret witness he'd managed to convince to testify in his next court case.

She laughed. "My dad made the cobbler. He—" she placed special emphasis on the word, "—has always been the chef in our family, even before he cut back on his classes at the university. He's a professor in the psychology department at Wayne State. Long ago, my mother was one of his students. A very romantic story—remind me to tell you about it someday. By the way three of my four older brothers are better cooks than my sister or myself. The last is hopeless in the kitchen."

Their laughter flowed around the cozy room. "Sounds like you have a charming family. Are you on the low end of the totem pole?"

Heather laughed. "You could say that. I'm the runt. I was always so eager to grow up. I got so tired of being bossed around."

"Here, let me carry that." He took the tray from her hands. "Fit punishment for being an out and out chauvinist." Quinn winked at her, unaware of the sudden heat he ignited within Heather.

Once the tray was placed on the coffee table in front of the sofa, Heather did the honors. Quinn relaxed, enjoying her natural grace. It was part of his job to recognize truth from lies and to be able to read people. Heather was genuine—and, God help him, she was exquisitely attractive. Not only that, but she was congenial, honest, direct, and compassionate.

Was it any wonder that Cynthia had responded to this woman's warmth? The bottom line was his daughter trusted Heather and so did Quinn. In fact, he was banking on her compassion, hoping for all he was worth that her heart was big enough to include his baby girl. With her help he might be able to reach Cynthia before it was too late.

"Quinn, why hasn't Cynthia been to school?"

Tension seemed to block his vocal cords as he focused on putting his feelings into words. Finally he said, "She's locked herself in her room. She only comes out when

I'm not home. She won't talk to me," Quinn said haggardly. "You've every right to say I told you so."

Heather could never do that. "At least you tried."

"Instead of talking to her, I yelled at her. I blew it! I was furious. I thought I might strike her . . . something I've never even considered before. I ended up sending her to her room." His hand shook so that he put down the mug he'd been holding.

"You had every right to be upset. You're involved in an emotionally volatile situation. Many people show anger when they're hurt or disappointed."

"My wife would have known what to do. But then, if Peggy were alive none of this would have happened." Instantly he wished he could retract the statement. He couldn't believe he'd said it aloud.

"You loved your wife very much," Heather said softly, seeing that he missed her still—and for some reason the realization made her extremely sad. "Does it hurt to talk about her?"

"Yes," he said, swallowing with difficulty. "How did you know?"

"You're forgetting my training involves good listening skills, looking beyond what's said, just as yours does."

He nodded, feeling very uncomfortable with the conversation. He was used to his thoughts remaining private.

"So tell me how I can help Cynthia. What is it you want me to do?"

"Heather, talk to her, please. I've got to find out if she has been taken care of. If she hasn't been to a doctor, would you arrange an appointment with your own gynecologist?" He scowled. "She bolted her bedroom door when I threatened to call Bob Grant, our family doctor."

"I see," she said, visualizing a scene that left the father infuriated and the child in tears.

"We need to find a solution. But how can I do that when I still can't get a straight answer out of her?"

"I agree. But Quinn, we don't want to scare Cynthia—perhaps frighten her into doing something she might come to regret."

As he ran a hand over his close-cut natural, the tremor was embarrassingly apparent. Just what in the hell *was* the right answer? "She can't get an abortion in Michigan without my consent or a judicial bypass."

"That's right. But there are other states beside Michigan," Heather repeated Cynthia's words.

Quinn's brows formed a straight fierce line, he pulled absently at his mustache. He was so long in responding that she said his name once more.

"There's no easy way out of this. I don't want Cynthia to have an abortion. But she's too young to be a mother and certainly not a wife."

Heather's heart went out to him. She recognized the very real pain she saw in his deep-set eyes and heard in his voice. She'd been so wrong about him. He wasn't the ogre she had thought.

"Well, we can't settle this tonight. Given time, you'll find a way to help Cynthia decide what to do. I want you to know I believe the ultimate decision should be Cynthia's. We're discussing her baby and her body and her life. Neither one of us can live her life for her." Heather watched his lips thin, but he didn't comment. "Quinn, I think it will be your love and support that will make all the difference to her."

"I hope so," he said, clinging to the thought and

warmed by her faith in him. His child's life seemed to be teetering on the verge of collapse.

"Cynthia's a good kid."

"Yeah, I think so, too. What do you know about the boy?"

"Nothing. Cynthia has kept his identity a secret."

"What?"

"Unfortunately, it happens. The girls are so in love with the guys that they try to protect them."

"Is that what you think she's doing?"

"Well, I don't know for sure. But I've asked her about him, and she never wants to talk about him."

"Does he go to Lawrence? Has she been seen with one boy around the school?"

"I'm sorry, but I don't know."

Quinn swore under his breath, unable to fully vent his frustration. He felt like slamming his fist against something, but destroying Heather's wall wouldn't change a blasted thing. His fifteen-year-old daughter would still be pregnant.

He sighed. "I realize I'm lucky you didn't slam the door in my face. I deserved it after the other night."

"We both have reason to regret our behavior." Heather put her hand over his where it rested on his thigh, unmindful of the intimacy of the action. "Let's forget it. I'm not proud of myself, either. And I'll do whatever I can to help."

Quinn stared at the small soft hand on his leg, amazed by the sheer volume of heat it generated. When he spoke his voice was a bit huskier than normal. "Thanks."

Heather withdrew her hand, suddenly realizing how

the action could easily be misinterpreted as being intimate, rather than comforting as she intended.

"I'm sure this is just a job to you, but Cynthia likes you and cares about you."

"I'm glad. I care for Cynthia. By the way—it stopped being just a job when I lost my temper the other night. Can't you use a friend?" Her smile was contagious.

His eyes were drawn to her soft full mouth, in spite of his better judgment. Intimacy between them wasn't possible. It would only complicate an already difficult situation. An inner voice commanded he take what the lady was offering and say thank you.

"Always," he said, speculating on the challenge. He surged to his feet. "I really should get out of here. I've imposed on you long enough. When can you talk to Cynthia?"

Heather stood also. "Is tomorrow morning too soon? Around eleven? I'm taking my two nieces downtown to the ethnic festival and shopping. They're about the same age as Cynthia. We should be able to talk then." She'd walked with him into the entrance hall. "What do you think?"

"Sounds fine. I appreciate what you're doing."

He marveled at how tiny she was. She barely reached his shoulder without the benefit of those stilts she called shoes. She might be a small woman, but there was no doubt that she was curved in all the right places. "Do you have a pen? I'll give you the address."

"Just a second."

Masculine eyes followed her with appreciation. Not only did she look good, she moved beautifully.

Busy wrestling with her heightened awareness of this

so-silent self-contained man, it took her longer than necessary to locate the pad and pen. Both were in their usual place on her desk. She was breathless as she handed him the writing tools.

"Will you be home in the afternoon? Around four thirty? I think we should talk after I've spoken with Cynthia."

"I've a partners meeting in the morning and paperwork to finish at the office. But I'll make a point to get back as quickly as I can."

They stood facing each other near the door. Quinn had shrugged into his jacket before jotting down the information she needed. When he raised his head, he found himself staring into the softest, warmest brown eyes imaginable. They were clear, so unguarded, so beautiful. Slowly he extended his hand. "Heather, thanks . . ."

"No thanks necessary." She smiled, drawing his gaze to her soft generous lips.

They were close—close enough for him to enjoy her woman scent. No perfume had ever been manufactured that could surpass her natural fragrance.

Did she taste as good as she smelled? Where did that thought come from? Had he been too long without a woman? Guilt had kept him celibate for too damn long. He couldn't sleep with a woman without feeling as if he were betraying his wife. It didn't make sense, but he couldn't seem to help it.

There was no mistaking what she requested from him. *Friendship.* And Heather would make the ideal friend. She was a warm, generous person. But she was also a very attractive woman. The male part of him wasn't about to let him forget that, either.

The problem came when he returned the pad and pen. The moment his fingers glided over her hand, his common sense crumpled like dry leaves in the wind. But it was the movement of her pink tongue moistening dry lips which proved too much of a temptation.

Quinn cradled her jawline, caressing it before tilting her face up toward his. He paused, his heart pounding like a jackhammer in his chest. He gave her time to withdraw if she wished. Yet when her lovely lips parted in surprise, desire blazed like a forest fire as he covered her mouth with his.

Quinn groaned his pleasure, his mouth moving insistently, yet seductively over hers.

Like a cold pat of butter in a hot pan, Heather sizzled, melting against Quinn. The cushiony softness of her breasts rested on his chest.

"No—" she gasped, suddenly realizing what she was doing. She pushed away from him.

Her eyes were wide pools, mirroring her confusion. Her mouth was ripe like a luscious strawberry, swollen from his attention. Her full breasts lifted with each breath she took, her nipples clearly outlined. She was at once the picture of feminine titillation and dismay.

"I didn't mean for that to happen," he said, his voice heavy with surprise and desire. "Good night." The door clicked softly behind him.

Five

"Stupid!" Heather admonished herself, squinting into the brilliance of the midmorning sun. She'd forgotten her sunglasses, and she was too far from home to turn back now. The sunglasses were only one of the half dozen small things that had gone wrong that day. Burnt bacon, lumpy grits, and a cut finger were not responsible for the tension headache forming above her right eye. Quinn Montgomery was the reason. She'd actually dreamed about the man.

Heather hadn't had that particular dream in years. When she was a girl, she used to have it often. But nowadays it was a bit of sweetness that carried over from her childhood. Her siblings had often teased her about it, especially her sister Gwen—but Heather hadn't minded. The dream was too special to be ignored. As silly as it had been, it gradually became a part of her.

Was she eleven or twelve when she first dreamed of her wedding day? It was a beautiful day, warm and sunny. In the dream she wore her mother's lace and ivory satin wedding gown. All of her family was present, even her great-aunt Naomi, who never seemed to stop talking and always called her father "boy." Everything was perfect.

Her handsome brothers smiled with love in their eyes.
She'd walked down the aisle on her dad's arm.

But last night's dream was different. When she reached
the floral-covered archway and her groom clasped her
hand with his strong fingers, his face was clear. It wasn't
shrouded in a heavy gray cloud as it had always been
before. And she hadn't awakened with the customary
smile on her face.

Quinn Montgomery had been in her dream. *Quinn!*
Heather had awakened instantly, trembling. She'd been
none too happy as she lay awake for hours, unable to go
back to sleep or push Quinn out of her thoughts.

As Heather peered around the car's sun visor, she wondered if she were falling for the parent of one of her
counselees. She prided herself on her professional demeanor. Damn, she knew better! She'd worked too long
and too hard to get where she was today. She couldn't
afford to jeopardize her career over a man.

Even if all things were considered favorable, the man
was just not right for her. The fact that he was a widower should have been a deterrent. He obviously hadn't
gotten over the loss of his wife. Had she forgotten that
because he considered his professional life more important than his child, Cynthia's world was coming apart?
That fact alone was a heavy negative as far as she was
concerned.

Face it, girl, Heather mused, Quinn Montgomery was
too downright attractive for his own good. With his
looks and his standing in the black community, he probably had women falling all over themselves to get next
to him.

Now if he would be so kind as to keep his sexy full

lips to himself, she wouldn't have a problem. But last night when he took her into his arms, it had taken forever before she had the good sense to push him away. How could she have been so reckless?

Quinn—an extremely articulate lawyer—was unable to express his innermost emotions. His determination to get help for his daughter had softened Heather's earlier view of him and touched her heart.

And last night, as his head had begun its descent, her tingles of glorious expectation had begun. He had hesitated a split second before his mouth had covered hers, and she thought for sure her heart had stopped. If there had been even a tiny bit of resistance within her, it vanished into thin air, leaving her unprotected and open to him. Her bones had seemed to liquefy as she welcomed his kiss and melted into his arms. He'd been like a magnetic field, irresistibly drawing her to him.

Why him? What made him so different? Never before had a man's kiss affected her so strongly or had his mouth aroused her so quickly, so effortlessly. She'd had no difficulty saying no to other men. Her ex-fiancé Kenneth had been the only man she'd made love with. The experience was such a disappointment it was best forgotten. The problem had not been with Kenneth, but with her. Heather had not been in love with him.

Quinn . . . Was it her imagination or had he cradled her tenderly against his chest? And why had he kissed her? Had she inadvertently encouraged his attention when she'd innocently touched his hand as they sat together on the sofa?

What was wrong with her? She hardly knew the man.

She didn't understand her response to him. By the time she turned off Jefferson Avenue toward Indian Village, Heather decided it was time to forget her childhood dream and Quinn's kiss. She was here to help Cynthia.

The house number was mounted on a high wrought iron gate, she noted as she turned onto the private drive in one of Detroit's most exclusive districts.

Cynthia was ready and waiting in front of the large tree-shrouded house. "Hi," the girl said tightly. Her high cheekbones were streaked with crimson blush while her full lips were outlined in black and painted a wild cherry. Makeup couldn't conceal the unhappiness in her eyes. Baggy striped bib overalls hung on her slim frame. A single strap held them in place and a dotted blue and pink T-shirt completed the look. Her thick black hair had been brushed behind her ears and held away from her face with a wide pink headband.

"Hi, yourself," Heather said with a smile. "How are you today?"

Cynthia mumbled a response, taking an exorbitant amount of interest in fastening her seat belt.

Heather maneuvered her car back onto the main road before saying, "I'm glad you could come. My nieces are about your age. Ericia is sixteen and Angela fourteen."

"Miss Gregory, I didn't ask to come. Daddy didn't give me an out. It was either come with you or go with him to see Dr. Bob."

"Well, we're going to have a fun day," Heather encouraged, hiding her annoyance with Quinn's high-handed methods. He certainly hadn't helped the situation. An uncooperative, resentful teenager was all she needed right now. "You can call me Heather since we're away from school."

Suddenly overwhelmed by feelings of betrayal and despair, Cynthia blurted, "I thought you were my friend! I thought I could trust you!"

"Hey, wait a second." Heather pulled over to the side of the street. "You're forgetting something, aren't you? You asked me to speak to your father for you. And that's what I did," she remarked gently as she turned to the unhappy girl. Tears pooled in the girl's large charcoal-gray eyes. Quinn's eyes, Heather caught herself thinking. "That's what you said you wanted, remember? Cynthia, what went wrong?"

With her shoulders hunched, Cynthia hung her head while tears trailed down her soft brown face. Yes, it was what she thought she had wanted, but she wasn't sure anymore. She couldn't tell Heather how rejected and disappointed she was because of it. She felt alone . . . so alone.

"Come here, honey," Heather said, opening her arms. The storm clouds broke the instant Cynthia felt Heather's comforting warmth. "Now, now," Heather said, her hand moved soothingly over the girl's soft black curls. Her permed hair was very thick and lustrous. Heather rocked her until her sobs eased and turned to hiccups. "Better?" Heather handed her a tissue. "Sometimes a good cry is just what one needs. It always helps me."

"You?" Cynthia said, busy blowing her nose and wiping her face.

"Sure. Did you think only kids have problems? Everyone hurts and feels pain from time to time. Everyone cries, even strong men like your dad."

"No way! He doesn't care about anything but his law practice."

"Your father has feelings, too, honey."

"Not him," she denied vehemently, recalling to Heather how he acted when her mother died. He'd cut himself off from her. It was like she no longer mattered to him, as if she wasn't hurting, too. "He didn't shed one tear even when my mama died," she ended bitterly, her eyes wide with pain. "Not once has he ever told me he loved either one of us. Not once!"

"Just because he didn't say it doesn't mean he doesn't feel it. Many men keep their feelings hidden . . . unfortunately," Heather explained, disturbed by her own compelling need to defend Quinn.

Both he and Cynthia had found a place in Heather's tender heart, even though she knew she had no right to feel anything for the man. Like so many young girls, Cynthia was going to have a baby while she was still just a baby herself. Quinn was a master at concealing his emotions. Apparently last night he had been desperate for Heather's help, which explained why she'd been able to witness a bit of the turbulent emotions churning inside him.

"Whose side are you on?" Cynthia snapped, unable to bear Heather's defense of her father.

"Your side. But that doesn't mean I'm against your father. Tell me what happened after you told him you were pregnant?"

"He sent me to my room. Later, he tried to ask me a bunch of stupid questions. He didn't do anything I thought he would. Everything went wrong. He doesn't care."

"Honey, how did you expect him to react?"

"I don't know what I—" She ended abruptly, turning her face away but not before Heather saw a single tear trickling down to her chin and drop into her lap.

"Was it what he said or was it something he didn't say that upset you so much?"

Cynthia pushed out her bottom lip. "It doesn't matter." Nothing was going the way she had hoped . . . nothing. It was all such a mess.

"But it does matter. You told me you wanted to talk to him about your pregnancy. Why didn't you?"

"I guess I just freaked," Cynthia insisted unhappily. "Then later he started cross-examining me like I was on the witness stand. It got me so mad. I just couldn't handle it, so I stayed in my room the rest of the week."

"He wants to help you, honey. He's your father and he loves you."

"How many times do I have to tell you? He doesn't love me," she shouted. "I'm just a reminder of my mother. I look a lot like her."

"Then she must have been very beautiful," Heather said, putting the car into gear. "You and your dad need to talk. Start by telling him how you really feel, then listen to what he has to say."

Cynthia pursed her lips and said, "Yeah, sure." Her talks with her father always started and ended with him lecturing her on her attitude and her behavior.

Heather squeezed the girl's hand before returning both of hers to the steering column. "Did you at least tell your dad about the baby's father?"

"So he can have him arrested? No way." Cynthia folded her arms across her small breasts. She didn't want to talk about this one minute more. "Tell me about your nieces. What did you say their names were?"

"A change in topic is not going to solve anything, Cynthia," Heather said firmly. "You have some decisions to make about the future. And it can't be put off much longer. From what you've told me, I guess you're about two months along. Right?"

"Mmmm," Cynthia mumbled, feeling as if she were being backed into a corner.

"You're not alone in this. You have the baby's father, me, and your own father."

"Look, can't we talk about something else?"

"Sure. But you should know that your dad asked me to make an appointment for you to see my gynecologist. I think you'll like Dr. Burnette. She's understanding, easy to talk to." Heather didn't see Cynthia's complexion take on a gray tint as she slowed the car and entered the residential area. "I made your appointment for Monday. I plan to go with you, so there's no need for you to worry." At Cynthia's silence, Heather decided to change subjects.

"I try to take my nieces out at least once a month," Heather continued in a sing-song voice. "We always have a good time." She turned into the drive of a large two-story brick home. "Their mother Gwen is my older and only sister. However I come from a large family—I have four older brothers."

"Wow! Is your sister like you?" Cynthia asked a bit anxiously while making no move to open the car door as she stared at the house.

"Some folks say we could be twins. They're wrong. I'm taller by a full two inches," Heather joked, grabbing her purse and pocketing her keys. "I'm sure you'll like Gwen and the girls."

"What if they don't like me?" Cynthia held back, not budging even though Heather waited on the pavement.

"What's not to like? Be yourself, Cynthia. No one can ask for more." Linking arms with the girl, the two approached the large Tudor home. "Relax, I'm right beside you."

The door opened before they rang the bell.

"The cavalry! Hallelujah!," Gwendolyn Carmichael exclaimed before giving her sister a big hug. "Take 'em out of here. They're driving me crazy. They've been at it all morning over some fool boy. I can't get a thing done," she complained, a sketch pad in one hand and colored markers in the other.

"Working on the new book?" Heather grinned, urging Cynthia ahead of her into the cozy, attractive home. "Gwen writes and illustrates children's books," Heather explained to Cynthia. "Cynthia Montgomery, my sister Gwendolyn Carmichael."

"Hi, Cynthia. Come in, come in." Her petite frame was swallowed inside a man's gray jogging suit. Fluffy pink slippers covered her small feet. Her hair had been cut short in the back and soft black curls framed a lovely face much like Heather's.

Gwen led the way into the sunny yellow kitchen at the rear of the house, pausing along the way to call up to her daughters as they passed the staircase.

"You don't know how much I cherish these Saturdays, Heather. Those two shopaholics drag me from one end of the mall to the other. They can never make up their minds and they absolutely hate everything I like. Teenage girls! Save me!" She eyed Cynthia suspiciously. "How old are you, sugar? Fifty-two?"

To Heather's relief Cynthia giggled, not offended by Gwen's outrageous teasing. Once they were seated around the table in front of the curved bay window, Gwen dispensed cups of coffee and hot chocolate.

"Auntie!" Angela bounced into the room, giving Heather a bear hug. "I didn't hear your car. Who's this?" she asked, reaching for a jelly doughnut and bypassing the blueberry and bran muffins sharing the platter in the center of the table.

"Cynthia Montgomery, Angela Carmichael," Heather said, eyeing her niece's patterned bobby socks, holey short-sleeved sweatshirt worn over a striped shirt and shorts. Like all the Gregory women, her two nieces had rich black hair and large caramel-colored eyes.

"Hi," Angela said between bites.

"Love the outfit, Angie. But, ah, when we're downtown you don't know me, okay?" Heather teased outlandishly, tugging on her niece's bushy shoulder-length ponytail.

"That bad, huh?" Angela grinned. "No problem. Now Ericia has to let me wear her red jeans. I'll tell her you said so."

"You'd better not. You two have been fussing all morning over some boy," her mother moaned. "Get your sister, please. No more arguing. I mean it, Angela Margaret," Gwen called after her, then turned to Cynthia. "Will you excuse us? I want to show Heather the new illustrations I started last night. Won't take a minute. Help yourself to a doughnut."

"Sure, "Cynthia shrugged, sipping her drink.

Once they were safely inside the study, Gwen said, "Now, sugar, tell big sister what's wrong."

"You brought me in here for this?" Heather said with one hand on her hip, avoiding her sister's probing gaze. She wasn't about to go into all those crazy emotions she'd been experiencing since meeting Quinn. And especially not with his daughter just down the hall.

"Stop cutting your eyes at me and tell me why you look so tired. Didn't you sleep last night? You've got dark smudges under your eyes. Is it Charles?"

"No, it's not Charles. And I'm *fine.*" Heather knew she was protesting too strongly, but she couldn't help herself. Gwen was about as subtle as the IRS when she thought one of her loved ones was keeping something from her.

"Hey, don't bite my head off! I was hoping it was Charles. When are you going to find a man you can get serious about?"

Heather laughed, going over and giving her sister a hug. "I love you, too, but will you please stay out of my love life. I didn't ask you what you and your hubby did last night," she teased.

"This morning you mean," Gwen laughed. "I'm so mad at that man I can't see straight. He went to the office today. The only time we have alone and he has to go to work. *Men!*"

"And you want *me* to try to get one of those? Sounds like plain aggravation."

"Stop trying to change the subject. Something is going on with you and I know it. You're counseling Cynthia, aren't you?" Gwen didn't wait for confirmation. She knew her sister. Heather took her job very seriously.

"Montgomery . . . hmmm?" Gwen tapped a slim finger against her lips. "Where have I heard that name? It's been just recently, too."

"Probably in the newspaper. Cynthia's father, Quinn Montgomery, is defending Clayton Jameison. It was written up in the *Free Press* this morning."

"Now I remember. Jameison is that wealthy industrialist accused of killing his wife and her lover." Heather nodded.

Gwen looked speculatively at Heather. "Judging by his pictures, Quinn Montgomery is a very attractive man."

"Will you quit?" Heather tossed back over her shoulder as she headed out the door. Recognizing the determination beneath the innocent question, Heather knew Gwen wouldn't stop until she knew every little detail. Heather wasn't ready to share her thoughts about Quinn—although she knew she couldn't keep him a secret very long since the two sisters had always been close in spite of the ten years between their ages. But for now her dream about Quinn, plus her confusing emotions were too new . . . too disturbing. "Cynthia is waiting and the girls are ready."

Hart Plaza was crowded as usual during the warm weather ethnic festivals. Although the tribute to the Hispanic culture had begun the day before, it was still in full swing. They toured the open-air booths with a wide variety of authentic dishes and viewed the crafts on display.

By the time they sampled the fare of at least a half dozen vendors and danced to the vibrant music provided by an authentic Latin band, located in the arena in the center of the plaza, Heather was no closer to understanding her absorption in Quinn than she was to explaining Cynthia's withdrawal.

She was so unresponsive to Ericia and Angela that Heather wasn't surprised when her nieces stopped trying to include Cynthia in their chatter.

The shopping excursion was a bit more successful but not much. Heather was proud of her nieces. Even though the outing turned out to be a disappointment, they both attempted to make it enjoyable. Heather promised herself that she would make it up to them. Maybe an overnight trip to Chicago. Heather almost chuckled as she imagined her two nieces let loose in downtown Water Tower Place. It was after six when she dropped them off and began the return trip.

"They hate me!" Cynthia insisted, her small chin lifted proudly and her mouth quivering.

"That's not true," Heather said softly.

"They didn't like me."

"Do you honestly think you gave them a reason to like you, honey?" When no answer was forthcoming, Heather said gently, "It takes a friend to make a friend. Sometimes you're the one who has to make the first move."

"That's easy for you to say. I don't have a mother like your sister or an aunt like you. No one to take me places or do things with me. And my dad's always working."

"You've got a father who takes care of you and loves you. And now you *do* have me. You can come to me any time. Plus, you have my home phone number, so use it."

Heather was suddenly reminded that Cynthia had spent

her formative years in boarding school among strangers. While some youngsters thrived in similar circumstances, unfortunately Cynthia wasn't among them.

Heather bit her lip to hold back the unvarnished truth. Cynthia was lucky, much luckier than so many kids without mothers or fathers to care about them. She lived in a nice warm house, had a place to sleep, and plenty of food to eat. She needed to realize that there were people without homes or jobs or clothes. But now wasn't the time to point out these truths to Cynthia. The girl wasn't in a receptive mood.

She was having a difficult time of it, and some young man had taken full advantage of her need for love. Maybe they were in love, but Heather doubted it.

They had stopped for a red light when Heather asked, "Does your boyfriend know you've spoken to your dad?"

"No," she shouted. "Why do you keep asking about him?"

"Cynthia, he has rights, too. After all, he *is* the baby's father. What does he want you to do?"

For a moment Cynthia looked as if she were about to burst into tears. The blare of a car horn behind them forced Heather's eyes back on the road, and as a result she didn't notice the girl's visible sigh of relief.

"Cynthia?"

"Look, I don't want to talk about him. Are you coming inside with me?" Cynthia asked as they turned into the drive. "Dad's already home." She indicated the black Mercedes parked ahead of them.

Six

"Yes, I'd like to speak to your father," Heather said, fighting the inclination to do just the opposite. Nothing would make her happier than postponing a face-to-face meeting with Quinn. She parked her ancient Firebird behind the black Mercedes. "Don't forget your appointment with Dr. Burnette is Monday at two. We can leave from school. I'll speak to your last hour teacher."

"You won't tell her that I'm—"

"No one else has to know just yet. But, honey, if you decide to keep your baby, it won't be a secret for long. And unfortunately our school doesn't have a program designed to meet the needs of pregnant students. But there are several such schools throughout the city." Heather patted her hand. "There really isn't a reason why you can't continue your education. Of course, you're welcome to remain at Lawrence—but we don't have parenting classes. And those classes help the girls learn how to become good mothers. And— Cynthia?"

"I'm listening."

"After you've seen the doctor on Monday, you, I, your dad, and the baby's father will have to talk about the future. A decision has to be made soon. We can't put it off indefinitely. It will be okay. I promise," Heather said reassuringly.

Cynthia looked at Heather with genuine horror, her eyes brimming with tears. "Nothing will ever be right again." Releasing her seat belt, she jumped out of the car.

Gathering her things, Heather frowned. Once she was standing outside the house beside Cynthia she insisted firmly, "That isn't true."

"Are you coming inside?" Cynthia asked, glancing back over her shoulder.

What could be worse than being fifteen and pregnant, Heather wondered as she followed the girl inside. It was strange how Cynthia could talk openly about her relationship with her father, yet she was so closedmouthed about the boy involved.

Cynthia didn't act as if she were infatuated with him. If anything, the girl was more concerned with her father's reactions to her pregnancy than she was in establishing a lasting relationship with her boyfriend. Something wasn't right, yet Heather couldn't quite put her finger on what it was.

Heather followed Cynthia into the large black marble foyer veined in gold. From what Heather could see the large, elegantly appointed house was beautiful but at the same time cool and not at all welcoming.

Her stomach fluttered with nerves as she listened to the girl call her father. She was no longer certain why she was there. Yes, they needed to talk. But not now, not here.

How could she face him after last night . . . after her dream? He made her feel things she had no business feeling for him. Why hadn't she said she would telephone him? A quick call later this evening would have served the same purpose. And it would have been a lot easier on her equilibrium.

"I'll check with Mrs. Thornton. She probably knows where he is." Cynthia hurried down the central hallway.

If the truth were known, Heather was afraid to see Quinn. She'd rather get in her car and speed away as fast as she could go. She couldn't afford to become emotionally involved with a parent. If nothing else his kiss had taught her just how vulnerable she was to him.

For so long she had yearned to fall in love with a special man. A man who saw life the way she did, a man who was able to give as well as receive love. A man willing to work at making a life together with her. Heather was no different than any other young woman. She wanted to be loved. Quinn Montgomery just wasn't the man for her. So why wouldn't her insides be still?

The front door opened behind her.

"Hi," Quinn said with a smile, somewhat breathlessly. He wore a navy blue jogging suit that did wonderful things to his broad shoulders, trim middle, lean hips, and hard muscled thighs. The color of his shirt seemed to enhance the hue of his eyes, so dark grey that today they appeared almost black. His strong full-drawn features stamped him distinctly male. Using the towel around his neck, he mopped perspiration from his face.

"Hello." Heather's heart pounded wildly in her chest. Her hand automatically tucked and smoothed braids away from her face. She was annoyed with herself for wondering if she needed to freshen her lipstick. Suddenly her denim skirt and pink cotton knit blouse seemed unimaginative and drab.

"Just get back?"

"Yes." Her small brows crinkled as she realized she was tongue-tied and trying to avoid his gaze.

"Where's Cynthia?"

"She went to find the housekeeper. She was looking for you."

"After sitting all morning, I needed a quick run. My study is this way." He took her arm and ushered her into a comfortable room just past the impressive staircase.

Heather hurried inside, hoping to get away from the tantalizing feel of his hand on her skin.

"Have a seat. May I offer you something?" His lips had tightened, his eyes never leaving the graceful lines of her soft shapely body. She was just as lovely as he remembered and just as desirable. He had spent last night thinking about her. For the first time in recent memory, he hadn't been consumed by memories of Peggy. The realization was somewhat disturbing.

"Nothing, thank you," she said, glancing around the book-lined masculine domain.

"I'll let the others know I'm here and then change. Be right back."

Heather seated herself on the cream leather sofa in front of the stone fireplace. The sofa and matching leather armchair were centered on an oriental rug in rich ivory bordered by blue and copper. A massive oak desk dominated the room. The dark brown leather chair behind the desk was the only piece of furniture that was well worn. Heather imagined Quinn in that chair surrounded by his law books and notes. A computer terminal was set up behind the desk, beneath a wide picture window.

Heather nearly jumped out of her skin when the grandfather clock in the corner chimed on the hour. She was a mass of nerves. She knew she had to get a hold of herself before she did something really stupid. Letting him kiss her last night was dumb enough. She couldn't afford to make any more mistakes where he was concerned, especially if she were to help Cynthia. Above all, Heather knew she must maintain her objectivity. And Cynthia's needs came first.

"That didn't take too long," Quinn said, returning with a tray in hand. He set it on the coffee table. He'd changed into gray stone-washed jeans and a pale gray turtleneck sweater. The color served to enhance his dark rich skin tone and his charcoal-colored eyes. He handed Heather a glass of iced tea from the tray. "How was your day?"

"It was pleasant, although I don't think Cynthia enjoyed herself."

"I think she's enjoyed herself too damn much already," he said tightly. "She left here upset with me. I suppose it's too much to hope that she didn't take it out on you?"

"She isn't having an easy time of it."

"What did you find out?"

"Nothing new. She won't give me any information about the boy. Not even his name. She's so guarded about him. It's almost as if she's trying to protect him."

"A good thing," he said thoughtfully. "When I get my hands around the little bastard's neck, he'll have plenty to answer for."

"That attitude will solve nothing, only alienate Cynthia even more. If we want to help, we can't force her to tell. Have you had any more thoughts about the solution to all this? Since abortion is out as far as you're concerned, are you advising her to keep the child or give it up for adoption?"

Quinn walked over to the fireplace, his drink forgotten on the tray. He stared down into the empty grate, his back to Heather. He hid the pain on his features, unaware of the anguish in his voice. "Hell, I don't know. I just don't know." He swallowed the lump in his throat.

Heather's heart ached for him and Cynthia. "There's still time to help her decide, Quinn. But for her own future happiness, I still think the ultimate decision must be Cynthia's."

"Cynthia is fifteen years old! What does she know about raising a child? Hell, I'm forty-two and making a mess of it."

Heather said evenly, "Our school doesn't have a specific program for pregnant girls. As I was telling Cynthia, there are several such schools throughout the city with very good programs. Although it would be wonderful if she could stay at Lawrence, we don't have parenting classes that help the girls learn how to become good mothers while continuing with their education."

"You're suggesting she keep the baby, aren't you?" Quinn asked sharply.

"I'm trying to explain the options and resources available."

"And you told this to my daughter?"

"Yes, don't you think she should know? This is her body after all."

"There's no doubt about that," he said dryly.

"I feel very strongly about Cynthia's rights. No well-intended judge or even concerned parent can fully comprehend the terror a girl goes through in this situation. But it all boils down to the fact that it's her life and her child. Quinn, she has to be able to live with this decision for the rest of her life."

"Do you think she's capable of raising a child?"

"With your help and support, yes I do. But it doesn't really matter what I think. What matters is what is right for Cynthia. She must make her own choice."

He swore heatedly, curling his hands into fists. "The toughest decision my daughter has ever had to make was choosing what jeans to wear!" After a time, he asked gruffly, "What about your doctor? Have you spoken to him?"

"Her. Cynthia has an appointment with my doctor on Monday. We'll leave school around one thirty. After her appointment, I thought of taking her for a quick sandwich and hopefully a good talk before bringing her home. Then later in the week, I'll make an appointment for the four of us."

"Four?"

"You, myself, Cynthia, and the boy."

"Okay," he sighed heavily.

Heather felt a surge of triumph at his agreement and momentarily almost lost the battle within herself. She'd tried so hard not to notice the way his jeans hugged his buttocks, his hard-muscled thighs. Even with his back to her, she'd found him wonderfully exciting.

But he really wasn't handsome, she mused. His nose was a shade too wide, his jawline too square, his eyebrows too bushy. But try as she could, she couldn't find a single thing wrong with his mouth. It was downright sexy, the bottom lip slightly fuller than the top. She recalled how his mouth felt against hers, the warm caress of his mustache on her face. Never had she been so aware of a man. He was a threat to her peace of mind. She couldn't be around him for long without wanting to be in his arms. But Quinn was off limits to her. So why couldn't she remember that small detail, she scolded herself angrily.

Quinn's eyes were dark, almost ebony, when he turned toward her. "It's all a bit difficult for me. But Heather, I want you to know I appreciate your help. I honestly don't know what I would have done if I had to handle this alone."

When she refused to meet his gaze, he asked, "Are you alright? You look angry."

Heather flushed. "I'm perfectly fine," she protested sharply. She tried to laugh it off and failed. "Let's not talk about me—I'm here for one reason and that's Cynthia . . . only Cynthia."

"You *are* angry," he declared softly. "And you've been avoiding my eyes constantly today. Why?" Sidestepping the coffee table, he stood in front of her.

"I think I should leave," she said, getting her things, suddenly unable to cope with her emotions.

"We haven't finished talking," he said, blocking her path.

"I have. Will you kindly move out of my way?" When he didn't, she sidestepped him and headed for the door.

He was there ahead of her, leaning against it, his large frame blocking the portal.

"Don't mess with me, Quinn!"

"You're angry and I'd like to know why?"

"You know why," she insisted. Her eyes were locked at the base of his masculine throat.

"Look at me, damn it."

"What is it you want from me?" she asked, forcing herself to look into the depths of his eyes. Her nostrils flared with temper, but she quickly found that she was inhaling the fresh scent of his dark skin. She bit her fleshy bottom lip, refusing to acknowledge the need to have his lips pressed against hers.

Quinn caught his breath. For a moment desire almost blazed out of control as he accepted just how badly he wanted this woman. He wanted to memorize every inch of her petite golden length, stroke her with his hands, worship her body with his own. His head filled as he yearned to taste all of her sweetness.

"What is going on in that head of yours?" Quinn said softly. "You're a beautiful woman, a desirable woman, and I assumed the attraction was mutual. Why shouldn't I kiss you here and now—unless you haven't been honest with me. . . . You told me there wasn't a man in your life. Is that the truth?"

"Yes . . . my lack of involvement with another man isn't the issue here."

"Tell me the issue, because I sure as hell can't find it."

She dropped her lids, her breath coming much too quickly. She felt compelled to protect herself from this man. He threatened her in ways she couldn't begin to describe, let alone understand. He clouded her mind to the point that she couldn't think at all. She wasn't even certain what disturbed her more, the man or the way he made her feel.

Heather considered herself a realist. He was Cynthia's parent. And she would be better served by reminding herself of that detail. Yet he was so very male, so utterly attractive that his masculinity drew her inexorably—and she was in way over her head. Her responses to him last night had proven that.

"You're angry because I kissed you last night, aren't you," Quinn said matter-of-factly.

"Yes, damn it! Where do you get off thinking I'm interested in becoming one of your women? My job is to help Cynthia, not satisfy you sexually. Cynthia's my only concern, Mr. Montgomery."

She had to make him understand that she took her work seriously. This was no game to her. She was furious with him and with herself. She didn't know how she was going to fight her attraction to him.

"This has nothing to do with my daughter or your job, Heather. This is between you and me. I felt it the second you walked into my office. I didn't plan to kiss you. It just happened."

"That kiss was wrong. It should never have happened."

"Heather . . . I don't mean to upset you. But I'm not sorry it happened. The timing was lousy—on that we agree. But you're a very special lady and the man in me recognizes that," he said, his voice deep and gravelly.

"It was a mistake."

"You kissed me back, Heather."

"I didn't—"

His hands were large but gentle as he caressed her cheeks, the length of her throat. "But you did and you know it. Sweetheart, what harm is there in wanting each other? I was awake for hours last night, thinking about you. Just looking at you makes me forget everything else. You walk into a room and my blood pressure goes up."

Quinn put his arms around her and took what he wanted most, her red-tinted full lips. Oh, she was luscious, her lips were as sweet as he remembered . . . sweeter. Her breasts were so wonderfully full and ripe. How had he managed to keep his hands off them?

Heather clung to Quinn, her senses whirling out of control from the pleasure, of it all.

"Heather . . ." he groaned. ". . . open your mouth for me. I want to taste you, all of your sweet mouth." Quinn shuddered with pleasure as he stroked his tongue over hers again and again.

"Quinn . . ." she whimpered. "Quinn . . ."

His body ached for release. He couldn't remember wanting a woman as much as he wanted Heather. There was something about her that went straight to his head.

With quick sure movements, he unfastened her blouse and unhooked the front clasp of her sheer lacy bra. His mouth was relentless on hers while he filled his palms with her cushiony softness.

"You're beautiful," he whispered, lowering his head.

Heather moaned with pleasure as he took her nipple into the warmth of his mouth. He circled the hard brown center over and over again, sending white-hot waves of desire through her body. She cradled his head, her fingers were in his thick dark hair as he sucked at her nipple.

"Daddy?" Cynthia's voice sounded through the closed door, shattering their sensuous haze and bringing them both back to reality in a hurry.

Quinn's voice was gruff when he said, "Just a moment."

With her back to him, Heather crossed to the armchair, straightening her clothes before she dropped into it. She was shaking so badly she had to clasp her hands in her lap.

Quinn opened the door to his daughter.

"Heather?"

She nodded.

"Mrs. Thornton said to tell you dinner will be ready in ten minutes." Cynthia glanced around her father to where Heather sat by the fireplace.

"Have her set an extra plate."

"No, I'm afraid I can't stay," Heather said, getting to her feet.

Quinn knew he had no choice but to accept her decision. He could already see the reproach in her cutting gaze. For a man known for his discipline, his behavior was totally unacceptable. What was there about her that destroyed his thought processes?

Heather's hands were trembling when she punched out Quinn's number on Monday.

"Williams, Burnstein, Montgomery, and Hersal."

It was five minutes and two secretaries later before Quinn came on the line.

"Heather? Something wrong?"

"I don't know. Cynthia missed her classes today. I called your home, but according to your housekeeper she isn't there either. Where is she?"

"She's supposed to be in school. I dropped her off this morning at ten to eight. She might have been held up by one of her teachers."

"Quinn, she isn't here," Heather said, forcing a professional calm she was far from feeling. "I've spoken to all her teachers, and according to them she hasn't shown up for school today. I've even had her paged. Quinn, Cynthia isn't in the building."

There was a lengthy silence.

"Quinn?"

"Do you think she is just playing hooky? Or do you think it's something more serious?"

"I don't know." Heather said with a disheartened sigh. "All I'm certain of is that she's not where she should be and she's been very unhappy."

"You think she might have run away?"

Mutual fear became a tangible thing that seemed to stretch across the miles. "Let's not jump to conclusions," Quinn said quietly. His stomach felt like a hard knot of tension. "I'll call you back as soon as I know anything."

"What are you going to do?"

"I'm going home. There might be a note, some clue to her plans."

"I'll meet you there as soon as I can. That is, if you

think I can be of help . . ." Heather waited, her heart heavy.

"Thank you," he whispered, his voice grave. "I have a feeling I'm going to need you."

Seven

"Miss Gregory?" As Heather nodded, the housekeeper said, "Please come in. I'm Mrs. Thornton." She stepped aside to allow Heather to enter.

Heather offered her hand, "It's nice meeting you, Mrs. Thornton."

The brown-skinned older woman smiled. She nodded her regal head, saying, "It's good to meet you, too, young lady. So sad it has to be like this . . . so sad. Mr. Montgomery's in his study."

Heather knocked briefly on the open paneled door before walking in. "Quinn. Any news?"

Quinn stood with his back to her, staring down into the grate. Logs were in place but they weren't lit. The afternoon sunshine spilled through the louvered blinds covering the windows. He didn't speak or so much as turn when she said his name. He couldn't. His throat muscles felt as if they were locked with despair.

The slump of his powerful shoulders, the open whisky bottle on the mantel were all indications that something was very wrong. Even though her heart filled with dread and she feared the worst, she went to him. He was hurting . . . badly. It never occurred to Heather not to respond to that need.

"Tell me." Her small slender fingers curled over his forearm. She could feel the tension of his large muscular frame through the layers of a navy blue wool suit jacket and cream silk shirt.

"She's gone. Cindy's run away." His tone was low and raw with pain.

"Oh, no." Heather unwittingly tightened her hold on him.

"I've made a mess of things."

Uncertain as to what to say, for she knew words couldn't bring Cynthia back or ease his fears, Heather remained silent while her tender heart went out to him.

"I handled this whole pregnancy thing wrong. I was just so angry, so upset that I didn't try hard enough to reach her." Slowly he turned toward Heather, allowing her to view the anguish he couldn't hide. His eyes shimmered with unshed tears, his face gaunt with worry. His stomach was burning as if it were on fire.

For once Quinn welcomed the pain. He'd let Peggy down. She had left Cynthia in his care. She trusted him to raise their daughter and keep her safe. He had failed. Over the years, he had become consumed by his own sense of guilt and grief that he had shut Cindy out.

Peggy's death had been such a shock. It had happened so suddenly. There had been no time to resolve the division between them. She had died angry and upset with him. That pain had been something no amount of time could ease.

"Quinn, it's not your fault. You made mistakes, yes. But you tried, you really did try to help her through this.

Besides, neither one of us is totally blameless. I felt something was wrong on Saturday. But I thought it was connected to her disagreement with you. Maybe if I had tried harder, I could have reached her. I don't know. But blaming ourselves is not going to bring her back any sooner."

"I'm scared for her, Heather. She's only a baby. She doesn't know anything about being on her own. I lost a brother to the streets. I won't lose my little girl. I can't . . ."

Heather silently prayed for Cynthia's safety as she squeezed Quinn's hand reassuringly. She held on to him, hoping he would allow her to share some of his pain. He was such a strong man, sometimes a bit too proud. He'd been alone for so long that he'd become an expert at locking his emotions deep inside himself.

Quinn hurt. Oh, how he hurt. She offered comfort and compassion. He didn't fight it, he simply accepted. There would be plenty of time later to analyze, but not now.

Where had it all gone wrong? Was it when Peggy died? All he had ever meant to do was love Cynthia, give her everything he and Peggy had planned for her long before she was even born. Cynthia . . . Quinn unwittingly clung to Heather's hand and a bitter sob caught in his throat.

"She'll be back, Quinn. I just know it."

By focusing on Heather's words, he was able to ease the pain in his stomach and allow himself to gain control of his emotions. He took slow, deep steadying breaths, forcing his lungs to empty, then fill again.

Suddenly, he dropped her hand and he moved away, embarrassed by his weakness.

Startled by the rapid change in his demeanor, it took Heather a few moments to recover. She had given as well as received comfort from his closeness.

Quinn was infuriated with himself. Why couldn't he be around her without baring his very soul to her. Hell! Another few seconds and he would have broken down entirely.

"Care for a drink?" he asked stiffly.

"It's a little early for me."

Quinn didn't allow himself to meet her frankly assessing gaze. He stared at the amber liquid in the glass he recovered from the mantel.

"I talked to as many of Cynthia's classmates as I could before I left school. No one has seen her."

He watched her as she sat in the leather armchair beside the stone fireplace. "I had the same idea. I looked for her address book, but I couldn't find it. I was hoping to find a name of a friend she might have turned to."

Heather couldn't tell him that Cynthia had no friends at school. The girl didn't have a clue as to how to make friends. "What makes you so certain she has run away?"

Heather was wearing a knee-length black straight skirt. Crossing shapely legs covered by sheer black hose, she unwittingly drew his gaze. She shrugged out of a mantailored, black leather jacket. Her silk blouse was tangerine. Her braids curled softly against her shoulders. Small gold hoops dangled in her earlobes when she moved.

"Cynthia left this in her room." He held out a single sheet of pink paper, silently cursing the tremor in his hand.

Heather read it twice. "She has to go away because

she couldn't tell you the truth? What truth? What could be worse than being pregnant?"

"How the hell should I know?" he growled in frustration. "You're the expert. Tell me."

"I wish I knew," she said thoughtfully. "What's being done to find her? It's too soon to call the police, I suppose?"

He said, "I've a few connections on the force, so I contacted them anyway. At this point I was told all I can do is stay by the phone in case she tries to call. I've checked with the airlines and the train stations." He thrust his hands into his pockets. "I don't mean to take this out on you. It isn't you she ran away from." He stared down at the patterned carpet for an extraordinary length of time. Finally he said impatiently, "I should be out there trying to find her!"

The telephone rang. Quinn grabbed for it. "Montgomery residence. Darnell? Any news?" He perched on the edge of the desk. Absently he loosened then removed a cream and navy patterned silk tie as he spoke into the receiver. His movements were jerky, disjointed, unusual for him. He shoved the tie into his jacket pocket, releasing the buttons near his dark brown throat. "No . . . keep at it. Call when you have anything . . . anything at all."

Heather listened, anxious but hopeful.

"That was a friend of mine, Darnell Hunter," he explained after returning the phone to its cradle. "He and three of my associates are out checking the truck stops, bus depots, and rest areas on all the major freeways surrounding Detroit. The patrol cars are out. They're all circulating a picture of Cindy."

"What about R.A.P. Hotline? The Runaway Assistance Program of Michigan? Did you call them?"

"Yeah. I want my little girl back . . . safe and in one piece."

"Quinn, please. You're tormenting yourself."

"I should be out there doing something . . . anything!"

"What if Cynthia calls and you're not here? What if she changes her mind and wants to come home? She would want to talk to you, wouldn't she? Quinn, I think you're really needed here. The police may even need more information."

"It's so damn frustrating."

Heather nodded.

"Quinn, how much money does she have?"

He straightened slowly, then said, "I don't know."

"Does Cindy have her own savings account?"

"She has a checking account. She also has a trust fund. Her mother and I started it for her when she was a baby. But she can't touch it until she's twenty-one. The insurance money went into C.D.'s for her after her mother died."

Heather ignored the last. "Her own checking account. Why?"

"Expenses. When she needs more, she just tells me and I have my secretary make a deposit into her account. She charges her clothes to my accounts."

"Are you saying she has access to your credit accounts, such as in a bank card? Quinn, she could have charged an airline ticket to South America by now." Heather knew she made him angry, but she didn't care.

"For heaven's sake, she's fifteen years old. How could you allow her access to so much money?"

Quinn stiffened at the disapproval all over her face. The truth hurt, especially coming from Heather. He cared what she thought of him. He wanted her respect. Obviously he was failing at that, too.

"Cynthia's my daughter. I trust her." Quinn's face was cold and unyielding. "How was I to know she'd take off like this? She has to have clothes!"

She had really ticked him off now. Heather pressed her lips tight in frustration. Determined not to let her emotions get the best of her, she asked, careful to keep her voice level, "How much does she usually have in her checking account? Twenty dollars? Forty? She couldn't have gotten very far on fifteen dollars."

"Just a moment." He went to the telephone and began punching out a number. When he completed the call, he said in a dry tone, "My secretary deposited six hundred dollars into the account this morning. She normally handles Cynthia's expenses."

Was it any wonder Cynthia believed her father didn't love her? His secretary knew more about his child than he did. Heather didn't have the heart to point that out to him. His dark face appeared haggard, as if he'd aged twenty years in the span of a few seconds.

"I should of had sense enough to . . ." his voice trailed off. He found the situation chilling. The buck stopped with him.

The quiet was unnerving. The only noise in the room came from the grandfather clock in the corner.

He couldn't hold back the words anymore than he could contain the pain. His voice was tight with self-loathing when he finally spoke. "I've been living on the fringes of my daughter's life. She did so well in school before we lost Peggy, always at the top of her class." He hesitated. "She despised the boarding schools I sent her to after her mother died. I just didn't know how to take care of a little ten-year-old girl. After that, she was always in trouble. I kept moving her from school to school." He paused, finding it difficult to go on.

"Quinn, you don't—"

"No, let me finish. When Cindy begged to come home, I let her. I didn't know what else to do. Over the years I've gotten into the habit of giving her what she wanted. I wanted her to have the advantages that I didn't have as a kid. Now I realize I've given her too much, and without adequate supervision. You're right. I've been a lousy father."

Although Heather longed to go to him, she couldn't. She'd done it again, accused him of being an inadequate father. "Quinn, I didn't mean to hurt you. I just want you to realize that Cynthia needs you. Now more than ever before."

There was a tap on the open door before Mrs. Thornton entered with a tray of coffee and plate of homemade cookies. She placed the tray on the coffee table in front of the sofa. "Thought ya'll could use a little something."

"Thanks, Mrs. Thornton."

"I heard the phone?" she asked anxiously.

"There isn't any news about Cynthia. I'll let you know as soon as we hear."

She nodded before leaving.

Heather moved to the sofa and began pouring coffee

from the sterling silver pot. She held out a cup to Quinn, who was pacing the length of the fireplace.

"Pacing won't bring her back any sooner. Maybe if we put our heads together, we can come up with a solid clue. Do you think she's alone?"

"Do you mean—"

"Perhaps she and the baby's father decided to run off and get married."

"Well, there's no mention of the guy in her note. I almost wish she were with him. At least I'd know she wasn't alone." Quinn frowned.

"Yeah, I know what you mean." She held out his cup.

"Thanks." He sat down on the cushion next to hers.

"On Saturday Cynthia got really upset when I explained that I wanted the four of us to sit down and plan the future. I suspect it has something to do with the boy. Quinn, she loves you so much, and she wants your approval, even if she's gotten herself involved with someone she knows you won't like."

"I don't even like considering that possibility." Quinn brooded, ignoring the coffee cup in his hand. As of yet he hadn't even been able to come to terms with the fact that his fifteen-year-old baby had been sexually active. But with some smart-ass punk? How in the world could he help her when he couldn't find her? His eyes and mouth were bracketed by worry lines.

"Cream, sugar?"

"I take it black."

"Mmmm, I'm sure that does wonders for your ulcer."

A crooked smile tugged at the corners of his mouth. His gaze traveled over the delicate lines of Heather's features. He found something new in her eyes each time he looked into their warm brown depths.

"I just wish there was some news," she whispered. "We just have to remember that Cynthia is a bright, gifted young woman. And we'll get her back. And then we'll help her through this together."

"Five o'clock," he said unnecessarily as the clock chimed. Quinn surged to his feet, putting the still full cup back on the tray. He roamed the room, his footsteps soundless on the Oriental carpet.

"Quinn, does Cynthia have a diary or journal?"

He stared at Heather hopefully for a moment. "Yes, she does. Do you think she might have left it in her room?"

"It's worth a look."

He grabbed Heather's hand and pulled her along with him. When they reached the foyer that opened on one wall to a wide staircase, the doorbell sounded. Their gaze locked in expectation for an instant before he hurried to the door.

"Quinn! Darling!" The elegant brunette hurled herself into his arms.

Heather stiffened as she watched the interplay.

"I'm so sorry, I came as soon as I heard. I was out shopping for the twins. Darnell couldn't reach me when he left the office. Oh, darling, you must be absolutely frantic. Has there been any news?" she asked, studying him with wide blue eyes. With every hair in place, she was immaculately dressed in a bright blue knit dress and matching coat. At five-nine, she was as slim and strikingly lovely as any runway model in New York or Paris.

"Nothing," he said, disengaging himself and ushering her inside.

"Heather Gregory, Elaine Hunter. Heather is Cindy's school counselor. Elaine and her husband Darnell are old family friends."

Heather smiled warmly, clearly shocked by her initial tinge of jealousy.

After the two had greeted each other, Quinn explained, "We were on our way up to Cindy's room. Thought she might have left her diary behind. It might give us a clue to her plans."

Heather volunteered, "I'll look."

"Thanks. It's the first door on the right, at top of the stairs. Would you care for coffee, Elaine? We were in the study." Cynthia's room was done in pink and white, very pretty and girlish. A search of the nightstand and dresser proved fruitless. Heather spotted the gilt-framed photograph on the vanity. It pictured a much younger Quinn with his arms around an unbelievably beautiful young woman.

Her slender frame, almost ethereal features, and striking coffee and cream beauty reminded Heather of Cynthia. In fact, she was holding baby Cynthia against her small breasts, a radiant smile on her lips as she looked into the camera lens. They were a trio filled with happiness and love.

Heather felt as if she been punched in the chest as she studied the other photographs. Quinn and Peggy had evidently been very much in love and thrilled by their daughter. She had no reason to be upset. It was no surprise that Quinn had been deeply in love with his wife.

He had told her as much himself. So why had seeing that love hurt so?

By the time Heather left the girl's room, she was convinced that Cynthia had taken the address book and her diary with her. Intent on taking a few moments to sort out her thoughts, Heather went into the formal living room to the left of the foyer. Above the marble mantel was a huge oil portrait of Peggy Montgomery. She was captured for all time in a stunning concoction of cool blues and silver. The colors in her gown were echoed in the elegantly appointed room. She represented feminine perfection, the pinnacle of beauty and black womanliness.

As she looked at the likeness, Heather wondered if Quinn would ever have room in his heart for a new woman, a new love? Somehow she doubted it. Any woman in her right mind would know that although he was handsome and he was sexy, he was not available. He still cared too much about his late wife. The one thing Heather prided herself on was her common sense. It was time she started using it.

Quinn was speaking on the telephone, when Heather returned to the study.

"Anything?" Elaine asked from where she sat on the sofa. She patted the place beside her.

"No. She probably took it with her." Heather asked, "Any word?" as she sat down.

Elaine sighed, shook her head. "He's talking to his late wife's sister in New York." Elaine was frankly curious about Heather. "We're summer neighbors. We own adjoining lots in Traverse Bay. In fact, my twin boys and Cindy practically grew up together on the beach," Elaine said, with Quinn's deep baritone in the background. "Peggy and I were close friends. Quinn and my husband Darnell have been friends since law school days."

Uncertain as to whether she should be hearing any of this, Heather picked up her cup, but put it down again. The beverage was cold. She occupied herself by lacing her icy hands together in her lap.

"Has Cynthia been in trouble in school again this year? She's had so many problems since Peggy's death." Elaine said, her concern evident. "I've tried to help her, but no matter how hard I tried I've failed to gain her confidence." Elaine's eyes were troubled.

"That may be because you're such a close friend of her father's. Cynthia's problems are a bit complicated. But please don't give up on her." Heather smiled, deciding she liked the other woman.

"I'm glad you're here. Quinn shouldn't be alone tonight. Life hasn't been easy for Cynthia and Quinn." Elaine waited expectantly, hoping that Heather would focus on the nature of her relationship with Quinn.

"Did you find it?" Quinn asked as he replaced the receiver.

"No, I'm sorry. Apparently she took it with her."

Weariness and disappointment were revealed in the lines of his body. He shoved both hands into the pockets of his trousers.

"Quinn, I've called the boys in East Lansing, told them to be on the lookout for Cynthia. They'll call if she comes to them."

"That was a good idea." Quinn gazed thoughtfully out at the fading afternoon sun. It had been hours since they discovered his daughter was missing. Everything looked as if she'd been gone since early that morning. With the approaching nightfall his anxiety intensified.

"Is there anything I can do for you before I leave?" Elaine asked. "I wish I could stay, but we have a business dinner tonight with the Bradfords. One of us has to make an appearance. But if you need me, I'll be happy to come back afterward."

"Thanks for coming over, Elaine. You and Darnell have done so much already." Quinn helped her with her coat. "Look, try not to worry," he said, resting an arm along her shoulders. "We'll get her back safe."

"Call when you hear. Promise?"

"Promise." He smiled at her affectionately, leaning down to kiss her.

"If it weren't for this stupid dinner, I wouldn't leave like this." Elaine brushed at the tears in her eyes.

"Stop it. I'm fine. Besides, Heather has agreed to stay. Let me walk you to the door."

"Alright." To Heather, she said, "I'm glad I had a chance to meet you. I hope to see you again, under less strenuous circumstances."

Heather nodded goodbye and watched as Quinn showed Elaine out, then wandered aimlessly around the room. Stopping at a bookshelf, she read the names on the spines of the books. Most were heavy law books, but there were also favorites of Heather's such as John Wideman, J. California Cooper and Martia Golden. But her thoughts were far away from this room. They were with Cynthia. She uttered a silent prayer: Please, Heavenly Father, let her be safe. Heather turned at the sound of Quinn's entry, hoping she looked calm and steady.

"Heather?" He approached her with long quick strides. "Did the phone ring while I was out of the room?"

"No one called."

He swore, crossing to the mantel. Picking up the near empty squat tumbler, he downed the drink in a single swallow.

She said his name softly: "Quinn . . ."

A vein in his neck throbbed as if he were gritting his teeth when he asked gruffly, "You *will* stay won't you?"

There was no hesitation on her part. She hated the misery she saw in his dark gray eyes. She nodded.

"For as long as it takes?" He couldn't begin to express how much her staying mattered to him. Pride be damn, he needed her.

"Yes . . ." Heather bit her trembling bottom lip. She was close to losing the hold she had on her emotions. She was feeling much too much. Tears were not far away, and they certainly wouldn't help the situation.

"Thanks," he said so softly she barely heard him. "Heather I want you to know—"

The telephone rang before he could finish.

Heather's eyes locked with his. Hope she didn't vocalize was transmitted to him. Quinn stopped the sound on the second jingle.

"Montgomery," he answered.

Eight

"Cindy? Is that you, baby?" Quinn whispered, his voice tight with emotions.

Heather gasped aloud and ran to him. He instantly looped an arm around her, pressing her into his side. She could feel his large body quiver as he listened carefully, but she didn't see the moisture flooding his gaze because she was blinded by her own rush of tears.

"Where are you, baby girl?" He paused, listening. "Are you all right? Good. Don't cry, peanut. No . . . no, I'm not angry. I want you to go introduce yourself to the manager of the station. Let him know you're waiting for your father. Find him! I want you looked after until Heather and I can reach you. Yes, she's here, hold on." To Heather, he said, "She wants to speak to you."

"Hello, Cindy. It's so good to hear your voice," Heather said, attempting to swallow her tears. "No, he's not mad at you. No. We both just want you back safe. No. Don't worry. It'll be fine once we've talked. Yes . . . yes . . . okay. Here's your dad." Heather returned the telephone to Quinn.

"Yes, I know where that is," he said, releasing Heather

momentarily to jot down information on a notepad. "It's going to take a while to get there. Yes, we'll be there as soon as we can. Don't forget about the manager. Hold on, baby girl. Bye."

Once he'd put down the telephone, he sat on the edge of the desk and held onto Heather. She offered no resistance. They silently shared a heady sense of relief and gratitude. Quinn sighed heavily, drawing strength from Heather. When they parted they both looked away.

"Where is she?" Heather asked, while pretending her legs weren't trembling.

"She called from a bus station in Dayton. She's going to wait there for us."

"I know a little bit about Dayton. I went to college down that way," Heather said before asking, "Quinn, how did she sound to you?"

"She's sounded fine—upset but fine."

Heather couldn't help smiling as she studied the relaxed lines of Quinn's face. If only he were able to put that love she saw in his eyes into words—the words that Cynthia needed to hear from her father.

"I've got to let everyone know she's safe." He reached for the telephone, then stopped suddenly. "Heather, Dayton is about a four-hour drive. We probably won't arrive until close to midnight. Do you still want to come?"

"Yes."

He smiled, evidently relieved by her answer. This time when he reached for the telephone, Heather stopped him.

"While you're taking care of things here I'll go on home and pack an overnight case. I need to check in with Mrs. Silvers, our school's principal, and let her know what's happened." Heather said softly, "I'm so glad she's safe."

"Me, too. I'll pick you up within an hour."

Seated at her desk, Heather had just hung up the telephone when the doorbell rang.

"Hi, all set?" Quinn like Heather hadn't taken time to change.

"Yes. My overnight case is over there. I'll just get my purse and jacket."

"Allow me." Quinn took the black leather jacket from her and helped her into it. He grabbed the bag she left at the base of the staircase.

They were both belted into their respective seats when he asked, "Did you make your call?"

"Yes, Mrs. Silvers sends her best wishes."

"She understands your reason for going?"

"Yes, now she does." She admitted with difficulty, "This case has become very personal with me." Pausing to take a fortifying breath, she went on to say, "I seem to have lost my objectivity. So I've decided to turn Cynthia's case over to another counselor when we get back."

"Like hell!" His brows came together in a deep frown.

"Quinn, I care too much. My feelings are involved. For me to do a satisfactory job I must be able to step back and view the situation clearly."

"Heather, I don't think now is the time to quit. My daughter's gonna need you. Cindy trusts you." And so do I, the last was a thought he didn't give voice to.

"She'll have my support. I don't plan to leave her high and dry."

"But—"

"I've some personal days. I decided to take them now in order to come with you. I wouldn't be here if I didn't think I could be useful."

"And later—after we're back. What happens then? You hand her case over to some stranger?"

"Quinn! I'm not deserting Cynthia. I hope to continue being her friend, a part of her life." Heather hesitated, knowing she couldn't very well tell him that it was her responses to him that disturbed her. She had found it easier to be frank with her administrator than with Quinn. But what choice did she have? She couldn't in all good conscience continue counseling Cynthia. It was unethical.

"Quinn, I plan to help her get her life back on track."

"Thank you." He was quiet, thoughtful for a time. "We're lucky, Heather. She could have so easily taken a plane across the country before she changed her mind."

"Yes. And she decided on her own that she wanted to come home. That's a very good sign."

He nodded, his eyes on the road as he headed for the expressway. "Music?"

"Please," she agreed, settling against the supple black leather seat.

"Have a preference?" He opened the glove compartment, indicating a selection of compact discs inside.

"Anita Baker?"

"Aw, yes, the sister is one of my favorites." When Heather handed him the C.D., her fingers accidentally slid across his smooth palm. "Soft." He said it so quietly that for a second Heather thought she had imagined it.

As music flowed gently around them, she concentrated on it, hoping to ignore the warm flutters inside of her.

"Tell me about yourself."

"What do you want to know?"

"Everything," he said with an unexpected smile.

Heather tingled with awareness, wondering if he were joking. Perhaps he was hoping to lighten the mood that had been so very tense the last couple hours. She'd be foolish to read more into the comment than idle curiosity.

"Heather?"

"That's easy enough. I was thirty last month—and I've finally gotten over the shock of it. My family believes in celebrating birthdays. Everyone in our family has a party, whether they want one or not."

Quinn's wide mouth curved into a half smile.

"My parents gave me this horrible party. Big balloons with 'Thirty and Over the Hill' printed on them. And the jokes! My brothers are such teases. But I must admit we did have a great time. Daddy makes wonderful cakes. This one was a three-layer affair. The darn thing could have been a beacon on a foggy night with all those candles blazing away. Overall, it was terrible."

Quinn chuckled, able to relax for the first time since learning of Cynthia's disappearance. Heather had that effect on him. He enjoyed her company. What amazed him was his own candor. He found himself opening up with her, sharing even private thoughts, which was out of character for him.

He asked, "What was it like growing up in a large family?"

He briefly took his eyes off the road to look at her. He sure liked what he saw. Heather Gregory was easy on a man's eyes. She probably had men tripping over themselves to get to her. The thought annoyed the hell out of him.

"Loud," she laughed, tucking several braids behind her ear. "I was a terrible tomboy. I used to follow my brothers everywhere, much to their annoyance and my poor mother's despair. I hated dresses and hair ribbons and patent leather shoes until I was thirteen." She paused, "But we were lucky. Even though both of my parents worked and there wasn't always enough money for all the things we wanted, there was plenty of love."

"Hmmm," Quinn murmured, settling back. "Sounds like a wonderful family." A smile softened the lines of his dark brown face. "Did you grow up here in Detroit?"

"Yes, I love the city," Heather said.

"I agree!" he laughed.

Heather smiled thinking how easy he was to talk to. "I was glad I had a chance to go away to college. It allowed me to grow up and gain some independence. Once I finished Central State in Wilberforce, Ohio, I moved to Chicago."

"That's a surprise. I assumed you were a Wayne State graduate."

"Nope. Although I'm in their doctorate program."

"What field?"

"Clinical psychology."

"Heavy. So why Chicago?"

"I wanted to prove myself. I couldn't do that here. At least, not with my father. And my four brothers were almost as bad as he was. Daddy's from the old school. He believes that a girl should live at home with her folks until she marries or dies, whichever comes first."

Quinn chuckled but didn't interrupt, enjoying the cadence of her soft voice.

"My older sister Gwen married while she was still in college. She swears her sole reason was to get out of our parents' house."

"Get out of here!"

Heather giggled, adding, "I'm not kidding. But it might help to know she's crazy about her husband Eric. They've been married close to eighteen years."

Quinn grinned, and Heather continued. "Even though I'm the youngest in the family, I'm not spoiled. Although," she said slowly, "I do like having my own way."

"The baby." He chuckled and shook his head. "That must have been a real hassle when you started to date. I pity the poor guys." He hesitated, "Almost."

Heather turned her head away, gazing out the window for a time. He didn't need to see the grin she couldn't hide. She felt almost like purring. He was certainly good for her ego.

"So?" Quinn prompted.

"What?"

"So how difficult was it for a guy to get past your brothers?"

"My brothers were very accommodating. So much so that one of them always managed to follow me on my dates. My own personal chaperone. I can't tell how much that did for my social life. I had none. Is it any wonder I went away to college the first chance I got and moved out of state for a while?"

Quinn roared with laughter. Finally he asked, still chuckling, "So why Lawrence?"

"Diane Rivers, my old college roommate, teaches at

Lawrence. She wrote and told me about the head counseling position. It was a promotion for me. By then, I had finally admitted to myself that I missed my family and friends. I'd been thinking about returning home for a while. Aren't you tired of me hogging the conversation?"

"I'll let you know when I'm bored."

Heather shivered, sensitive to the husky warmth in his tone. She hadn't completely accepted her interest in him. She certainly hadn't planned on caring about him. For so long, her family, her career, and her work toward her doctorate had been the center of her orderly life. Now suddenly all that had changed. Her world had become extremely complicated. If she wasn't careful, she'd end up falling for him, and that would be nothing short of emotional suicide.

Even if she wasn't Cynthia's counselor, she was not looking for a broken heart. She'd told herself that her response to Quinn's caresses and kisses were unimportant, told herself that the attraction between them was best forgotten. Quinn was not emotionally free. It was surprising he didn't still wear a wedding band.

"I, for one, am glad you found your way back to Detroit. Have you ever been in love?"

Heather was at a loss for words. Suddenly she was grateful for the advent of darkness. She concentrated on the passing scenery rather than the virile man beside her.

"No. For a time I thought I was. It was while I was in Chicago. I became engaged to a very nice man for all the wrong reasons."

"What happened?"

"I wanted to be married and I cared about him. It was

not enough. It took me awhile to figure it out. In the process, I hurt him and myself."

"Don't be so hard on yourself," Heather was relieved when he asked "Why a private school?"

"The challenge. Lawrence lives up to its reputation. We're just starting to make our school financially accessible to minority students. I'm committed to that goal. There are too many children falling through the cracks in the public school system. They're lost in a maze of paperwork. I know it isn't a problem exclusive to Detroit. It's happening all over the country. Our African-American children's needs must be addressed. Especially our males."

"It's a relief to know someone is doing something positive rather than complaining. Our jails are packed with kids who were determined to be making something out of their lives. They go about it in the wrong way. It's not that they lack intelligence, just guidance."

"Honey-lamb, I don't believe it. We actually agree on something." Heather laughed.

He grinned. "I haven't heard that expression in years."

"My great-aunt Naomi is full of old sayings. But seriously, scholarship money is the key. I'm determined to double our minority population next year."

"If anyone can do it, you can."

Heather smiled, warmed by the compliment.

"I think it's important that successful African-Americans give back to their community."

"I couldn't agree with you more." Although his pro-bono cases weren't something he normally discussed, Quinn found himself telling Heather about a recent case. "I got involved in a drug case where a perfectly innocent family man lost his truck due to kindness. He let a buddy borrow it, unaware that the guy was using. It was seized by the police."

"Oh no! Did he get it back?"

"Oh yeah, but we had to go to trial to get it back."

She flashed him a brilliant smile. "I'm surprised you have the time."

He shrugged, "How is the dissertation going?" he surprised her by asking.

"Slowly. I've been volunteering at the Crisis Prevention Center. I started to help gather information for my dissertation. But it's much more than that now. I've found it helps me, far more than it does those troubled youngsters. The children I work with have attempted suicide at least once."

Quinn's respect and admiration for this woman constantly grew.

Heather made herself comfortable, kicking off her high heels and tucking a leg beneath her. She leaned her head back against the seat cushion.

The sweet soulful melody, "Giving You the Best That I Got" whirled around them. Their silence was relaxing. For a time they weren't governed by fear or worry.

Quinn inhaled the sweetness of her scent, longing to caress her soft skin. He contented himself by reaching over and lifting a thin single braid from where it rested against the side of her soft neck. He fingered it, rubbing his thumb over it.

Heather glanced at him. The question on her lips was never voiced. His gaze was on the highway stretching before them. The deep rich color of his skin was lost within the dark interior of the car. She didn't need to see him to know that he was so intensely male. His profile would only attest to that. Quinn . . .

She let her thoughts fly, allowing herself the freedom to wonder what it would feel like to be his . . . his woman exclusively. Her imagination soared as she mentally gave herself over to the fantasy. She could almost feel herself lying in his arms, her nude body wrapped around his lean muscular length. Just the thought of Quinn's wide long-fingered hands smoothing over her skin down her body made the tips of her breasts swell, becoming so hard and achy that she could feel them through layers of her clothing.

Oh, Quinn . . . If only he would move his hand from where it rested on his thigh to her breasts. She was dizzy with yearnings for him to palm her softness, squeeze her, then worry her tingling nipple by tugging on it. She swallowed the moan rising in her throat. Instead, Heather wiggled in her seat, quickly crossed her legs, holding her thighs tightly together.

She had to stop this recklessness. Just because she had experienced his kisses and his caress and found so much pleasure from them didn't mean she wanted a relationship with him.

She was no different from most women. She wanted a loving closeness with one special man. A relationship that might someday lead to marriage and a family of her own. Why was she even thinking about this now?

She had to stop! She should know better than to sit next to the man and fantasize about his long fingers caressing, not her braid, but the very heart of her femininity. She squirmed in her seat.

"Restless? Want to stop and stretch your legs?"

His deep voice sent shivers down her spine.

"I'm fine."

"Do you braid your own hair?"

"Oh, no, I don't have the skill or the patience. My aunt Naomi does it for me. Her fingers are still as quick and skilled as they were when she used to pick cotton as a girl in Georgia. My mama's folks are from down there."

"She does a wonderful job. I like your hair that way. Reminds me of another place, another time."

"Ancient Africa?" she asked with a tilt of her head.

"Yeah," he sounded somewhat taken aback. "You read the history?"

"Oh, yes. Van Setima and George James are my favorite authors. How can you know where you're going if you don't understand where you've been? Someday I'm going to take that study-tour of Egypt. I want to see the Nile."

"You, too?" Quinn laughed softly. "I have a minor in African history. Unfortunately it's almost impossible for me to find time to read anything outside of the law. Egypt at this point is a dream vacation for me."

He snatched another look at Heather. No, Heather wasn't just beautiful. She was intelligent, honest, and very generous with her warmth and her time. The more he learned about her the more he wanted to know.

If a man weren't careful he could easily find himself deeply, irrevocably in love with Heather. Quinn scowled. There was no doubt about the fact that he wanted her. What sane man wouldn't want to make frequent and intense love to Heather Gregory?

But he also knew there was no room in his heart for

a new love. That part of his life was over. It had ended
the day his wife Peggy was buried. The pain of that loss
had never healed. And quite frankly at this late date he
no longer expected it to.

But Heather. She was different, very special. She was
intriguing. The woman's mind fascinated him.

After a time he said, "You're awfully quiet."

"Just thinking. I wish I knew why Cynthia ran away.
How can we help her when we don't know what's really
bothering her?"

"She's pregnant. At her age that should be enough."

"There's more to it."

"Such as?"

"That's just it, Quinn. There's a missing piece to this
puzzle. I can't figure out what it is."

"I know I've done a lousy job with my daughter in
the past."

"I'm not criticizing you. I accept my part in this. Remember, she didn't come to me, either. She was upset
on Saturday, but she didn't trust me enough to tell me
why."

His voice was cold, without emotion when he finally
said, "I'll do whatever it takes to help my daughter."

"I hate it when you use that icy tone. It makes you
seem so distant, uncaring."

"What do you want from me?" He scowled, glaring
at her before returning his gaze to the road.

"Listen with an open mind, okay?" When he remained
broodingly silent, she sighed softly. "Please . . ."

He couldn't see her urgency, but he heard it in her
voice.

"I'm listening."

"I know you love Cynthia and want her back. But she desperately needs to know how much she matters to you, Quinn. And she needs to hear it from you."

"I'm not good at putting my feelings into words."

"Think about Cynthia. Think about how important this is to her." Heather paused. "There's more." She swung one leg nervously.

"What?"

"Cynthia thinks you somehow wished she had died rather than her mother. Don't you see, she's doing what you've done since learning of her pregnancy . . . blaming herself."

Dark smoke-colored eyes bore into brown ones before he was forced to return his attention to the highway. The silence that had risen between them was deafening.

"Nothing can bring her mother back," Heather said softly. The pain in his eyes was unmistakable. "But your love and assurance can give Cynthia the courage she needs to face the uncertainty ahead. Please, don't freeze her out."

"I don't do it intentionally!"

"I know." She hesitated, not wanting to rouse his temper, but determined to help him repair his relationship with Cynthia. "No matter how resentful or angry she might seem when we find her, she needs to know that you love her regardless of the worry and disappointment she's caused you."

"Is there anything more I should do—Cut my chest open and bleed all over the place?" His sarcasm was razor sharp—the air around them seemed to crackle with tension. He held the steering wheel with such force it was surprising it didn't break into two equal parts.

"If you love her, show her," Heather persisted. "Let her see into your heart."

Quinn's hands clenched the steering wheel. "I can't believe we're still having this stupid conversation."

"A little while ago, you were willing to do just about anything to get her back. Have you changed your mind?"

"No—but I warn you, I'm no good at this kind of thing."

She could see him slowly relinquishing his grip on the wheel, his long strong fingers, once again guided the car with an expert ease.

He leaned back, rounding out his shoulders. Only Quinn knew his temper was still simmering, his emotions raw, and his stomach felt like it was boiling. He searched in his pocket for an antacid.

Heather was also affected by his mood. Her throat was filled with unshed tears. He had every right to his anger. The things she had said to him were hard for any parent to take. But somehow her concern for him and Cynthia had gotten mixed in. She wanted to help him so badly.

Also, she was treading a thin line between breaking Cynthia's trust. Helping Quinn understand his daughter was critical. She suspected she'd already blown it. She consoled herself with the hope that Quinn's effort might win Cynthia over. Face it girl, you are messing in the man's business.

Darkness enveloped them as they approached the Michigan-Ohio border. As Quinn's anger dimmed, guilt reared its monstrous head. This wrenching emotion was something too familiar for him not to recognize. He'd let Peggy down—now he had done the same thing to their baby. No matter how hard he tried he couldn't forget. Why had he insisted that Peggy . . .

"Quinn, I'm sorry." Heather's voice interrupted his thoughts.

"I am, too," he said quickly. "I didn't mean to snap at you. The truth is a little hard to take right now," he said, rubbing his jaw, roughened by the day's growth of beard. He reached out and touched her cheek with the hard knuckles of one hand in a very gentle caress. "I trust you. Forgive me?"

"There's nothing to forgive."

"I've made some serious mistakes with my daughter's upbringing. I'm not trying to duck my responsibilities," he said candidly. "Do you really think Cindy is serious about this boy?"

"I wish I knew." Heather's brow wrinkled as she thought. "What I can't figure out is why she didn't mention him when she called. She didn't ask us to contact him."

"Hell, I can't figure out how it happened. She's home every night."

"I do believe, Counselor, that babies can be conceived during the daylight hours."

He laughed in spite of the seriousness of the subject.

"Quinn, no one can monitor a teenager every second of the day. Their need for independence keeps getting in the way."

"Heather, I don't know what's going on in my own child's life," he said with difficulty. "I've spent so many hours working, and evidently not enough with Cynthia. I didn't even know she had a boyfriend until you told me she was pregnant. I want her safe."

* * *

Every time Cynthia thought of facing her father, her eyes flooded with tears. Had she done the right thing? Maybe she shouldn't have called. . . . If she weren't such a baby, she'd take the next bus leaving Dayton. It was heading west. Los Angles seemed like a good place, warm and far away. Problem was the people she cared about were back home. She wished she were home right now, wished she'd never left. How was she going to tell her father the truth?

Cynthia was grateful for the noise in the bus station. It covered the sounds of her sniffles. She sat slumped in a chair, her shoulders hunched, her face buried in a magazine. Rifling through her oversize leather bag, she searched for a tissue. When she couldn't find a dry one, she settled for the wadded one she had shoved in the pocket of her jacket. She had made such a mess of things.

She'd backed herself into a corner. There seemed to be only one way out of it . . . to run. Careful that her father didn't discover what she was up to this morning, Cynthia had managed to squeeze only a change of clothes and underthings into her school bag. Once her father let her off at school, she had taken a local bus to the bank, cashed a check, then headed for the Greyhound station. She didn't dare go back home for her things. Mrs. Thornton would have called her father right away.

She'd been so scared that she'd taken the first out-of-state bus she found. All she knew was that she had to get away.

It wasn't as if she wanted to run away—she had no choice. But the farther she traveled from home and her father, the lonelier she became. When the bus stopped in Dayton she got off. She was scared, really scared. For the first time she faced the prospect of life on her own. Cynthia panicked. That was when she called her father.

As she sat shredding tissues, she knew that it was only a matter of time until she had to deal with her father. He was already angry. Her stomach knotted as she realized just how much she dreaded facing him and Heather. She need to think. Plan what she was going to say. Time was running out for her.

Cynthia gathered her things and rushed over to the restroom. She ducked into a stall and waited until the room was quiet before she moved to the sink.

She looked awful. The makeup she'd applied with such flair that morning was streaked—gold, blue, and green shadows were smudged across her forehead, where she had wiped her eyes. Using a dampened paper towel, she tried to clean her face. Every time she thought of facing her father her eyes, already red and swollen, filled with fresh tears.

"Hey, are you okay?"

Cynthia jumped.

"Sorry, I didn't mean to scare you, girlfriend. You okay?" the teenager asked. Her young thin face was covered with pimples under a heavy layer of makeup. Her blond hair hung in unclean tangles to her shoulders. Her jeans were not fashionably torn as Cynthia's were. The rip in the fabric came from constant use, just as the fabric stiffness was not due to sizing, but rather a lack of washing.

"Yeah," Cynthia said, around a sniffle.

"I saw you in the lobby. I'm waiting for my bus. Hey, you look kinda upset. I ain't doggin' you or nothin'. If I'm poking my nose in where it doesn't belong, just say the word. I'm out of here. But hey, I know what it is to need a friend."

Cynthia was too caught up in her own misery to take notice of anything more than the other girl's sympathetic attitude. The hardness in her pale blue eyes testified to experiences far beyond her years.

"You by yourself?" she asked, eyeing Cynthia's designer clothes, leather sneakers, and oversize leather carry-all. An expensive gold locket hung on a thick diamond-cut gold chain around Cynthia's neck. The delicate gold and diamond tennis bracelet on her wrist was duly noted.

"Yeah, but I'm okay now. I just got kinda scared for a moment."

"Hey, I understand. I'm alone, too. I'm headed for the Big Apple. I'll be here all night. My bus doesn't leave until seven tomorrow mornin'. I was on my way out to get a burger. Want to come?"

"I'm expecting my father. He's going to meet me here."

"I thought you said you were alone?" she said sharply.

"I am," Cynthia said, when she saw the other girl's frown.

"Look, it's up to you. I just thought you could use a friend."

"I've got time. My dad won't be here for a while. He's driving down from Detroit."

"Cool," she said, looking quite pleased with herself.

"Just give me a second to clean my face."

"I'm Eva. What's yours?"

"Cynthia," she answered, splashing water on her face.

When she was finished she ran a quick comb through her hair.

The two girls threaded their way through the crowded terminal. A group of passengers had just arrived—family and friends were on hand to add to the confusion.

Cynthia started to tell the manager where she was going, but the woman was busy on the telephone. Besides, she'd be back soon.

Cynthia didn't see the hand motion the girl made to a slim man, leaning against the wall.

"There's a burger place just down the block," Eva said, holding the outside door open for Cynthia.

Nine

It was much cooler, almost nippy since the sun had gone down. Cynthia zipped her color-blocked parka close around her throat. The sidewalk around the station was congested, the streets were filled with evening traffic.

"Are you from around here?" Cynthia asked.

"Yeah," Eva answered. "I'm going to my sister's. She and her old man said they had a room for me. My ma's dead." She walked with her shoulders hunched, her hands in her pockets.

"Mine, too," Cynthia said, softly. "I'm from Detroit. I've only been gone a few hours and already I'm homesick."

"First time away from home?"

"Not really. I never traveled by myself though. When I've gone away to boarding school, my dad always took me."

"You a runaway?"

Cynthia shrugged, not answering. She didn't really want to talk about why she was here alone. Besides, whenever she thought about her father and what she'd done she started to cry. She was determined not to make a fool of herself by acting like a crybaby. The other girl would think she was really stupid. After all, she was older—maybe even seventeen.

The restaurant was one of a popular nationwide chain. And it was busy. Hungry for the first time since leaving home, Cynthia ordered a double cheeseburger, fries and a large chocolate shake. Eva ordered a Coke.

"I thought you were hungry?"

The girl shrugged. "I'm a little short."

"Short?"

"On cash. Got to make what I have last."

"Oh," Cynthia said in surprise. "I have enough for both of us." She extracted a fifty dollar bill from her wallet, unaware of the other's interest in its contents. "Go ahead. Order whatever you'd like."

"Hey, thanks." Eva smiled, taking a quick glance back over her shoulder.

They found an empty booth near the rear. Eva quickly took the seat facing the front entrance. Cynthia, busy taking off her jacket and getting comfortable, didn't look around. Her companion chatted away, but her eyes were on the slim young man who had been following them. He sat at a booth by the door, sipping slowly from the soft drink in his hand.

Munching on fries, Eva asked, "So why were you crying in the John?"

"I got in trouble so I ran away."

"What kind of trouble?"

"Look, can we talk about something else?"

"Sure, just thought you could use a friend."

"I can. It's just I did a dumb thing, okay?"

"So you ran, huh?"

"Yeah. What do kids do around here for fun?"

"Not much. That's why I'm cutting loose from this dump."

"Are you running away, too?"

The girl laughed. "No need. Me and my old man don't get on. The smart-ass is always trying to run my life. Hey, I'm sixteen. I don't need an old fart like him trying to beat my ass every time I'm a few minutes late. Hell, half the time he's so drunk he don't know if I'm dead or not. I say good riddance." Eva had a mouth full of food. "You gonna eat that?"

Cynthia shook her head, passing over the half-eaten sandwich. Eva wasn't like any of the girls Cynthia had met in boarding school or even at Lawrence. She was different. She wasn't afraid of anything. Cynthia liked her. Finally, she had found someone who wanted to be her friend.

Quinn exited the interstate, following the secondary road to the gas station in order to refuel and stretch stiff muscles. Even though it was after nine, the station was busy and he had to wait for a free gas pump.

While Quinn was occupied with the car, Heather used the ladies room on the side of the building. When she rejoined him, he was pocketing money.

"Hungry?" he asked, holding her door open.

"Do we have time to eat?"

"I can eat and drive. Can you eat and ride?"

"Sure can."

Mrs. Thornton packed sandwiches, coffee, and fruit juice. The basket is behind my seat. Sound good?"

"Very."

Quinn positioned the basket where she could reach it before starting the car. "Hope you like sliced turkey and swiss."

"Anything . . ." She smiled, handing him a sandwich before getting one for herself. "How much farther?"

"Little over a hundred miles. We should reach Dayton around eleven."

They exchanged worried looks.

"I won't feel right until we can see for ourselves that she's safe."

"That makes two of us." He washed his sandwich down with a healthy swig of apple juice. "It's nightfall and that makes me uneasy," he said speeding along the interstate.

Heather ate slowly, her thoughts miles ahead with Cynthia. When she finished, she foraged in the basket. "Grapes—Want some?"

"Nope. You go ahead."

She nearly choked on the fruit in her mouth when he said "If I didn't know better I'd think the men in Detroit have lost their eyesight as well as their good sense."

"Where did that come from?"

"An opinion. Something wrong with that?"

"There you go, trying to put me on the defensive. I'm gonna have to watch out for you, Counselor."

"Professional defect. Do you date?"

"Yes, as I'm sure you do. My brother is always fixing me up with one of his buddies. Did I tell you my twin brothers Carl and Bruce Gregory both play professional football?"

"No, you didn't—but I recognize the names. Carl

plays with Detroit and Bruce plays in Minnesota. I'm impressed."

"Why? Because they play sports professionally?"

"Because you survived childhood with those two around. They're huge."

Heather laughed. "Our house was never quiet. Ever since Carl married, last year, he's become a notorious matchmaker."

"And . . ." he prompted.

"And nothing." She looked over at Quinn.

"Well?" she prompted.

"Well what?"

"Do you date?"

"No."

"Oh, yeah," she said dryly. "Pull the other leg."

Quinn laughed in spite of himself. "Why can't a woman believe a man when he tells the truth? I have no reason to lie. You know as well as I do it takes time to develop and maintain a relationship."

"I suppose you have a point."

"My case load is unreal. There's no such thing in my life as free time." He sighed. "I don't know how, but that's got to change. I'm just beginning to realize how unfair I've been to Cynthia. If I'm not careful, I'm going to lose my daughter."

"You're forgetting something, aren't you? Cynthia loves you."

Heather couldn't stop herself from asking, "When you said you're not dating, were you telling me that you're celibate?"

"Yes. Why do you sound surprised? You having difficulty with that?"

"Frankly, yes."

"Casual sex doesn't do it for me, Heather. At least, not anymore."

"I suppose anything is possible."

"You say that because I'm a man. You wouldn't have any trouble believing another woman."

"You're wrong."

"Oh, really? Think about it. I had no trouble believing you, sugar dumplin'."

"You've made your point," Heather said reluctantly.

Sipping from her soft drink, Eva asked, "A kid like you must get everythin' she wants. Right?"

"Like me? What does that mean?" Cynthia asked, suddenly uncomfortable.

"Nice threads. Plenty of money. I'm no fool. You got real gold around your neck. Who's your daddy? Some big shot, huh?"

Extremely uneasy, Cynthia began gathering up her things.

"Where you going?"

"I'm done. I'm going back to the bus station."

"Hey, look. I didn't mean nothin'. I was just askin'," Eva said, hurrying to keep up with Cynthia.

They were on the sidewalk when Cynthia said, "You don't have to come. I know my way back."

"It's cool."

Cynthia frowned and watched the girl start off without her. For a few moments she stood undecided.

"Hey, wait for me," Cynthia called.

The wind was brisk and it stung her cheeks. Eva was

just disappearing into the dark night when Cynthia dashed after her.

Eva was several blocks away. She didn't stop when Cynthia called out to her. She ducked into an alley. By the time Cynthia reached the narrow dark alley that ran down the center of the dilapidated L-shaped building, Eva had vanished.

Without a moment's hesitation Cynthia continued on, wondering if Eva had gone through the side door. Dumpsters were piled high with trash, garbage littered the ground. Music blared from the bar housed on the ground floor.

Cynthia looked around uneasily, but there was no sign of Eva. A long sleek car was parked at the rear of the building. Where could Eva have gone? She couldn't be inside the bar, could she?

Now what? Could she get back to the bus station on her own? It couldn't be that far away, could it? Cynthia was beginning to doubt the wisdom of being so far away from the streetlights. Movement within the dumpster caused her to turn around and head back to the safety of the sidewalk.

She'd taken only a few steps when she found her exit blocked. A tall, lean man stood in such a way that his back was toward the street. She couldn't make out his features, but he had red hair. Eva stood next to him.

"What's going on?" Cynthia asked, shifting her heavy bag from one shoulder to the other.

"You did real good, baby. Real good," he drawled. Although the compliment was for the other girl, his eyes never left Cynthia. "Don't worry, Daddy will take care of you later, sugar."

"Eva, who's this man?" Cynthia asked, looking nervously from one to the other.

"I ask the questions." He laughed as if he'd just told a joke. "My girl here tells me you're all alone in the world. Need some looking after. I'm your man. I take care of my girls. The street ain't safe for a pretty thing like you, baby. Not to worry. I'll be your sweet daddy, I'll take care of you, sugar."

"Look, I don't know what you're talking about." Cynthia said, too scared to take her eyes off of him. Something about him made her flesh crawl. "Let me pass, please," she said as she approached cautiously.

When she tried to dash by, he grabbed her by the back of her jacket and swung her around roughly. Off balance, she suddenly found her back against his front, his arm across her rib cage. He muffled her screams with his hand. "It's alright, baby. No one is going to hurt you."

"Get the money." He motioned with his head. Eva rifled through Cynthia's things and found the wallet in an inside zipper pocket.

Cynthia screamed again. "No! That's all the money I have!" She had close to seven hundred dollars in that wallet. Cynthia tried another scream as she fought desperately to get away.

"Be still, little girl, before I give you something to yell about, like a fat lip."

"I want this," Eva said, holding up a silk blouse. "You said I could keep her stuff."

"Yeah, yeah, come on—before someone comes."

"I want the gold chain and the locket. I saw it. It's around her neck."

"No!" Cynthia cried. "You can't have it!"

Cynthia kicked and twisted her body as much as she could. Her father would never forgive her if she lost the locket. Her mother's picture was inside that locket. Panic set in when she realized what they could do to her besides steal her things. She was in danger—there was no one around to help her. Frantic with fear, Cynthia sank her teeth into the man's hand and pushed him as hard as she could.

"Bitch!" he roared, ripping the gold locket and chain from around her neck. Swearing viciously, he shoved the screaming Cynthia as hard as he could, hurling her slight frame toward a nearby Dumpster. She slammed head first into the unyielding metal, and crumpled onto the trash-littered concrete pavement.

Before he reached again for the unconscious Cynthia, someone yelled from the window overhead: "Hey, what goin' on down there?"

Eva said urgently, "Let's get the hell out of here before somebody calls the cops."

"Finally," Quinn sighed when they reached the city limits.

"Please, Dear God, let her be safe," Heather prayed aloud.

Waiting for a traffic light to change, Quinn said softly, "I stopped praying the day I lost my wife. But today I haven't been able to do anything else."

"Is that the bus station over there?"

"Yes, I think so."

"Nervous?" she whispered, once he'd parked in the large dark lot behind a row of buses.

"A little," he said quietly. He reached for her hand, in need of her support and reassurance. Heather gave both, returning the slow steady pressure of his fingers against her own.

"Remember, show her what's in your heart."

He nodded. "Let's go."

"You mean to stand there and tell me you let my daughter walk out of here without trying to stop her! What the hell kind of place is this!" Quinn was livid, his whole body pulsed with it.

The security guard and the bus station manager exchanged a look before the manager said, "She walked out of here of her own free will. It's not my job to stop her. Besides, as I told you before, she probably left while I was on the telephone. I didn't see her leave. It's not my fault."

The security guard added, "Yeah. It got crowded for a while there. I saw her when she went into the bathroom after Sue, the manager here, asked me to help keep an eye on her. She just disappeared."

Quinn clenched and unclenched his jaw.

"Are you certain she didn't return later?" Heather asked sharply.

"Positive."

Quinn took Heather's arm and pulled her toward the front door.

"But Quinn, we haven't talked to—"

"We talked to everyone." He swallowed the rage and fear coursing through his bloodstream.

"Where are we going?"

"Police station."

Quinn's face was set, devoid of emotion. His mouth was taut, his back straight as he concentrated on driving. She wanted to say something to him, reach him in that cold distant place he found within himself—a place that he kept hidden from others. Yet her own feelings were too involved, and silence lay between them like a fog, thick and clogging, until it seemed to weigh down even the air they breathed.

Quinn jerked the car to a stop along the curb. His voice was frustrated and angry as he asked, "Was that two left turns and a right at the light?" For a man trained to remember the tiniest detail, he couldn't recall a few simple directions.

Heather knew his furor wasn't directed outward but at himself. It was too dark in the car for her to see his features clearly, yet his pain was clear in his voice.

"Left at the next two lights then a right at the next corner," Heather said soothingly. She reached out and stroked the hand resting on his knee. It was a tender caress meant to comfort.

He clasped her hand tightly for a few seconds, inhaling slowly, before releasing the pent-up air trapped in his lungs. Slowly he opened his hand, allowing her soft slim fingers to glide across the surface of his wide smooth palm. Ever so briefly he laced his fingers through hers, then released her and returned his hand to the steering wheel.

Their visit to the police station proved to be an exercise in acute frustration. There was no shortage of teenagers reported missing. Quinn made sure Cynthia's name now topped the list. They left the station armed with the addresses and phone numbers of the local shelters and a map of the city.

"That was a waste of time! I want my daughter found . . . now! Anything could have happened to her." His long strong legs moved quickly down the block toward the car.

Heather hurried to keep up with his rapid ground-eating pace. In heels, her five-two frame was no match for Quinn's six-two, long-legged strides.

"They're doing the best that they can. Thanks to our visit they have a picture of her and a car out looking for her. There is nothing more that can be done for the moment."

"Look what it took to get a car out there? Hell, I had to practically call the mayor. You heard them! They don't believe she's still in Dayton! They think she's on her way to L.A."

"Quinn, that's because a girl fitting Cynthia's description boarded the bus tonight. It's possible."

"It's highly unlikely. She's here—I'm going to find her if it's the last thing I do."

A police station held no mystery to him. He'd dealt with them too many times in his work. The difference was that this time it had gotten personal. Too damn personal for his peace of mind. His baby was out there. And he wanted every cop in Dayton out looking for her.

Quinn reached the car, then looked around, surprised that Heather wasn't right beside him. When she caught up to him, he asked, "Do you think she was on that bus to Los Angeles?"

"No. I think she's here in Dayton. But it was a good

idea for the authorities to fax Cynthia's description on to California, just in case."

Quinn nodded. "I don't know why I took this list. Cynthia wouldn't be in any of these places. Why would she go to a shelter?"

"It's a place to start looking," she said.

"She's able to pay for a room. Our time would be better spent calling the hotels and motels in the area."

"Quinn, the shelters are a start. There aren't that many for runaways. It shouldn't take long and we can show them Cynthia's picture."

"Okay," he said tiredly.

Heather got into the car and sagged against the seat. She was every bit as tired as he was. But the lateness of the hour wasn't worth worrying about. They had to find Cynthia—and tonight if possible. Whenever Heather thought about her alone on the streets, she shuddered. It was downright scary. How could Cynthia have put herself at risk like this? And for what? Quinn knew the worst. He knew she was pregnant. He accepted it. Why couldn't Cynthia see that?

"What do you think happened?" Quinn asked, once they were under way. "What made her change her mind?"

"Quinn, she's confused and very unhappy. I think she got scared at the prospect of facing you. That's why she originally involved me in this, remember? She knows we're on our way. So I don't believe she's left Dayton."

"She wants to be found, Heather. I know she does. I heard it in her voice. So we're talking about a few hours. What the hell happened?"

"We'll find out," Heather said evenly, controlling her

fear for Cynthia. She had to stay steady if she was going to help the girl and her father.

Unfortunately there was no sign of Cynthia at the shelter. Quinn and Heather showed her picture around. It quickly became apparent that the few kids who were willing to look at Cynthia's picture exhibited a measure of distrust toward adults. The night counselor at the last shelter suggested that they have pictures of Cynthia printed on flyers to be hung or passed out in places frequented by teens.

As they emerged from the last shelter, Heather paused to pull her jacket tight around her against the wind, which seemed to cut right through her. The car was several blocks ahead of them. She practically had to run to keep up with Quinn.

"Quinn!" she gasped as her ankle twisted.

He whirled around, managing to catch her, thus breaking her fall. "You alright?"

"No!" she snapped. "I twisted my blasted ankle trying to keep up with you. Ouch!" she cried, after trying to put her weight on the foot. "Now look what I've done."

"It's those silly shoes you women wear. Those heels must be four inches high," he said, lifting her up and into his arms.

"Three," she corrected stiffly, lacing her fingers behind the strong column of his neck.

"Why do you need the damn things?"

"If you were five-two and most of the students you counseled were taller than you are, you'd wear them, too." She wasn't about to admit that vanity had a lot to do with it. She'd always wanted to be tall.

Quinn hid a smile.

She felt so stupid. He had enough on his mind without having to take care of her.

In a few moments Quinn had her tucked inside the car and he slid behind the steering column. "Let's have a look at that ankle."

Exasperated with herself, she wondered why she hadn't worn jeans. And what difference would that have made when she tended to wear heels even with jeans? The only flats she owned were aerobic shoes—and they were at home in the back of her closet.

With her leg propped on his thigh, Quinn carefully removed her shoe. His large hands were gentle on her tender flesh. "Wiggle your toes. Great. It's swollen, but it looks as if you've only twisted it." Quinn continued to cradle her small foot in a wide palm, his fingers caressing her soft skin through her hose.

"We need to get you to a hotel and that foot into some water. A good soak and an elastic bandage is all you need."

Quinn caught himself, mastering the urge to explore the tempting length of her leg. She had such beautifully shaped calves and firm thighs. He imagined the skin along the inside of her thigh was incredibly soft and smooth to the touch. He breathed in sharply he put a firm rein on his thoughts.

Heather was disappointed when he released her. For a short time she'd forgotten everything but him as she'd indulged her senses in the pleasure of his hands on her body.

Quinn chose a downtown hotel. It was nearly 2 A.M. Heather's ankle was throbbing so badly that she doubted she could put her shoe back on, let alone walk inside. Quinn settled the matter—he carried her. Her face heated when they registered at the reception desk. Their rooms were on the second floor. He didn't put her down until they were inside her room.

"They probably think we're honeymooners," Heather said in embarrassment.

"With separate rooms?"

"Connecting rooms," she said, from the edge of the double bed.

"Well, what do you think?" he asked, looking around.

"It's fine."

"Be right back. I'll get the bags."

Heather was beat and tempted to curl up across the bed. But that would have to wait.

He knocked briefly before turning the key in the lock. Heather was busy flipping through the telephone book.

"It shouldn't take too long to call the motels and hotels in the area."

"That foot needs to be soaked."

"Quinn, we don't have time to waste. If we can we've got to find her tonight. I've started on the first half of the alphabet, why don't you take the last."

Sharing her sense of urgency, he recognized that time was the enemy. Cynthia had already been left too long on her own. Quinn grabbed his bag and left saying, "Good luck."

Little more than an hour later, Quinn knocked on the outside door. "Just a second," Heather called, hopping over to the door on one foot. "Come on in," Heather said, before hopping back to the telephone. "Sorry," she said into the mouthpiece. "Do you have anyone fitting that description?" She waited, listening. "Thank you." She hung up.

"Well?" he asked hopefully, having completed his own list of numbers.

Her eyes were as disappointed as his. "Nothing. You?" When he shook his head, she had to bite her lips to keep from crying. "Quinn, I'm so sorry."

"Me, too."

"I just don't understand. It's as if she just disappeared."

"People don't just disappear. Something happened. I won't rest until I find out what it was. She wanted to come home, damn it—I know that much." He didn't dare voice his worst fears—that somehow Cynthia might have been hurt, robbed, or raped, kidnapped, or even murdered. He shuddered while his stomach felt like it was boiling.

"Yes, she did. And we must remember that. We'll find her, Quinn," Heather said softly. He looked so tired.

He nodded. "One good thing came from all those calls. I found a twenty-four-hour drugstore not too far from here. Now if I can find an all-night diner."

"Are you hungry?"

"Sure, aren't you?"

"It's so late. I can wait till morning."

Quinn tossed her room key on the dresser before going into the bathroom, all without comment. She heard the splash of water in the bathtub. "You soak that foot while I'm gone. I'll get the elastic bandage, Tylenol, and food. Anything else?"

"You're awfully good at giving orders, aren't you?"

"About as good as you are, sugar dumplin'. Salad and soup?"

"And a chocolate shake."

"Need any help getting into the tub, Sugar?"

"No!"

Quinn left chuckling. Heather laughed, too. After the many hours of anxiety they'd endured, they both could use something to smile about.

And she'd gone and twisted her ankle! Just how much help could she be to him now?

Ten

Heather was in the tub when she heard Quinn's knock on the outside door.

"Come in," she called.

"It's locked, honey."

"Oh!" She hurried as fast as her sore foot would allow. "Just a second," she called, dripping water all over the bathroom floor. "Ouch!" she cried, having broken a nail as she tried and failed to open her locked overnight case on the bed. Where was her purse? The key was in the bottom of her purse.

"What's wrong? Are you alright?"

"I just broke a nail. Hold on—I have to find the key to my case."

"Take your time," he drawled. "I'm not going anywhere."

By the time Heather located both her purse and the key, and exchanged the towel for her thigh-length peach toweling robe, her nerves were a little raw. Hobbling to the door, she opened it only to find the hall empty. "Quinn?"

He rattled the knob of the connecting door. Heather jumped, realizing that her nerves were more than raw, they were jagged. Slamming the outside door with more force than necessary, she took a deep breath before opening the other door.

"Hi," he said, lifting one of two bags he carried. His dark smoky gaze moved leisurely along her petite frame. He hesitated for just a second too long on the base of her satin smooth neck. She looked good, all soft and sweetly scented from her bath.

"Sorry I took so long. I think I fell asleep in the tub." Heather pushed a thick fall of braids away from her face. She was propped against the dresser, her weight on the uninjured foot.

"How's the foot?" He made no effort to enter her room.

Heather smiled up at him. His strong chin was darkened by black stubble. His eyes were practically hidden by downcast lids, and thick curly lashes almost caressed the top of his high cheekbones. His wide full lips were moist from where he'd just brushed them with his tongue.

Heather decided that he was much more appealing than whatever was inside those bags he carried. Talk about sweet brown sugar.

"Heather?"

"Hmm?"

"How's the foot?"

"Much better," she said.

He nodded. "Good. I got lucky—I located a print shop where we can take Cindy's picture tomorrow."

"Oh, Quinn—that's good news."

"I also found an all-night diner and the drugstore—all without getting lost. Bought some Epsom salts for that foot." He held out the bag. "Soak your foot again in the morning and then wrap it. It will feel like new." He offered the packages. "Good night."

"Aren't you going to stay? Eat some of this food?"

The lines around his nose and mouth deepened. He looked almost haggard. There was a sadness in his eyes that he didn't even try to conceal.

"Quinn," she said catching his hand and tugging him inside. "Get in here and help me eat this."

Quinn smiled, captivated by the sultry dark glance she gave him from beneath her long lashes. The same look African women had no doubt given African men since the beginning of time. He watched fascinated by her bare legs as she limped over to the small table near the window.

"Sit," she said, pointing at one of the two chairs. Peeking into the bag, she sniffed. "Smells good."

He wouldn't sit down until she was seated across from him.

"Chocolate shake, my favorite."

"Mine, too."

She handed him a cup of creamy New England clam chowder and a salad, hoping the aroma would stimulate his appetite. Neither said much as they shared the late night supper.

Quinn was the first to finish. He glanced at his watch. "I think I better get out of here so you can get some sleep." He was on his feet, collecting the empty containers.

Heather touched his sleeve before he could move away. "You don't have to rush off. It'll be light in a few hours. Besides, I doubt I could sleep anyway. Are you sleepy?"

"You need the rest."

"So do you. But that isn't what this is all about, is it, Quinn?" she said softly, watching him closely. "First, you were reluctant to eat with me, and you're the one who insisted on going out for food. Now you're hurrying away." She swallowed the lump in her throat, before whispering. "Please, don't shut me out. Talk to me. Let me share the worry and the pain. I feel it, too."

"Heather, I don't think you know what you're asking," he said tightly, focusing on the wall above her head.

"You're upset—and with good reason. Let's talk about it."

Quinn looked at her then, really looked at her. He saw the sorrow, the anxiety, and the fear pooled in her eyes. She genuinely cared about Cynthia . . . and about him. It had been a long time since he'd felt that kind of caring from a woman. He'd missed it. But he didn't trust himself enough to reach out to her.

She got up slowly and moved to stand in front of him before she said, "I know you hurt inside." She rested her palms against his chest, using his strength for support. As Heather looked up into his dark eyes, she realized she had fallen in love with him. Suddenly nothing else seemed to matter.

Quinn shut his eyes, closing out the sight of her golden beauty and her innocent sensuality. The chemistry between them was of the high voltage variety. He hadn't even tasted his food, his senses had been so tuned to her softness.

It had driven him nuts wondering if she had anything on under that robe. He knew her full breasts were unbound. He'd enjoyed their natural movement. Her nipples had puckered against the terry cloth. Was her lush bottom bare or partly covered by a skimpy pair of panties? The soft fragrance of her skin was hypnotizing. Her braids formed an ebony cloud around her shoulders. He imagined them across his pillow, her head cushioned against his shoulder. His body tightly sheathed within hers.

All that made him male demanded that he touch her, caress her, claim her. If he stayed, there would he no stopping him. He wanted her, badly. At the moment he wasn't willing to put his control to the test. Besides, he desperately needed her help and support in locating Cynthia. He couldn't afford to antagonize her with unwanted sexual advances.

"My sole reality is that my baby is out there alone. And there isn't a blessed thing I can do about it." Abruptly he was trembling with fear and rage and guilt. "How can I sleep? How can I go to bed tonight and pretend Cynthia isn't out there unprotected?"

Heather's arms went around his slim waist. Her slender ringless hands moved soothingly across his back. "We'll start looking again as soon as it's light. Quinn, she may be alone, but we know she has enough money to pay for a decent room." Silently she prayed for the teenager's safety. "We'll keep on looking until we find her."

Quinn held on to her. She was such a little thing. The top of her head barely reached his shoulder. But the compassion and the warmth she offered made her worth her weight in gold.

"Yes, we *will.*" Every time he closed his eyes he saw his daughter's face. No matter what she'd done, he still loved her.

"You did all the driving. You've got to be exhausted."

"I can't rest until I know she's safe." Quinn steadied

Heather before he took a step back from her enticing warmth. Desire should be the last thing on his mind. Yet he ached for the kind of sweet explosive release he instinctively knew Heather could give him. He was a hot-blooded man. And he knew he couldn't accept her sweet companionship. What he wanted was to make love to her . . . tonight.

Dropping down to the bed and tucking her bare legs beneath her, she said "Okay, we'll pass what's left of the night together. We can play cards, tell old stories about college days." She didn't want him to leave . . . she didn't want him to spend what was left of the night brooding.

He swallowed before he said, "Girl, you get in that bed and get some rest."

Heather shook her head, tightening the sash around her waist and resolutely crossed her arms beneath her plump breasts. "We're in this together."

The action redirected his interested to the bounty of her softness. His eyes bore into hers, taking in the sexy pout of her soft mouth. Was the bottom lip slightly fuller than the top? Both—he decided after considerable study—were luscious, full, and so inviting. Her pink tongue briefly moistened the succulent bounty. Quinn's nostrils flared as he fought the hunger licking at his insides, leaving him hard and throbbing with desire to taste her mouth.

"Stay," she said softly, determined to hide the shock of her recent discovery. She'd been charmed by his smile, intrigued by his intellect, amazed by his strength, dazzled by his thoughtfulness, and thrilled by his wit. He was unlike any man she had ever known. Suddenly she couldn't bear to see his pain. She longed to ease that heartache.

Her small chin lifted as if she were quite willing and

able to meet the challenge in his heated gaze. Humor caused his mouth to lift for an instant. She would win any battle of wills between the two of them. All she had to do was look at him with those soulful eyes and he was lost.

Although amused by her determination to have her own way, he couldn't seem to look beyond the expanse of her soft brown shoulders and the silky length of her throat. Her skin was like liquid gold, rich and creamy smooth. He studied that tender spot at the base of her neck, perfect for a man's tongue . . . his tongue. Quinn ached to make her purr with pleasure—satisfaction he alone could give her.

Each night since their very first kiss, he'd been unable to sleep until he allowed his thoughts of Heather the freedom to roam. And the memory of how she felt in his arms flooded his senses with pleasure.

Tonight Quinn was hurt and angry with his daughter. His sense of defeat was enormous. And it was overshadowed by a crushing sense of fear. Even though it shamed him to admit it, he knew he needed Heather. If he so much as kissed her tonight, he wouldn't be able to stop. He was so hot for her, he could take her right here and now—on the bed, on the floor, in the damn bathtub. He didn't much care where. He wanted Heather Gregory just that badly.

He cursed the conscience that wouldn't permit him to use her. And in so doing, he ignored the dictates of his body demanding he do whatever was necessary to eliminate the discomfort of his arousal.

No matter how willing and ripe for the taking she

might look curled up on the bed, making love wasn't an option. Abruptly, Quinn turned to leave.

"Quinn—"

"Breakfast at six," he said tersely, walking through the open doorway between the rooms. He didn't wait for a response.

He slammed his bathroom door closed behind him. Stripping with little regard for his clothes, Quinn turned on the shower. He couldn't breathe easy until cold water coursed down his scalding hot flesh.

Heather remained where she was—her heart heavy with love, disappointment, and an odd sense of relief. At least Quinn was using his head—at least he had his priorities straight. For a dangerous instant, she'd forgotten her reason for being in Dayton with him. She'd forgotten everything but how he made her feel.

By mutual yet unspoken agreement they left the door between their rooms open, although neither breached the other's privacy.

When Cynthia opened her eyes, her head felt as if it were about to explode. She whimpered in pain.

"Wake up, baby," the elderly black woman said. "This 'ere cool towel 'elp ease t'at pain in your 'ead."

Cynthia had no choice but to obey. "Where am I?" She discovered her voice was so hoarse she could hardly speak.

"Don't you be frettin'. Miss Mattie looks out for you. Ain't nothin' gonna' 'urt ya 'ere. Lay still, but don' go back to sleep."

Cynthia's head hurt so badly and she hurt all down

her left side. It hurt to move. Suddenly the nightmare in the street flooded her mind, and she gasped aloud as the horrible fear and betrayal returned.

"I knows that side stings a bit, too. I cleaned it and put some ointment on it."

"I remember . . ." Cynthia mumbled.

"Shush. Mattie ain't gonna let no one bot'er you. Just close thems pretty eyes and rest."

As Cynthia felt the cool dampness of the cloth and the woman's soothing sweet humming, her eyes drifted and she slept.

All too soon the older woman was shaking her awake again. Cynthia's head hurt so bad all she wanted to do was sleep. But the woman wouldn't let her sleep for long.

Early the next morning, she needed to use the bathroom. She was so dizzy that she would have fallen without the elderly woman's assistance. She was so tired, so tired. She was so grateful when the woman let her sleep.

When she awoke again, the late afternoon sunlight peeked in from the frayed edge of the drawn shade. Cynthia lay on a lumpy sofa, a patchwork quilt covering her. Her eyes slowly moved around the cramped but very neat one-room apartment. A tiny kitchen area took up one corner of the room. A narrow bed off to the side, a chest of drawers, and nightstand comprised the bedroom area. The living room consisted of a sofa and an old battered rocking chair. Aged photographs graced chipped water-stained walls. The floor was covered with faded blue linoleum which buckled in the center of the room. The old scarred furniture gleamed from lemon-scented polish—everything was old but spotlessly clean.

"Ain't much," the older woman said. She was seated

in the rocker, a crochet hook speeding along the top row of the pink and white afghan pleated neatly in her lap. "But enough for an old woman. Now tell Miss Mattie how you feels, puddin."

"Better."

"Headache all gone?"

"Still hurts. But not like before," Cynthia said, sitting up very slowly.

"What yo name?"

"Cynthia," she said, suppressing a moan. "How did I get here?"

"I hears ya screaming down in the alley. I yelled out to leave ya alon'. Called Joe downstairs in the bar to go out t'ere and see about you." She frowned, "I can't get up and down 'em steps too good no more. So Joe brought ya to me. Wants me to calls yo peoples?" Her black watery eyes were filled with kindness.

"They took my wallet, my bracelet, and my mother's locket." Tears slowly trickled down Cynthia's brown face as she realized that her dad was going to be furious when he found out. And she had seven hundred dollars in that purse. He would blame her for all of this. And he would be right. If she hadn't run away from home, none of this would have happened.

"Did he see my bag? My clothes and makeup were inside."

"Nope."

Cynthia's lips trembled as she realized she was left with nothing more than the clothes on her back.

"You knows t'at man and t'at gal?"

"Him, no, but I met Eva in the bus station. She invited me to go with her, get something to eat. He must have been following me. I'm not sure. All I remember is trying to stop him. I bit him hard and then he pushed me. I hit my head."

Tears filled her eyes. She groaned because her head hurt when she cried. Stupid! Stupid! She'd gone and given her father another reason to be disappointed in her. Another reason to be sorry he had her for a daughter. She might look like her mother, but she wasn't like her at all. She made one stupid mistake after another. No wonder her father didn't want to spend any time with her. She couldn't blame her father for not being proud of her. She'd never done anything in her whole life to make him proud.

What was she going to do? How could she go home? Seven hundred dollars gone. Her father had told her to stay in the bus station. And she disobeyed him once again. She couldn't go back home now. She couldn't!

"Now . . . now. Can't nothin' be t'at bad," Miss Mattie cooed. "From around here, child?"

"No."

"Want me to call yo peoples?"

Cynthia shook her head, making herself wince. "No. I don't have anyone to call." She had trusted that girl, Eva or whatever her name was—and she had tricked her. Now she was too scared to face her father. After all the things she had done, he'd never forgive her. Not ever. "Excuse me, Miss Mattie, I need to use your bathroom?"

"Go 'ead. Need help?"

"No, ma'am." Cynthia tried to return the woman's grin, but failed.

When she returned having freshened up as best she could, Miss Mattie was at the stove stirring a large fragrant pot. The kitchen, like every inch of the tiny apartment was clean and gleaming with care.

" 'ungry? Got nice bit of beef stew and biscuits. I makes me own. Although my touch is not as light as my mama's. Lord, t'at woman could make some biscuits. Come, sit down, puddin'." She motioned to the small card table and two straight-back chairs jammed into the kitchen area.

Cynthia found it best to move very slowly.

"I 'pect you still a bit dizzy. T'at's a good-size lump on the side of your 'ead." Miss Mattie placed the steaming hot food in front of her. "Got some buttermilk and lemonade in the icebox."

"Lemonade, please."

She chuckled. "Nice to see you 'aven't lost your sweet tooth," she said opening the aged refrigerator.

"Thank you. And thanks for taking care of me."

"Glad to 'elp. You looks like such nice young thang."

Cynthia did smile then. Miss Mattie reminded her of Mrs. Thornton. She had always been kind to her. Maybe she didn't have a mother like the other girls. But she did have Mrs. Thornton and she had a friend . . . Heather. And she had a father. If only she had thought about them before she'd run away. But how could she stay? She had told so many lies. Now it was too late to go back. Her father couldn't forgive her, and Heather was bound to be disappointed in her. No amount of wishing could push the calendar back.

"How old ya, Cynthia?"

"Fifteen."

"Why ya out on the street like t'is? Police lookin' for you, gal?"

"No, ma'am."

"You run from home?"

Cynthia's head snapped up too quickly, causing her eyes to fill with tears. "I don't feel so good." She dropped her head onto the table. "Please, do you have an aspirin?" She was so tired and she hurt all over.

"Just a minute." When Miss Mattie returned, she said, " 'ere, take t'is."

Whimpering, Cynthia complied. "I need to lay down."

"In a few mo' minutes. But first we gonna' get some food into ya. Ain't eaten a spoon full of nothin' since you been 'ere. Now come on, baby. Just a little stew."

Cynthia did feel better after she had eaten. She just couldn't eat very much. Once she was comfortably arranged on the sofa, she could hardly keep her eyes open.

"Go ahead, sleep do a body good."

Cynthia woke sometime later. Her head was clear and even her side had settled into a dull ache. "Any stew left?"

"Plenty in the pot." Miss Mattie smiled from where she was seated at the kitchen table reading her Bible.

Cynthia returned the smile. She was almost finished eating when Miss Mattie asked, "Why you run, puddin?"

Cynthia stared at her. "You have no right—"

"Long as you in my house, ya respec' me and listen to what I got t'say."

Cynthia was immediately humble. "Yes, ma'am."

"What yo' plans?"

"Don't know." Cynthia realized that she didn't have so much as a toothbrush to call her own. How in the world was she going to take care of herself? She had no money. No place to stay.

"Not on drugs? I didn't see no needle marks on ya. But t'ey's ot'er kinds of fool stuff young folks take nowadays to get high. Well?"

"No!"

"So why'd you run?"

Cynthia clamped her mouth closed. She wasn't being disrespectful, she just couldn't answer.

Miss Mattie clucked her tongue against the roof of her mouth. She pursed out her lips. "Kids nowdays sees and knows too much. Ain't got no business knowin' all t'at. Havin' babies for t'ey grown.' She didn't notice Cynthia avert her eyes. "Does everythin' too early, makeup, tight clothes. Too grown, I tell ya. And ends up sellin' t'eir bodies when thangs gets rough for 'em. Can' run away from your troubles, puddin'. Just be waitin' on down the next block."

"You don't understand."

"Can't understand unless ya won' be telling me. But don't worry about t'at now. Finish eating yo supper, child. Got more if'n ya want it."

"I can pay you. I got five dollars. I found it tucked in my pocket."

"Keep yo money. Ya gonna' need it more 'n me." She picked up her Bible and her glasses, then began reading the text. In spite of her eighty-odd years, her warm brown skin was still soft and unblemished. Her glossy thick white hair was brushed back away from her fine-boned face and French-braided into a single neat pleat.

Over breakfast Quinn and Heather decided to visit the hospitals in the area, as well as hotels and motels they'd called last night before circulating pictures of Cynthia. They were still in agreement that she couldn't have left on that late night bus.

"How's the foot?"

"Better," she smiled. "Thanks to you." She'd soaked it again that morning. And Quinn had wrapped it for her. Heather had even managed to get her shoe back on.

Neither one of them had gotten much rest. Quinn had been on the telephone most of the night, staying in contact with Detroit and the Dayton police. There had been nothing to report. He looked tired, the skin around his mouth and eyes were pinched and strained. Even on the drive to the diner before breakfast he was popping antacids like candy. Heather shared his worries.

"I think we should add the shelters for homeless women and children the police told us about to our list."

"Are you crazy?" he exploded. Tossing the necessary bills for their meal on the table, he got to his feet.

"Quinn?"

"I said no."

Heather quirked a brow at him.

"Ready? By the time we finish with the hospitals in and around the city, the print shop should be open and we can get the posters made. It's a good thing I thought to bring along that pack of her school pictures."

Heather waited until they were outside on the sidewalk before she said, "It can't hurt to try the homeless shelters."

"It's a complete waste of time."

"It's worth a try," she insisted, refusing to back down.

Quinn scowled. It hurt too much to even think of his little girl feeling that desperate . . . that alone. Gently pressing his hand against the small of her back, he spanned her slim waist, urging her forward toward the parking lot. Heather looked fresh and attractive in slim-fitting stone-washed jeans and a white silk blouse with large turquoise buttons down the front. Her black leather jacket protected her from the crisp morning air.

"I know it's not pleasant to even think about your Cynthia being desperate enough to have to go to a homeless shelter, Quinn. But we can't just turn our backs on any possibility. No matter how remote it seems we have to try. Honey, please." The endearment slipped out as she turned toward him, looking up into his dark handsome face.

"Let me think about it, okay?"

Quinn's wide shoulders and hard chest was covered by a wheat-colored cotton sweater and his long legs and lean hips were encased in navy blue jeans. He carried a denim jacket over one shoulder and on his feet were white athletic shoes. He looked rugged and outdoorsy, not like the smooth sophisticated lawyer she knew him to be.

"Alright Quinn, maybe we should split up so we can cover more ground. I could rent a car."

"Uh-uh. I prefer to have you with me—we work well together." He sighed, opening the door for her. "Maybe we'll get lucky. Or the police will find her. Someone has to have seen her."

Quinn gave Heather the map and the list. "You navigate, I'll drive."

There was no sign of Cynthia at any of the hospitals. Heather and Quinn were both relieved by that stroke of luck. Their next stop was the police station. There was simply no news. So they moved on to the printer and then started working on their list of hotels and motels.

At noon Quinn stopped at their hotel.

"Why are we stopping here?"

"Sugar dumplin', you're beat. Get some sleep. I'll finish up. There are only a half dozen more places to go."

"Alright," she said, too tired to argue the point. "Good luck," she called as he pulled back into traffic. "Bring her back safe."

Heather wasn't sure what woke her. She was curled up on her side, one arm tucked under the pillow. She frowned at the phone on her nightstand. It was silent. When it rang again, she realized the sound was coming from Quinn's room.

"Hello?" she said breathlessly, having run to catch it. Her robe was loose belted around her waist.

The hiss of the shower, the jeans and sweater Quinn had worn were on the chair, alerting her to his return.

"Yes, this is Mr. Montgomery's room. Can I help you?" A noise behind Heather made her turn around. Quinn emerged from the bathroom.

"Oh . . ." Quinn said. His deep brown torso sported a towel which stopped at midthigh. It hung low on his trim hips. His stomach was taunt and firm, his shoulders broad, his chest smooth and hairless.

Heather forced her eyes away. Quivering in response to his masculine beauty, she said in a whisper, "It's the desk. They want to know if we'll need the rooms another night?"

The look in his eyes was explanation enough. Evidently he hadn't had any luck in finding Cynthia.

"Yes, we're staying on," she said into the telephone.

Eleven

"You were sleeping pretty good there, girl, when I looked in on you," Quinn said, caressing the softness of her nape beneath the heavy fall of her braids.

She smiled, liking the teasing warmth in his voice. They were so close she could smell the scent of his freshly washed body and feel the heat of his brown skin.

Quinn hadn't failed to note how sexy she'd looked, sleeping on her side, her lovely golden limbs bare. Dark hair spilled over the pillow, her pretty brown eyes hidden beneath black lashes, her soft lips slightly parted as if waiting for his kisses. It had taken considerable effort not to crawl into bed with her. Yes, he wanted to make love to her. But at that moment, what he wanted and needed most was to hold her in his arms and in turn be held by her. Just as he was doing now.

Heather sighed taking a step away, even though she welcomed the closeness. Although aware of the question in his gaze, she watched a single drop of water roll down his chest, slow at his flat male nipple, before continuing down his taunt concave stomach. She didn't lift her eyes until the bead of moisture disappeared in the few crisp strands of black hair visible above the bath towel knotted low on his hip. The thick masculine proof of his arousal was unmistakable.

Their eyes met. Heather was the first to look away.

Quinn's body throbbed with the force of his emotions. Heather's robe had come undone. His hands were balled into fists as his dark hungry eyes stroked the full swells of her beautiful breasts.

"Don't look at me like that," he said, gruffly.

"Like what?" Her voice was husky with feminine yearning as she struggled to gain control of her breathing.

"Like you want me to make love to you," he said with a rough throaty urgency as he cupped her shoulders and drew her against his damp bare chest.

Quinn lowered his head until he could bury his face in the wonderfully scented hollow at the base of her throat. He tongued her there, loving the taste of her creamy golden flesh.

Heather gasped from his open-mouthed caress and shivered as he glided along her neck, tantalizing the throbbing vein down the side. He scraped the soft skin, causing her legs to tremble.

"You taste so sweet . . . so sweet," he said in a deep throaty whisper. "I want to taste you all over." He kissed her cheek, down the side of her face to her small yet firm jawline. His wide palm stroked down her body from her tiny waist to her amply curved hips and shapely thighs. She was a gorgeous woman. And he intended to make her his woman.

"Please . . ." she moaned. She balanced on tiptoes, stretching as high as she could in order to gain access to his firm lips. She pressed her mouth along his jawline, his chin, his throat.

"Kiss me," she demanded. Lost in the softness of her flesh, it took him a moment to recognize what she requested. Dropping his head, he didn't hesitate to give her his mouth. He growled deep in his throat as she moved her lips over his. He intensified the kiss. He parted her lips and she welcomed his fierce hunger, and the rough velvet of his tongue. Heather thought she might faint when he laved the corner of her mouth over and over again. She was a mass of tingling nerve endings by the time he stroked her tongue with his own. He left her weak with need and vibrating with pleasure. Her robe and bra were on the carpet along with his towel.

"Heather . . ." he groaned. Quinn couldn't seem to get enough of her. He repeatedly caressed her wonderfully soft buttocks. He told her clearly and explicitly how he wanted to please her.

"Oh!" she exclaimed when he lifted her petite length until the apex of her thighs could cradle his solid heat. She quickly locked her arms around his strong neck, pressing her lips there just below his ear.

"Feel what you do to me—you make me so hard. I can't think of anything but you. Feel me baby, feel me," he said, rubbing against her heat. Kissing her again and again, finally he said, impatiently, "Kiss me back, pretty girl. I want your tongue in my mouth."

She eagerly granted his request. Eventually he let her down, controlling the slide of her body against his own.

Heather caressed his chest, teasing the flat ebony nipple with the edge of a nail. Quinn's blood seemed to flow with a scalding force through his body. He loved the way her skin felt against his, loved the wonderful softness of her unconfined breasts pillowed against the hard muscle of his chest. Loved everything about Heather.

She made him feel things that he'd long ago given up on ever feeling again. In fact, he honestly couldn't remember ever wanting a woman this badly. He was desperate to have her beneath him. The sheer intensity of his hunger for her was disturbing. He'd nothing to compare it to. His senses were more alive than ever before. Their kisses were unbelievably sweet, almost magical. If necessary, he could easily settle for kissing her all night long.

So what was his hurry? This wasn't how he planned it. And yes, he had planned to make deep passionate love to her someday. But not now. Certainly not here in Dayton while his daughter's fate was unknown. And not while his mind was divided with worry over Cynthia. It wasn't the right time for them. Heather should be wooed with flowers and romantic candlelit dinners and long leisurely walks in the moonlight. She deserved the best. He intended to give it to her.

Quinn stepped away, running his hand over his hair. He tried not to look at her but he found he couldn't forgo even that small pleasure. He cleared his throat loudly, although knowing what he needed was to clear his head. He stared into the smoldering warmth of her caramel-colored eyes.

Heather was shaking so badly she was grateful for the bed behind her. Sitting onto the edge, she waited, uncertain why he had stopped. She certainly hadn't wanted him to.

Quinn fought against the need to cover her body with his own. He forced himself to breath deeply and evenly.

Only the thin layer of a sheer black lace panty concealed the softness between her thighs. He'd already waited an eternity to have her.

She swallowed with difficulty, not even considering shielding her body from him. "Why did you stop?"

It hurt like hell to say it, but he said it nonetheless. "Heather, I don't want you regretting this later."

"I'm not a child, Quinn. I know what I want. I want to be with you as much as you want me. The only thing I ask is that we use some type of protection."

"That's been taken care of," he said opening a drawer in the nightstand and placing a foil package on the bed. Before she could voice the question in her eyes, he answered, "While I was at the drugstore last night, I thought I'd take care of the matter just in case the situation presented itself. Honey, I didn't plan this. Hell, our timing stinks. But I won't lie about it either. I've wanted to make love to you from the second you walked into my office. The feeling ain't goin' away. But you're entitled to candlelight and romance—not a hotel room in Dayton."

"Honey, I don't need those things to make me happy," Heather answered. "Please, let's not wait any longer." She didn't move, didn't breathe until she felt his hands tracing down her neck, along her shoulders. Heather whimpered in reaction as he lay down on the bed, covering her mouth and body with his.

He palmed her breasts, stroking his fingertips over her cushiony softness, never quite giving her the full caress she craved. His mouth was hot and sizzling on hers. She moaned with pleasure. Her breath caught in her throat as she waited, hoping for the sweet pressure of his hands on her sensitive nipples. She gasped when he finally squeezed a hard brown nipple between his thumb and forefinger, then shivered in rapture as he took her into his mouth and suckled, then he sponged the sensitive peak over and over again.

Heather groaned from the hot sweet pleasure he gave her, instinctively crossing her legs to ease the throbbing pressure within. Even though Quinn felt as if his own body were on fire, he took his time, moving tenderly from one breast to the other before returning to once again lave then suckle.

"You've the softest skin in the world," he whispered. When he found a small ebony mole just below her right breast, he couldn't stop himself from tonguing it. You're so beautiful. I could look at you for hours and never want to stop." His eyes caressed her, then his lips replaced his hands and he licked the underside of her breasts before eventually moving down her rib cage. He circled her belly button using the rough edges of his tongue. Quinn kissed his way down to the edge of her bikini panties. His hands stroked her inner thighs, parted them—her golden skin was as delicate and as succulent as a ripe Georgia peach.

"Quinn—" Heather gasped, moving her hips as the heat within grew to alarming proportions. She needed him. . . .

He felt the tiny shiver that shook her body as her nails dug into his back. He refused to be rushed. He'd waited too long for this . . . for her. He ignored the dictates of his own body and concentrated on pleasing Heather. He cupped her sex, caressing her mound. He smiled in deep satisfaction when he discovered her panty was soaked with the nectar of her desire for him. With unsteady fingers, he removed the cloth veiling her feminine secrets.

Quinn's heart raced with excitement. She was exquisitely made. He let his fingers play through the thick black curls. Gently, he parted the dewy folds, trailing a finger over her damp heat before focusing his attention on the tiny center of her desires. Quinn caressed her, giving her the exact pressure she craved.

"Quinn . . . oh . . . no more . . ." she whimpered, stroking his back and shoulders.

"Yes, more, much much more." He replaced his hand with his mouth, loving her until she cried out his name as she climaxed, her heart pounding madly within her chest.

When she opened her eyes, he was smiling down at her. His eyes were hot with need. "Come here," she demanded, reaching out to him. There was no doubt in her mind that she loved this man, loved him with every part of herself.

"You're so wonderful." Her soft hand caressed his upper body, and her mouth was soft and warm on his chest.

He dropped his head unable to resist a quick suck of her bottom lip. He took the tender lip into his own mouth and tongued the corners and the fleshy inside of her mouth, filling his senses with the power of his need.

Heather ran her soft hands along the taunt muscle of his inner thighs, hesitating. Blood pumped vigorously in his veins as her hands moved closer to his sex. Quinn wondered if the expectation might be more than his nerves could take. He wanted her soft hands firmly on his manhood, stroking him to the point of bursting. When her fingertips brushed over him, Quinn sucked in his breath, unable to contain a deep throaty groan of pleasure. His body expanded even more as he forced himself to fill his lungs with air.

Heather loved the feel of his firm male flesh and her desire increased as she caressed him, moving her hands up and down his shaft intent on giving him absolute pleasure.

"Yes . . . Heather . . . yes," he whispered as she gently cupped him. "Harder," he groaned. "Yes, like that." Quinn shivered, eyes closed.

When Heather caressed the full crown of his sex, Quinn growled, pulling her beneath him, covering her body with his. His kisses were hard, insistent. Her mouth flowered under his onslaught. Quinn trembled, then shuddered when she ran her nails down his spine. He released her mouth, his breath coming in rapid pants.

She placed a series of moist kisses against the base of his throat, then paused, to lave a hard male nipple with her soft wet tongue, before moving to the other and repeating the action. Unable to tolerate more of the delicious torment, Quinn spread her thighs. He positioned her so he could explore her intimately, first with his fingertips and then with the broad tip of his sex. Again and again he stroked her, determined to prove to her how good it could be for them. When she cried out with pleasure and pleaded with him to take her, Quinn nearly lost control.

Their gaze locked in silent communication, expressing a mutual need and excitement. Their mouths came together first, exchanging blazing hot kisses. Her pulse soared as Quinn slowly filled her. He kept a firm rein on his own need, allowing her time to adjust to his size. As her sleek satiny warmth welcomed him, he gritted his teeth, struggling for control. He tried to ignore the dictate of his body demanding he lay claim to what was his alone. She was like liquid velvet, hot and sweet.

Quinn said her name aloud as he began deep determined thrusts, filling her to the point of bursting, giving her all that he had to give without hesitation. She met the savage hunger within him. The female challenged the male in this ultimate contest. Love was clearly the victor—for Quinn's relentless need to conquer was conquered by her as sparks of passion ignited and burst into uncontrollable flames, consuming them both as one. There was no longer Quinn or Heather. There was no longer male or female. They were a single unit, plunging into the most exquisitely sweet release.

Quinn lay spent, his body completely relaxed. Stroking her back, he realized he was happy for the first time in a long time. Heather had managed to find a place in his heart.

He brushed soft, full lips swollen and tender from his kisses. He toyed with her braids as he absently wondered if he would ever get his fill of Heather. Already he wanted her again.

She sighed. Quinn might not love her yet, but he cared for her deeply. And Heather was confident love would come in time. He was a marvelous lover. She was so glad they hadn't waited. They both needed the pleasure they found together.

When she shifted a bit, Quinn rolled onto his back and brought Heather with him. She now lay comfortably against his chest. He placed a sloppy wet kiss on her neck.

Heather giggled before catching his bottom lip and suckling. Her maddening tongue rekindled the fire in his loins. She bit him playfully.

"Ouch!" he murmured thickly. His hand traced her spine, enjoying the texture of her skin, the interesting dip where her body flared into utterly feminine buttocks. "If you don't stop that, you will get more than you bargained for."

"More?" Her mouth slid along his jawline to his earlobe. She teased the outer shell, then captured it between her teeth, to lave it seductively.

"More," he repeated. All he could focus on was the glorious feel of her breasts on his chest and the incredible softness of her inner thighs against his sex. His heart hammered wildly. He felt himself lengthen, thicken in readiness for her.

Heather purred softly deep in her throat.

Quinn chuckled. "Do you have any idea how sexy you are?"

She was too busy warming the base of his throat with her tongue to answer. But she stopped when she felt his intimate long-fingered caresses. Quinn surprised her by positioning her above him and letting her receive the full force of his passion. Heather moaned, arching her back.

"Good?" he asked urgently. He lifted his upper torso so that he could support, himself on his elbows and tantalized the elongated tip of her breast with his mouth.

Heather couldn't form the words to express what she was feeling. Quinn took her silence as an indication that she wasn't receiving all that she needed. He intensified his suckling at her breast and surged powerfully within her, causing an exquisite torment that traveled through her bloodstream.

On and on the pleasure went until Heather reached her climax ahead of Quinn. She held on to him, glorying in his shattering release. When it was all over, she collapsed against him, her cheek resting above his heart. Quinn hugged Heather tightly as their breathing gradually slowed.

Quinn found his lids too heavy to remain open. He massaged her nape beneath the heavy fall of her braids.

"What time do you want me to wake you?"

"I'm not going to sleep. The flyers won't he ready until after six. Then I thought we'd go back to the bus station. Talk to the cleaning staff. Someone has to know something. And I want to be back out on the street by nightfall. What do you think?"

"Makes sense. We can post Cynthia's pictures in the bus station."

His thick lashes covered his eyes, when he said, "I just need to rest my eyes for a few moments."

"Mmmm," she mumbled, curling up next to him.

When Miss Mattie turned off her small black and white television, Cynthia was finished drying the dishes.

The girl's mind wasn't on what she was doing. She fretted about the long night ahead. She had nowhere to go. Nowhere to sleep and not enough money for a hotel room or even enough to buy breakfast tomorrow morning. What was she going to do?

She couldn't expect Miss Mattie to let her stay until

morning. She'd already been so kind to her already. Besides, Miss Mattie was having a hard enough time taking care of herself without a stranger to feed.

This was her own fault. If only she'd been more careful. If only she hadn't run away in the first place. How was she going to find a job? And what could she do? She hadn't even finished the tenth grade. Her father was always harping on education.

Tears filled her eyes, flooding her gaze as she thought of her father. She never doubted for a moment that he had come to Dayton last night to take her home. What worried her was what he'd done when he hadn't been able to find her. Had he gone to the police? Were they looking for her, too? Or had he and Heather turned around and gone back? He was bound to be angry—perhaps angrier than ever before. She'd just wanted him to notice her . . . now he wouldn't ever speak to her again. He probably hated her.

Looking up from her needlework, Miss Mattie frowned as bitter sobs tore at the slender girl. "Come 'ere, puddin'." She patted her bony knees.

Cynthia rushed to her, dropping down on the floor beside her. She held Miss Mattie close, letting her cheek rest against the woman's lap, hiding her face like a child in the folds of her apron.

"Go 'ead, cry. Cry it out," Miss Mattie soothed her gently. It was only after a torrent of scalding tears that Cynthia began to quiet. "Cain't be t'at bad."

"You d-d-don't u-u-nders-t-t-and," she sobbed brokenheartedly. "I don't know what to d-do! I can't go home. I ca-a-n't."

"Why baby?"

"I—"

"I don't know what's troublin' ya so. But I help if'n I can."

Cynthia's tears slowed, but they didn't stop completely. Every time she thought of all the mistakes she'd made, how she let her father down, she cried harder. Once she quieted and caught her breath she asked, "Miss Mattie, what should I do?"

"Go home to yo family."

"I only have Daddy. My mother died when I was little."

"Well, he's family, ain't he?"

"Yes, ma'am," she hiccuped.

"Call him. Tell him ya wanna come home."

One of the cleaning ladies at the bus station recognized Cynthia from her picture. She remembered seeing her leaving with another girl around ten.

Heather and Quinn later learned from the police that Cynthia had left the bus station with a well-known teenage prostitute. The girl fit the description of a young woman currently being sought for possession of drugs and for being an accomplice in a series of armed robberies.

Quinn and Heather spent the night much as they had the night before on the streets, only this time they passed out flyers with Cynthia's picture printed on it. They made one more stop at the police station, in the wee hours of the morning, before heading back to their hotel.

"I don't believe it! This whole thing is turning into a nightmare!" Quinn said, highly frustrated as he followed Heather inside the room.

"If they knew about this girl, why hasn't she been arrested? That's what I want to know," Heather muttered, rubbing her temple. She had a headache that wouldn't quit. She was beat. She wouldn't have been the least bit surprised if a strong gust of wind sent her into oblivion. Her nerves were as frayed as Quinn's.

"The criminal justice system doesn't work like that, pretty girl. Besides, they don't really know if it's the same kid. Do you have any idea how many kids we saw tonight?"

"Too many! It's time someone dealt with this issue. Quinn, the light on the phone is blinking."

Quinn reached for it while Heather looked on anxiously. "Yes, the message? Thank you." He said, while dialing, "It's from Mrs. Thornton. She wants me to call home. Mrs. Thornton. What? Thank God!" Quinn cried, dropping the phone. "Cindy called and she's still here in Dayton," he said to Heather as he retrieved the instrument. "I'm sorry, I got so excited I dropped the phone. What was that address? Yeah, I've got a pen." He grabbed the one Heather held out to him, her smile every bit as wide as his. His hands were trembling as he wrote. "Okay, repeat that address for me. Got it. Yes . . . yes. Right away. Bye."

"How is she?" Heather pressed.

"She's fine as far as Mrs. Thornton could tell. Cynthia called home about eleven. Mrs. Thornton has been trying to reach us. Come on, let's go get her."

"Yeah," Heather said with feeling. They were under way when she asked, "Where has she been all this time? Why did she leave the bus station? Why didn't she wait for us last night?"

"I don't know. Cynthia didn't say very much. Get the

map. It's in the glove compartment. Yeah, look up this street for me. It shouldn't be too far from Main, close to Jefferson, I think. I know I've seen it. I can't remember where."

"It's close to the bus station."

"Okay." Quinn concentrated on his driving. He pushed everything else to the back of his mind. His plans centered on finding his daughter.

They stopped in front of a bar housed on the lower level of a rundown building.

"It's a bar," Heather said worriedly.

"Same street address. But I've got an apartment number. Stay here. I'll be right back."

"No! You're not leaving me here alone in the car at three in the morning," Heather insisted, ignoring the throbbing of her still tender ankle.

"I'm just going around the side to see if there's another entrance. I'll be within hollering distance."

Heather got out of the car and locked her side. She stubbornly limped along beside him.

Quinn slowed his steps and took her hand in his.

They discovered the side entrance down a nearly deserted alley. Heather jumped when a foraging cat hissed from the lid of a Dumpster. Quinn gave her hand a reassuring squeeze.

Where once there was a lock on the door there was now a gaping hole. The knob kept the door closed.

They shared an anxious look before Quinn led the way up the narrow poorly lit stairs to the second floor landing.

"Apartment 4." Quinn realized his heart was turning cartwheels in his chest. With an equal measure of dread and anticipation, his stomach tightened to form a ball of acid and tension. "Here." He pounded on the door.

Heather was every bit as anxious as he was. The response took so long that she began to worry that they might not have the correct address. Or even worse, that Cynthia had gotten scared and disappeared yet again.

A magnified blurry eye filled the peep-hole. "What ya wants 'ere t'is time of nigh'?" an elderly voice shouted through the closed and firmly bolted door.

"I'm Quinn Montgomery. I'm looking for my daughter Cynthia." He rocked back and forth impatiently on the balls of his feet. He ran damp hands down the leg of his jeans. He heard a muffled conversation behind the portal, but for the life of him, he couldn't make sense of what was being said.

It seemed to take forever—but it was only a few moments before the chain was dropped and no less than three deadbolt locks were disengaged.

"Daddy!" Cynthia yelled before the door was completely opened. Then she hurled herself into her father's eager arms.

Twelve

Quinn held Cynthia fast. The girl sobbed out her relief while Heather's eyes filled with tears.

Quinn ran a hand soothingly over his daughter's hair, his own eyes wet as she clung to him.

"Oh Daddy . . ." she wailed. "I didn't think I would ever see you again."

"I'm here, baby girl. I'm here," he said softly, trying to calm his high-strung daughter. She was so much like her mother, and precious to him. He felt as if he could breathe easily for the first time in what felt like months.

"Ain't t'at nice." Mattie Cummings dabbed at her eyes.

"Heather!" Cynthia sped into Heather's arms. "I'm so glad you're here."

Heather held her tightly. "You gave us a scare."

"Ya'll come on in 'ere," the elder woman urged.

"Thanks," Quinn said, ushering Heather and Cynthia inside. He kept a protective arm around the girl's shoulders. Cynthia smiled up at him. "Introduce us, little girl."

"Mrs. Mattie Cummings, this is my father, Quinn Montgomery. And my friend, Heather Gregory."

"It's a pleasure, Mrs. Cummings. I'm sorry we came

so late. I hope you understand why we thought it couldn't wait until morning." Quinn shook hands with the elderly woman, careful of frail arthritic fingers.

"We're so grateful to you for keeping Cynthia safe," Heather said, momentarily cradling the woman's hand in her own.

Miss Mattie beamed. "Pleased to meet ya. Sit a spell."

Heather and Quinn shared the sofa with Cynthia in the middle.

"Miss Mattie has been taking care of me since I got robbed in the alley last night"

"Robbed!" Quinn and Heather said simultaneously.

Quinn asked "What happened—"

"Were you hurt?" Heather interjected.

Cynthia dropped her head, nervously clasping her hands in her lap. "I left the bus station to get some dinner. I went with another girl who said she knew a restaurant just down the street. Eva told me she was waiting for the bus to New York. I didn't know it was a trick."

"And . . ." Quinn prompted impatiently.

"They took my purse with all my money in it. My clothes. Daddy, I'm so sorry. I know you told me to stay at the bus station."

"You said they?"

"She had a friend who must have followed me into the alley."

Quinn lifted her face, pushing her hair away. He studied the bruise near her temple, the scrape on the side of her neck, and the dark smudges under her eyes. She'd lost weight. Weight she couldn't afford. She was too thin as it was. "They hurt you?"

Cynthia could see the rage in her father's eyes and shivered.

"Cindy?"

"Yes, Daddy. But not too bad. When I wouldn't give him my locket he pushed me hard and I fell and hit my head and scraped my side."

"Swellin' gone down. But she got a goose egg on her 'ead," Miss Mattie said from her place in the rocker. "I 'eard her yellin'. Called Joe who takes care of the bar downstairs. Told 'im to get out t'ere quick, see about the baby. 'E brought her up to me. 'Hem bastards nearly killed t'is 'ere baby." She rocked to and fro, pausing to say, "Kept wakin' her up ever' few ours. Check 'er."

"Show me your side." Quinn's voice was gruff.

"It's better, Daddy." But she showed him the scrape along her side. His long strong fingers gently lifted the gauze to study the jagged scrape.

"Still hurt?"

"Just a little."

"Have you seen a doctor? Sounds like you might have had a slight concussion."

"Doctor's cos' money. Ain't got no insurance. I looked after her best I could," Miss Mattie said proudly.

"So Cynthia has been with you since last night?" Heather asked.

"Sure has. Didn't eat much a t'all."

"Was the incident reported to the police?"

"For what? 'udlums didn't wait for no police. Why you t'ink I keeps 'hree locks on 'hat door? Ain't safe no more, ain't safe."

"I'm so glad it was *you* who found her, Mrs. Cummings."

"Call me Miss Mattie. Ya got yourselves a good girl . . . real good girl. Just a little unhappy now. But a good girl." She smiled fondly at Cynthia. "Can I gets ya and the lady frien' somethin'? Don't takes but a minute to puts on some coffee."

Cynthia spoke before either of the adults could respond. "Heather isn't Daddy's girlfriend, Miss Mattie. She's *my* friend." The girl didn't see the look that passed between Heather and Quinn.

"Tea?"

"No, thanks. Did you make that quilt on the bed. It's beautiful," Heather said with a smile.

"Yes'm. Made it with scraps from my c'il'ren's and 'usbands clothes. T'ey all dead now." She wiped at a tear.

"It's lovely," Heather said warmly.

The elderly woman smiled.

Getting to his feet, Quinn said, "I'm just trying to think of a way to show you how grateful we are for your care of Cindy." He asked awkwardly, "I'd like to pay you for Cynthia's food and board."

"Put that there money away, young man. Did what a good Christian would. Lord'll always make a way."

"Let me at least pay you for the food. My daughter may be light as a bird, but I know she doesn't eat like one," Quinn said with a smile.

" 'Ush now! You just takes some time to find out w'at really the matter with t'is little gal. Don't want her runnin' away no more."

Quinn looked at his daughter. Her eyes were suddenly glued to the floor, and she was holding Heather's hand. "Yes, ma'am. That's what I plan to do."

Heather went over and kissed her smooth brown cheek. "Miss Mattie, thank you. It scares me to think of what could have happened to Cynthia if it weren't for you."

Quinn extracted a business card from his wallet. He handed it to the elderly woman. "Please call me if you ever need anything. My home number is on the back."

She smiled, tucking the card into the pocket of her robe.

"I mean it. Perhaps you'd like to come and visit Cindy? You'd like that wouldn't you, baby girl?"

"Oh, yes, Daddy."

"Miss Mattie?"

"We'll see," she said, lifting her chin. But her eyes were twinkling.

"Fair enough. Cindy, get your things. We've kept Miss Mattie up long enough."

Cynthia's eyes filled. "I only have my jacket. They took everything. My money, my clothes—even my gold locket with Mommy's picture inside."

Quinn's brow creased in a frown. "The important thing is you're okay."

"Miss Mattie, could Quinn and I take you out for a meal tomorrow? Once we've all gotten a little rest?"

Mattie Cummings grinned from ear to ear. "Yes'm. Just give me a call and I get ready fast."

"We look forward to it. Good night," Quinn said offering her his hand.

Cynthia kissed and hugged her before following Heather out.

"We'll stand here while you lock up."

"Bye." Miss Mattie smiled her thanks and hurried to do just that.

Quinn followed them down to the bottom of the stairs. Cynthia trembled as they walked through the dark alleyway.

"You're safe, baby girl," he said, softly, taking her hand.

The three of them squeezed into the front seat with Cynthia once again in the middle.

"Hungry?"

"Daddy, I've eaten already. I'm just tired."

"We need to get your head x-rayed. We also have to report the robbery to the police."

"Can't it wait? My head doesn't hurt anymore. I just want to take a bath and go to bed. I haven't slept in a real bed in so long."

"Heather and I haven't gotten much sleep either, young lady. If you ever pull something like this again, I will turn you over my knee and make more than your head hurt. You understand me!"

"Yes, sir." Cynthia answered with a slight smile.

"Maybe if I'd done a little of that when you were little we wouldn't be in this mess. We still have to deal with your pregnancy."

"Quinn," Heather said softly.

"And you owe both of us an explanation. But not tonight." Quinn started the engine.

"Daddy," Cynthia said in a tiny voice, "I'm so sorry."

Rather than pull away from the curb, Quinn looked down at his daughter's bowed head. He put a finger under her chin and lifted her face. "I know you are. I'm sorry, too, about a lot of things. And I'm very thankful that you're safe. You could have been seriously hurt. You scared the hell out of me. I don't want to lose you, nor

do I want anything to happen to you. I love you, kid."
He kissed her on the forehead.

"I love you, too, Daddy," Cynthia said in a wobbly
voice, too scared to hope that he would still feel that way
once she told him everything.

Heather was silent, unwilling to intrude on this private
moment. A soft smile tilted her lips—she was profoundly
pleased that Cynthia and Quinn were communicating at
last.

"I suppose we can wait until we get back home to
have Dr. Grant check you out. We all could use a little
sleep. Okay, Heather."

"Sounds fine to me."

By the time they reached the hotel, Cynthia was doz-
ing with her head on Heather's shoulder and Heather was
doing the same, only her head rested against the win-
dowpane. Quinn was smiling as he parked in the hotel
lot. It looked as if he'd end up carrying both of them up
tonight.

"Wake up, ladies. We're home—at least for what's left
of the night."

As they walked to the entrance with Cynthia leaning
sleepily against his arm, Quinn noticed Heather was
limping badly. He put his free arm around her waist.

"Do you need me to carry you?"

"No—I'll soak the ankle again before I go to bed."

"What's wrong, Heather?"

"It's nothing to worry about, honey. I twisted my ankle
last night." They were nearing the front desk when she
said to Quinn, "There's no need to get another room.
Cynthia can share mine."

"Baby girl?"

"I'd like that. I'd rather not be by myself."

"Okay. We can get what clothes you need in the morning." Quinn waited until they were in Heather's room before he said, "Try to get some rest. We'll talk in the morning. I want to know how you want to handle your pregnancy." To Heather he said, "Can I speak to you privately for a moment?"

"Good night, Daddy," Cynthia called before disappearing into the bathroom.

"Let's go into the other room." Quinn closed the connecting door after them. Leaning against it, he placed a hand on her shoulder. "Are you sure she won't be an imposition?"

"Never that. I happen to love her, too."

Quinn smiled. "Yeah, I kind of thought so." He cradled her face in his palm, stroking the mole at the corner of her mouth. She had such wonderfully soft full lips. Heather smiled up at him. Quinn wasn't satisfied until she was close and tight in his arms, her body a sweet caress against his.

"I don't think I could have made it through this without you." He brushed her mouth with his.

Heather melted against him, comfortable with letting him support her. She welcomed his foraging tongue. He teased the enticing corners of her mouth—but he didn't deepen the kiss, he merely played.

"This afternoon—well, I want you to know it wasn't planned. But it happened. And Heather, I'm so glad it did. It was good, so good for me. How was it for you?" His voice was so soft and deep, she had to strain to hear him, as he caressed her cheek with his hair-roughened cheek. "It's been a long time since I've been with a woman. I hope I wasn't too rough. I tried not to rush you, but I was so damn hungry for you."

She lifted her mouth toward his for another warm kiss. "You made it wonderful for me. I'm glad it happened, too. I wanted you, Quinn Montgomery." Her voice was seductive.

He took a deep, wet kiss—enough, he told himself, to last through the empty night.

Heather wanted to spend the night locked in his arms. Although he hadn't mentioned love, she thought of him as her lover and her friend. And it was enough for now. "I should get back to Cynthia," she whispered.

"I know," he said huskily, ignoring that part of him that demanded he keep her where she belonged . . . with him.

But from now on Cynthia came first. He made some serious mistakes with his daughter. That would all have to change. Everything else would have to wait including his work and his personal life. That was the way he vowed to keep it. So as much as he wanted to make long leisurely love to Heather and get their relationship on a solid foundation, he knew Cynthia was in more need of Heather at the moment than he. Besides, it was too soon for Cynthia to learn about their involvement.

"Good night," he said, his voice thick with desire. "Try to get some rest. Okay?"

"You too," she said, caressing his cheek. "Night."

Heather could hear Cynthia splashing in the tub when she returned. Heather realized that she needed a few moments alone to collect her thoughts, sort through her feelings.

She felt like she was on a merry-go-around and couldn't

get off. Not only had she become personally involved with a parent, she'd fallen in love with him. And to make matters worse, she had made love with him.

Their lovemaking had only served to intensify her feelings for him. Her heart raced as she remembered what it was like to be in his arms, his body within hers. Heather's face heated. She'd nothing to compare it to.

Her only sexual experiences had been with Kenneth, the man she'd thought she would marry. That had been years ago, before she returned to Detroit. As she thought of Quinn and what she felt for him, she knew there was no comparison between the two men. Quinn was a wonderful lover. But that wasn't what made the difference for her. The difference was with her and what she felt for Quinn.

"Hi." Cynthia was swamped by the large bath towel. "I hope you don't mind, I used the unopened toothbrush I found on the cabinet and your toothpaste by the sink."

"Use whatever you like." Heather removed a nightshirt from her overnight case. "I have an extra nightshirt. You're welcome to it."

"Thanks," Cynthia said. "I washed my underthings and hung them on the bar over the tub. Was that okay?"

Heather smiled, trying to ease the girl's nervousness. "Sweetheart, if you want to talk—"

"I'm all done in the bathroom," she interrupted.

"Okay." Heather collected her robe and nightshirt.

"What side of the bed would you want?"

"Doesn't matter."

When Heather emerged Cynthia was curled up in bed, but she wasn't asleep. The girl was clearly exhausted. The last few days had taken their toll. Heather could also see that Cynthia was upset, but she couldn't force the girl to share her worries. Heather sat down on the opposite edge of the double bed and began lotioning her legs and arms.

Finally Cynthia asked anxiously, "Are you mad at me, Heather? For running away?"

"Honey, I was disappointed that you picked this way to show us that you were unhappy. But no, I'm not angry with you." Heather was reluctant to ask the next question, but knew it was crucial. "You're alright, aren't you? I mean that man in the alley, he didn't try to force himself on you, did he?"

"No!" The girl shuddered. "He settled for pushing me into the Dumpster and taking all my money and my gold locket with my mother's picture in it. That was a Christmas present from my father. And my bracelet! How could I forget that?"

Heather nodded. "I'm glad he didn't really hurt you."

"I just wish it were all over."

"But it is, isn't it?"

"No . . ." Cynthia hesitated, staring down at her hands, unable to meet Heather's gaze. "I lied."

"About what?"

"Everything. It was all a lie."

"About what?"

In a rush of tears, Cynthia confessed. "I'm not pregnant. I never was. I've never even slept with a boy."

Heather blinked. Cynthia not pregnant? The plastic bottle of lotion she'd been holding thumped to the carpet.

Why hadn't she guessed? She was a trained professional, for heaven's sake! If not at first, then certainly when the girl panicked when faced with that doctor's appointment. It made perfect sense.

"I'm sorry, Heather. I'm so sorry . . ." she whispered as tears rolled down her cheek. She whimpered, "I wanted my daddy to . . ."

"I know you did, honey," Heather said, going over to her. She held her close. She understood only too well.

Professional experiences had shown her that children were capable of dangerous and sometimes deadly actions in the hopes of gaining their parent's love or attention.

Heather waited until she was quiet before she said gently, "Cynthia, I know you didn't mean to hurt anyone. But you've got to tell your father."

"I know. In the morning—"

"No, honey. Tonight. After what you put him through, he has to be told now. You owe him that much."

Cynthia's dark gray eyes, so like Quinn's, flooded with tears once again at the thought of facing him. Her voice was trembling when she said, "It was wrong, I know that now. I should never have run away. I'm sorry."

Heather stroked her back until she calmed. "It's time to tell your father the truth. Don't worry—I'll be right beside you. It won't be so bad."

Cynthia nodded. "I ran because I didn't think either one of you would ever forgive me. I guess I couldn't live with it. Do you hate me, Heather?"

"Never . . . I'll always be your friend," Heather reassured. "I'm so happy you're safe."

"Will you still care about me when we get back?"

"There's no doubt about that," Heather said with a wide smile.

Cynthia smiled back. "I like you so much. Could we do things like before?"

"Of course, but first I want your promise that you'll

never run away again. If something is bothering you, tell your father. He loves you so much." Heather squeezed her hand. "Let's get this over with."

Quinn was beat, yet he knew he was too wound up to sleep, so he decided to get a few calls out of the way. He was on the telephone with Cynthia's aunt when he heard the knock on the connecting door.

"Joan, I'll have Cynthia call you as soon as we get home. No, I promise. Okay, bye."

For an instant his heart beat wildly in his chest as Heather filled his mind. But he pushed those sensuous thoughts aside as he opened the connecting door.

"Hi, baby. Can't sleep?"

Cynthia shook her head, but she didn't speak.

He sent a questioning glance to Heather. Cynthia was hanging on to her as she followed the girl into his room. He quizzed her with his eyes.

"Cynthia has something to tell you, Quinn." She silently pleaded with him to be patient, although she doubted he understood. She urged Cynthia forward.

He watched as his daughter nervously twisted her hands, and tears began running down her soft brown cheeks. A sob tore from her throat.

"What's wrong, baby girl? Did something else happen last night? Did that man in the alley—"

"No," she said quickly.

"Then what?"

"Oh, Daddy," she wailed, "I was so scared!"

"I know, baby girl, I know," Quinn said softly, reaching out to cradle her against his chest, his hand moving soothingly over her slim shoulders. "You're safe now. No one is going to hurt you."

"I have to tell—" She cried even harder.

Quinn tried to soothe her, saying, "It's alright, Cindy. Don't cry. You're going to make yourself sick. Remember, you're carrying my grandchild inside of you."

"No, D-D-Dad-d-y—"

"Huh?"

"I ran away because—"

"It's going to be alright You don't have to face this pregnancy alone. We'll find a way together."

Heather longed to help, to tell him the words Cynthia was having such a difficult time getting out. But she didn't. If Cynthia and her father where going to repair their relationship, the girl had to be honest with him.

"Go ahead, Cynthia," Heather encouraged softly, but her eyes were on Quinn. "Remember, your father loves you."

Quinn looked at Heather, sensing there was something she was trying to tell him. He waited, not knowing what to do or say to make it easier for his daughter.

Taking a deep breath, Cynthia managed to say, "I ran away because I d-d-didn't think you would forgive me for wh-what I've done."

"Cynthia, running away didn't change how I feel about you," he answered, his voice thick with emotion. "I know I've made mistakes since your mother passed. . . ."

"Oh, Daddy!" Cynthia sobbed harder. "I got so scared when Heather made that doctor's appointment—" She pressed her face into his shirt.

Quinn held her, giving her time to collect herself.

"I d-didn't think you would want me to stay if you—"

"If what, baby girl?"

Fresh tears spilled down her cheeks, wetting his shirt. "It was all a lie! All of it." Cynthia couldn't bring herself to look at him.

It took Quinn a second to realize what she had said. He gripped her shoulders, holding her away from him so that he could see her face.

"You're telling me that you aren't pregnant?" His brows lifted in shock.

"Yes, sir," she whispered. Her whole body shook as she looked up at her father.

Quinn didn't know what to say. He wasn't even sure what he was feeling at that moment. Relief was foremost in his mind as he realized that his daughter wouldn't have to face the most difficult decision of her young life. For that he was supremely grateful.

"Quinn—"

"It's alright, Heather. I'm not angry," he said, softly. "I'm disappointed in you, Cindy. But I'm glad you're not pregnant. Really thankful." He surprised her by giving her a hug.

"I'm sorry, Daddy. Really sorry." She sniffed. "I promise never to do anything like this again."

He lifted her chin in order for her to meet his gaze. He voice was firm when he said, "I don't expect you will. You did a very reckless and foolish thing. You used Heather to get back at me. And you put yourself in unnecessary danger. I don't like it. We'll discuss your punishment when we get home. Go to bed," he ended gruffly.

"Yes, Daddy," Cynthia whispered, turning to leave.

"Cindy, just because I'm disappointed in you and intend to put you on punishment doesn't mean I don't love you." He paused. "Good night."

Heather watched a muscle jump in his neck as if he were clenching his teeth. He looked so tired. "It's going to be alright, sweetheart," she whispered softly.

"Always the optimist." He smiled, knowing he didn't dare touch her. He longed to hold her close—he hungered for her warmth. Instead, he said, "Night. Sleep well."

They all slept late. It wasn't until they were lingering over coffee after breakfast that Heather had an opportunity to speak with Quinn privately. Cynthia had gone to buy a change of clothes in the hotel's boutique.

"Quinn, talk to me."

"I don't think you want to hear what's going on in my head."

"I know you're disappointed . . ."

"It would be embarrassing, that is, if it hadn't been so damn dangerous." He shook his head wearily, then said, "After we make the police report and have a meal with Mrs. Cummings, we should be on our way."

"Cynthia has been confused and unhappy. That's why she did what she did."

"She has been manipulative."

Heather heard the hurt and disappointment in his voice. "Quinn—"

"There's no excuse for what she did. The hell she put us through these last few days, Heather. There never was a baby!"

"But isn't that wonderful?"

Quinn stared at her. "Yeah. But how do you solve something like this? Beating her behind might make me feel better, as would locking her in her room until she's twenty-seven," he said drily.

"You could try talking to her, taking some time with her. Try letting her know how much you care about her. Do it now. So she'll know she doesn't have to tell lies in order to get your attention. She needs you, Quinn, more than ever before."

Quinn nodded, agreeing with every point Heather made, but he was still furious. The cold calculation involved in his daughter's behavior terrified him. He'd defended too many similar types in court. It was the deliberateness of her actions that he found intolerable. He also felt a strong sense of personal responsibility and guilt for what she'd done.

"Quinn, she had to have been desperate to risk her life as she did. Cynthia couldn't face you. She couldn't face either one of us. Quinn, she could have died alone on the streets. And we probably would never have known what happened to her. We're so lucky! Think of all those kids we saw out there, while we were trying to locate Cynthia. It's scary."

He accepted that he had to find help for Cynthia. And he had to change his own habits. He had to cut back on his hours at work. He had to make time for his daughter. The sight of those lost kids was something he would never forget. Cynthia was his little girl. Yet his anger and disappointment just wouldn't vanish.

"Heather, I can't overlook this. She was vengeful and selfish. I have a right to be upset about it."

"Quinn, I just don't want you to be so hard on her. I

think she's suffered enough and shouldn't be punished when she gets back home."

Getting to his feet with the food check in his hand, he asked, "Are you ready?"

"Yes," Heather said, rising.

"Did you get any sleep last night?"

"Not much. How about you?" She'd heard Quinn pacing throughout the night.

Quinn shook his head, handing the cashier a large bill. "Doesn't matter. We'll be home soon, then we all can get some rest."

The police station proved to be an ordeal for the girl. But with her father's support, Cynthia made the robbery report. The meal with Miss Mattie was a welcome respite. By early afternoon they were on the road and headed toward Detroit.

It was after dark when they reached Heather's condo. All of them were exhausted. Cynthia was asleep in the backseat when Heather got out of the car. Heather was a bit uneasy as Quinn walked her to her door.

Unlocking her front door, she said, "I'd ask you in, but I know you have to get Cynthia home." She broke off, looking into the smoldering depths of his dark eyes.

He was studying her mouth, imagining himself catching her bottom lip between his even white teeth, savoring its texture and softness before he completely covered her mouth with his, plunging his tongue inside, thoroughly investigating the sweet interior. He moaned huskily.

"Quinn, don't."

"I'm just looking . . . wishing. I want you tonight, sugar dumplin'. Would you let me stay and make love to you if I asked?"

"Yes," she whispered, trembling at the raw passion in his voice.

He smiled, pleased by her response. "Sleep tight. I'll call you tomorrow." With that he was gone.

Thirteen

"Can I join you?" Diane Rivers didn't wait for Heather's reply but took the empty chair across from her at the lunch table.

Heather looked up from the tuna salad she'd been toying with rather than eating. "Hi, Diane." Her thoughts had been far from the noise and activity of the staff lounge.

She'd spoken to Quinn again last night on the telephone, just as she had every night since they returned last week from Dayton. His deep sexy voice was the last she heard every night and the first she wished to hear each morning. As crazy as it seemed, she had fallen even more deeply in love with him—and they hadn't been able to spend any time together. But tonight would be different. They had a dinner date, and she was looking forward to being with him.

"I'm glad you're alone. I need to talk to you." Diane was a very lovely toffee-toned black woman with thick black hair. She said, picking up her fork, "I want some answers and only you can give them to me."

"Problem?"

"You tell me! I know that sounds a bit crazy, but I really don't know what's wrong. It's Charles. He's been so remote. Have you noticed?"

"I can't say I have. He may be a bit self-absorbed. But I'm sure there's nothing wrong," Heather said, purposefully vague.

"You're his best friend. If anyone would know what's wrong it's you."

It was true that he'd been upset when Diane didn't appear at the panel discussion or the school dance following. Surely he was over his snit? Heather was ashamed that she didn't know the answer. She'd been too involved with Quinn and Cynthia to spare a thought to little else.

"Has he confided in you?"

The two old friends knew each other very well. Yet Heather was frankly surprised by Diane's attitude. Maybe she did care about Charles more than she was willing to admit. "Exactly what's bothering you?"

"He's just been so evil! I don't know what I've done to offend him or why he's so angry with me."

Before Heather could begin to formulate a response, she saw the man in question heading in their direction. They usually shared the lunch table. Charles was engrossed in conversation with the English department head and hadn't apparently seen them. When he looked up, he frowned. Then he bypassed their table to join an another group of teachers near the window.

"Did you see that! That's what I've been talking about. You two eat lunch together every day, but today he sees me here and suddenly he prefers to sit next to Glendale.

HERE'S A SPECIAL INVITATION TO ENJOY TODAY'S FINEST HISTORICAL ROMANCES— ABSOLUTELY FREE! *(a $19.96 value)*

Now you can enjoy the latest Zebra Lovegram Historical Romances without even leaving your home with our convenient Zebra Home Subscription Service. Zebra Home Subscription Service offers you the following benefits that you don't want to miss:

- 4 BRAND NEW bestselling Zebra Lovegram Historical Romances delivered to your doorstep each month (usually before they're available in the bookstores!)

  - 20% off each title or a savings of almost $4.00 each month

  - FREE home delivery

  - A FREE monthly newsletter, *Zebra/Pinnacle Romance News* that features author profiles, contests, special member benefits, book previews and more

- No risks or obligations...in other words you can cancel whenever you wish with no questions asked

So join hundreds of thousands of readers who already belong to Zebra Home Subscription Service and enjoy the very best Historical Romances That Burn With The Fire of History!

And remember....there is no minimum purchase required. After you've enjoyed your initial FREE package of 4 books, you'll begin to receive monthly shipments of new Zebra titles. Each shipment will be yours to examine for 10 days and then if you decide to keep the books, you'll pay the preferred subscriber's price of just $4.00 per title. That's $16 for all 4 books with FREE home delivery! And if you want us to stop sending books, just say the word....it's that simple.

It's a no-lose proposition, so send for your 4 FREE books today!

4 FREE BOOKS

These books worth almost $20, are yours without cost or obligation when you fill out and mail this certificate.
(If the certificate is missing below, write to: Zebra Home Subscription Service, Inc., 120 Brighton Road, P.O. Box 5214, Clifton, New Jersey 07015-5214)

Complete and mail this card to receive 4 Free books!

YES! Please send me 4 Zebra Lovegram Historical Romances without cost or obligation. I understand that each month thereafter I will be able to preview 4 new Zebra Lovegram Historical Romances FREE for 10 days. Then if I decide to keep them, I will pay the money-saving preferred publisher's price of just $4.00 each...a total of $16. That's almost $4 less than the regular publisher's price, and there is never any additional charge for shipping and handling. I may return any shipment within 10 days and owe nothing, and I may cancel this subscription at any time. The 4 FREE books will be mine to keep in any case.

Name _____

Address _____ Apt. _____

City _____ State _____ Zip _____

Telephone ( ) _____

Signature _____
(If under 18, parent or guardian must sign.)

LF0296

Terms, offer and prices subject to change without notice. Subscription subject to acceptance by Zebra Home Subscription Service, Inc.. Zebra Home Subscription Service, Inc. reserves the right to reject any order or cancel any subscription.

You know as well as I do that he can't stand that man. Heather, why is he acting this way?"

"Diane, calm down." Heather sighed. "I'm sure whatever is bothering him can easily be settled between the two of you."

Heather couldn't tell what she suspected—that Charles had fallen deeply in love with Diane, and that he resented her relationships with other men. Charles would hang her from the nearest tree.

She was beginning to feel as if she were almost in the same situation herself. She loved Quinn, but their relationship was still so new. What if he found out she loved him? Heather didn't want him to know her feelings anymore than Charles wanted Diane to know his.

And then there was the problem of Cynthia. At the moment she needed emotional stability and support. Heather didn't think she was ready emotionally to deal with a woman in her father's life, especially when that woman was Heather. Cynthia would probably view her as a threat.

"And how do you suggest I do that? He barely speaks to me! I've tried to talk to the stubborn man, but he only stares at me with a dense look on his face, as if he doesn't know what language I'm using! The jerk! Oh, why do I care?" she fumed, taking a bite of her sandwich. "Men! I hate them all!"

"What about that sexy advertising executive you were dating? I thought he was really something," Heather said between bites of salad.

"Frank? Too possessive. I went out with him twice and he started making demands. You know how I feel. When they start asking questions it's time to say goodbye. Oh, he was good in bed—but so are a lot of guys."

"So why worry about Charles? I've never known you to get upset over a man."

"He's different, and we've been such good friends. I just don't understand. Heather, why won't you tell me what's wrong?"

"As you said, we're friends. I can't break a confidence."

Heather didn't want to be in the middle of their mess. She knew that Charles wasn't about to share Diane with the half dozen men she fancied. He wanted to be the only man in her life. So why couldn't he just tell Diane that and leave Heather out of it?

"Thanks a lot!" Diane said looking terribly hurt "I thought we were friends! I even wrote to you about this job when you were in Chicago. And this is the way you repay me? Some friend you are."

"Honestly, Diane. What's wrong with you? You know good and well you don't want to get involved with any one man. Or have you suddenly fallen in love with Charles?"

"Don't be silly. He's the only real man I know. He's honest, straightforward, and the best-looking thing around. I'm not trying to get in his way. I just want our friendship to continue. He's the only man I've ever been able to depend on. Besides, he understands me. But he's not looking for a commitment," she finished with a wistful smile.

If she weren't so upset about Quinn, Heather was certain she would have burst out laughing. Talk about crazy!

But at the moment she was a bit fed up with the silly games these two were playing with each other.

"Girl, you either want the man or you don't. I don't think he's willing to let you play with his emotions, Diane. Isn't that what's really bothering you? You've met a man that can say no to you and mean it."

"That isn't true!"

"Well now, there's nothing to worry about, is there?" Heather said, collecting her things. "I've got to go. I've a meeting with Mrs. Silvers within the hour and I haven't completed the final revision for the summer school schedule. Are you going to teach the computer work-study this summer?"

"Yes . . . some of my best students are involved. Are you planning on working?"

Heather shook her head. "I'll be concentrating on my dissertation all summer long. At the rate I'm going, I'll be a little old lady before I've finished making sense of all the data."

They reached the corridor outside the staff lounge when Diane placed a detaining hand on Heather's arm. "I'm sorry. This isn't your fault. I shouldn't have dumped all of this in your lap. But don't you see, I need your help. Please, Heather."

The hallway was crowded, and Heather had to stay close in order to make herself heard. "Frankly, Diane, I don't see how I can help you. You've got to talk to him. Only he can you tell you what's on his mind. Besides, even if he does care about you, and I'm not saying he does, but if he does, then you have to give something of yourself in return. He's no different from anyone else. We all want to be first in that special person's life."

They'd reached the counseling wing. "I think you should really think hard about your motives, girlfriend." Heather squeezed Diane's hand.

"Will you speak to him about me?" Diane begged. "Tell him that I'd like for us to talk?"

"Yes. But give it time, okay?" Heather suggested, then waved and followed the side corridor.

"Heather, a Mrs. Backster from MADD called. They'll be happy to aid the team of volunteers for prom night." Joan Wilson, the secretary, serviced all five counselors.

"Great! Thanks, Joan."

"You've a student waiting in your office, the Montgomery girl. And these are for you."

Heather looked up in surprise as she handed her a florist's box tied with a peach ribbon. The middle-aged woman smiled teasingly. "New man?"

"Thanks."

"Don't thank me, thank Mr. Wonderful," she laughed.

Heather smiled, her eyes reflecting her excitement. "Will you please tell Mrs. Silvers that I won't have the summer school schedule until later this afternoon. I'll bring it over when I'm done."

Heather fought the urge to take a quick peek at the card as she jockeyed around two co-workers chatting in the doorway of one of the offices. Her office was the corner one at the end of the corridor.

"Hi," she said, closing the door carefully behind her. "You been waiting long?"

"Just got here." Cynthia returned her smile. "You busy?"

"I've always got time for you, kiddo. How are you today?"

"So, so. I spoke to my new counselor today, Mrs. Van Ervin."

"And?"

"I don't like her. Why can't I have you?"

"You know why. We've already been over this a hundred times. We're friends now. Our relationship is a personal one, not a business one. You've got to be a bit more patient. Give her a chance."

"We're still going tomorrow?" she asked hopefully.

"Naturally. Tour of the Museum of African-American History, followed by lunch downtown and a movie, right? You nervous about staying over tonight with my nieces?"

"No . . . well, a little. What if they ask about me running away? What will I say?"

"They don't know about it. Just have fun. That's why you're going, right?"

Cynthia grinned. "I have to go or I'll miss study hall." Cynthia gave Heather a quick hug before asking, "Who sent the flowers? A man?"

Heather gave a weak laugh. "A friend. How are things between you and your dad?"

"Better. Although he's still upset about what I did."

"He has that right."

"But he's not giving me any space. He's been home for dinner every night this week. He does his work at home now, after I go to bed. He's even taken to checking my homework."

Heather held back a laugh. "Honey, you wanted his attention and now you have it."

"Are you on his side?" Cynthia asked sharply.

"Nope. I'm on both your sides."

"I wanted to do things with him and talk about stuff. I wanted to know he cares about me. I didn't ask for a jailer."

"That's all a part of it," Heather said quietly.

"Once he gets bored with playing father, things will be back to the way they were before," Cynthia said dryly, but her eyes were filled with worry.

"Oh?"

"Yeah. He won't have time for me again."

"I think you're wrong. Remember, your father loves you. That won't change, no matter what."

Cynthia nodded. "I've got to go. See you in the morning," she called as she ran out.

Heather sighed. Quinn loved his daughter—but it looked as if time and some much needed therapy would eventually prove it to the girl. Now all she had to do was convince Quinn.

"Quinn . . ." She said his name aloud, reaching for the long box. Inside she found a dozen long-stemmed tangerine-tinted roses. Beautiful, she thought lightly touching the tender buds. Her hands were trembling when she opened the card: *Tonight . . . Quinn.*

"Oh, yes . . ."

"You look good . . . really good," Quinn said softly. He sat across from Heather at the candlelit table, enjoying her beauty.

Two tiny orchids were pinned above one ear and her hair was swept to one side, allowing him to view the expanse of her creamy golden neck and shoulders. Her dress was a thin-strapped, silver, chermuse sheath that seemed to have been made to caress her soft curves. A waterfall of tiny silver hearts dangled from her earlobes and silver chains on her wrist were her only jewelry.

"Thank you," she said with a warm smile. She lifted the glass of sparkling champagne to her strawberry-tinted mouth.

"Are you enjoying yourself?" Quinn knew he sounded like a broken record and felt like a kid on his first date. He'd planned their evening down to the last detail, hoping to make her brown eyes sparkle like semiprecious stones.

And he hadn't been disappointed when they boarded the *Star Gazer* for an evening of dinner, dancing, and moonlight while the boat made a leisurely cruise down the Detroit River.

"Very much so." Her eyes shimmered like diamonds. "The food, the wine, and especially the company are all exceptional. And the view!" She referred to the twinkling lights along the Canadian coastline.

"I've missed you this past week," Quinn said, before confessing somewhat awkwardly, "This evening was meant to show you how grateful I am to you for all you've done to help me and Cindy."

Heather dropped her lids, hoping to hide her hurt and disappointment. The last thing she wanted was his gratitude. What she longed for was his love. She wanted to be a part of his life and she wanted him to be a part of hers. But she said none of these things. It was too soon. Besides, love was something that had to be given . . . freely.

"How did Cindy do in school this week? She's been an angel at home. I hardly recognize my own kid."

"Very well. She's trying to make up for her mistakes. She seems happier—I congratulate you." Heather lifted her glass to him. "Knowing how you feel has made a world of difference to her."

"I'm trying. Although it hasn't been easy, especially now that her elaborate hoax has come out. Whenever I think of what she did I get angry all over again."

Heather's long lashes fluttered down briefly, concealing her eyes. They were wide and velvety brown when she said, "She can't handle your anger, Quinn. She's still too unsure of herself."

"Yeah, I know. What do you think of Mrs. Van Ervin, the new counselor?"

"She's good. Have you met her?"

"Yes. She seems competent," he said dryly. "She recommended that Cynthia and I consider professional help. A family therapist." A ball of tension had formed in his midsection. He had a feeling he wasn't going to like what Heather was about to say, but he preferred the facts unadorned. "Do you agree?"

"Yes. Naturally, she and I have talked about Cynthia. The therapist was my suggestion. Cynthia has had some serious problems. It would be naive of us to believe that they will just go away."

His eyes seemed to bore into her. "So you think my daughter should see a psychologist."

"Yes, I do. She needs to be able to talk out her problems."

"Can't she do that with Mrs. Van Ervin?"

"Quinn, Cynthia needs therapy. She can only benefit from having a trained professional with whom she can work through her feelings . . . about herself, about you, and about the loss of her mother at such an early age. You know all the new challenges teenagers have now—drinking, taking drugs . . ."

"I wish you hadn't turned her case over to someone else."

"I didn't have a choice. It's unethical to work with a child that I'm so personally involved with—I've lost my objectivity."

"I can't find anything wrong in your caring about my daughter. She loves you—you know that."

"And I love her, too. That's one of the major issues—I can't be her counselor any longer." She sighed. "Quinn, when a girl loses her mother, she—"

He interrupted, "Do you know this Dr. Ann Johnson that Mrs. Van Ervin recommended?"

"Yes, very well. Ann Johnson and my mother are partners. I've also worked with her and observed her many times. She's an older woman, specializing in counseling teens. She's thorough and has a high success rate. But she insists on involving the entire family."

"Are you saying she will want to see me, too?"

"Yes. She doesn't work exclusively with the child. Don't worry, I'm sure you'll like her. She's been written up in several leading psychology journals."

Quinn scowled. He wanted what was best for Cynthia, but at the moment he wasn't sure what was best.

"Please, Quinn, just meet Ann Johnson. Talk to her before you decide."

"Okay, I'll meet her. But that's all I'm promising."

"Thank you." Heather smiled, lightly caressing his fingers as they worried the stem of his water glass. "I'm glad you haven't told Cynthia about us, Quinn. I don't think she's ready emotionally to handle it."

He nodded, looked at her closely. "You don't feel it's a bit dishonest?"

"No. Because neither one of us started out to deceive her. Our being together wasn't planned."

He frowned, hating the omission, but feeling helpless to do anything about it. "It isn't fair to you, pretty girl. You shouldn't be a damn secret."

"We don't have much choice."

The waiter put in an appearance at their table. "Would you care to sample either our chocolate chip cheesecake or rum raisin pudding?"

"Cheesecake," Quinn said without consulting her.

"Quinn!" She attempted to look annoyed, but her smile gave her away.

He chuckled. "Come on, Heather—you know you're dying for a piece of that cheesecake. Huge chocolate chips," he teased, unable to look away from her soft mouth.

Heather couldn't hold out against his infectious laughter. She giggled. "You know me too well."

He smiled slowly, his thumb ever so subtly stroking the delicate skin of her inner wrist.

It was impossible for her not to recognize the subtle change in his mood. Her cheeks flamed as she thought back to their lovemaking. She'd experienced the full force of his masculinity. She'd wanted him then . . . and she wanted him now.

"I've missed you." His voice was low, seductive, revealing the raw hunger and disappointment he had experienced every night since they had been intimate. Long lonely nights that left him awake and aching for her sweetness.

"You're embarrassing me," she whispered.

"Why?" He took her small hand into his. "Because I'm man enough to admit that I want you?" His declaration sent a quiver of sexual excitement moving from him directly to her.

"Stop!" she whispered. "We're in a room full of people."

"No one can hear. I ache to hold you, to love you. Don't you want me?" His voice was as deep and dark as his skin and exquisitely masculine.

"Oh, Quinn," she said breathlessly.

"Answer me."

"Yes," she said very softly, yet matched the smoky fires in his eyes with a sultry glance of her own.

Quinn found he had to clear his throat before he could speak. "Heather . . ." he began, only to be interrupted by the waiter with their desserts. She would have withdrawn her hand, but he held onto it. The thick pad of his thumb worried the sensitive flesh between her thumb and forefinger.

Quinn released her hand so that she could use her fork. He sat watching her, fascinated by the movement of lips and tongue as she ate. His senses went into overdrive and he found he had to look away. Just knowing she wanted to be with him as much as he wanted her left him drunk with desire.

"Mmmm, delicious." She smiled at him. "Gonna win the Jameison case?"

"Quick change of topic, baby." Quinn smiled. "Well, it's hard to tell. We should be able to wrap it up next week, then it's up to the jury. The waiting can be torture, especially for my client. He's been through enough."

"I should think so. Being accused of murdering your wife and her lover isn't an everyday occurrence."

"Especially when you're innocent." Quinn said, pushing his plate to the side. "Let's get back to discussing Dr. Johnson. You say she's your mother's partner?—I didn't realize your mother was in private practice."

"Oh, yes. She handles all kinds of clients but is particularly interested in substance abuse cases. In fact, my goal is to someday join Ann and my mother's practice. That is, if I ever finish my dissertation."

"Coffee?" the waiter asked.

Quinn grinned at her and went so far as to fold his arms over his chest, but said absolutely nothing.

Heather laughed. "Herbal tea, please," she told the waiter. "Quinn?" she asked sweetly.

"The same, thank you." Quinn waited until they were alone before he quizzed, "Was that for my benefit?"

"The laughter was at your expense. The tea, no. I happen to prefer herbal tea, Counselor."

Quinn seemed satisfied with her answer. "All your course work done?"

"Yes."

"Family loyalty won out?"

"Naturally. I didn't even consider going anywhere but Wayne State. Of course, my advisor is one of my father's colleagues. But my father has warned me that I'll receive no preferential treatment. Did I tell you that my father was once my mother's teacher? That's how they met."

"Romantic."

"Very."

"You're a romantic." He smiled. For some unknown reason that pleased him.

"Are you laughing at me?"

"Never that," Quinn defended, stunned by the discovery that he wanted to be the only man to set her heart racing and her pulse whirling out of control.

He experienced a swift ache in his midsection when he reminded himself that no matter how much he wished differently, he had nothing to offer emotionally. His heart wasn't whole.

Yet his breathing accelerated as the memories of Heather beneath him filled his head. Her soft, sweetly scented skin had been bare and his manhood had throbbed with the power of his desire for her. They'd searched for and found a mind-shattering release as one. Quinn had never experienced anything like it . . . not ever. The experience had left him hungry—always ready for more of Heather.

But would an intimate, mutually satisfying, exclusive relationship keep her happy? He could give her everything she wanted . . . everything . . . except love. Love meant marriage, and that part of his life was over.

The seductive rhythm of the band on the upper level floated down to them.

Heather smiled dreamily. "The music sounds great."

"Would you like to go upstairs and dance?"

What a marvelous idea, Heather thought—a legitimate excuse to be in his arms. "Oh, yes," she said. A huskiness entered her voice, causing his eyes to darken even more.

Quinn rose from his chair and held her chair for her. He was so close that his breath warmed her cheek. His nostrils flared. Jasmine or orchids? He couldn't decide. Whatever the scent, it mixed with her body chemistry to become an erotic temptation to his senses.

Quinn guided her with a slight pressure of his hand in the small of her back. He didn't speak, concentrating on the graceful sway of her hips as she mounted the stairs ahead of him. There wasn't a doubt in his mind that her behind was as soft as it looked. He knew for a fact it was softer.

When they reached the small dance floor, he took her in his arms with more haste than grace. What was there about her that affected him so strongly? She was no great beauty. Hell, that was a lie. Heather was beautiful inside and out.

Her appeal went beyond the physical. It was her incredible sweetness and sincere wish to help others that he admired most about her. Her ability to give so unselfishly of herself and keep on giving fascinated him.

"What a great band," she said, from where her cheek rested against his chest.

"You move well," he murmured, dropping his head in order to enjoy her scent.

"So do you," she said, lifting her head. Her soft thin braids ever so subtly caressed his throat.

Quinn struggled with his desire. Heather couldn't help but feel his arousal, but she didn't pull back. In fact, Quinn felt the tiny shiver that went through her as his thigh glided smoothly between her slightly parted legs as he swayed with her in time to the music.

"I know I shouldn't feel guilty about taking the night off and enjoying myself. I've spent so many Friday nights in the library." She laughed.

"Let's get some fresh air," he said sharply.

Many of the guests were taking advantage of the star-studded deck. Quinn and Heather found a somewhat se-cluded spot near the bow of the boat. Quinn inhaled deeply. He felt her studying him through the thickness of her lashes.

"Quinn, is something wrong? What happened in there?"

It was that blasted word that had triggered his memory. Guilt . . . He ate it daily, breathed it constantly, and prob-ably perspired it nightly in the form of nightmares. He couldn't get away from it. Hell, it wouldn't let go of him. Peggy . . .

Quinn held himself responsible for his wife's unhap-piness before she died. He had done the only thing he could have under the circumstances. Yet Peggy was dead—while he was very much alive, able to enjoy an-other woman's kisses . . . another woman's body.

"Sometimes it helps to share problems," Heather

coaxed. She placed pink-lacquered nails on the navy sleeve of his jacket.

Quinn looked out at the churning water far below them. "I can't," he whispered. His throat closed around his inner agony. He surprised himself when he reached for Heather and held her against him.

Fourteen

"Tea?" Heather asked as she placed her evening bag and wrap on the rocking chair.

He seemed to fill the archway leading into the living room.

"Quinn?"

He caught her hand before she could move farther away. "I've missed you. I know it's only been over a week since we were together. Ten days that have felt more like a year." His voice was gravelly with need when he asked, "Have you missed me, baby?"

He didn't give her time to respond. His lips were warm and possessive as he covered Heather's mouth with his. The caress was glorious, but it wasn't enough, not nearly enough. He traced the outline of her full lips with the tip of his tongue as if memorizing each delectable detail. Quinn pushed past the barrier of her teeth, delving into the delicate lining of her mouth. She was luscious, sweeter than the finest wine, yet so potent that she went straight to his head.

"Heather . . ." he whispered, stroking the velvety warmth of her tongue with his own until they were both weak with unfulfilled yearnings. "Tell me," he demanded in a deep throaty voice. "Tell me you want me just as much as I want you. Tell me you want me to make love to you."

"Yes . . . oh, yes," she said breathlessly. "I've missed you so much."

Heather was a quivering mass of desire as sexual tension flooded the pit of her stomach. Her feelings ran so deep for this man that she needed to be with him, needed to please him in every way a woman can please her man. Her hands tunneled under his suit coat, exploring the long length of his back from shoulder to waist, enjoying the hard muscle beneath the silk of his shirt.

"Heather . . ." His warm firm mouth slid slowly down her neck, lingering at the base. He ran his tongue over the scented hollow, causing tiny shivers to explode deep inside of her.

If it weren't for his support, Heather probably would have collapsed at his feet in a heap of unfulfilled longing. Quinn didn't seem particularly bothered by her weight as she leaned into him. In fact he swung her off the floor, one arm beneath her knees, the other around her waist. His mouth never left the enchanting place where her neck and shoulder joined. She was sweet, so sweet, he thought as she looped her arms around his neck. He gave her one hard impatient kiss before he took the stairs two at a time.

Heather bubbled with laughter of pure happiness. At last she was where she wanted to be most of all—in his arms.

He grinned down at her but didn't slow his pace. Heather rubbed her cheek against his chest, fascinated by the strong even rhythm of his heart as Quinn carried her into the softly lit bedroom at the end of the hall.

They came down on her double bed together, laughing. It was so good to be together. No worries, no intrusions, just the two of them.

Heather, who had landed on top of Quinn, sobered suddenly and shivered with anticipation as Quinn planted a series of kisses down her neck. She gasped, arching backward and turned her head to the side.

She whispered his name as he unzipped her dress and pushed it out of the way, exposing her golden beauty in a pale pink strapless lace bra, pink lace panty, and pink lace-edged garters. He groaned his appreciation and kissed the top swells of her full breasts and her thighs above the black lace-edged stockings.

Her heart was so full of love that she hugged him, pressing her lips against his chin, his nose, his jawline, whatever she could reach. He quickly lowered his head, giving her total access to his mouth.

Although he didn't share the love she held close to her heart, she was nevertheless thrilled by his gifts of passion and tenderness. A part of her would never give up hope that one day she would have his heart. But for now her feelings must remain under lock and key.

Heather's hands were shaking as she loosened his tie, unbuttoned his shirt, then pushed it down his arms. She ran her hands over his bare chest down to his trim midsection before she placed her soft lips on his collarbone. She unfastened his slacks while kissing the hollow at the base of his throat, biting him gently.

Quinn growled his pleasure, a low throaty sound when

her soft wet mouth tongued and circled his nipple. Her tender efforts ignited white-hot flames.

"I wanted you so badly that first time, I thought I was going to die from the wanting. I can't believe it's possible for me to want you more. But I do—right now."

Quinn parted her lips to savor her unique flavor. Heather . . . He found her tongue and stroked it against his, slowly in and out of her mouth, a provocative prelude of what was to come.

She'd gone limp by the time the kiss ended. Her breathing was quick and uneven. He rolled, taking her with him. She lay on her back, her limbs bracketed by his muscular thighs. He focused on her earlobe, removing the earring to replace it with his mouth. Unhurriedly he tasted it, eventually tracing the delicate outer shell with his tongue before suckling the lobe.

Quinn moved lower until his cheek rested on the softness of her breasts. He cradled her in his big hands, holding her breasts together and burying his face between their cushiony softness. He nestled against her. Quinn's heartbeat quickened, and he lifted his head to look at her. Long thick lashes rested on the high slope of her cheeks, and her mouth was as ripe and succulent as crushed strawberries—wonderfully full and swollen from his kisses.

"Look at me." He waited until she complied, then said, "Now tell me what you need."

Heather gasped as air quickly rushed from her lungs and she trembled with warm anticipation.

"Tell me, baby. I need to know what you like and how you like it."

Her experience was so limited that she wasn't comfortable vocalizing her thoughts. She pressed her lips against his neck, hiding a blush as she eventually whispered close to his ear, "Like in Dayton."

Quinn nodded. "You want it slow and deep, sugar?"

"Oh . . ." She blushed deeper.

"There's no room for embarrassment in this bed. Tell me," he demanded, giving her a tantalizingly sweet kiss. "I want to please you."

"Yes . . . Quinn, please . . ."

Quinn's body was throbbing with the intensity of his desire. He could detect a slight tremor in his fingers as he removed her lacy underthings. Slowly he journeyed over her from rounded shoulders to small feet.

"Your skin is the color of spun gold, satiny smooth . . . wondrously soft," he said, tracing the path his hands had followed with his wet open mouth. "You're beautiful."

By the time he returned to her lips, she had to feel his bare skin against hers. She pushed at his shirt. "Hurry, Quinn. Please . . . hurry."

He stood and quickly finished undressing himself. Heather's eyes touched every inch of his dark brown length from his tightly curled close-cut natural to the strong cords of his neck, his broad shoulders, wide chest—down to his trim middle and lean hips and his engorged sex thick with passion for her. Quinn's thighs were muscled, his calves long, and his feet were narrow. Heather instantly decided it was Quinn who was the beautiful one. And tonight he was hers.

"Oh, Quinn," she said, with her arms welcoming when he returned to lie down beside her. Her eyes sparkled with love. "I want you . . ."

Quinn didn't think he could wait an instant longer. His kisses sizzled, hot and deep, fierce with longing. "Can

you feel how much I want to be inside you? Can you?"
He rubbed himself against her.

"Mmmm . . ."

"Oh, sugar, I intend to make you purr for me tonight,"
he said, thrusting his tongue into the wet warmth of her
mouth.

She touched him, reacquainting herself with the texture, the feel, and finally the taste of Quinn. Heather
circled his flat ebony nipples, raking over them with her
nails before laving each in turn with her tongue, biting
him playfully and causing him to gasp in pleasure. His
heart pumped like a wild thing inside his chest.

"No more," he growled, holding her tightly and giving
himself time to gain control.

"Quinn?"

"Give me a second," he said, tenderly caressing her
nape beneath her braids. He recalled Spike's film, *She
Gotta Have It,* and almost laughed aloud. In his case the
"she" was he. He was about ready to explode. If he
didn't get some of Heather Gregory and soon . . . For
this one special night they belonged to each other. She
was his . . . his alone. And he was hers.

Heather placed soft butterfly kisses behind his ear,
along his neck, down to the supersensitive spot at the
base of his throat.

He did laugh then, a deep throaty laugh. "I've got to
have you, sugar." Quinn caressed down the side of her
body, around her waist, eventually cupping and squeezing
her soft behind. His tongue thrust into her mouth, while
he parted her legs with his own, exposing the delicate
bounty of her inner thighs.

She gasped at the gentle pressure he applied to her

vulva with his knee. She was so hot and empty. He took a hard raisin-brown nipple into his mouth, licking the sensitive peak, generating a tremendous heat within her. Eventually he suckled. Heather bit her bottom lip to keep from screaming out her pleasure.

As Quinn suckled, he also stroked her. He played in the soft tight curls between her thighs, taking his time before his long lean fingers slowly caressed the slick soft folds of her femininity. She was as lovely as a dew-kissed rose and just as wondrously soft and gloriously wet. Heather voiced her pleasure in a seductive moan as he concentrated on the highly sensitive nub, the very heart of her desires. He stroked her until she cried out, convulsing in a series of rippling orgasms.

Her climax served to increase his excitement. Quinn held her close, soothing her until she calmed. He whispered, "I like you like this . . . so hot and wet."

Although she was still trembling, Heather gave him a warm, loving kiss.

"Touch me," he whispered huskily, eager for the feel of her soft hands on his heated flesh. Heather licked his neck while she caressed his chest. He held his breath when she moved down to circle his navel before tangling her slender fingers in the thick hair surrounding his masculinity. His breath stopped altogether when she lightly traced the length of his pulsing manhood. He was dying for her. "Heather, please, take me. Take me into the warmth of your hand."

Heather wanted to give him pleasure. She closed her soft hands around his shaft and caressed him with the same loving tenderness he'd shown her moments before. Quinn's eyes were tightly closed. He was unable to focus on anything but the erotic massage she gave him. When she worried the smooth crown with her fingertips and then her mouth, Quinn's whole body stiffened in sweet agony.

"Enough!" he said, lifting her against his side. He held her still while his breath came in rapid pants.

Heather felt the swift uneven beat of his heart. It matched her own. He held her close until his breathing slowed, then he lifted thick black lashes. His pupils were like rich, dark smoke, smoldering with passion as he studied her. Her soft thighs circled one of his as she pressed her damp heat against him.

"Now! Quinn . . . now."

She was burning for him. If he didn't take her soon, she would perish from the wanting. Thrilled by her responses to him, Quinn gave her a long searing kiss before he reached for the small foil package he'd hastily tossed on the nightstand earlier. Heather waited while he put on the protection. But by the time he parted her thighs and positioned himself, Heather was sobbing out her relief, running her nails impatiently down his back.

"Open your eyes, sugar," he managed raggedly as his body pulsated with the full force of his desire. "I want you to look at me as I make you mine." He groaned with pleasure as he slowly penetrated her, submerging himself in her marvelous moist heat, his heart racing like a bucking bronco. Once he was deep inside of her, he forced himself to wait, to give her time to adjust to his size. The last thing he wanted to do was hurt her.

Heather said his name as she curled her limbs around his. She loved the feel of him inside of her, yet ached for the force of his lovemaking. He flooded her senses, filled her head and her heart, leaving room for nothing more. At last they were together. Quinn's nostrils flared as he inhaled the earthy scent that was their desire for each other. While he paused, his body pounding with an urgency that demanded he immediately ease the crushing weight of his hunger for her.

Heather sobbed, instinctively tightening her body around him, pressing her hips against his and stroking his nipples with her fingertips. Quinn wasn't sure if it was the huskiness of her voice, or the sensual stroking against his highly sensitive nipples, or the movement of her hips, or if it was the provocative caress of her inner muscles that led to his undoing. Whatever the cause, it was more than enough to push Quinn into an all-consuming rhythm, intent on taking all she had to give and in turn be taken by her.

He lifted her, cradling her hips in his large hands and coaxing her into meeting his slow, deep thrusts. Quinn dropped his head low enough to give each of her aching nipples a thorough licking before pulling first one and finally the other deep into his mouth to suck, sending shock waves vibrating straight to her womb. She tossed her head from side to side and held on to him as tightly as she could.

"Heather . . . oh, sugar," he groaned, each new thrust bolder, more determined than the last. She was heaven on earth, Quinn decided, intensifying his pace, responding to a mutual goal to give the utmost pleasure. Faster and faster they rode wave upon wave of white-hot desire, giving more and more while enduring the wonderfully sweet torment.

Heather was the first to plunge into the whirling pool

of ultimate gratification. Quinn was right behind her. She held him tight as his body shuddered with release. His mouth meshed with hers a split second after she declared her love for him.

Ever so slowly Heather floated like a leaf carried by the wind on a brisk spring evening. Very gradually their bodies calmed. Heather curled like a small contented kitten against Quinn's side, her head on his shoulder as she caressed the thick black hair at his nape. When she would have kissed him, he stopped her, moving until he could look into the dark beauty of her eyes. He marveled over the way she made him feel.

Giving in to the lure of sleep, her lids dropped and she dozed, wrapped in her lover's arms. Quinn wasn't so fortunate. As his body temperature cooled and the tension in his loins dissipated, his thoughts were a mass of contradictions.

Lately all he could think about was Heather. She filled the empty place inside of him. As he watched her rest, he knew that once again she had captured him so totally, enchanted him so completely that he hadn't thought past the necessity of satisfying them both. It was good with them . . . too good. So good that it scared him. It was Heather—her spirit, her earthiness, and her essence proved a continuous source of fascination for him.

The problem was that when Quinn was with Heather he tended to forget everything else including Peggy. It wasn't like he hadn't slept with other women since his wife's death. But they were nothing more than occasional empty sexual encounters, the sole purpose of which was to relieve the swelling in his groin. So empty that he discovered he preferred celibacy. Heather had changed all that. She'd managed to engage his body, his mind, and his heart. He cared about her. He even valued what she thought of him, as a father, as a man.

Quinn held his breath when Heather shifted, snuggling closer to him. He was angry with himself. Their lovemaking left him feeling as if he had betrayed Peggy in some way. Peggy, his wife, his only love, and the weight around his neck that continued to drag him down.

Oh, he'd heard Heather's softly vowed confession of love. And he despised his momentary selfish delight in her declaration. How in the world was he going to deal with it? Didn't he have enough to feel guilty about? Sighing, he leaned over gently caressing her mouth with his.

"Heather?"

"Hmmm . . ."

"Sugar, don't go to sleep, at least not yet. I have to go."

"Why?" she said drowsily. Frowning, she pushed her braids away from her face.

He made no effort to retrieve his things. "I don't think I should spend the night. Things are complicated, and we agreed it's too soon for Cynthia to learn about us."

Alert now, she lifted up on her elbow so she could see his face. She held the peach lace-edged sheet over the lush swells of her breasts.

Quinn smiled, and a tender light entered his gaze. Her natural sense of modesty was only one of the things he found endearing about her.

Heather's heart quivered with the fear that she might

have slipped and told him how she felt about him when she climaxed. She couldn't have, could she?

"We agreed . . . remember?" He seemed baffled by what he saw in her eyes.

"Yes, I know," Heather said quickly. She was suddenly flooded with relief. She hadn't told him. "I don't understand what one has to do with the other?"

Quinn chuckled. "Have you forgotten the plans you and Cindy made for tomorrow morning?" He gave her a hard kiss.

Heather laughed—yes, she'd forgotten everything, everything except Quinn. Sliding back into his arms, her head against his shoulder, she traced the length of his upraised leg with a fingertip.

"We can set the clock and get up early." Her hand moved upward, an open caress.

Quinn held his breath, captivated by the movement of her hand. His heart drummed loudly as he waited with delicious expectation. When she caressed high on his thigh, his manhood began to harden.

"Quinn?"

He couldn't speak. At least not until her soft open palm smoothed over his waist completely bypassing that once again pulsating focus of his masculine passion.

She placed soft butterfly kisses down the side of his throat. One, two, three, by the fifth kiss Quinn had turned so that her lips met his. His mouth opened over hers and his kisses were of the deep tongue-thrusting variety.

It took her a few moments to recall her thought. "Cynthia's at my sister's. The girls will probably sleep late. You can call Gwen in the morning, arrange to pick up Cynthia yourself and bring her back here. Perhaps you might consider joining us for breakfast, Counselor," she ended breathlessly. Quinn was yet again drawn to her exquisite mouth. Each new kiss was deeper and longer than the one before it.

"I want so much to sleep in your arms tonight," she managed to whisper.

Quinn took her hand and placed it where he wanted it. "You will," he said, his voice low and thick with desire.

The doorbell was loud and intrusive in the quiet bedroom. Heather stirred, reaching for her robe. It wasn't in its customary place in the armchair beside the bed.

Black dress slacks and a white silk shirt were flung across the back of the peach chair. Black silk male briefs were on the cushion, along with her things.

She blinked, suddenly wide awake. Her eyes went to the clock-radio: nearly nine o'clock. No! She had set it for seven. What happened? Had she failed to pull out the stem in back?

It can't be Cynthia, she thought as she hurried into the connecting bathroom for the peach terry cloth robe on the hook behind the door. She managed to splash some water on her face before she raced back into the other room to the window. Her bedroom overlooked the front of the building. Beside the curb was her sister Gwen's car, and the girls were inside.

"Quinn!" Heather was trembling so badly that it took her a few seconds to get her arms into the sleeve of the robe.

"Hmmm," he said from beneath the pillow he had over his head.

"Cynthia is at the door!"

"It's probably only the paper boy."

"I don't have the paper delivered! My sister's car is in front of the building. I can't see the door from here, but she must have decided to drop Cynthia off."

Quinn swore, sitting up in bed. "What time is it?" he asked, the sheet stopped to his waist.

"Ten to nine. I don't know why the clock didn't go off! What are we going to do? She can't find you here!"

"Don't worry," he said, rising. "She was bound to find out that we're involved. So we just deal with it."

"No! Not now! It's too soon. Please hurry, honey." She tossed him his briefs. "If I can get her into the kitchen, you can slip out the front."

He scowled at that idea. "Go on ahead. I'll be down in a second."

Heather was still shaking when she unlocked the door for Cynthia.

She waved to her sister and nieces as they drove away. "Hi Cynthia. Come on inside."

"Sorry—I know I'm early. But Mrs. Carmichael and the girls had dentist appointments this morning. They decided to drop me off on the way. Save Dad a trip."

"Oh," Heather said, trying to calm herself. She walked through the living room opening drapes as she went. "Come on back to the kitchen while I make some hot chocolate and breakfast. Hungry?"

"Nothing for me. I ate hours ago."

"Well, you can keep me company. Come on." Heather

led the way. If she could just keep Cynthia in the kitchen . . .

Cynthia made herself comfortable on one of the high stools in front of the counter while Heather nervously searched through the refrigerator.

"I had so much fun. We stayed up all night watching videos and doing our nails. What do you think of this color combination?" Cynthia held her hands out for inspection.

"Interesting," Heather said diplomatically, glad for the youthful happiness and enthusiasm she saw in Cynthia's sparkling eyes. "You get any sleep?"

"Not much. It was even better than I thought. I'm so glad Ericia and Angela asked me to spend the night. You know how nervous I was about going." She giggled. "They wanted to come with us today, but Mrs. Carmichael said no." Grinning for all she was worth, Cynthia said, "It's my turn to spend the day with you. Just the two of us, doing girl stuff."

Heather nodded absently, distracted as she listened for the sound of Quinn's footsteps. Had he gone yet? What if she hadn't impressed upon him how important it was for him to leave? Oh, dear . . . it was all her fault. She should have known better than to let something like this happen. Cynthia just wasn't ready.

"May I use the phone, please? I want to catch Daddy before he leaves the house. Save him a trip."

"Ah . . ." Heather went completely blank for a second.

"Morning," Quinn said from the doorway, his suit jacket flung casually over his shoulder. His jaw was darkened by the black stubble on his chin.

"Daddy!" Cynthia's startled gaze swung from him to Heather.

Heather, suddenly aware of her nudity beneath her robe, tightened the belt around her waist.

"Mrs. Carmichael dropped me off. She and the girls have a . . ." Cynthia stopped. "Why are you here?" she asked slowly as realization dawned on her. "Why are you here?—"

"Cynthia," Heather interrupted, "you don't understand."

"You're sleeping with each other," Cynthia accused, noticing her father's disheveledness. "I hate you. I hate you both."

"Sit down," Quinn said in a voice that didn't tolerate argument.

"Daddy, she's *my* friend. Why?"

"Heather and I don't have to explain ourselves to you, young lady. We care about each other, and that is all you need to know about it—"

Heather interrupted, "Quinn, please. She deserves an explanation."

Cynthia turned on Heather. "I don't need your help," she shouted. "You tricked me. I thought you liked me, loved me even! You used me to get close to my father. I already had a mother! I don't need another one. If it hadn't been for me, you would never have even met my daddy. Well, I don't want you to pretend to be my friend. Do you hear me, I don't need you."

Heather breathed heavily as if she'd been running. Cynthia's taunts hit home. They were close enough to the truth to be painful. She had no business falling in

love with the girl's father in the first place. And now she
was forced to see Cynthia suffer because of it.

"You've said enough. You owe Heather an apology."
Quinn's jaw was tight with frustration.

"No, Quinn, please. Not now."

"Not ever!" Cynthia cried, tears streaked across her
face.

"Go stand by the car! I'll meet you there in a minute.
It's parked in the back, next to the carport."

"I don't want to—"

"You heard me, Cynthia Ann."

Cynthia stormed out of the room. They heard the front
door slam behind her.

"Little brat!" Quinn huffed, smoothing a hand over
his hair. "Heather, I'm sorry."

"I'm sorry, too. Go to her, Quinn—she needs you."

"I wish I didn't have to leave you like this."

"Cynthia has to come first. She's so afraid of losing
you. That's what she thinks is happening here."

He quickly bent, brushing his mouth briefly against
Heather's. "We'll talk—soon." Quinn followed his daughter out.

Fifteen

Heather rubbed tired eyes. Even though her desk was still littered with end of the semester reports that needed her immediate attention, she was making inroads. She found it was simpler to stay late rather than cart it home.

"Hi." Charles had seen her car in the parking lot and decided to come back and check on her. "What ya doin' here this late?"

"Can't you guess? A month before summer vacation and look at this. I'll never make it."

Charles chuckled. "Don't I know that feeling."

"Finished with practice?"

"Yeah." He was dressed in gray sweats, the school logo was printed across his chest.

"How's the track team looking? Think we'll beat Lincoln?"

"As long as we're standing still, we look great. Trouble starts when we high jump and sprint. Need I be more specific?"

Heather giggled. "No, I get the point. Haven't seen much of you lately."

"Been busy," he hedged.

"Have a moment now?"

"For you, sure." He sank down into the chair in front of her desk.

Heather doubted he would be so accommodating if he knew she intended to discuss Diane. She had enough problems of her own without getting in the middle of a relationship that had nothing to do with her—but she'd made that stupid promise to Diane. So now she was stuck. Diane had already stopped her twice to ask, since the lunchroom incident, if Heather had talked to him.

"You're awfully quiet. Problem?"

"You're not going to like this."

"A mystery?" he said, propping one leg so the ankle rested on the knee.

"It's Diane."

"Not interested," he said tightly.

"You started this, Mr. Randol, when you pulled that nasty stunt in the teachers' lounge last week. Publicly embarrassing Diane. How could you? The whole school has been buzzing. What exactly is your problem?"

Charles was on his feet. "Time out! I won't discuss that pretty little slut with anyone!"

Heather had never seen him so upset. "Okay, you don't want to talk. Just sit down and listen for a moment."

"Go ahead!" he sneered, dropping back down. "Give me an earful of what the injured, sweet Miss Thang had to say. I can hardly wait."

"Be fair, Charles."

"You wanted to talk—so talk. By the way, you haven't asked about my current lover, Melissa. She's really hot."

"I'm not interested in Melissa. I thought her name was Beverly?" Heather frowned, then snapped, "Not that I have a thing against any one of those gorgeous empty-headed baby dolls you like to play with, but believe me, no woman wants to be involved with a man merely to ease his sexual desires."

"Melissa knows the score. We have a good time together. She's not interested in my bank balance. Not everyone is looking for true love like you, doll-face."

Heather ignored the dig. She'd found love, but she had to admit it wasn't doing her much good at the moment. She'd spoken to Quinn every evening since Cynthia had stormed out of her place last Saturday morning. Their discussions centered around what had happened. Nothing personal about the two of them. But what really worried her was Cynthia.

The girl was constantly on Heather's mind. And she hadn't seen her all week. Heather missed her and blamed herself for the child's unhappiness. She should have seen it coming. But no . . . Heather had been too caught up in her feelings for Quinn. She never should have persuaded him to stay the night. And what had happened to the blasted alarm?

Oh, Quinn . . . She ached for soft, sweet words from him telling her that what they shared was as special to him as it had been to her. Talk about a woman with an attitude. Heather was beginning to get one, especially since Quinn was acting as if they hadn't slept together. Men!

"Diane doesn't want your money. You think any female who shows an interest in you is after those big bucks your folks left you, kiddo."

Charles came from a very well-to-do family. His grandfather had started the profitable pharmaceutical company.

"I hate to tell you this, Heather. But your friend's only interest in me is to wrap me around her beautiful little finger. If I had any sense, I'd give up coaching and concentrate on living the good life. Spending the winter skiing in Aspen, the summer in the south of France, the fall in the Caribbean—then I wouldn't have to put up with manipulative females like Diane Rivers."

Heather laughed, tucking a braid behind her ear. "Will you quit! You'd be institutionalized within a month for boredom. What do you care about jetting around the world? The kids need you, and you know it. You're good at what you do, Charles. And what's more, you love the work."

"Thanks for the vote of confidence, but . . ."

"Be for real," Heather said, getting up and coming around the desk. "You think I don't know about those inner-city youngsters you work with at the Community Center and the Urban League? Or the athletic programs you donate your time and money to on the weekends? Now let's get back to the real issue."

"It's your dime, but don't expect me to change my opinion of your girl."

Heather suspected he was using his anger like a protective shield. She certainly didn't want him hurt. But she suspected it was already too late. Charles was in love with Diane.

"Well?"

"Diane's confused and extremely hurt by your sudden coldness. She wants to know what she's done to offend you. Perhaps you'll be kind enough to contact her to discuss the matter with her." Heather was tempted to say, and leave me the hell out of it.

Charles asked, with his eyes boring into Heather, "You didn't tell her how I feel about her, did you?"

"No way! You know I wouldn't betray your trust." She sighed, leaning back against the edge of the desk. "Diane deserves your honesty."

"She doesn't deserve a damn thing from me! We're not lovers. As far as I'm concerned, we aren't even friends." The pain in his voice was unmistakable.

Although Diane claimed to want his friendship, Heather wondered if she knew what she wanted from him. Diane was terrified of commitment. Her mother's failed marriages had left a lasting impression on the young Diane. Rather than become involved with one man, she tended to juggle them. Only Charles was different. She sighed. "Why does love have to be so darn complicated?"

"I'm hardly qualified to answer that," he said, shoving his hands into his pockets. "What difference do my feelings make to her? Heather, I'm not about to play her game."

"I can't tell you what to do. But I do know she was hurt by the way you've slighted her. If the two of you could just talk, maybe you could explain what you want and need from a relationship."

"Do you know what you're asking? You're asking me to open myself up to all kinds of pain. Thanks, but no thanks, friend."

Heather went over to him and rested her hand on his shoulder. "I'm not asking you to do one single thing that you feel isn't right for you. I don't want you hurt."

"She's not about to change. Nor am I about to give her a weapon to use against me," he said stubbornly.

"I understand all that. But you're the one whose attitude has changed. Diane hasn't a clue as to why things aren't hunky-dory between the two of you. Until now, you've done an outstanding job of hiding your feelings for her. What happened?"

"I just can't take it anymore. I'm fed up with pretending to be her friend just so I can be near her. I'm sick to death of her cheerfully parading a new lover under my nose week after week. I may be in love with her, but I won't put myself through that kind of hell. I'm not taking any more crap off her. I've had it," he swore harshly.

Heather gave him a comforting hug, much in the same way she would one of her brothers. "I'm sorry. Forget what I said. I'll think of something to tell Diane."

"You're sweet and loving," he said in exasperation. "Why couldn't I fall in love with you? It would have been a lot simpler."

"I've asked myself the same question about you, old friend." Suddenly Quinn filled her thoughts. "Unfortunately we find each other about as exciting as dishwater."

They laughed.

"Let's get out of here. I think I've seen all the paperwork I can take for one day."

"Sounds good to me."

Heather collected her purse and locked up. They chatted about school as they made their way out. They reached her car first.

"You've decided to see Diane, haven't you?"

Charles nodded. "Yeah. Maybe I've been unfair to her by not explaining myself."

"Good luck, my friend."

Charles bent and gave Heather a quick kiss. "Thanks, I need it."

"Don't forget. Dinner, Saturday night."

"Home cooking—I can't wait. Too bad Melissa doesn't know how to cook. See ya." He waved, moving toward his car.

"Heather, you've outdone yourself, doll-face. I have only one problem. I may become a permanent fixture in your dining room. Not to worry. Just stick a few stray flowers in my hair and use me as an exotic centerpiece," Charles said, eyes twinkling. "Stop laughing. I'm serious." He leaned back in his chair, a wide grin splitting his handsome brown face. "I can't move!"

"Just imagine the headlines. Charles Alexander Randol III, of the illustrious Bloomfield Hills Randols, gives up his esteemed coaching career at Lawrence High to take his rightful place . . . centerpiece extraordinaire." Heather giggled. "You really are a nut, Charles. But I love you anyway."

"You joke, but I have a catastrophic announcement: I don't have room for that delectable rum pound cake your dad sent over." He groaned and rubbed his slender middle.

"And just how did you know about that cake? You peeked in my refrigerator!" She placed her hands on her hips in mock outrage. "For that you will help me clear the table and fill the dishwasher." Heather rose and began collecting the serving dishes.

They had shared a relaxing meal. Charles hadn't mentioned Diane once. Heather hadn't asked any personal questions. She wasn't about to make that mistake twice.

If Charles's week had ended anything like hers, it was best forgotten. She'd lain awake night after night, until she received the nightly call from Quinn. She was desperate to see him and she missed Cynthia. She couldn't stop worrying about her.

"What's the matter, doll-face?"

Heather, busy covering the leftover food, looked up and asked, "Why can't all men be like you or my brothers?"

Charles's brows shot up with apparent dismay. "Man trouble, hmmm?"

"Yeah. I did something really stupid. I'm involved with the parent of one of the kids I used to counsel."

"He's not married, is he?"

"I haven't completely lost touch with reality. He's a widower. Cynthia Montgomery's father. I turned her case over to Jane Van Ervin. But not before I fell in love."

"Sounds like a lucky guy to me."

Heather smiled. "There are a few problems beside my unprofessional behavior."

"You're human. You're allowed to mess up. So what's the deal?" Charles began loading dishes into the dishwasher.

"Cynthia and I were getting close—until she found out that Quinn and I were lovers. She threw a fit. That was last weekend."

"And?" he prompted, watching as she calmly filled the coffeemaker.

But Heather wasn't calm. Her hands were trembling and she knew she was close to tears. All because she wondered if she had made a horrible mistake in trusting Quinn. Had she fallen in love with a man who didn't care about her? She had tried to be so optimistic about the future of their relationship. Now she was having serious doubts. Did he blame her for asking him to stay?

"Heather!"

"What did you say?"

"After the kid threw the fit, then what?" he reminded her impatiently.

"Nothing. I haven't seen her all week. I'm worried about her. She already has some heavy problems—she doesn't need this." She grimaced. "Although I've talked to him on the phone every night this week, he seems so impersonal. I know that he must be a parent first. He's clearly focusing his time and energy on his daughter, which is wonderful. She needs that right now, she really does."

Heather sighed, recalling the magical evening they had had together, concluding in the most tender lovemaking imaginable. Her mind told her one thing, her heart another.

"Charles, I'm scared. I feel like I've waited a lifetime to find this man. I love him and I don't want to lose him."

"Be patient—the kid's bound to come around."

"I love Cynthia. I don't want to see her hurt."

"Does he know how you feel about him?"

"Does Diane know how you feel?"

They stared at each other for a time, then broke into hysterical laughter.

"Just what are we laughing at?" she asked.

"Who knows, but it beats the hell out of crying."

They worked in companionable silence. Heather arranged the dessert and coffee tray while Charles stored the food in the refrigerator.

"You know, there's no point in worrying about this. The kid will come around, given enough time. And if you need me to talk to the guy, no problem. I'll straighten him out for you."

"That's exactly what I don't want you to do. But thanks. You're an awfully special guy, you know that?"

He frowned, shoving his hands into his pockets as he leaned against the counter.

"Charles, that was a compliment."

"Yeah. Finished?"

"Will you carry the tray into the living room, please? I'll follow with the coffeepot."

Heather paused to switch on the lamps. Having deposited the tray on the coffee table, Charles began pacing the room.

"Coffee?" She held out a cup.

He moved to sit beside her on the sofa. Suddenly he said, "I spoke to Diane. I stopped in between classes."

Heather started, her cup halfway to her mouth. She put the cup safely back on the saucer. "That didn't give you much time to talk."

"Didn't take long. It isn't going to happen for us, Heather. She doesn't want the same things from life that I do. She's not ready to settle down."

"Are you talking marriage?"

"Yeah. But it has to be with the right woman. Diane isn't that woman," he said emphatically.

It seemed as if she couldn't control her love for Quinn or her need to be with him, anymore than Charles could halt his love for Diane. Heather had no trouble understanding his hurt and disappointment. It was etched across his features. At that moment she would have liked to shake some sense into Diane Rivers.

"Oh, Charles. I'm sorry. I'd hoped that . . ." The doorbell interrupted her before she could finish.

"Expecting company?"

"Nope. I won't be a moment."

The bell rang a second time before she reached the door.

The past several days had been the most frustrating of Quinn's life. His daughter had tried her best to turn both their lives into a living hell. It was almost as if she were testing his love for her. But he knew how badly Cynthia was suffering. She was angry, hurt, and jealous. Despite what she had said and done, he knew Cynthia still loved Heather and missed her terribly.

If the truth were told, the only way he'd managed to cope with the situation was due to his nightly talks with Heather. His time on the phone with her had been the only peace he'd had, even though the sound of her voice heightened his longing for her. He wanted her. She was constantly in his thoughts.

He kept remembering little things about her, such as the way she liked to sleep on her side with her petite frame curled into a ball, her arms around her legs, rich ebony braids trailing across the pillow. He found it very natural, sleeping with her, her back against his front. He lay awake at night recalling her scent, the softness of her skin, her tight hot sheath. He would become instantly erect and would remain so throughout the night. His head was full of intimate details of the two of them together. But his torment wouldn't end there.

He often woke with her scent in his nostrils, her voice echoing inside his head because he'd dreamt about her. His dreams of Heather were more vivid, more erotic than the memories of sexual encounters he'd had with other women.

He was tired of lying awake while his sexual desires waged war with his good intentions. No matter how he looked at it, the bottom line was that Quinn wanted Heather. Yet when dawn's first light crept into his bedroom, his resolve to be there for his daughter was uppermost in his mind. He had to help Cynthia while she still cared what he thought. It looked as if she would have months of therapy ahead. His personal life would just have to wait. Quinn was determined to be the best father he could be. Cynthia needed him.

It was too much to ask that a young beautiful woman like Heather wait until he had his life together. And then there was Peggy. She would always be a part of him. Their connection hadn't ended. He had a responsibility to her that defied the grave.

Even though he knew his heart wasn't whole, he needed Heather. His heart and soul might belong to Peggy, but his body and his mind were Heather's alone. Oh, how he'd missed her . . . She was so warm, so loving. When she had given herself to him, she had done so because she loved him. Everything she had done had proven that love to him.

On the drive over, he had been unable to think of anything but Heather. She deserved better than she was getting from him. At the moment he had nothing to offer her. Damn it all—he didn't want to let her go. No matter how many ways he looked at the situation or how much he needed to be with her, Quinn knew he couldn't ask this of her. It wasn't fair to her, he thought as he walked to her door and nervously waited for her to answer.

"Quinn!" Pleasure washed over her, and her hands automatically reached out to take his and pull him inside.

His mouth didn't lift into the engaging smile she'd come to appreciate. Nor did his eyes soften, although they journeyed over her petite frame, then repeated the maneuver, much slower the second time, as if he might have missed a tiny essential point.

"Hi," he said gruffly. She looked stunning in a turquoise caftan of polished cotton, threaded with gold. It draped her soft sweet curves and complemented the beauty of her golden skin. The front of her head was decoratively wrapped in a matching swatch of cotton, while her ebony braids swirled around her shoulders. She was absolutely gorgeous.

Heather drank in his prominent dark features just as intently, her soft gaze caressing him. His lean hips were encased in tight-fitting jeans, and his broad chest was covered by a pale yellow cotton pullover sweater that did marvelous things to his smooth skin. His somber air kept her from walking into his arms and pressing her lips against his for a quick sweet kiss.

The rattle of utensils against a dish in the living room gave Quinn pause. "Sorry. I didn't realize you had guests."

"No problem. Come in." Heather linked her arm with his. "How's Cynthia?"

"She's having a hard time of it. She misses you so much. But she refuses to pick up the phone and call you. Stubborn!" He sighed, saying softly, "She's placed all the blame for our being together on you."

"It's understandable," Heather said, smiling to hide her regret. "Has she started therapy yet?"

"Yes."

"That's a relief. Did she accept my nieces' invitation tonight for their pajama party?"

"Yeah. The girls talked her into it. I think she was afraid she'd run into you."

"I'm glad she decided to go. Gwen and the girls will see that she has a good time."

He nodded, his eyes on her mouth, feasting on the generous curve and glossy red color. His hand automatically tightened on hers.

Heather wasn't aware of Charles's presence in the archway until Quinn stiffened. The heat of his eyes flared as he watched the other man's approach.

"Hi," Charles said casually.

"What the hell is going on here?" Quinn demanded.

"Nothing's going on," Heather said, hastily making the introductions.

"Why is he here?"

"Charles is my friend. I've told you about him." Heather explained, shocked by his anger.

Both men were very tall. They shook hands while eyeing each other. Charles topped Quinn by a good two inches. Quinn was broader in the shoulders and chest.

Charles said, "I understand congratulations are called for, Counselor. You photograph well on camera. I caught your interview on the afternoon news."

"Hmmm?" Heather turned a quizzical gaze at Quinn.

"Jameison was aquitted," Quinn explained, struggling to hold on to his temper. He didn't like Charles being here . . . didn't like it one bit.

"Quinn! How wonderful." Her sweet smile was directed his way.

In spite of himself he was warmed by her praise. "Thanks," he said, then turned to Charles. "So you're the man my daughter says all the girls call hot? She had a crush on you during the first semester."

Heather laughed, trying to relax. "You do have that effect on our students, Charles. Maybe it's those deep-set black eyes and the dimples," Heather suggested. "Cynthia Montgomery is Quinn's daughter."

"The tall pretty girl with the purple and green eyelids and horrendous backhand?" he asked politely.

"That's her," Quinn said tightly.

"She was in my tennis class last fall." Charles's eyes went inquisitively to Heather's hand on Quinn's sleeve before meeting her anxious eyes.

"Join us, Quinn. I was about to serve dessert. I had rum pound cake—that is, until I answered the door. Charles, did you leave any?"

"There might be enough for two tiny pieces," Charles teased.

Once the men were seated on opposite ends of the sectional sofa, Heather excused herself to collect another cup.

She returned as Quinn was asking, "Should I apologize for spoiling your evening?" It was a masculine challenge.

"Not if it's meaningless," Charles said evenly.

Heather handed Quinn a cup of coffee. His gaze momentarily linked with hers, as if he were searching for an answer to some unspoken question.

"I've followed a few of your recent cases, Counselor," Charles said. "I'm amazed at your ability to put criminals back on the street. My sympathy remains with the unfortunate victims."

"Cake?" Heather interrupted, darting Charles a warning look.

Quinn was clearly in his element. "I agree that victims are, on occasion, unfairly treated by our judicial system. That's one of the major reasons I've concentrated on criminal cases in the last five years—to stop some of these injustices. Everyone deserves his day in court, rich, poor, even the criminally insane—and I do my utmost to provide the best legal defense available." Quinn paused thoughtfully. Then he said, "I gather you weren't pleased with the outcome of the Jameison trial."

Heather relaxed, recognizing the respect in Charles's eyes, even when his negative response came readily. She didn't listen to their discussion. Quinn alone held her interest.

The second she'd seen his face, her feelings for him took over. She loved him, and she missed not being able to see him and be with him. Heather didn't resent the time he spent with Cynthia. In fact, she respected him more for trying to make up for past mistakes. He had to put Cynthia and her needs first right now, but despite her best intentions Heather was beginning to feel a little resentful. She didn't want Quinn to forget about her—she so wanted to be a vital part of his world.

When she refilled her own cup she emptied the pot.

"More coffee, gentlemen?" She rose, the near empty ceramic pot in her hand.

"None for me. It's time I shoved off." Charles smiled at her warmly. "The spread was fabulous, doll-face."

The sight of Heather's smile warmed the far recesses of Quinn's soul. But the pleasure was mixed with pangs of jealousy.

"Glad you enjoyed it."

To Quinn's increasing annoyance, the smile remained on her soft lips and was reflected in the depths of her eyes.

"Nice meeting you, Counselor." Charles offered his hand.

"Same here," Quinn replied coolly.

The two men shook hands.

"Be right back." Heather walked Charles to the door. In the entrance hall, Charles said, "I enjoyed myself."

"Good."

In a lowered voice Charles asked, "He seems like a nice guy. Just be careful. I don't want you hurt."

"You're sweet." She took his hand and whispered back, "I'm sorry about Diane. It's still not too late. If . . ."

"It's too late." In a louder tone Charles said, "Thanks for caring." He gave her a quick kiss.

She kissed him back, caressing his cheek. "I love you, you know."

Neither had been aware of Quinn watching their exchange from the archway. Nor did they see him turn, his hands balled into fists as he stalked over to the mantel.

"Do you think it would help if I called Diane?"

"No. I want you to stay out of it."

"Alright." She stepped back, opening the door for him. She watched him make his way to his car before closing the door.

Sixteen

Although Quinn stared at the painting above the mantel, his thoughts were hardly the tranquillity depicted in the oil. Seeing her in another man's arms had been equivalent to waving a red flag in front of a bull. Quinn pulsed with rage. He wanted some answers, and he wasn't in a patient mood. Just what in the hell kind of game was she playing with him? He wasn't some untried boy. He wasn't about to let her take him on an emotional rollercoaster. Just because he cared for her didn't mean he was stupid!

Heather was behind him. He didn't need to turn and look. He knew that she was there. His attraction to her, his awareness of her was so potent that he knew he could have found her blindfolded in a crowded room.

Despite his anger, the last half hour, while he'd been making idle conversation, his interest had centered on the seductive mole at the corner of her soft mouth. Did she have any idea how it aroused him?

"Would you like more coffee?"

Her gentle touch on his arm caused a shaft of fire to shoot down its length, directly into his bloodstream. She was more potent than any drug, more addictive than a

narcotic. Damn it, she'd lied to him! The face he turned
to her was cold with jealous fury.

"What kind of game are you playing?"

Heather stared at him. Her eyes were the color of
melted caramel. Her pink tongue came out to dampen
dry lips, unwittingly lingering in the corner of her mouth,
near but not quite touching that mole.

Quinn suppressed a groan as red-hot rage mixed with
white-hot desire and gripped him with equal force. He
wanted to plunder his tongue deep into the moist warmth
of her mouth. But he also wanted to shout his outrage
at what he'd witnessed between her and her so-called
friend.

He did neither. He merely glared down at her from
the length of his prominent nose. Why in the hell should
it matter so much? What difference did it make who she
kissed and claimed to be in love with? He didn't have a
right to listen to a private conversation. It wasn't any of
his business who she slept with. He should never have
touched her in the first place. She left him so tied up
emotionally that he didn't know his head from a hole in
the ground.

"What do you mean?"

"Forget it!" He stalked past her to the liquor cabinet
where she kept an array of crystal decanters and glasses.
"Do you mind?" He didn't wait for a response, but filled
a glass with amber liquid. He had no idea what it was.
In fact, he didn't care. Surely if his stomach was on fire
with alcohol he could ignore how much he still wanted
her.

She followed him. Her hand touched his before he
could raise the glass. "You never drink unless you're up-

set. Sweetheart, what's wrong? Why are you so angry? If anyone should be upset, it should be me. I'm the one who has been alone all week."

"Don't!" He jerked away. "Let's get one thing straight. I've never lied to you." He hissed, "Did you think you have me so crazy about you I'd let you do anything you pleased? How big of a fool do you take me for?"

"Quinn—"

He cut her off, saying, "What I would like to know is why? If you're sleeping with the bastard, say so, damn it."

Heather couldn't move or even defend herself, shocked by the sheer force of his rage and the unfounded attack on her character. Eventually she said, "Charles and I are friends . . . good friends. I've never lied about that or anything else for that matter."

"Are you sleeping with him?" he yelled at her.

"I'm sleeping with you!" she yelled back.

"I heard you tell him that you loved him. You told me the same thing." He paused before adding maliciously, "In the position we were in, sugar, a man doesn't forget what he hears." It had been when she had reached an explosive climax and he'd been a split second away from his when she'd sobbed out her love for him. No, there was no mistake. Maybe he should have said something at the time rather than throw it in her face now. Damn it, she was in the wrong—not him.

Heather blushed. "I do love you," she said softly. "I just didn't realize I said it out loud."

"You can't be in love with both of us! What's the deal here? Isn't one man enough for you? You need two chasing behind your skirts?" Quinn couldn't seem to stop himself from taking his hurt and frustration out on Heather. But what they'd had was so rare. Why was she throwing it away like this?

He swore viciously as he thought of how gullible he'd been. He'd believed she loved him. He'd needed to know that she cared for him and valued him as a man . . . her man. Every single time he heard her voice on the phone this past week, he wanted to get into his car and come to her . . . experience her sweet magic once more. It wasn't as if he didn't want to come, he couldn't. And she'd been busy entertaining her boyfriend.

Her face was turned away from him and the pain he caused. When she spoke, her voice reflected the depth of her unhappiness. "I don't lie . . . ever. If you intended to hurt me, congratulations. You've done an exceptional job." She bit her trembling bottom lip and her eyes shimmered with unshed tears. "I think it would be best if you leave *now!*" Damn his arrogance! She'd done nothing to deserve this kind of treatment from him. And she wasn't about to take it.

In one quick movement Quinn pulled her up from the sofa and into his arms. Heather cried out, unable to forge resistance. She found her breasts crushed against his chest, his head bent low as he kissed the side of her neck, his nostrils flaring as he inhaled her unique scent.

His voice was rough, heavy with emotion when he said, "Forgive me. I lost it for a while there." He knew better than anyone that he didn't have a claim on her. She wasn't his woman, no matter how badly he wished it. When she tried to move away, he tightened his arms. "Please, sugar. Let me hold you. That's all I want, just to hold you." His pride be damned. He had none when it came to Heather. Now was all the time they had and he refused to give up that little bit.

Sighing, she leaned against him. Heather no longer had strength to fight with him. What was the point? He owned her heart. She tilted her head back, lifting her face toward his. She brushed her mouth over his, seeking the hot masculine bounty. Unable to resist the soft temptation, Quinn groaned, deepening the caress. Heather shivered with pleasure. Oh, yes, his kisses were everything she needed, hungry, demanding, and so very male.

"Quinn," she said his name around a sigh as she realized how desperately she'd missed him. She was back where she belonged—in her lover's arms.

Quinn groaned his pleasure, sucking her fleshy bottom lip into his mouth. His tongue reacquainted itself with the honeyed secrets of her mouth before taking possession.

Her breasts swelled with longing, her nipples hard peaks of arousal as she pressed into him, rubbing against his chest. She could feel his heat even through their clothing. It felt wonderful, but she ached to feel his bare flesh against her breasts. She sucked his bottom lip into her mouth, tugging and nipping at it with her teeth. Her hand dropped to the hem of his sweater. She slid underneath and didn't slow until she could caress his warm skin.

Quinn shuddered, forcing himself to break the seal of their lips. He caught her hands. Another soft caress and he wouldn't have stopped until he had her beneath him, giving her what they both needed to feel complete. Quinn groaned in bitter frustration. His hands were shaking when he retrieved the glass of liquor he'd left on the mantel.

"Honey—"

"Heather, I know I'm making a mess of this tonight. I can't believe I lost my head like that. That wasn't suppose to happen."

"You've known all along that Charles and I are friends."

"This isn't about Charles. It's about Cindy."

"Oh!" she said, sitting down. Fear and uncertainty rushed over her. "Has something more happened?"

"Cindy hasn't bounced back from the incident on Saturday morning as I'd hoped."

"Have you spoken to Ann about it?"

"Yeah. Dr. Johnson feels counseling may take some time. And she definitely wants me involved." His mouth tightened when he said the last.

"How do you feel about that?"

"I'm not thrilled, but I want my daughter to get better."

Heather smiled, very pleased by the news. But Quinn wasn't smiling. And he didn't think she would smile either when she heard his decision.

"It's going to work out for the best—I just know it. Now tell me about Cynthia."

"Cindy's still very upset." He frowned. "She loves us both. And she's scared."

"You don't think she's going to run away again?" Heather couldn't quite keep the anxiety out of her voice.

"No, nothing like that," he assured quickly. "Cindy's jealous of my feelings for you and yours for me. She isn't interested in sharing either one of us. I've tried to talk some sense into her and gotten nowhere. She's not reasonable about this thing." He threw his hands up in frustration.

There was more, much more—but it affected not only Cynthia but him as well. He wasn't able to reveal how adamantly Dr. Johnson believed their problems were linked to Peggy's sudden death. She encouraged them both to pursue grief therapy. Quinn wasn't about to admit that he was the holdout. While he'd do whatever was necessary to help his daughter, that didn't mean he was willing to share his private thoughts about Peggy.

"What's Ann recommending? Grief counseling?"

Quinn was startled, so much so that his heart jumped. As much as he cared for Heather, there were some things he just couldn't tell her.

"Yeah," he said gruffly, then changed the subject. "Cindy's placing all the blame for our being together Saturday on you. As if I'm just an innocent victim in all this. I can't seem to make her see the truth."

"It never should have happened."

"Our making love?" he asked sharply.

"No, honey. But you wanted to leave and I stopped you. I persuaded you to stay the night."

"I wanted to stay. I wanted to be with you." He didn't add that his feelings on the matter hadn't changed in the least. He still wanted her.

Heather fretted. They hadn't planned to become involved with each other. Now Cynthia believed she was trying to take her father away from her—that Heather was a threat to her place in her father's life. With more therapy her views were bound to change. But like Quinn said, that would take time . . . lots of time.

"Quinn, I should have insisted that you leave." Heather blinked away tears.

"Sugar, none of this is your fault. Cindy panics at the idea of losing me to you. I've gone over and over this with her, but she gets so upset she can't hear a word I'm saying."

He released a rush of pent-up air before he said in exasperation, "Giving her whatever she wanted was a lot easier than finding time to be both parents to her. Hell, that mistake nearly cost me my daughter. When I think about what could have happened to her out on those streets alone, I break out in a cold sweat."

Their eyes met in understanding.

"Heather, I'm struggling to change the past. Or at least I'm trying to change it. Cynthia has to come first with me."

Heather held her breath, dreading where this might be heading.

"I've gone over this time and time again. The truth is Cynthia can't handle my involvement with any woman right now."

"Especially not me."

Quinn nodded with difficulty. He couldn't quite believe how deeply Heather had gotten beneath his skin. His need for her seemed to be constant, and ever-growing. Frankly, he hadn't a clue as to how to control it. He'd come to depend on her warmth, her strength, her willingness to listen. And the few times they'd been intimate, he'd felt truly happy, whole inside. He couldn't even sleep at night until he'd spoken to her.

She heard the regret in his voice, yet Heather was hurting so badly she couldn't speak. It seemed as if they were both caught in a trap with no easy way out. Heather loved Cynthia, too. But she didn't want what she and Quinn had to end. Not now, when they were so close to finding real happiness.

"Please, don't think I'm allowing my child to dictate my personal life. That's not what's happening here."

"No, I don't think that," she said heavily. "Cynthia's needs of course must come first."

"Even before my own," he added with difficulty. How in the world was he going to stay away from Heather? She was quiet for so long that he asked, throatily, "Heather . . . ?"

"You're right. She needs you. Right now, I'm a threat to her." Heather didn't acknowledge the crushing weight of unhappiness within her. She and Cindy weren't in competition for Quinn's love. What Heather wanted and needed from him was very different.

"This therapy thing takes time. We could be talking about a few weeks, months, maybe even years. There's just no way of knowing how long."

Heather's heart ached, filled with fear as she waited for him to finish. "Are you saying you don't think we should see each other?"

"It's not fair for me to ask you to wait," Quinn said, his voice taut with emotion.

Was he looking for an easy way out? He hadn't claimed to love her. She had been the one to spill her innermost thoughts to him, not vice versa. The pictures of him and his late wife flashed through her mind. Was that why?

"You don't have to ask. I'll wait because I love you."

The silence between them was astronomical.

"What do you expect me to say?" he roared defensively. "I know damn well you're not interested in sneaking around. I respect you too much to even ask such a thing of you." His stomach was burning as he struggled with his own emotions. He cared about her. He didn't want her hurt. "This isn't how I want it either." He scowled, then said, "But I can't ignore Cindy."

They both knew Cynthia had suffered from his emotional neglect. What Heather didn't know and he couldn't tell her was that he'd had spent years trying to lose himself in his work, unintentionally forgetting his responsibilities to his child while trying to forget his guilt over the unresolved issues between himself and Peggy.

"Quinn, I'm not disagreeing with you. You don't have a choice. The professional within me admires the strides you've made to repair your relationship with Cynthia. Given time, I'm positive you'll succeed."

Heather was proud of him, pleased at the efforts he had taken to heal the rift between himself and Cynthia. But she was also afraid that what they had was over. She didn't want it to end.

"But, Quinn—I'm a woman, too. And that part of me is not letting go. I can't help it," she said with difficulty, fighting not to cry. "I don't want to lose you."

Quinn didn't want to lose her either. He wanted to be the man in her life . . . the only man in her life. "I can't ask that of you. It's not fair."

Heather closed her eyes. When she opened them, they shimmered with unshed tears. She wouldn't cry, not now.

Quinn kept his hands deep in his pockets. He ached to hold her. But he knew better than to touch her. No matter what he decided intellectually, emotionally and physically he couldn't stop himself from taking her sweetness.

"Cindy's angry at you now," he said, "but that won't last because she also loves and respects you. Be patient, Heather. She'll come around."

Heather nodded, refusing to put any more pressure on him. He knew how she felt. That would just have to be enough for now.

"I know she said some hurtful things . . ."

"They're forgotten. We all say things in anger we regret later. You know I don't want to take you away from her."

No one could ever take the place of Cynthia's mother. Yet Heather would be less than honest if she didn't admit to herself that she'd entertained fantasies of marriage to Quinn, which always involved having a solid friendship with his daughter. She'd even dreamed about it.

"I know." Quinn stared down at the carpet. "It's late. I should be going."

Heather didn't argue. She walked with him to the foyer.

"Have big plans for summer vacation?" he asked, not sure he wanted to hear the answer, especially if her plans included Charles.

"Most of my plans involve the word processor. I hope to complete my dissertation."

"All work and no play," he chanted, a smile tugging the corners of his wide mouth. His dark eyes never left her face.

Heather managed a weak smile. "Oh, I always have time for my family and friends. How about you and Cynthia?"

"We hope to spend some time at the cottage on Traverse Bay."

Quinn's gaze locked with hers before moving to her mouth. "Take care of yourself. I'll call from time to time, if that's okay with you?"

"I'll look forward to it," she said around the lump in her throat. Her arms were crossed beneath her breasts.

"Good night, sugar." He leaned forward and brushed his lips gently over hers.

"Goodbye," she said, choking back tears.

"No, not goodbye." Quinn's voice was thick with yearning.

Heather's heart ached as she watched him leave. Although she wholeheartedly agreed with his efforts, that still didn't slow the tears that flooded her gaze and rolled down her cheeks.

As the weeks went by, Quinn's nightly calls came to mean a great deal to Heather. While their talks were a means of staying abreast of each other's lives, they were also extremely frustrating. It was as if they'd made an unspoken agreement not to discuss the yearnings to see each other and be together. They had both accepted that it just wasn't possible.

When Quinn learned that Heather would be one of the chaperones for Lawrence's sophomore class overnight bus trip to Toronto, he asked if she could keep an eye on Cynthia for him. Heather wasn't sure how that would work out, considering Cynthia wasn't speaking to her.

But Quinn thought it was a perfect time for the two of them to heal the rift—which in his opinion had gone on entirely too long. Heather agreed. But she knew this was something that couldn't be forced. It had to come from the girl. With only a few days remaining on the school calendar, Heather doubted Cynthia would reconsider. It seemed as if the girl had built a wall of resentment against Heather.

Heather couldn't help wondering if it was childish on her part to leave it up to Cynthia to make the first move. Her instincts told her differently. Friendship was a gift.

Charged with the task of making certain that all eight of the fifteen- and sixteen-year-old girls assigned to her returned in one piece the following day, Heather settled into her bus seat, Benita Porter's novel *Colorstruck* open in her lap. But her gaze was on the passing scenery, and her thoughts were with Quinn.

She tingled, remembering their telephone conversation from the night before. It had been extremely late when her bedside telephone had rung. She'd just drifted off, not quite asleep, but not awake either. Her voice was husky with feminine sweetness. He apologized for waking her. Quinn had been working at home and forgotten the time, but she hadn't minded.

She lay curled on her side in the dark, listening to the heaviness of his masculine voice. When he asked what she was wearing she'd almost forgotten how to breathe.

Heather had told him without hesitation, wishing she could have modeled the pale blue lace nightgown for his viewing pleasure. His voice had dropped even lower as he murmured a throaty endearment. For a time they were both quiet, listening to the other's breathing. Sizzling heat of shared desire had crackled along the telephone wires. It came from explicit memories of their lovemaking and was white-hot with need so long denied. They wanted each other and they both felt the other's longing. Suddenly they began speaking at the same time. But Quinn didn't ask and Heather didn't offer. They ended the call soon after that.

"Is this seat taken?" The faint tremor in the girl's voice indicated an uneasiness.

They'd been under way for some time now. Heather had chosen to sit toward the back of the bus, hoping for a bit of privacy. She had seen Cynthia avert her head when she first spotted Heather. The slight hurt, but Heather ignored it. There was no mistaking her surprise.

"No, help yourself." Cynthia wasn't one of the girls assigned to Heather's group. "How have you been?" she asked over the giggles and nonstop chatter around them.

"Okay," Cynthia said, staring down at her hands. "You?"

"Busy," Heather said with a smile. "But fine otherwise. I've missed you."

Cynthia looked at her suddenly, her gray eyes very dark. "I missed you, too."

Heather was thrilled. It was good just to look at her. Cynthia's brown skin was so smooth and pretty. Her hair was cut even shorter than Heather remembered, but it was curly and very flattering. The only makeup she wore was a bit of mascara and rose-tinted lipstick. But her eyes were so full of sadness that Heather felt as if her own heart would break. Heather forced back her own tears. This child was so precious to her.

"I never meant to hurt you, honey."

Cynthia was quiet for so long that Heather sighed with regret. It was enough that Cynthia had made the attempt. So Heather asked with more cheer than she felt, "Ready for summer vacation?"

Cynthia nodded, but she didn't look at Heather. "I've been busy with therapy group and Angela and Ericia and Daddy. The girls and I love it when he takes us roller skating. You don't mind me being friends with them?"

"No. Why should I?"

"But they're your nieces."

"Yes, but you're forgetting something."

"What?"

"I want you to be happy."

"I'm sorry, Heather," she whispered. "I said mean things to you."

"Don't worry about it. It's over."

"You're not mad at me?"

"No. You have a right to your feelings."

"I just don't like you and Daddy . . ." she looked away. "Well, you know. I don't think it's right."

"Why, Cynthia?" Heather asked, careful to keep her voice low.

"I just don't like it," she said, turning back and tilting her chin stubbornly.

"Okay," Heather said, realizing she wasn't ready to talk about her feelings with her.

Cynthia frowned, silent for a time. Finally she found the courage to ask softly, "Could we still be friends?"

"Is that what you want?"

"Yes . . . please . . ." Cynthia bit her lip as tears filled her eyes.

"Okay, then," Heather said with a welcoming smile.

Cynthia returned the smile, brushing impatiently at her tears. "I'm glad."

"Me, too. But I want you to know, my feelings for your dad have—"

"I don't want talk about you and Daddy," she insisted. "Did Ericia and Angela tell you that I came to their pajama party?"

"They did. Sounded like you all had a ball."

"At first I wasn't going to go. But Mrs. Carmichael called and invited me. Boy, am I glad I changed my mind. Angie and Ericia are so silly." Cynthia giggled, reaching for Heather's hand.

Striving to hide her frustration, Heather talked to Cynthia about her nieces. She so wanted for Cynthia to realize that she wasn't standing between her and Quinn.

The overnight trip included a visit to the Ontario Science Center, the CN Tower, and shopping and lunch the next day at the downtown Eaton Center.

Even though Cynthia wasn't in the group assigned to Heather, nevertheless they managed to spend time together. Quinn's name wasn't mentioned.

It wasn't until the drive home the next afternoon that Heather had an opportunity to speak privately to Cynthia. The bus was so noisy with music and singing that there was no need to worry about being overheard.

"What do you think of Dr. Ann?"

Cynthia smiled. "I like her. She really listens to what I have to say. And she wants to know how I feel about things."

Heather smiled.

"I met your mom, Dr. Gregory."

"Oh, really?" Heather smiled.

"She looks so young, you two could be sisters."

Heather laughed. "Everybody says that."

Cynthia hesitated before saying, "I told Dr. Ann about you." Peering anxiously at Heather, but not quite able to meet her gaze, she said, "I hope you're not upset?"

"It's alright, honey. That's all a part of therapy. The idea is to talk about the hurt, get it out in the open so it won't hurt so much. I'm just glad you're able to trust Dr. Ann."

"That's what Dad said." Suddenly Cynthia looked at her hands. She apparently hadn't meant to mention him to Heather.

"Quinn and I care about each other, Cynthia. It's okay to talk to me about him if you want. We can't very well pretend he doesn't exist, now can we?"

"No, I suppose not." When she spoke again, she surprised Heather when she revealed, "Dr. Ann and I talk about my mother a lot. I really miss her."

Heather could see the sorrow in Cynthia's eyes. She wanted to hold her close, take away some of the loss. Unfortunately life wasn't that simple. Nor would that approach help Cynthia. Talking was the best way to work through the pain.

"Dr. Ann talks to Daddy, too, about my mother. But he never says much," Cynthia told Heather in a whisper. "I just wish he would talk to me about her. There are things I would like to know about her. I know he loved her, too. I just don't understand why he won't even talk to me about her."

"Sometimes talking about someone you loved very much after they're gone is very difficult. Your parents loved you and each other and that just doesn't go away.

But maybe someday your dad can talk to you about your mother. Be patient with him, okay?"

Heather suddenly remembered the portrait of Peggy Montgomery in their family home. Quinn never talked about his late wife, not even to her child. Apparently it hurt too much. He was still grieving for his lost love. Heather hurt so bad she wanted to cry, for she couldn't stop herself from worrying if she had given her heart to a man who wouldn't ever be emotionally capable of loving again.

Seventeen

Heather padded across the wet tile flooring to the pool-side lounger. She spread a beach towel over it and leaned back so she could watch the antics of the three girls still in the water.

Cynthia and her nieces had become inseparable, although Heather and Cynthia's friendship wasn't as strong as it once was, but it, too, was flourishing.

With the school year behind her, Heather concentrated on her dissertation and volunteer work at the Crisis Center, trying her best not to worry about the future.

"Wow! It's hot!" Cynthia exclaimed as she came to perch on the side of Heather's lounger.

"Did you ask her?" Angela and Ericia asked.

"Good grief! I haven't had a chance. Besides, I told you I didn't want to do it." Cynthia dried her hair with the towel Heather had dug out of a huge beach bag.

"I would ask what's going on, but I have a feeling I really don't want to know." Heather tried to look stern but burst into laughter as she handed out more towels.

"Cindy has the most wonderful idea, Aunt Heather. Say yes! Please say you'll do it!" Ericia bounced down next to her aunt.

"You just have to. I'll simply die if you say no, Auntie," Angela said.

Cynthia didn't say a word, she just looked from one to the other.

"Go ahead, Cindy, tell her. Auntie's cool. She'll understand." Angela gave Cynthia a little push.

"Yeah, tell her!"

"Oh, alright. But I don't see why I have to do the asking."

"It's your cottage!" This response was simultaneously announced.

"Heather, Daddy was going to take me up to our cottage on Traverse Bay for three weeks. But now he started a new case in Washington—the one where the congressman's son is accused of rape. Anyway, he doesn't know if he'll finish before the summer is over." Cynthia hesitated, twisting the towel in her hands.

Heather was careful to keep her features even, yet her heart did a flip-flop. The mere mention of his name affected her. "And?" She placed her sunglasses on her nose.

"I told the girls about it and they want to come, too. Only we can't go alone. There are three bedrooms, plenty of room for all of us. Anyway, we thought you could volunteer to go with us. Then Daddy and Ericia and Angela's folks will let us go. We all promise to leave you time for your paper."

"Please, Auntie," Ericia added.

"Pretty please!" volunteered Angela.

"There's plenty of kids around and things to do. We'll be at the beach or the tennis courts all day. Out of your way, " Cynthia added.

"Say yes," the girls begged, kissing her cheeks until she covered her face, giggling.

"Stop that. Let me think about it for a minute, okay?"

Unfortunately for Heather they watched her like a hawk.

Heather sighed, knowing when to accept defeat. "It sounds like a great vacation for all of us. But only if you three keep that promise to give me some time for my work."

"We will! Thanks, Auntie," her nieces cheered. All three rushed her with more hugs and kisses.

"Wait! Don't get too excited. I said I'd go. But you girls have to clear it with your folks. If they agree, we go. If not, forget it. We won't take advantage of Cynthia's dad. He may not want three wild teenagers on his property. Now let's get back to the condo and change. I promised Mrs. Thornton I'd get you home by three, Cynthia. Angie and Ericia, you two have piano lessons this afternoon. And I've got to get over to Wayne State. I've an appointment with my advisor."

Heather reminded herself that when he called tonight, she would suggest that he consult with Cynthia's therapist before making a decision—just as a precaution to be certain the time away wouldn't jeopardize the girl's progress. His calls were something she continued to look forward to. And now that he was in Washington, even more so. Unfortunately their talks couldn't take the place of the hot kisses and sweet lovemaking they once shared. But Heather was far from giving up on this man or his child. She loved them both too much.

Much to the girls' delight, their folks did agree. In fact they all thought it was a great idea as long as Heather was up to the challenge.

"We're here!" Angela cried as they pulled into the extensive drive. The impressive stone and brick house was high on a ridge overlooking Traverse Bay. It was clearly a showplace and nothing like the cottage Heather and her nieces had expected. The house as well as the grounds were well taken care of judging by the condition of the perfectly groomed lawn and lush flower beds.

"Every girl for herself. Start unloading," Heather called, opening the trunk of her ancient Firebird. "Careful of that laptop computer, Angie."

The great room was sectioned off into spacious living, dining, and kitchen areas. A wide stone fireplace was centered on the portion of the outside wall that was not given over to glass looking out on the bay.

"Look, Aunt Heather, a pool!" Ericia said from the rear patio doors that opened onto a large redwood deck.

"Do you like it?" Cynthia asked Heather as she put down her suitcases. "Daddy had it redecorated after my mother died."

Heather gave the girl a quick hug. "It's beautiful. And it was awfully nice of your father to let us use it. You must thank him for all of us when you call him to let him know we've arrived safely. You two need to call your folks as well."

"Now?" they wailed.

"After dinner will be soon enough," Heather said, hiding her amusement.

"Where is your room, Cynthia?"

Cynthia led the way down a short hallway on the left, past the very modern kitchen. The girl's bedroom was spacious and beautifully furnished with a single white wrought-iron and brass bed. The dresser, vanity, and rocking chair were all white wicker.

"Very pretty," Heather said, taking in the apricot and cream curtains and bedspread. The floor was carpeted in cream shag. "Did you pick out the colors yourself?"

Cynthia beamed with pleasure. "Yes, but Mrs. Hunter helped me. This way."

They went through the connected cream marble bathroom into the gold and cream guest room. The comforter, drapes, and armchairs were in shades of gold, the carpet was cream.

"Perfect! Ericia and I can bunk in here." Angela bounced excitedly on one of the twin beds.

"Come on, Heather, I'll show you where you're to sleep." Cynthia pulled her along the hallway back through the living room to the far end of the house and toward a narrow flight of stairs that she hadn't even noticed earlier. The top of the stairs disappeared from view.

"It's Daddy's loft. You're going to love it," Cynthia said, tugging on Heather's hand.

The umber carpeted staircase led to a huge bedroom-study that was done in nut brown, oyster, and touches of cinnamon. A huge brass king-sized bed faced a glass wall overlooking the bay. Built-in bookshelves flanked a large fireplace adjacent to the bed. A wide rolltop desk and comfortable armchairs stood opposite the fire-place.

"The bathroom is huge." Cynthia opened the pat-terned-glass door at their right. "But it doesn't have a tub, just a shower stall. If you want a bath, you'll have to share with us. Do you like it?"

Heather laughed. "What's not to like? Are you sure your dad won't mind?"

"Of course not. He wants you to be comfortable. I just hope he can make it up for the Fourth of July picnic the Hunters always give. Oh!" Cynthia's hand flew to her mouth. "I forgot—I have a letter for you. It's from Daddy. He wrote it while he was home last weekend. I'll be right back."

Heather was shaking so badly she had to sit down on the bed. Was it her imagination or was Cynthia being more candid about her father? She was changing. Did that mean she was becoming more secure in her rela-tionship with her father? Could it only be a matter of time until she was able to accept Heather's involvement with Quinn? As she absently stroked the rich velvet com-forter, memories of the large dark, handsome man washed over her. Oh, how she missed him. She ached to be back in his arms.

She still couldn't believe that she'd told Quinn how she felt about him the last time they made love. She certainly hadn't meant to tell him. Yet the words had poured from her, overflowing the bounds of her heart. She shivered in reaction to the sensual memories. Oh . . . the way he had made her feel. She'd been aware of only him, his deep rhythmic possession. When the instinctive tightening of her inner muscles had sig-

naled the warm rush of her release, she'd been unable
to withhold even a part of herself. Her control had shattered, and all her love for him flowed forth in a verbal
declaration.

"Quinn . . ." She said his name softly, pressing her
fingertips to her lips. Their lovemaking had been so glorious. He'd given a part of himself to her. Damn it, she
didn't want to give him up.

Heather had told him she understood, and she did.
She didn't resent his decision. Nor did she resent Cynthia for the strain she had placed on their involvement.
But she would be lying to herself if she didn't acknowledge how much it hurt not being able to see him or to
be with him. Yes, the hurt was there. But she refused
to dwell on it.

"Here!" Cynthia's curly head appeared at the top of
the stairs.

"Thanks. Is all the luggage in?"

"Yeah. Angie and Ericia are unpacking. I should get
busy myself. Hey, we might still have time to walk down
to the beach before dinner." She was gone before Heather
could respond.

Her hands were trembling when she broke the seal of
the envelope. She had to run damp palms down the sides
of her jeans before she removed the single sheet.

Hi sugar. You have guts—more courage than I
have. Imagine volunteering to take on three teenage
girls. I wish I could have gone along to help you
out, but you should find everything you need. Mrs.
Matthews was to have cleaned the place and stocked
the refrigerator and freezer. Give her a call if you

have any problems. The Hunters are right next door. Cindy knows the phone numbers.

Feel free to stay as long as you like. The house would just be sitting empty.

I probably shouldn't ask, but I can't stop myself. Are you enjoying our late night talks as much as I am? Do you have any idea how much I miss you? How much I want you? Quinn.

"Oh, honey, I miss you, too," Heather whispered, pressing her face into the pillow. She'd heard his deep masculine voice just last night. But what she had most wanted last night—as she wanted every night—was for his arms to be around her and his wide mouth to be tasting hers.

Within a week they settled into a comfortable routine. Before breakfast Heather and the girls swam in the pool and spent the mornings together. After lunch the girls went off to play volleyball or tennis with their friends. There was no shortage of teens in the vicinity. Heather took advantage of the girls' absence to work beneath the shade of the wide umbrella of the redwood table on the patio.

This was where Elaine Hunter found her. She'd skirted the thick shrubs which bordered two properties. "Oh, I'm interrupting. I saw the kids on the beach and assumed you could use the company. Wrong, huh?"

"Nope, I could use the break," Heather said with a welcoming smile. "These figures are starting to run together."

The two had known each other a short time, but once Heather had gotten over her initial jealousy of Elaine on the night of Cynthia's disappearance, Heather discovered she liked her. Remembering how kind Elaine and her husband had been to Quinn during the time Cynthia was missing had warmed Heather's heart.

"Come inside. I've got the air conditioner going and iced tea ready to pour," she said, closing the laptop computer and putting her notes away.

"Sounds wonderful. Ninety-eight again today. Can you believe this Michigan weather?"

"Probably snow tomorrow."

They both laughed at that.

"What are you working on?" Elaine gestured toward the textbooks and mounds of paper.

"My dissertation. I've been at it for over a year now. In fact, I'd hoped to finish it this summer. But I think I'm going to need more data to support my view," Heather said with a sigh. "Looks like I won't finish until the fall now." She led the way into the kitchen.

"Doctoral candidate, hmmm. I'm impressed. What field?"

"Clinical psychology. Have a seat." Heather indicated the dining area. "I'll get the glasses."

Once they were seated, Elaine said with a smile, "That sounds interesting. Are you planning to give up counseling?"

"No, at least not for a while. I enjoy working in the school system, and I especially enjoy working with teens. I hope to do both by eventually joining my mother's practice as a part-time psychologist."

"So what's your paper about?" Elaine sipped her tea.

"Teen suicide. I've been volunteering at a teen suicide Crisis Prevention Center and learning a lot. Would you like a cinnamon roll? The girls made them this morning. They've suddenly developed an insane urge for cooking. Or should I say, I may be the one going insane before they're finished."

Elaine laughed. "I'll try anything once."

Heather raised an eyebrow in warning, but passed over the plate of goodies.

"These are really good!" Elaine said munching.

"Amazing, isn't it?"

"Your nieces are delightful. They came over to help me weed the garden, a thankless chore if ever there was one. Anyway, I like them. It's easy to spot the family resemblance. They're so pretty. And their friendship has made a world of difference to Cynthia. I haven't seen her this happy in years. And I suspect you have a lot to do with that."

"Thank you. And for that compliment, you can have another cinnamon roll." Heather beamed. "Somehow I have a hard time believing those three girls were interested in pulling weeds—more like big-game hunting. Am I right?"

Elaine knew exactly what she meant. Her twin sons Kevin and Keith had invited their handsome college roommate up for a few weeks. "Probably."

"Their motivation is named Gary. Are the girls making pests of themselves?"

"No, nothing like that."

"I'll speak to them."

"Whatever for? There was a time when Cynthia was little that she practically lived in our house. She and my boys were always up to no good." Her blue eyes reflected her amusement. "We've spent every summer up here since the children were in diapers. I'm afraid your nieces were disappointed today. The boys drove up to the Sault Sainte Marie with some college friends. They won't return until this evening." Elaine popped the last bit of roll into her mouth. "Are you finding any time to enjoy yourself?"

"Oh, yes. I'm having a wonderful time."

"Have you heard about our annual barbecue? We have it over the Fourth of July weekend. You and the girls are coming, aren't you?"

"Mmmm, Cynthia told us about it. The girls and I are looking forward to it. If you need help, let me know. I'd be glad to do whatever I can."

"Thanks, I'll keep that in mind. I just hope my husband is coming. Darnell is busy on a new case. It's always a case. If he forgets that next weekend is the Fourth of July, I'll be the one dragging him into court. Honestly! Is Quinn flying in?"

Heather, refilling their glasses, nearly dropped the pitcher. "I don't know." Somehow she managed to give Elaine her drink without mishap. "More lemon or sugar?"

"Both, thanks. Take my advice and don't fall in love and marry an attorney. Oh, they make excellent providers, but on the whole they're workaholics. My husband and his best friend, Quinn Montgomery, are the worst of the lot." Elaine looked up, realizing Heather was extremely quiet. She saw the single tear slide down Heather's cheek before she wiped it away.

"Heather? What did I say?"

"Nothing." Heather had gotten up and moved to the patio door, her back to Elaine. She took slow calming breaths, hoping to get her emotions under control. "I don't know what's wrong with me." Her voice was muffled by the hand she pressed to her trembling mouth.

"It's Quinn, isn't it?"

"Your warning is a little late. I've already fallen in love with him."

"I was only teasing," Elaine hurried on to say. "Quinn is a very attractive man, a wonderful man."

"But a man who has no room in his life for a new woman," Heather said in frustration.

"Honey, life doesn't always cooperate. Come on now, dry your face. If you like we can always discuss the price of pork chops," Elaine said gently.

Heather joined her at the table with a somewhat wavering smile. "I didn't mean to come apart on you. When you mentioned his name, the tears just came from nowhere."

"We don't have to talk about it."

"It's alright. I probably need to talk. I've been holding it in for so long."

"Quinn knows how you feel?"

"Oh, yes. But there are complications. We've decided to put our relationship in cold storage for a while."

"But why?"

"Cynthia . . ." Heather flushed, recounting the embarrassing morning Cynthia discovered she and Quinn were lovers.

"Surely Quinn hasn't allowed Cynthia to control his personal life!"

"No. But she's been through so much, and she needs him now."

"Do you think therapy is helping?"

"Yes. Given time, I think Cynthia will be fine."

"For that we're all very, very thankful," Elaine said. "Heather, Cynthia isn't the only one who's suffered since Peggy's death."

"Quinn."

"Yes," Elaine said evenly. "He's been through hell."

"I see," was all Heather could manage to say. She didn't dare ask more. It was bad enough to fear that he was still in love with Peggy. It would be too much to hear the words—because then all her hopes for the future would be crushed. Yet Heather had to know. "Do you think he's still in love with Cynthia's mother?"

"How can I answer something like that? I don't know. He and Peggy had a good marriage. And they loved Cynthia very much. Then Peggy died very suddenly," Elaine said with sadness in her voice. "There's something about her death that still bothers Quinn. I'm not sure what it is. He won't talk about it."

Yes, that sounded just like Quinn, Heather decided thoughtfully.

"I hope I haven't discouraged you. Because I'm really glad about the two of you."

"Oh, Elaine, I miss him so badly. Our only contact these days is the telephone. And since we've been here, I haven't spoken to him at all." Heather swallowed back tears. "I know I'm being silly, but I can't bear not talking to him. It's too much! But it's all we have right now." Heather brushed impatiently at the tears spilling down her cheeks.

"I'm so sorry. I had no idea you two were going through this kind of torment. It must be just awful."

"No, it's not awful. I'm just weepy today." Heather took a deep breath. "I thoroughly agree with Quinn. Cynthia has to be his number one consideration. I want her well and happy just as he does." Heather trembled with emotion as she whispered, "I know I shouldn't expect anything of him right now. Quinn has enough to contend with. But a damn phone call! Why can't he call me?"

"Give it time. I saw the way Quinn looked at you the night Cynthia disappeared. And I've heard the warmth in his voice whenever he mentions you. Heather, you're important to him."

But Heather wanted his love. That was what she really wanted, more than telephone calls, more than anything else in the world. She would be willing to wait forever if she just knew he loved her.

"It hasn't been easy for you, Heather. I know that. Quinn has so much anger and bitterness inside of him that he can't seem to let go of the past. Please, don't give up on him."

"As my great-aunt, Naomi always says, I feel like I'm between a rock and a hard place."

"You've been so good for Cynthia. I think you're good for Quinn, too. I, like you, happen to love the guy. So promise me you won't make any decision just yet."

Heather nodded.

"Good! Just kick back and relax. Enjoy your vacation." Glancing at the kitchen clock, Elaine jumped up. "Got to go. I'm expecting a call from Darnell." She gave Heather's hand a reassuring squeeze. "Talk to you soon."

"No matter what happens between Quinn and myself, Elaine, I'm glad he has friends like you and Darnell."

Eighteen

The girls were involved in a noisy game of Scrabble when the telephone rang that evening.

"I'll get it," Heather said, reaching for the instrument at her elbow. She'd been reading an article on teen suicide in a recent psychology journal. "Montgomery residence."

"Hey, pretty girl." Quinn's voice was deep, arresting to her sensitive ear.

It took her a second to regain the use of her blocked vocal cords. "How are you, Quinn?"

"The question is how are you? Still in one piece?"

"That's debatable," she said as casually as she could manage, considering her breath had been trapped in her lungs. "Would you care to switch places?"

"Not in this life!" His deep masculine laughter sent shivers of awareness through her nervous system. "Have everything you need? The house clean, refrigerator and cupboards stocked?"

"Perfect. You've a lovely home. It's a shame you couldn't make this trip with Cynthia. She would love for you to be here."

"I somehow doubt that. The kid's been beside herself

with excitement. Something to do with teenage girls and boys, know what I mean?"

"All too well. Elaine sent Gary, her boys' college roommate over with a casserole and the girls have been whispering and giggling all evening. And I understand there's a fifteen- and sixteen-year-old brother and sister living a mile or so down the road."

Quinn chuckled softly. "The Sanders kids. Have you been able to do any work on your paper?"

"Yes, but it's going slower than I would like. That has nothing to do with the kids. More to do with research."

"The kids aren't taking all your time?"

"No, they've been very good about that. I manage to put together a few hours between lunch and dinner." Heather looked up to see Cynthia watching her. "Cynthia's right here. Just a minute, please." She got up, putting down the phone. "Hurry, it's long distance."

"You're cheating! That's not a word, Angie!" Ericia screeched at her sister, sending her into a peal of laughter.

"How about popcorn?" Heather headed for the kitchen as the girls cheered their approval.

There was no point in pretending she was unaffected. For a moment she'd forgotten everything in the pleasure of hearing Quinn's voice after so long. But one look at Cynthia had reminded her that the call was to his daughter. If Heather hadn't answered the telephone, she wouldn't have spoken to him at all. That realization hurt . . . badly.

Elaine had requested she give him time. Time for what? To hurt her even more? No, Heather wasn't the self-sacrificing type. In the past, when a relationship wasn't right for her, she had always had enough pride to walk away. That was what she had done when her engagement had gone sour. Why was it so different now?

Perhaps she was the one who was different. No, it was Quinn. She couldn't turn her back on him. She cared about him too deeply. The simple truth was her heart belonged to him. It was too late to ask for it back.

But what was she supposed to think? Or didn't he expect her to notice that he hadn't called her in two blasted weeks! And there was no way she could call him. The only time she was alone was during the afternoon while he was probably in court. If only there was an extension in the loft where she slept.

Heather felt totally confused. It was driving her crazy wondering if Quinn was still in love with his late wife. She was no closer to finding an answer now than she'd been weeks ago. Maybe it was better if she didn't know . . .

And there were Cynthia's ambiguous emotions toward her. When Heather had been on the telephone, Cynthia had looked at her with a combination of curiosity, love, resentment, and a bit of jealousy. At the moment Heather didn't feel sure about anything, except that she would be spending another night in Quinn's bed, without him.

With Independence Day weekend fast approaching, the girls insisted they each needed a new outfit for the barbecue. On Thursday they drove into Traverse City to do the necessary shopping.

Later that night the girls decided to give each other an extensive beauty treatment. Heather had gone out for a walk along the beach, and when she returned she found each young face smeared with what looked to be a mixture of oatmeal, honey, and egg.

"Having fun?" Heather tried to keep a straight face, but failed.

"This is work," Cynthia announced, adding more of the mixture to her unblemished face and neck and shoulders.

"Smells more like breakfast. What all did you put in there?" Heather turned up her nose at the unusual color.

"All natural ingredients. We've got eggs, oatmeal, honey, beer, garlic, and avocado blended in," Ericia explained.

"Used your dad's imported beer, did you Cynthia?" Heather asked with amusement.

"He won't mind when he sees how gorgeous we are."

"Would you like to try some?" Angela offered.

"I think I'll pass this time. Have you tried putting it on a cookie sheet? It would probably taste great except for the beer and garlic."

"Oh, Aunt Heather!" Ericia giggled.

"I'm going to bed. Oh! Put the kitchen and bathroom back the way you found them when you're finished, please. See you beauties in the morning."

Heather was halfway up the stairs when Cynthia ran after her. "I forgot to tell you. When Daddy called I reminded him of the Hunters' barbecue on Saturday." Cynthia beamed, unaware that Heather's heart had stopped beating. "Gosh, I really miss him. I can't wait for him to see how much my backhand has improved since Keith has been coaching me."

Was Quinn coming? Could he find the time? He was involved with a very important legal defense. They had even seen him being interviewed on a national news broadcast earlier in the week. "Is he flying up?"

"He's not sure. But I'm keeping my fingers crossed. He said he'd call tomorrow night, one way or the other." Cynthia started to give her a kiss on the cheek but at the last second reconsidered. Instead she blew a kiss, then dashed back into the bathroom to join the others at the mirror.

Heather was pleased with Cynthia's increased poise and confidence. It was amazing how much she had grown in such a short few weeks.

Heather paused on the landing, considering the very real possibility of seeing Quinn soon. She had been furious with him the other night. Tonight she wasn't angry. Tonight she felt lonely. She missed him desperately. She longed to show him, as a woman shows her man, how much she loved him and needed him. If he came, she could do none of those things. They wouldn't have time alone together. She would have to ignore the urgent yearnings to be back in his arms.

As she sank in the nearby armchair in the unlit bedroom, Heather recalled their romantic dinner together and later their lovemaking. Her mind was flooded with remembered pleasure.

Later as she curled up in bed, holding his pillow close, Heather accepted that even if he did come to Traverse Bay this weekend, nothing would change. Her body might ache for his lovemaking, and she might crave his sensuous caresses—but they wouldn't make love. Her breasts ached against the bodice of her nightgown as her heightened senses refused to forget the weight of his chest pressed against them or the wonder of wrapping her legs around his lean hips while feeling his hard masculinity deep within her, filling the emptiness and loving her as only he could.

Friday was the longest day on record. All evening long Heather's eyes strayed to the silent telephone. The girls were engrossed in shaping and polishing their nails and didn't notice her anxiety. The phone stayed silent. Quinn didn't call.

"The others are all there, Aunt Heather. Hurry or we'll be late." Ericia watched as Heather put the cherry topping on the cheesecake.

"What she means is Gary's there," Angela said.

"Now look, you." Ericia put her finger in her sister's face. "I've had enough of your teasing."

Heather had about enough, too. She hadn't been able to sleep until dawn and felt like doing a bit of yelling herself. "Ericia, please—why don't you go on ahead. I'll be along in another couple of minutes. Cynthia, will you and Angela cover the salads with plastic wrap?"

"You're going to change, aren't you, Aunt Heather? I mean you're going to wear a bathing suit like everyone else, aren't you?" Ericia chewed on her lower lip as if she had just considered the possibility that Heather might not. The idea was apparently too horrible for words.

"Of course. Honey, stop worrying—I won't embarrass you in front of your friends. I've done my nails, hair, and makeup. All I have to do is change. Hey, why don't you and the girls take the food over to the Hunters? I'll meet you there in say, ten minutes?"

"Oh, alright. Come on, gang." Ericia picked up the largest bowl. She was dressed like the others in beach gear, and like the others her tennis outfit and shoes were in one of the carryalls beside the patio door.

Her sister was just about to announce her objection to the plan, but a censoring look from her aunt caused her to grab the Jell-O mold and hurry over to collect her bag.

"Cindy, aren't you coming?" Ericia asked impatiently.

"In a few. You guys go ahead. I'll wait for Heather."

Ericia didn't argue. She was out the door and hurrying her sister along.

Cynthia said, "The last bowl is covered. Is there something else you want me to do before we leave?"

"No, not really. As soon as I wash these few dishes I can get ready. I hate to leave the kitchen a mess," Heather said, preoccupied with looking for the lid to the pie plate.

"Go ahead and get ready. I'll finish in here." Cynthia began filling the sink with sudsy water.

Something in Cynthia's voice caused Heather to stop what she was doing and look at her closely. "Honey, is something wrong?"

"It's no big deal. Honest!" the girl said, picking up a dishcloth.

"Anything that causes you to have that unhappy look on your pretty face is a big deal." Heather placed an arm around her shoulders.

Cynthia rested her cheek on Heather's forehead. "If we take too long, Ericia will be mad. I'm beginning to agree with Angie. She has been a real pill since she met Gary. He doesn't even like her for a girlfriend. He already goes with a girl at college."

Heather was relieved. Gary was too old for her niece. Besides, she didn't want to see Ericia hurt.

"Boys!" Cynthia sneered. "I hope I never fall in love."

Heather laughed softly. "Don't worry about Ericia. She's got a good head on her shoulders. So, what's really bothering you, kiddo?"

"Daddy! He didn't call last night. Do you suppose something bad happened to him?"

"I think if he were ill, we would have been called."

"Why didn't he call? If he were coming, he would have caught the first plane out of D.C. It's after twelve and he still isn't here."

"Cynthia, I'm sure he's done his best to get away. But you have to remember, your father is an extremely important man. A lot of people depend on him. He's working on a delicate case. He might not be able to get away right now." Heather didn't say Quinn's name, she couldn't—just the sound of it hurt.

"Yeah, I know. But things have been so great lately. Why does he have to go and spoil it!" Cynthia pouted, tears of frustration ran down her soft brown cheeks.

"Honey, your father isn't trying to hurt you."

"Oh, I suppose I'm being a brat. But Heather, I get scared." She stopped abruptly. Suddenly she seemed fascinated by her pink-lacquered nails.

"Scared of what?"

When she didn't answer, Heather turned her so she could look into her eyes. "Are you frightened that things might go back to the way they were before you ran away?"

Cynthia was quiet before she spoke. "Yeah," she confessed. "Now we do things like a family. He even lets me run with him in the mornings before he has to go into the office. I hate getting up at five thirty, but we talk while we run. And I'm getting pretty good. Naturally I'm not as good my daddy, but I'm improving." She paused for breath. "He doesn't stay late at work anymore. He makes it home for dinner every night. He brings a lot of work home, but he doesn't do it until late after I'm in bed. Heather, he's teaching me how to play racquetball, and I'm teaching him how to roller blade."

"Stop worrying. This new case has taken him out of town for a couple of weeks. He's coming back. And when he does, just tell him how you feel. It's important that you let him know how much you want to continue spending time with him. Your dad loves you, dear heart. You mustn't forget that."

Heather was touched by the enthusiastic kiss and hug Cynthia gave her.

"I love you so much," the girl whispered.

Cynthia didn't want to even think about the time they weren't friends. She'd missed Heather every single day. She hated fighting with Heather and couldn't bear the thought of their friendship ever ending. As Cynthia clung to Heather, she thought about her mother. She was gone forever. Dr. Ann had helped her see that no amount of wishing or misbehavior could bring her mother back.

"I love you, too, sweetheart." Heather gave her a hard squeeze. "You alright, now?"

"Yes," she smiled.

"Well, I'd better get changed or we'll be in trouble. I won't be long."

Heather was as good as her word. She changed into a one-piece black suit trimmed in wide, patterned gold bands that were embroidered with fuchsia flowers at the neckline and the waist. The bodice plunged into a low, expansive vee in front and back and was cut high at the hip, making her shapely legs appear longer. Her braids were held away from her face by a colorful gold and black foil scarf that Heather tied into an elaborate wrap. She wore a very full sheer black skirt trimmed in the same patterned thick gold band. She limited her makeup to flame-colored gloss and mascara. After checking her bag for tennis gear and shoes, Heather was ready. She ran lightly down the stairs, but she was brought up short at the bottom.

Cynthia had her arms around Quinn's wide shoulders. The girl's face was glowing with happiness.

"Oh, Daddy, I've missed you!" Cynthia's laughter echoed pure joy as she jumped up and down, still holding on to her dad.

"Yeah, I got that message. I missed you, too, baby girl. Hey, let go. I'm an old man, remember." Quinn jokingly staggered as if he were about to fall.

Cynthia laughed and gave him a loud kiss on the cheek before letting her hands drop gracefully to her sides.

Quinn looked up to encounter Heather's shocked brown eyes.

At last . . . Heather said silently with her eyes as Quinn thought that very same thing. They both knew he shouldn't have come and the reasons why.

He'd boarded the plane in Washington not fully comprehending his own actions, yet knowing the case he was involved in could make or break his professional career. He'd come anyway. He had to see Heather.

He'd survived for weeks with the smell of her lingering in his nostrils, the taste of her in his mouth, the memory of her soft curves burned in his brain. He couldn't stay away a second longer.

Heather's hungry gaze moved over him, remembering every detail of his long muscular frame, filing away for future consideration the slight changes in him. His skin was darker as if he'd been out of doors as much as he could. Yet the lines around his eyes were pronounced as if he been working late into the night and gotten little sleep.

Was it her imagination or did his shoulders seem broader, barely able to contain the powerful sinew beneath his gray, short-sleeved, knit shirt. His waist seemed slimmer, but his thighs were as taut and well defined as she remembered.

"Look, Heather—he made it! Isn't it wonderful!" Cynthia ran over and hugged her.

"Yes, wonderful."

How in the world was she supposed to handle this? She'd promised to keep her distance for Cynthia's sake. Yet despite what Elaine had told her about his devotion to his late wife and despite the fact that Cynthia was standing right next to her, Heather's heart raced with excitement. He looked too good to be real. But he hadn't called her once since she'd been here. She needed those nightly talks . . . needed to hear his voice . . . needed to know he still cared about her. Hadn't he realized that by not calling he had taken everything away from her. She had been left with nothing to hold on to.

"Hello, Heather," he said softly in that deep sexy voice she had come to adore.

"Hi. As you've might of guessed, we didn't expect you."

"I wasn't sure I could make it. That's why I didn't call last night. I didn't finish working until the wee-hours. I caught the first flight out this morning." He didn't smile, but his dark eyes drank in her golden beauty. It had been too damn long. "You're looking exceptionally fit for a woman living on the edge of her dissertation."

Although he was teasing, his gaze was anything but casual. His eyes lingered on her generously full rose-tinted mouth before eventually moving downward to the soft full lines of her sexy frame. His body responded immediately with desire for her. Some things didn't change. His hunger for Heather was one of those things.

"Where is everyone?" Quinn had to force his eyes from her. A year in a harem wouldn't quench his thirst for Heather, he decided hotly. Quinn hadn't even looked at another woman since he'd met her. She alone possessed the kind of warmth and sweetness that kept him coming back for more.

Cynthia answered, "At the Hunters. I was waiting for Heather. You're coming to the barbecue, aren't you, Daddy?"

"Sure."

"Hurry then. Get changed into a bathing suit. No business suits or ties allowed." Cynthia pointed a warning finger at him, but her wide smile told its own story.

"Right." He tweaked her nose before retrieving the overnight bag he'd abandoned by the door.

"I'll get the other salad." Cynthia dashed toward the kitchen.

Quinn paused when he realized Heather was standing on the bottom step. The staircase led to the loft. His charcoal eyes deepened even more as he realized she'd been using his room. The thought of her in his bed sent his pulse soaring. He knew what it was like to make love to this beautiful lady. What he didn't know was if he could stay away from her.

Heather could feel her face heating as she hastily stepped down and out of his way.

"Do you mind if I change in the bedroom?"

She shrugged, drawing his gaze back to her plump breasts. Sexual tension caused their sensitive peaks to stand out against her swimsuit. She gasped as his eyes stroked the engorged tips of her breasts as thoroughly as he'd once licked them. When his tongue came out to dampen dry lips, Heather quickly moved.

"It's your house," she managed to say, hiding the tremor in her voice. Her long lashes flicked wide when she recognized they had a problem. Quinn had to sleep somewhere, and the most likely place was in his own bed.

As if reading her thoughts, he said, "I'll take the sofa tonight. It opens into a full-size bed. All I ask is bathroom privileges."

"Of course." She headed toward the kitchen. "Come on, Cynthia. We'll meet your dad over at the Hunters."

Nineteen

"Congratulations, darling," Elaine whispered in Heather's ear as she dropped down beside her on the beach after an exuberant volleyball game. "I don't recall seeing any woman work so hard at staying away from a man."

Heather groaned, dropping her head to rest on upraised knees. For several hours she'd done her best to prove to herself that she was unaffected by him. It was stupid. Lying to herself hadn't made a bit of difference. She was still crazy in love with the man.

"Was I so obvious?"

"Not to the others, but then none of them know just how much you care for him. Have you two had a chance to talk?" Elaine asked.

The others were busy taking down the net or gathering and stacking driftwood for the huge bonfire planned for nightfall.

"No—but if there was something he wanted to discuss, he would have taken the time to call me. Evidently he had nothing to say to me," Heather hissed, determined to hang on to her anger.

"So that's it. Darling, ignoring him isn't going to get you what you want."

Heather frowned. She'd refused to play tennis on the off chance that she might have to partner Quinn. She'd used Elaine's needing help with the food as her excuse. She had even gone so far as to limit herself to a short time in the pool, leaving as soon as Quinn's sleek frame sliced through the water. Heather was ashamed of how purposefully she overlooked the empty place at his side at the barbecue in favor of squeezing in between her nieces.

Why was she acting like a teenager? She was so angry that she couldn't seem to stop herself. She wasn't being ridiculous—she was merely honoring their agreement. He asked her to keep her distance, and she was doing just that.

But what if she weren't able to keep up her end of it? What then? Her feelings for him were difficult enough without sexual desire getting in the way. She literally ached for him, craved the kind of sweet magic only he could provide. He was more than a terrific lover. He worked at pleasing her. It did no good to caution herself against him—she couldn't help wanting him.

"I know it isn't my business, but I care about you two. I truly believe he cares for you, Heather. It's in his eyes. Can't you feel him watching you? He follows you with his gaze. And I for one think it's romantic."

"What's romantic?" Elaine's husband Darnell asked, putting an arm around his wife's shoulders. Quinn was right behind him and he sat down near Heather.

"You, my darling, who else?" Elaine smiled at him, snuggling back against his side.

"You don't expect me to believe that, do you?"

"And why not? It's absolutely true."

Darnell looked over at Heather, a wide smile on his even features. "Enjoying yourself?"

"Yes, very much," she said. "The weather has been super. The girls and I love it here."

Busy trying to avoid staring at Quinn's compelling profile as he relaxed in close fitting cut-offs, his long hard thighs almost touching hers, Heather tried not to note the way the muscles in his arms were displayed to perfection in a short-sleeved blue cotton shirt that he'd left open down to the middle of his chest.

"How's life in Washington, old man?" Darnell asked.

"Intense."

"Not working too hard, are you?" Elaine asked.

"No. I've managed to do a little running, racquetball. Another week or two and we can wrap this thing up."

"You both work too many hours. It's not good for you."

Darnell laughed. "Darling, a man needs his work. It's the challenge. Heather, Quinn tells me you're responsible for the smile I see on Cynthia's face these days. Elaine and I love her like one of our own. And we're grateful for all you've done for her."

Heather forced a polite smile. "How generous, but I certainly can't take credit." Gratitude! Was that what Quinn felt for her? No wonder he hadn't called, the snake. In the beginning he'd desired her. Now even that had ended. It was over between them. Why had it taken her so long to realize?

Heather jumped to her feet. "Excuse me, I think I'll help the kids collect wood." She was off, oblivious to the streaked beauty of the sky as the sun began its descent.

* * *

Orange-red flames danced into a sky as dark and endless as a pool of liquid sapphires. The pulsating wails of Stevie Wonder poured from the portable cassette player.

Heather watched the kids jumping and twisting to the music. Loneliness tore at her tender heartstrings as she took note of the two other couples. The Hunters and the Sanderses enjoyed a special closeness as they took in the seductive appeal of the sultry, summer night. Her toes curled in the sand still warm from the hot sun. Her thoughts were with the man a short distance away.

He was stretched out with his back resting against a boulder, an idle hand on his thigh. Heather didn't have to look at him to feel his brooding deliberation.

Quinn resented that she had time for everyone but him. He was experiencing a sharp sense of disappointment. Why was she so distant? He barely had a chance to speak to her all day, and never privately. Damn it, he missed her. Didn't she feel the same? She was acting as if he'd mistreated her. What did she have to be angry about? Or was she simply tired of waiting?

"Hasn't this been the best day!" Angela exclaimed as she and Cynthia joined Heather.

"The best." Heather smiled quickly.

"I can't remember when I've had such a great time, in spite of the heat," Cynthia said, mopping her wet brow. "It was just super."

Heather looked from one to the other before returning her gaze to the slowly dying embers. She was glad someone was having fun. She couldn't remember ever being so miserable.

"The twins are driving up to Mackinaw Island in the morning," Angela said. "They're going biking around the island. Wouldn't it be great if we could go, too, Cynthia?"

"Yeah."

They both turned hopefully to Heather. "Can we?"

"Huh?"

"Go biking around Mackinaw Island with the Hunter twins," Angela begged. "Please, please, please."

"Have you been invited?"

"Sure, if you and Dad give the okay." Cynthia said, blissfully unaware of what the innocent coupling of their names had done to Heather.

"Please, Auntie, say yes. It's only one day. Maybe we can have lunch in the Grand Hotel and get fudge."

"Sounds like fun. But Cynthia, you must get your father's permission. I can't speak for him."

The girls beamed. After conspiratorial whispers, they went to sit with Quinn.

Heather couldn't help chuckling. She'd been worried about Cynthia being away from therapy. But apparently the vacation was doing her a world of good. All three girls couldn't be happier.

"He said we could!" the girls shouted, then asked each other at the same time, "what should I wear—"

"Decide later," Heather interrupted. "The fire has died and we should be leaving, especially since you have a long drive ahead of you. What time are the boys planning on starting out?"

"Seven." Angela frowned.

"That early?" Heather laughed, brushing herself down. "Where's your sister?"

"Here I am," Ericia called, having just returned from one last swim.

"Here—put this over your shoulders. It's getting cold." She gave her a beach towel.

"Guess what? Aunt Heather and Dad said we can go biking with the twins on Mackinaw Island."

"Hey! That's really hot." Ericia beamed. "We can pick our outfits out tonight. Can I borrow your pink and green overalls?"

"Sure. Hey, Angie . . ."

Heather put her arm around Ericia's shoulders. "Honey, I'm counting on you to look after the other two. You're the oldest and most responsible."

Ericia beamed at her aunt. She gave her a quick kiss on the cheek. "I'll keep those two in line."

The girls collected their things, while Quinn helped put out the fire and Heather worked with Elaine to clear away the remains of their meal.

Once they'd finished their farewells, the chattering girls went on ahead.

"Ready?" Quinn asked, Heather's beach bag in one hand and empty salad bowls in the other. Heather was cradling the remains of the cheesecake in the crystal pie server.

"Mmmm," she nodded.

"Those nieces of yours have really brought Cynthia out of her shell."

"Yes." Heather smiled her approval of Cynthia at him.

"Lady, that's the only smile I've gotten from you all day." Quinn groaned as he saw the tiny frown forming on her forehead.

"I'm surprised you agreed to the trip to Mackinaw Island."

"I wouldn't if I thought there was something to be concerned about. The Hunter twins are good kids. I've watched those two grow up. They'll take good care of the girls. Are you concerned?"

"Not really. I trust the girls. It's just that if anything happens to those girls, my sister Gwen will kill me. Are you sure they'll be safe?"

"Stop worrying. Mackinaw is roughly two hours away. If there's a problem, we're close enough that we can always drive up and get them," Quinn assured her, careful not to touch her. "Okay?"

"Okay."

This was certainly the longest night in history, Heather decided as she stood by the patio screened door. She glanced back at the four glued to the television set, sharing a huge bowl of popcorn. "How can you eat that stuff after all the food we've consumed today?"

The girls didn't hear the question. They were rolling on the floor and screaming with laughter at some new comedian on the *Tonight* show.

"It's a good program. Come and join us," Quinn said from his place on the sofa with his bare feet propped on the coffee table.

"No, thanks." Heather slid the screen door open and stepped out onto the patio. She'd changed into magenta cotton slacks and pale pink cotton knit sweater. Ebony braids swirled around her shoulders as she looked up into the cloudless darkened sky. It was a beautiful night—a night for lovers.

It was quite late when Quinn stood in the screened door studying Heather. The rhythmic creak of the patio swing blended with the night sounds. Heather sat lost in thought.

"The girls have finally decided on what they're going to wear and have gone to bed," he said, stepping outside. He offered one of the tall imported beer bottles he carried.

"I don't know how they expect to get up at six. Not one of them has been out of bed before eleven for the last two weeks." Heather laughed.

Enjoying the warm sound, Quinn joined her on the swing, taking a healthy swig of his drink.

Heather didn't have to look at him to know how well his shirt hugged his upper torso, nor did she have to inhale his fresh scent to recognize his masculine appeal.

"Ericia's growing up so fast. It's hard to believe she'll be seventeen in October."

"Yeah, I know what you mean." He smiled, unwittingly drawing her eyes to the seductive curve of his mouth, partly screened by his thick mustache.

Her heart accelerated as she thought of how that tiny bit of masculinity felt against her skin. She shivered as the warm rush of memories spiraled beyond the limits she had placed on herself. Clear recollections filled her head of Quinn's mouth between her breasts, the roughness of his tongue warming her breasts and her aching nipples before he took each one into his mouth and suckled with hard sweet suction. Heather trembled. She adored the feel of his mouth on her body.

"Good?"

She blinked. It took her a few seconds to clear her mind and realize what he was saying. She managed a quick sip of the brew, wondering why she took it. She hated beer. "Yes, especially on a hot night like this." With a smile she said, "No wonder the girls used this as the major ingredient in the all-natural face mask they coated each other with the other night." Heather laughed at the face Quinn made.

"Pretty night," he murmured softly.

"I should go inside." She spoke her thoughts aloud as she realized that wasn't what she wanted. She longed to stay right where she was, with Quinn.

"Stay . . . please." He tried not to think of just how much even a few minutes alone with her meant to him.

"Are the girls asleep?"

"They're in bed, which is distinctly different. There was plenty of giggling going on when I checked on them before I came out."

They exchanged a smile.

"When we were little, I remember my folks taking us kids on picnics to the state park in Bay City. We had a ball. We used to run up and down the hills. It was such great fun. We would play on the beach all day. At night when the stars came out, they seemed so much brighter, bigger than in the city . . . like tonight." Her glance strayed to him. She found herself asking, "Why don't you ever talk about yourself? You've never told me about your parents . . . your brother."

"It's not a pleasant story, Heather."

"That's it? That's the whole story?"

"Yeah." He took a deep swig from his beer.

"I've told you about my whole life. You've told me nothing!" Heather stared at him, unable to accurately read the shadows in his eyes.

Quinn was tempted to lift the small hand that lay on her lap and press a kiss into its center. Instead he slowly finished his beer and placed the bottle on the table at his elbow.

One of Cynthia's accusations, made months before, suddenly came to mind. She told Heather that her father hadn't cried when her mother died, hadn't shed a single tear. Maybe he didn't know how to cry. Did he keep the pain and bitterness locked inside? If so, that certainly explained his ulcer.

Heather broke the silence. "It's believed that a man's life expectancy is shorter than a woman's due mainly to his inability to express, thus release his emotions."

"Where did you hear that? On the *Oprah Winfrey* show? You don't honestly believe that, do you?"

"Of course I do." She shifted, unintentionally brushing her leg against his hard muscular thigh and quickly moved away.

"I intend to live to be a very elderly gentleman." He grinned. "Want this?" He indicated the nearly full bottle she was holding.

"I prefer iced tea."

His senses flared as he drank from the bottle, wishing it were her mouth he was covering with his own, exploring its sugary depths. Now that they were finally alone, he was aching from her. But he made no move to touch her.

Heather stared down into the gentle rippling water in the pool. He was too attractive. Quinn probably had women falling all over themselves to get next to him. Oh, why was she tormenting herself this way? She needed to get as far away from him as she could.

"You're awfully quiet. What's wrong?"

"Good night, Quinn."

"What do you mean, good night? We haven't said a half dozen words to each other today." He caught her wrist, gently massaging the soft inner flesh. "Stay with me. Let's watch the sunrise. The breeze is so nice off the bay."

From the instant he'd arrived, she'd struggled against her feelings for him. Frankly she was exhausted from the effort. She couldn't seem to stop loving him. She longed for him to be everything a man can be to a woman . . . lover, friend, someday . . . husband. But he was denying her even a corner of his world.

She didn't look at him. She couldn't. Her emotions were too close to the surface.

"Heather?"

"This is ridiculous. We can't stay out here all night."

"Why not? I've missed you, pretty girl."

"Oh really? That's news to me." She glared up at him. "You haven't called me once since I've been here. Let go of my hand," she hissed, absolutely furious with him.

"Woman, you're driving me up a wall!" he said in exasperation.

"Good!" she snapped at him, trying to ignore the way her skin still tingled from his caress. She folded her arms beneath her breasts. "You've annoyed the hell out of me for weeks!"

They were both on their feet now.

He couldn't help himself, he needed to touch her. He

cupped her slim shoulders. He swore when she tried to pull away. "Stop that!"

"You stop!"

"Why are you so angry? And it can't be over a telephone call."

"Why not? It's all we have." She stopped, realizing her voice was trembling.

"Heather—"

"Those calls made me feel as if you cared about me," she whispered, unable to look at him.

"I do care about you. That's not the issue. I didn't call because I thought it would be easier on both of us." He sighed. "Those calls were starting to mean too much. They left me lonely and miserable without you. I thought if I didn't call we both would cool down a bit. I'm sorry. I didn't do it to hurt you." When he tried to pull her close, she held him at arm's length. "Baby, don't be mad. Let me hold you. Give me that much."

"Oh, Quinn . . ." she said in a whisper, fighting for control of her emotions. "It's pointless. We have an agreement."

"I know, but I can't help myself. You've kept me away from you all day. Give me some of your sweet sugar, girl." The lower half of his body seemed to have conquered his brain. His breath warmed her lips, but he didn't take them. He needed her precious offering.

Heather shook her head, in spite of the sweet yearnings inside demanding her surrender. She swayed, like a moth circling a flickering flame, coming closer, ever mindful of the danger that could destroy it. His mouth represented the fire, a temptation she had promised to resist.

"The girls—"

"Are in bed," he finished for her. "Heather . . ." He lifted her chin.

Heather sighed in defeat, curling her hands around his neck and pressing her fingers into the thick, crisp hair at his nape. She went up on tiptoes to bring her mouth against his. His lips were cool, firm yet soft and dangerously inviting. His tongue was waiting, eager to remind her of the sensual pleasure he alone could give.

Quinn cradled her. "Oh, Heather . . ." His kisses were like a meteor shower, raining sparks of heat, light, and wonder over her.

They were so absorbed in each other that neither noticed Cynthia standing by the screen door. Her hand went to her mouth as she realized what they were doing. She spun on bare feet and raced back to her room.

Eventually he eased away, but only long enough for Heather to regain her breath. When his lips returned to hers, she played with his tongue, teasing, tasting, then suckling. Quinn growled, rubbing his thumbs against the hard peaks of her breasts. Oh, yes . . . yes. Quinn lifted her so he could cradle her soft buttocks in his palms, fitting his arousal between her soft thighs, and erotically massaging her feminine mound. Heather moaned so sweetly, making him wonder how had he survived without her these past weeks? How?

"No!" she gasped for breath. They couldn't make love.

"Heather—" All he could focus on was her and the sweet pleasure of being back in each other's arms.

"We can't do this, Quinn—especially with the girls in the house. Let me down." She didn't breathe until her feet made contact with the flooring. She was trembling so badly, she would have fallen if he hadn't been supporting her.

Heather knew that it wasn't only the girls holding her back. She didn't have much pride left, but she wasn't about to beg him to change his mind.

He held his mouth taut as he fought the fury of his passion. "Alright. I'll make up the sofa bed in the living room. You take the bed in the loft."

"But it's your room. I can sleep downstairs."

They squared off like two old war enemies, tired of fighting but knowing no other way to settle their differences. And they knew the problem had nothing to do with who should sleep where but had everything to do with the fact they both yearned to be in the same bed.

He surprised her when he said, "Okay . . . you win." He rubbed at the tense muscles in his neck. "Good night."

Twenty

Heather quietly opened the door to the guest room her nieces shared. Both girls were sound asleep. The screened windows had been left open, the ceiling fan hummed softly overhead. Heather watched them lovingly before tiptoeing through the bathroom which connected the two bedrooms.

Cynthia was lying facing the wall, her arm flung over her face. She was careful not to move. She was too upset to talk to Heather, especially after seeing her father and Heather kissing. Cynthia told herself that if her father just had to have a woman friend, Heather wouldn't be so bad. But Heather would be taking her mother's place, wouldn't she? Cynthia could never agree to that. She loved her mother.

But Cynthia also loved Heather. Was it wrong of her to want Heather to be her new mom someday? Because that was what she wished sometimes. It was something she hadn't even told Dr. Ann.

Heather bent and pulled the sheet over her bare legs before she tiptoed out and closed the door softly behind her, unaware of the tears that soaked the girl's pillow as she cried herself to sleep.

Quinn had opened and made the sofa bed with fresh linen. A summer blanket was folded at the foot. The screened patio door had been left open, and huge ceiling fans circulated the night air.

Heather kicked off her sandals before shedding her clothes down to her blue lace-edged teddy. She sighed, curling up in the center of the bed and hugging her knees to her chest. It had been an exhausting day. Like a fool, she'd tried to outrun her feelings for Quinn. All for nothing.

Seeing Quinn again had proven that neither time nor distance nor even the possibility that he might still be in love with Peggy had changed what she felt. She was hopelessly in love with the man.

Hot and sticky, she impatiently brushed a braid away from her damp forehead. God help her, she was jealous. She wanted what had once belonged to his wife. She wanted the man and the girl. She wanted to watch Cynthia develop into a well-adjusted, happy young woman. She longed to be the woman Quinn reached for during the night—the woman sharing his life and his dreams for the future. She especially wanted to carry his sweet brown babies. She hadn't planned for this love, but she couldn't change it.

And tonight, no matter how difficult it might be for her to admit, she knew that despite it all she wanted to be with Quinn. Heather wanted to sleep in his arms.

Telling herself she would only take a shower and leave him undisturbed if he was asleep, Heather's feet sank into the thickly carpeted staircase. It wasn't a question of whether or not Quinn would welcome her appearance in his room. Her problem was much more basic. She wanted his love. It probably would be better for them both if he were sleeping.

The drapes were pulled back and the windows open, taking advantage of the cool breeze off the bay. A full moon illuminated the room. Quinn was stretched out on his stomach. His head rested on upraised hands, and his face was turned away from the stairwell that opened into the room. The top sheet was at the foot of the large brass bed. He was nude. The bare expanse of his six-two masculine beauty caused her to catch her breath and pivot sharply. She was shaking so badly that by the time she reached the bathroom, she had to lean against the patterned-glass door for support.

Even with it closed, she could still see Quinn's deep brown torso gleaming in the moonlight. His trim waist flowed into bold curves of firm buttocks and long expanse of muscled thighs, strong calves, and narrow feet. Every inch of him so wonderfully familiar.

"Get a grip, girl" she scolded herself, turning on the full force of the shower spray. She scrubbed her body with unnecessary vigor. She was still trembling when she switched off the hot water and let ice cold water cascade down her heated flesh. By the time she dried herself she was shivering with cold, but trembling in wild expectation.

As she creamed her skin with perfumed body lotion, Heather tried not to think of his hands and mouth on her body. She stood for the longest time in the dark, letting her eyes adjust and giving her breath a change to slow. She'd changed into the mauve satin, lace-edged, thigh-length gown and robe she'd left hanging in the bathroom. Her heart was racing as she cautiously opened the door and considered making a dash for the stairs . . . naturally without so much as a glance at him.

When her toes curled into the carpet, she realized she was in trouble. Quinn had shifted. He was on his back now, one hair-roughened leg bent at the knee, his hands at his sides. He didn't say a word. He waited. But his dark eyes scrutinized her with raw masculine hunger that was unmistakable.

"I didn't mean to wake you." She didn't move. She couldn't tear her eyes away from him.

"The girls?" he asked softly.

"Asleep . . ." her voice trailed off. She was forced to swallow but she couldn't seem to divert her gaze.

Quinn felt no compunction about his nudity. His body demanded that he take what he needed while his heart warned him that he would never get enough of this woman. She made him feel things he had never felt before. He'd been wrong to board the plane in D.C. thinking he'd come to terms with his need for Heather. He been wrong . . . so wrong.

After one look at her this morning, he finally acknowledged the depths of his feelings and passion for Heather. As he lay watching her, he trembled, imagining her cries of pleasure, her soft body convulsing beneath him as her carefully constructed defenses shattered in a billion pieces.

This had nothing to do with Cynthia. Nothing to do with his love or devotion to his child. No, this was between him and Heather. And it was extremely elemental.

He'd spent too much time away from her, denying his feelings for her. So he concentrated on her golden beauty draped in that unnecessary bit of fluff. His nostrils flared and he eagerly inhaled, hoping to catch her scent. His eyes smoldered. He was trembling . . . losing control. Abruptly he jerked his head away, rolling onto his side, away from her. He ground his teeth in mute frustration, forcing himself to ignore the urgent dictates of his manhood.

There was no doubt that he wanted her, but he wanted her willing. And he appreciated her respecting his wishes to let Cynthia come first before their own needs. The problems weren't hers. They were his.

The effort of not touching her caused beads of perspiration to appear on his forehead, the taut muscles in his throat to stand out as he clenched his teeth. Quinn's entire body seemed to throb with need. He left it up to her . . . either go or stay. Finally, unable to bear the agony of having her there and not being able to touch her, he grated impatiently, "Go to bed, Heather."

"Not alone." She came around the foot of the bed. Her eyes collided with his. "I'm tired of fighting my feelings. I want to be here . . . with you."

Slowly Heather let her robe glide down her arms, then she slid first the right and then the left strap of her short nightgown off her petal-soft golden shoulders. The lace-edged bodice clung to the voluptuous swells of her body, then slid away from her chocolate-brown nipples, slipping down past the thick black curls veiling her womanly mound before it fell past her smooth thighs and calves and pooled at her feet.

Quinn released a harsh groan. "Pretty girl, you're even more beautiful than I remembered." Then he took huge gulps of air into his lungs, for it seemed while she disrobed he had forgotten to breathe.

How badly did he want her, she wondered. Would he

let his head rule his heart and fight his desire for her? She was taking a chance by offering herself to him. It was too late to stop now.

"That stuff about a cold shower is a lie. It didn't do a thing for me. I still want you."

Quinn's slow smile brought her eyes to the shape of his mouth and caused her heart to race wildly within her chest. "I could have saved you the torture. I tried it not half a hour before you came up." He patted the bed. "Care to share a little body heat?"

Her dark eyes were full of laughter and love as she dropped into his eager arms. "Come on, Counselor. It was ninety-eight in the shade today." She traced the shape of his mustache with a slim finger.

"Mere technicality," he murmured, pressing his lips against the base of her throat. He called forth every bit of his remaining self-control not to crush her to him. Now wasn't the time to rush, but to savor. His mouth covered hers and leisurely explored the mole at the corner that had been driving him mad with desire, before sucking her fleshy bottom lip into his mouth. He bit it, then worried the spot with his tongue. But the sweetness of her mouth overwhelmed him. He wasn't satisfied with teasing. They'd been apart for too long. He was starving for her and soon took ravenous kisses.

He sent primitive fire as old and hot as the African sun pulsing through her bloodstream. Her entire being was suddenly alive, drinking in the taste, the feel, the smell, and the fierce heat of the man. Quinn was her man . . . her own black prince . . . her heart.

Heather caressed his dark length. She ran her sensitive fingertips over the smoothness of his shoulder, savoring the sinew and ripples of his back. Her senses flamed as she smoothed her palms down to his flanks.

He voiced his approval as she moved her hands over him. But when her soft hands cupped and gently caressed his most sensitive points, he found himself shaking from head to toe. Her fingertips were as wonderfully light as the wings of a butterfly. She made it so good for him . . . too good almost as he clenched his teeth. Heather enclosed his erection in her soft hands and gave him the firm caresses he craved. He was so close to letting go, his entire body shuddered and he quickly captured her hands, clasping them around his neck and holding her close to his wildly beating heart.

Heather held on to him, pressing her soft breasts into his chest, rubbing her nipples against him. She answered the unmistakable message he communicated with his tongue by taking it into her mouth and sucking.

Quinn's hands roamed down the sides of her body until he reached the soft flare of her hips. She filled his hands as if she'd been made especially for him. Possessively he cupped and squeezed her lush behind, urging her up against his surging masculinity.

"Quinn," she said, knowing this sweet loving was what she had been waiting for, needed since the moment he arrived. "Please . . ."

He paused, staring into her eyes, losing himself in their warm depths. When he lowered his head to worry the delicate skin behind her earlobe, Heather trembled in response. His tongue felt like hot velvet as he trailed down the side of her neck to the base of her throat. She found herself holding her breath as he continued downward toward her full aching breasts.

She tingled with sensation as he followed the outer curve of her breasts, his mouth hot and wonderful. She couldn't hold back a moan when Quinn's mouth closed over her nipple. He tantalized each peak in turn. She whimpered as the empty place inside of her demanded to be filled. The wet washing of his tongue, the tender scrape of his teeth, the sweet suction on her highly sensitive nipple intensified her longing to such dimensions that she gasped his name aloud. Quinn concentrated on Heather. He fought the hunger to possess and in turn be possessed. He needed this as much if not more than she did. He had been forced to go too long without her. He needed her.

Heather's fingers unknowingly pulled on the short hair at his nape, her fingers wound within the soft thickness. Quinn was oblivious to the pain she caused, his long fingers between her spread thighs, stroking between the damp curls, following the slick folds of her body. Oh, she was hot. But Quinn planned to make her hotter . . . wetter. He replaced his hands with his mouth.

She couldn't contain her sweet pleasure. He gave her exactly what she needed and where she needed it. Her nails scraped into Quinn's shoulder blades as her senses soared and her entire body shuddered with a wonderfully sweet release. Quinn covered her mouth with his, containing her cries of absolute pleasure.

He couldn't wait a half second longer. Quinn pressed slowly into her until he filled her as completely as she filled his heart. Their joining created a tenderness and warmth that was ageless . . . eternal . . . beautiful.

Her name rumbled from his throat as they came together, establishing a driving rhythm that was mutually satisfying. Too satisfying Quinn decided, gritting his teeth. In another few strokes he would explode. He slowed or tried to.

"Quinn . . ." she complained. He soothed her with a long, deep kiss. But Heather refused to be slowed. She was burning up with fever . . . a fever to be consumed by him. She stroked his nipples and licked his throat while quickening the alluring movement of her hips against his surging strength. Quinn groaned, unable to resist her urgency. If she wanted it quick and rough, that was what she was going to get. He lifted her thighs so that she was completely accessible to his full force. Sweat poured off him as he worked to satisfy her.

"Oh . . . oh," she whimpered close to his ear. Her instinctively tightened inner muscles sent him over the edge. Quinn's control crumbled as they reached a violently sweet completion together.

The warm soft breeze coming through the window was soothing. It was a lovely night, a cloudless night. Heather rested in a tangled heap beneath Quinn. Gradually her breathing quieted, and with her cheek against his chest, she focused on the steady rhythm of his heart.

Lacing his fingers into her thin loose braids, he gently tugged until she lifted her lips for a poignantly tender caress. She smiled, thoroughly pleased by the satisfaction she read in his eyes. With a contented sigh, she turned onto her side with her back against his front, his long legs curved possessively around hers, his arms cradling her against his chest.

"Sleepy?" He pressed his lips into her hair.

"Mmmm." Long ebony lashes drifted down. "But I can't sleep here with you."

Quinn unconsciously tightened his arms around her. "Sleep. Let me worry about the girls."

"But—" Heather's mind was so hazy with fatigue that she couldn't seem to organize her thoughts.

"Shush, I'm here . . . sleep."

She did, unaware of the man who watched her through the night.

The morning sun was high in the sky, Quinn noted as sweat poured off him. He ran with rhythmic ease across the hard-packed sand. His body felt loose, his muscles worked in perfect symmetry, his heart beat vigorously. Another half mile and he'd start back. His pace didn't slow. He knew what his body was capable of. What he couldn't begin to understand was his heart. His feelings were so chaotic he was unable to contain them. Each stride served to loosen the tension from his body. But the real war raged on inside his head.

He'd left Heather's side just before dawn, while the sky was still inky black with just a hint of violet. She was curled around her pillow like the sexy kitten he once likened her to. She'd been exhausted—and with good reason. After only a few hours of sleep, he'd awakened her and they'd made love again. For one enchanting night he had forced back all thoughts, all fears, and concentrated on one thing—making love to Heather.

Heather . . . Her name slid from his lips with the anguish and bittersweet longing lodged in his heart. He was deluding himself if he thought one night could eliminate a lifetime's worth of longing. Heather was just so special. It had gotten so bad that he could no more control his need for her anymore than he could halt the flow of the wind or yank the stars from the heavens.

What was that song? "Just one look, that's all it took," he hummed to himself. He swore impatiently. He was worse than a kid at Christmas. Heather entered a room and his carefully constructed equilibrium flew out the nearest window.

Last night she'd stood beside the bed, simply looking at him. He'd forgotten everything. All he knew was that he had to make love to her. In truth, the second he had heard the water hit against the glass shower stall, his thoughts had gone wild. Through the patterned-glass door he watched the way the water sprayed along her petite frame. Saw the beads of moisture falling onto her upturned face, into her dark hair, down her neck, over her shoulders, around and over her full round breasts, then along her satiny smooth middle, into the ebony curls between her rounded thighs, along her beautifully shaped calves and small feet. Quinn had been fully aroused long before she opened the bathroom door.

When Quinn had left her side, he'd closed the drapes, then pulled on pajama bottoms and a robe before going down to the sofa bed. There had been no point in borrowing trouble. Cynthia was getting stronger each day. More confident than ever before. But Cynthia continued to see Heather as her friend, not as his lover. Perhaps he should discuss it with the therapist. His last thought before he went to sleep had been to wonder if he really cared what anyone thought of his relationship with Heather . . . including his child.

The girls' giggling attempt in the kitchen while trying to be quiet roused him. He'd joined them and shared a breakfast of runny eggs and burnt toast and orange juice. Quinn had persuaded the girls to let Heather sleep.

After assuring himself that they had enough money to rent bikes and have lunch and dinner out, he waved them off. But not before administering a stern warning to the Hunter twins to take care on the freeway and watch out for the girls. Quinn managed to slip Cynthia his gold card in case of an emergency and reminded all of them to return no later than eight that evening.

He grinned as he thought of Heather's nieces. They were so much like their aunt that he couldn't help the affection that welled inside of him. The girls were young, but with a budding beauty that might one day rival the beautiful woman asleep in his bed. For an instant he imagined his son suckling at Heather's breasts. They could make such sweet babies together.

"Dear God," he prayed softly, "Help me . . . I love her." He stumbled, almost sprawling facedown on the sand as he recognized his feelings. He was in love with Heather.

No! Please . . . not that. Anything but that, he moaned as if in agony. He couldn't go through that kind of torment again. Once was enough for any sane man. He swore expansively, his stride no longer strong or even. The roar of his refusal was like a thunderstorm mushrooming inside his head.

Pivoting sharply, Quinn ran into the surf while anguish rose within him as swiftly as the water level. He plunged full force into the crashing waves as hot tears blinded him. He wouldn't love again! He couldn't. He'd rather burn in the fires of hell than endure that acute state of vulnerability. How could he have done such a dumb-ass thing?

He had loved Peggy, given her his entire heart. Her sudden loss had nearly destroyed his sanity. He remembered her as she looked the night before her surgery. Her soft pleas replaced the roar of the surf.

"Don't! Please, Quinn, don't make me to go through with this," she had begged as hot tears streamed down her cheeks. Her large black eyes were like limpid pools of misery and fear. It was as if she'd predicted her own death.

He didn't understand her reluctance. He loved her and wanted her to live. He came from proud, strong men . . . warriors. He wanted her to fight the cancer that threatened her life and their lives together. He wouldn't even entertain the idea of not sharing the years ahead with her and their baby girl. Peggy was too young to be facing death . . . too young.

Perhaps he wouldn't have experienced such guilt later if he hadn't been the one to discover the lump in her breasts. But he had. And he'd insisted that she undergo the double mastectomy. Peggy resisted, refusing to even consider facing life with vital parts of herself missing. They'd argued over it, including the day of the surgery. She'd cried and pressed her small hands protectively to her breasts.

No matter how many women the doctor had persuaded to talk with her while she'd been in the hospital, women who lived full productive lives after this type of surgery, Peggy was frightened. She was terrified by the possibility of being disfigured, of still having the cancer, and most of all convinced regardless of what he said that Quinn would eventually stop loving her.

In the end Peggy signed the consent forms because she was unable to withstand the pressure Quinn placed on her. Vanity be damned, he thought, Quinn wanted his wife alive, breasts or no breasts. He believed he could cope with anything as along as he had Peggy.

On the morning of the surgery, Peggy had kissed Quinn and Cynthia as if she never expected to see them again. She'd clung to him, her eyes swimming in tears, hearing but not accepting his unwavering insistence that she would be fine.

Elaine and Darnell had waited with him through the surgery while he'd sent Cynthia home with Mrs. Thornton. Although his stomach had been a hard ball of tension, he couldn't swallow anything, not even antacids. He'd gone to the chapel, prayed as hard as he knew how that she be spared, constantly reassuring himself that he'd done the only thing he could.

When he'd returned to the waiting room he discovered he'd lost his wager with God. Quinn had gambled with Peggy's life and lost. She had died on the operating table from heart failure. They'd been unable to revive her. A young, healthy woman was dead . . . a vital part of himself had been buried alongside her.

Five years hadn't altered the trauma of that day nor had he been able to forgive himself for forcing her into the surgery. Maybe she would have lived only a few months without the surgery. No, he thought, he'd wanted her alive. He just wished she had forgiven him, trusted him. Not leaving him alone wondering if she ever would have forgiven him. Quinn couldn't forget, nor had he forgiven himself.

Quinn eventually dropped exhausted on the beach. The sun dried the moisture from his skin and hair as he sat brooding over his options.

He'd really messed up. When it came to love, he didn't even know the ground rules. Logic and factual deductions didn't apply. If he had had any sense at all, he wouldn't have gone near Heather Gregory in the first place. Considering his past history, he was crazy to have even kissed her. His good intentions had lost out to his hot-blooded attraction to her. But he had wanted her so badly that night in her condo, he had stopped thinking and let his hormones take over.

Quinn couldn't handle the fact that Heather made him feel things not even Peggy had made him feel. It was a different kind of love. It was deep, it was hot, it was damn scary.

So now what? Just this morning he entertained the idea of bringing their involvement out into the open. That was before he knew he was in love with her. Heather deserved better than what he had to offer. She deserved a man who was whole on the inside. A man who could give her the kind of love and lifelong commitment she needed. She deserved a wedding ring and bridesmaids and babies . . . lots of babies. She deserved the very best.

How was he going to find the strength to let her go?

Twenty-one

Heather sat with her feet tucked under her, deep in thought. A mug of coffee cooled on the low table in front of her. The revised dissertation rested in the unopened folder beside her.

She'd awakened late that morning, with thoughts only for Quinn. Was it any wonder? The pillow next to her still held his scent and she was satiated from his love-making.

How could she have actually thought she could stay away from him? She actually believed that she was immune to his seductive smiles and dark eyes. It was only a matter of time until her emotions took over. There was no room in her heart for regret. She'd given herself to him . . . asking for nothing in return . . . but hoping someday to have his heart.

When the patio door slid open, Heather turned toward the sound. Her eyes collided with his. A tingling started in her toes, and went right through her.

"So, sleeping beauty is up and about," he teased, his voice heavy with emotion. Although determined to keep his heartache to himself, he failed to prepare himself for the impact of seeing Heather so soon after discovering how he felt about her. One glance into her brown eyes and he was ready to beg if necessary for more of her sweet loving.

She went over to him, her soft smile inviting. He was dressed in black shorts and sleeveless T-shirt. "Good morning—or should I say good afternoon since it's nearly noon?" Her arms moved up his damp chest to lock around his neck, her eyes focused on his beautiful mouth.

"You'll get wet and gritty," he warned, yet he made no effort to avoid the irresistible offer in her upraised face. He bent his head, needing to sample her mouth. His hands rested low on her spine where her small waist flared into shapely hips.

Why now, after all this time? He'd been without a woman for more years than he cared to count. Yet Heather had managed the impossible. She filled the empty spaces inside of him.

But he owed her so much already. She was responsible for the present closeness he shared with his daughter. She'd even given them the push needed to get them into therapy. And even though she wasn't Cynthia's counselor anymore, she continued to give the feminine support and love his daughter so desperately needed.

Quinn was nobody's fool. He'd experienced enough women to know that Heather was one of a kind. As he looked into his special lady's eyes, his emotions seemed to fuel a warmth and tenderness that he hadn't known he was capable of. As her name and scent went to his head, he knew how much he needed her and didn't want to let her go . . . not ever. She was compassionate and generous. She provided a tranquility that had been painfully absent from his life. She made him laugh. She made him feel.

Quinn's hold on her tightened. What began as a simple kiss deepened, becoming much more. Heather opened her mouth to him, responding to his urgency. She gave no thought to withholding even a tiny portion of herself. Quinn explored the cool smooth surface of her teeth before delving into the warmth of her mouth. Yes—oh, yes, he thought as he found then stroked her tongue with his.

Heather . . . Heather . . . he said her name inside his head. If he had her, he would have all the woman he would ever need.

When he finally lifted his head, he couldn't think beyond his hunger for her. "I can't seem to stop wanting you."

Heather was busy bathing the wide planes of his chest with searing hot kisses. His scent was so earthy and male, she longed to once again know his lovemaking. They exchanged a series of electrically charged kisses that left them both weak with desire.

Fingers laced, they crossed the width of the living room and mounted the stairs to the loft. They helped each other undress. Her top and shorts closely followed his things.

When he pulled her down on top of him onto the recently made bed, she said against his mouth, "Hurry, baby." Each velvety brush of her tongue over his declared her urgency.

Quinn chuckled, one ebony brow lifted as he rolled with her, until he stared down at her from the length of one muscular arm. "What's the rush? Didn't get enough last night?" But even as he asked the question, he knew her eagerness couldn't match his. His restraint was sadly lacking. His hands were trembling as they moved down her back.

She giggled unashamed of her desire for him. Her arms tightened around him, bringing her hips into contact with his. She closed her eyes as she rubbed the aching tips of her breasts against his chest, causing delicious shivers of pleasure to pool between her thighs. He hadn't touched her there, yet she was ready for him.

Whatever Quinn had been about to say was forgotten. He gently cupped her shoulders and ran his mouth over the fullness of each breast. He kissed his way down her body. Each nipple was treated to his unwavering devotion, first circling it over and over again with his tongue, then suckling intently. Heather could only moan with pleasure as increased fire licked at her womb.

Although intent on tantalizing them both, he was quaking to be inside her sweet body. She was so wondrously hot that he sank into her in a kind of desperation—it was almost as if he feared she might vanish. Heather gave freely of herself, silently vowing her love for him with each seductive movement of her hips. They challenged each other, not holding back any part of themselves. They each concentrated on pleasing one another. But the passion couldn't be contained . . . it was too exciting, too sizzling hot to last for long. All too soon they were forced to give in to it. Heather's small frame shuddered in mind-shattering pleasure and Quinn was close behind—his own climax was amazingly sweet.

When he could speak, he asked, "Did I hurt you?" He looked down at her with heavy-lidded eyes. Their limbs intertwined and their bodies still joined.

He studied her flushed cheeks. Rose tinted her swollen lips and the thin ebony braids spread across the pillow. He smiled. But the smile didn't quite reach his eyes, they remained dark, almost brooding.

"Quinn?" she questioned, lifting a hand to his stubbled cheek.

"Mmmm, I need a shave and shower. Care to share? The shower, that is?"

Heather didn't have to be told that something was bothering him. Apparently he didn't plan on discussing it. Heather told herself there was no reason to worry. Quinn was a private man. He wasn't used to sharing his thoughts, his worries. She would just have to accept that about him.

Maybe he just needed time. She cautioned herself to take it one small step at a time. They were together now, so she could afford to be patient. As long as she could keep on seeing him, spend time with him, she could cope. She could deal with Cynthia's objections to their relationship and she could even deal with her own doubts about his feelings for his late wife. Or at least she thought she could. The one thing she couldn't handle was not being a part of his life. She reassured herself that he'd proven again and again how much he wanted her.

Heather giggled when he tugged her along with him into the bathroom. She adjusted the spray of the water while he lathered the lower half of his face. Although he worked methodically, he studied her mirrored length from where he stood at the sink.

"Save me some hot water," he said, enjoying the curves of her behind before she disappeared inside the stall.

She'd finished rinsing suds from her body when he joined her. She smiled as he ran his smooth jaw against her creamy wet throat. His shoulders blocked the spray.

"Miss me?" he teased, his gaze momentarily caught in hers. Quinn began soaping himself before he settled her against him. She was so tiny, she didn't reach his shoulder.

But she was all woman and she aroused powerful sensations within him. Emotions so consuming that Quinn hated the thought of losing her. Love was too damn painful. He'd survived its loss once, just barely. Quinn seriously doubted he was capable of doing so again. Yet he refused to even consider giving her up. He was being selfish, but he couldn't help it.

"Are you sore, sugar?"

She smiled, her heart softened by his concern. "A little," she admitted with a blush. "Did the girls get away smoothly? I didn't hear them leave this morning."

"No problem. They each had a day's worth of money and warnings to take care." He shivered, enjoying the feel of her soapy hands caressing his chest. "They're under orders to be back no later than eight. Kevin and Keith are reliable kids."

"I'm glad one of us was awake. I can't believe I slept at all, especially with the girls in the house," she confessed, her face hot with embarrassment.

"Stop that." Quinn grinned, his open palm following the wet length of her spine. "Our privacy wasn't violated. I moved to the sofa bed just before dawn."

"Thank you." She sighed in a rush of relief. "I was so worried—" She pressed her lips to the base of his throat. The hot flick of her tongue had him erect and hungry against her soft belly. "Did you eat?"

Quinn turned her toward the spray, rinsing them both. Heather was trembling, not from the temperature of the water but his hot tongue laving her neck.

"I breakfasted with the girls." He cupped her hips, lifting her up and positioning her limbs around his waist. His breath warmed her neck as he investigated its silky wet length.

"Quinn—" she gasped as she felt him surge against her moist femininity.

"Too sore?"

"No . . . Hurry . . ."

He groaned low in his throat as he slowly gave her what they both wanted.

"You're insatiable," she gasped into his neck.

"Uhh-huhh." She was right—He couldn't get enough of her. Yet he knew deep in his heart that he didn't want her hurt. And if he didn't let her go, that's exactly what would happen. He'd end up hurting her. That was something he refused to do. Quinn's heart ached as he made love to Heather for the very last time.

Their loving was exquisitely slow. He did his utmost to make it very good for her. Lost in the pleasure Heather voiced her love to him as she reached her release just seconds before his quaking climax. When Quinn eventually allowed her feet to touch the wet tile, his kiss was brimming with love . . . tenderness . . . despair.

Heather clung to him. Was it possible that she loved him more than before? The water was starting to cool as she ducked around him, soaped herself quickly before rinsing off.

"Where you going?"

"I'm starving." She grabbed a warm towel from the heated bar.

"Ah, food—the essence of survival."

"Chicken salad?"

"Mmmm."

She leaned inside to press her soft lips against his, ever so briefly, before leaving to dress and start their meal.

Heather was slicing fresh pineapple when Quinn appeared.

"Need help?"

Heather's smile was warm with love. Her eyes danced as she enjoyed the way his faded jeans hugged his hips and thighs. A short-sleeved cream knit shirt covered his chest. "Hope you're hungry."

Their lovemaking had been glorious, more wonderful than ever. Heather was happy. Happy to be back with him. Thrilled at the prospect of spending the next few hours alone with him. But Quinn wasn't as carefree as she would have liked. Something was still bothering him. It was in his eyes.

He towered over her as she worked at the counter in bare feet. His dark gaze warmed her shoulders and throat left bare by a strapless peach sundress. Quinn frowned, knowing that making love had merely taken the edge off his wanting. Even though his body was satiated, his heart and soul were in need.

But what really alarmed him was that he was so captivated by Heather that he had trouble remembering Peggy. She was no longer fresh in his mind. His feelings for Heather went even deeper than those he had for his late wife. He no longer woke in the night wishing for Peggy. His tender thoughts and amorous fantasies had all been directed toward Heather since the instant she walked into his office.

And now that Heather had taken his heart, his sexual needs rode him hard. He found nothing could ease the ache, not work or sports, nothing except making hot sweet love to Heather. What could she be getting out of their complicated relationship but heartache?

"Taste." Heather brought a bit of the sweet fruit to his lips. "Good?" Her eyes sparkled.

Long ago Peggy's eyes had sparkled as Heather's were doing now. Peggy had been there for him from the very first. Without her encouragement and her financial support, he probably wouldn't have made it through law school. He owed her. She'd had such a hard pregnancy with Cynthia. But she had been so happy as their baby grew inside of her. He remembered Peggy's contentment after Cynthia was born and suckling at her breast. Guilt along with despair surged painfully inside of him.

"Honey?"

"No, thanks." Quinn quickly moved past Heather.

But not fast enough. She saw the anguish on his features. Icy tentacles of fear squeezed her tender heart. She didn't have to be told he was thinking of Peggy. She knew.

"What do you need me to do?"

"The table, please. I'm almost finished here. Then we can eat."

They worked in silence.

"Looks good," Quinn said, when she brought in the

plates filled with chicken salad and garnished with freshly sliced fruit topped by walnuts and cream.

Heather smiled, determined to obtain the utmost enjoyment from their time together. The girls would be back before nightfall. And she wouldn't let anything spoil this special day. "Would you bring in the rolls?"

"Sure. How about a white wine?"

"Sounds good. Your home is very lovely, Quinn. Cynthia told me you've had it redecorated."

His nod was his only response as he headed around the counter into the kitchen area.

She fretted despite her best efforts to the contrary.

"Tell me about your case in D.C."

He did, but halfheartedly. His mind was clearly on something else.

Heather's fork clanked against the side of the plate when she finally gave in to her mounting fears. "Quinn, talk to me—tell me what's wrong."

He got up from his chair and went in the kitchen. He returned with an open bottle of whisky.

Her fear was in her throat when she asked, "Are you feeling guilty?"

"What the hell!"

"Well? What am I suppose to think? You're acting as if you're sorry we made love. It's a little late for that now. You wanted me as much as I wanted you." She wasn't going to cry! She wasn't! Quinn was so long in answering that Heather yelled, "Admit it! You feel guilty about making love to me!"

Quinn scowled. She was closer to being correct than she knew. He did feel guilty. But his guilt had nothing to do with what he felt for her.

"I know we agreed to wait until Cynthia finished therapy—"

"This has nothing to do with my daughter."

"Then what is it? Are you wishing I were Peggy? You are, aren't you!"

He stared at her, not quite believing what he just heard. Pain sliced through him. He couldn't speak for a moment.

"I guess what I want to know is when you make love to me, do you wish I were her?"

Quinn said, with his body taut with tension, "You have no right to question me about Peggy! None!"

Heather felt as if he had slapped her. "I'm tired of tiptoeing around it! You've been acting weird since you came downstairs. What else am I supposed to think? You won't talk to me!" She threw her napkin down beside her plate.

"What do you want from me? My gut sliced up in little pieces and hung out to dry?" Quinn felt violated. "Look, I know you deserve an explanation." He hesitated, taking a steadying breath, and instead of reaching for the hard liquor in his glass, he reached to take her hands. The thick pad of his thumb massaged her soft skin. "Please, try to understand. This has nothing to do with how I feel about you. I care about you. But there's so much I can't talk about."

Heather read the turbulent emotions that had become his companions over the years. He was hurting. She wanted to go to him, slide onto his lap, put her arms around him and hold onto him, and hope he found some comfort in their physical contact. But that was impossible.

She chose to tell him what was in her heart. "I love you so much."

"Heather . . ." He sighed, in need of her warmth, desperate for her acceptance. He was weary, bone weary of carrying around this pain. But as much as he wanted her, as much as he loved her, if he stayed in her life he was bound to hurt her.

He should have his butt kicked for starting something he knew he couldn't finish. He should never have touched her in the first place. No matter how much it cost him emotionally, he was going to have to protect her from himself.

"Don't shut me out, Quinn. Please . . . don't push me away."

"I have nothing to offer you."

"Yourself."

"Don't you see? I can't ever give you what you want. Marriage or babies." His voice was rough, laced with bitterness. "It's not fair to you. You deserve so much more than I'm capable of giving."

"Baby, I'm not asking for the world. I only want what you feel you can give. It will be enough." Heather was hurting so bad it took everything she had not to cry. But she sensed her tears would push him even further away.

"That's my point." He tucked a stray braid behind her ear, smoothing it tenderly. "I'll end up hurting you. I don't want to do that to you, sweetheart. I care about you too much."

He couldn't handle any more guilt. And he couldn't give her what she was entitled to. Hell, it was quite possible that he might never be able to reconcile his part in Peggy's death. How could he ask her to wait for him to come to terms with his past? He'd been on this same treadmill for five long years, and there still was no end to it.

"I never asked for a commitment. Where is this coming from? I want what we had last night and today. I'm not talking about the sex. I'm talking about the caring and the sharing. Once we're back home, we'll find a way to be together. What's wrong with that?"

Quinn said through his teeth, "Plenty!" He cupped his glass. But he didn't lift it to his mouth. His stomach was on fire and his heart ached. "I would be doing all the taking and you would continue to do all the giving. You deserve better."

"What I deserve is some honesty. Why do you feel responsible for Peggy's death?" Heather felt his reaction in the tensing of his muscles before he hid behind a wall of indifference.

He grabbed his glass. He crossed to the doorwall, staring out toward the bay. The water was choppy, waves crashing against the rocks. The sun was no longer visible, hidden in the clouds.

"Haven't you got it yet? My past is my own. It's none of your business!"

Heather inhaled sharply, incredibly hurt. Her eyes stung from suppressed tears. Finally she said furiously, "Your marriage may not be my business. But if you think my feelings for you stop at the bedroom door, you're mistaken!" She began clearing the table as if her life depended on it.

He moved to block her way. His nostrils were pinched with frustration. "Heather, you're unhappy. I can't live with that. It has to stop. I won't hurt you day after day, week after week!"

Heather was every bit as angry as he was. She pushed her way past him, careful not to slam a plate upside his hard head.

"Well?"

"What do you want from me, Quinn? You want me out of your life? Is that what this is about? You've discovered you desire me sexually but emotionally I leave you cold. What's your problem, bro? Your conscience can't take it?"

"Is that what you think? You really believe that I'm capable of that kind of deceit?"

"All I know is that I love you and want to be with you. But I can't. You're letting something that has absolutely nothing to do with our relationship tear us apart. It's not fair." She wanted to scream at him . . . to make him see what he was doing to them both. She swallowed the tears in her throat, forced herself to go on. "You've constructed a wall around yourself. I'm not strong enough to push through it, and it's too high for me to climb over. I can't reach you." The tears came quickly but she brushed them away.

Quinn couldn't look at her. He shoved his hands into the pockets of his slacks, his legs apart, his forehead a network of creases as he stared with unblinking fascination at the mosaic tile flooring.

When he spoke his voice seemed to come from far away, deep within his soul. "The past won't let go of me, baby. I've done everything short of chopping my head off to forget. I can't forget." Why couldn't she see that he had no right to even consider making pretty little brown babies with her? He wasn't a free man. "Maybe five years seems like a long time to you. But to me it's like yesterday. I loved Peggy. I didn't want to lose her. I wanted her to live. All I wanted was for her to live." Quinn stopped suddenly, shocked by what he had done. He shouldn't be talking to Heather about Peggy. "It's far from over for me."

"Maybe the first step is talking to the therapist. Getting some grief counseling." When he glared at her, she said, "Not for my sake but for your own . . . and Cynthia's. She deserves to talk to you about her own mother. Quinn, share the pain of your loss with her."

"Enough!" His large frame quivered with the harshness of his emotions. "This is about you and me, Heather!"

She didn't say anything more, she couldn't. He'd as good as pushed her out of his life. There was nothing she could say or do to stop him. He'd made his choice. What he didn't want was her.

She was in so much pain that she wanted to run from it, get away from this house . . . away from his lack of caring and trust in her . . . away from the hopeless despair threatening to drag her under.

"I didn't expect this to happen. Suddenly you were in my life and I couldn't get around my attraction for you."

"Sexual attraction."

"How can you keep saying that? I care about you, damn it! I care about you more than I ever thought I was capable of caring." He was in love with this tiny spitfire of a woman. Heather had somehow managed to weave her way inside of him until she became the very core of his existence. She had wedged herself so deeply in his heart that she had become a part of his soul.

"Then why can't you trust me?"

"I do. You know me better than anyone on this earth. I've told you more about, who and what I am. But . . . Peggy. I can't!"

The sliver of hope that had briefly blossomed in her heart was scattered like the unprotected petals of a rose in a harsh wind. "So it's over."

"Heather, don't you see? I'm too damn hungry for you. I won't be satisfied with an occasional night together. I'm not wearing any halo. And if you think that I'll stand back and watch you dating other men, you're wrong," he grated harshly. "Besides I have a daughter to consider. Cindy's been through enough. She's right in the middle of this thing between us. It's not fair to any of us. And you deserve much, much better."

The silence was deafening.

"If I want to make the connection from Metro, I'd better get a move on."

"You're leaving."

"Yes . . ."

The pain was worse than anything she had ever thought possible. Heather struck out at him in her grief. "You're right. I don't deserve this. And you don't deserve me. I just wish to hell I'd never met you!"

It was useless to pretend one day things might be different. Somehow she would accept his decision. It would no doubt take the rest of her life to manage that feat.

"Goodbye, Quinn," she said as she walked past him. She walked down to the nearly deserted beach, never once looking back. The afternoon and the night stretched ahead as she dropped onto the sand. Clouds rolled in, tears ran down her face.

Twenty-two

It was late, but Heather doubted she had the energy to undress. She compromised by kicking off her heels and lying across her bed. She'd stayed later than planned at the Crisis Center. Tomorrow was a work day and she could no longer sleep late in the mornings. September, with its cooler nights and bright sunny days, had brought a return to normalcy that Heather welcomed.

Congratulating herself on getting through the day without dwelling on what she couldn't change, she jumped when the telephone on the nightstand rang. As she lifted the receiver, she realized her hands were trembling. It wasn't him, she scolded herself. They hadn't spoken since that disastrous July weekend. Late night calls from him were a thing of the past.

"Hello?"

"Heather, I know it's very late, but—"

"Cynthia?" Heather's heart was beating so fast she had to take a quick breath to calm herself. "What's wrong, honey?"

"It's Daddy!"

Heather sat up straight. "What about your father?" When Cynthia's answer didn't come fast enough, Heather demanded, "Has something happened to Quinn? An accident?"

"Nothing like that. But we rushed him to the hospital. It's his ulcer, it's bleeding on the inside. And they want to do surgery. Please, Heather . . . please come." Cynthia was weeping.

"Of course. Just tell me where you are and I'll get there as soon as I can."

"We're at Henry Ford Hospital."

"You're not alone, are you?"

"Miss Mattie and Mrs. Thornton are here. And Mr. Hunter brought us."

Heather issued a sigh of relief. Miss Mattie had come for a visit at the end of the summer. After much prodding, she agreed to stay on as Mrs. Thornton's assistant. The two had become substitute grandmothers to Cynthia.

"Hurry—"

"I'm leaving now."

Heather was so upset that she had to calm herself before she could start the car. Getting into an accident certainly wouldn't help anyone. As she exited the John C. Lodge Expressway just before West Grand Boulevard, she hoped she had her own emotions under control. But by the time she reached Cynthia in the upstairs waiting room, there wasn't a doubt in Heather's mind that she was still very much in love with Quinn Montgomery.

Cynthia rushed into Heather's arms, weak with fright.

"How is he, baby?"

"He's in surgery."

Heather held her tight as she sobbed out her fear. "Calm down," she soothed. "He's strong and he's going to be alright," Heather vowed. She had said her own prayers on the way over.

Once Cynthia had quieted somewhat, they walked arm and arm over to where the ladies were seated.

Heather greeted the two elderly women warmly. "I'm so glad you two are with Cynthia. Sit down, honey." She patted the place next to her.

"I so glad ya came. T'is little gal wouldn' believe us," Miss Mattie said. Heather noticed how nice she looked in a pretty blue dress and hat.

Mrs. Thornton nodded. The two had become friends. "I thought we were going to have to put Cynthia in the next bed beside her dad's."

Cynthia clung to Heather.

"Where's Darnell? I thought you said he drove you here?"

"He's on the telephone."

"What happened?" Heather looked from one concerned face to the other.

"Mr. Montgomery has been off his food for a while. Stomach always hurting, but he won't go to the doctor."

"Mrs. Thornton's being nice. Daddy's been a real bear ever since he got back from Washington. Every week he gets worse. Tonight was when he started throwing up blood. I knew he was feeling bad when he asked me to call Mr. Hunter to take him to the hospital."

Heather frowned, unable to conceal her own fears. "And you couldn't get him to see his doctor before this?" Heather was beginning to feel sick herself. She couldn't stand it if something happened to him. Why didn't he take better care of himself?

"I really did try." Tears pooled in Cynthia's dark gray eyes, eyes so like Quinn's.

"I know you did." Heather hugged her.

Heather knew better than anyone how downright stubborn Quinn could be. He had walked out of her life, walked away from her love. That kind of hurt didn't just disappear. It lingered. And now she was scared, so much so that she didn't ask how long he'd been in surgery. She closed her eyes and continued to pray for his recovery.

"Do you think he's going to die?" Cynthia whispered.

"Stop t'at kind of talk, gal. He be fine, just fine," Miss Mattie insisted. "The Lord lookin' out for 'im."

"My mother died on the operating table. So I know it can happen," Cynthia insisted, wiping at her damp cheeks.

"Listen to me," Heather said, turning her young face toward hers. "Quinn's a strong man. He's in overall good health. He's going to get through this. We're going to be very positive. No negative thoughts allowed."

"Oh, Heather." Cynthia collapsed against her. She whispered so others couldn't hear, "I knew you would come. I love you so much. And I know you love Daddy. I just wish you two would make up."

Heather was thankful that Darnell Hunter chose that moment to return because she was totally lost for words.

"I'm glad you could come. Cynthia was frantic." He gave Heather a hug.

"Darnell. Have you any news?"

"Nothing. They wheeled him up over an hour ago. We should be hearing something soon."

"How's Elaine?"

"Fine . . . Well not quite. She's home recovering from

the flu. That's why she's not here with us. Can I get you ladies some coffee?"

It had taken Heather what was left of the summer to get herself together. Weeks of heartache and disappointment. Empty days without him and even lonelier nights. It seemed the harder she tried not to think of him, the more readily he came to mind.

Heather considered herself lucky. Quinn had been generous with his daughter. Heather and Cynthia saw each other on a regular basis. Heather had been the one to take her shopping for her school clothes. Heather had been the one to listen to the girl's dreams for the future. They talked about all sorts of things. Everything that was except Quinn. By unspoken agreement, Quinn's name was never mentioned. That is until tonight.

"Cynthia?"

She'd been standing near the window. Cynthia jumped, whirling around. "Yes, Dr. Grant. How is he?"

Heather was right beside her.

The doctor had been their family physician for a number of years. "He's made it through surgery just fine. He's in temporary serious condition."

Relief seemed to wash over them. Heather and Cynthia held on to each other.

"When can we see him?"

"Not for a few hours. He's in the recovery room."

"Thank you, doctor." Darnell offered his hand.

Heather quickly added, "Yes, thank you."

"When?" Cynthia asked with youthful impatience.

"He'll be in a great deal of pain when he wakes up. You may want to wait until morning before seeing him."

"Whatever you think best." Darnell looked at the others. "Why don't I take you ladies home? You've got to be exhausted."

The two older woman were clearly in need of rest. Cynthia had so much nervous energy that she couldn't sit longer than a few minutes. Heather was still in such a state of shock that her emotions were chaotic.

She was finally at the point where Quinn Montgomery wasn't her first thought every morning or her last each night. Yet she couldn't seem to stop herself from loving this stubborn man, not even when she knew he couldn't ever return her feelings, and it hurt like hell—but Quinn being ill hurt worse . . . much worse.

"We'll wait, Mr. Hunter. Cynthia's too upset to leave without seeing her father," Mrs. Thornton said, while Miss Mattie nodded in agreement.

"No. You ladies go on ahead," Heather volunteered. "I'll stay with Cynthia and bring her home after she has seen her dad." Like Cynthia, she wasn't about to leave the hospital until she'd seen for herself that Quinn was alright.

"Then it's all set." Darnell nodded. He whispered near Heather's ear, "Call me if there's any change."

She nodded, knowing he meant if Quinn took a sudden turn for the worse. Her stomach knotted with fear.

Cynthia was so quiet once they were alone that Heather said, forcing a reassuring smile, "It won't be much longer before you can see for yourself that he's alright."

Willing herself not to cry, Heather decided she had done too much crying already over that blasted man. All the tears in the world wouldn't change how he felt. Yet she, like his child, couldn't draw an easy breath until she knew he was out of danger.

"His ulcer has been bothering him a lot. He doesn't eat right, skips lunch, and has just coffee and a muffin until dinner time. I hear him at night. He walks the floor until late. He has been miserable since the two of you stopped talking."

"Where did you get the idea that I have anything to do with this?"

"Heather—at least be honest with me. Stop treating me like a kid."

"No . . . I . . . I didn't mean to treat you unfairly. I just don't understand where you got this idea from."

"I've got eyes. I live with him and I spend time with you. Before we went on vacation at Traverse Bay, I knew you and Daddy talked all the time. Heather, I'm not stupid," Cynthia said impatiently. "But since we've been back, it's been terrible. It's like I can't mention his name to you without you getting upset. And Daddy's even worse than you. Now he demands to know everything that you and I do . . . what you said . . . what you have on. He's always asking me questions about you. Why can't you two make up?"

Heather didn't know what to say. She had no idea what to think of Quinn's behavior. Why would he care when he was the one who insisted their relationship had to end? Heather looked at Cynthia. "You've changed your mind?"

"About you and Daddy? Yes. My daddy's so unhappy. I don't like seeing him this way."

"Thank you, Cynthia. It's nice to know you no longer believe I'm trying to take your father away from you. I appreciate your trust. But it's over between us." Heather swallowed with difficulty, her heart felt so heavy. "But it has nothing to do with you. Your father and I don't have to be friends to love you. So honey, don't worry about it. We're both adults—and we've made our choices," Heather ended as calmly as she could manage.

She'd lived on hope for months. No more. It had ended last summer, and she had come to accept that. It didn't matter that she still loved him. What mattered was he no longer wanted her. Nothing was keeping them apart but Quinn. Although Quinn apparently still found her desirable. Evidently that was all it was . . . desire.

"Miss Montgomery?" a nurse asked.

"Yes, ma'am."

"Your father's awake now. You can see him for a few minutes."

"Thanks! Come on, Heather."

It wasn't until they reached his room that Heather began to doubt the wisdom of her presence. She questioned whether Quinn would welcome even a brief visit from her. They hadn't parted very amicably. The very last thing she said to him was that she wished she'd never met him. Heather hung back, allowing Cynthia to go ahead.

Dr. Grant was just leaving. He cautioned, "He's still groggy from the medication. So only stay a few minutes." The nurse was just finished getting him settled when they entered. Cynthia slowly approached the bed.

Quinn's rich dark brown skin had taken on a grayish tint. He looked to be asleep, but he opened heavy lids groggily when Cynthia said his name and took his hand.

Heather remained near the door, taking in all the changes in him. He was thinner, much thinner than she remembered. Heather made no move to approach the bed.

"Daddy, how do you feel?"

"I'm fine, baby girl. It's just the medication making me sleepy," he said thickly, then groaned softly.

"Daddy, I was so scared."

"I'm . . ."

"Heather is here with me." But Quinn didn't hear her. He was asleep.

"Heather!" Cynthia spun around in alarm.

"He's fine, honey. But he's sedated. He needs to get lots of rest so he can heal properly." Heather was in danger of crying herself. She was just as grateful as Cynthia to see for herself that he had made it through surgery. "Come on, honey. Let's get you home."

As they walked arm in arm to the car, Heather gave Cynthia's hand a reassuring squeeze. "I know it's tough seeing him sick like that. But remember, he's going to get a little stronger every day. Before long he'll be just like new."

Once they were under way, Cynthia sighed. "I forgot to ask what time visiting hours are tomorrow morning."

"Morning? What about school? Your father won't like it if you miss classes."

"Just this once. I have to make sure he's okay."

"Well . . ."

"Please, Heather."

"This one time. After this, your visiting hours will have to be after school hours, correct?" Heather didn't want to leave Quinn alone in the hospital anymore than Cynthia did.

"Thanks. I just want to make sure."

Heather brought Cynthia to the hospital the next morning. Although she spoke to his doctor, she didn't see him herself. Quinn had a quiet night and was definitely on the mend. For nearly a week Heather dropped Cynthia off at the hospital after school and picked her up after visiting hours each evening.

When Cynthia questioned her as to why she hadn't visited Quinn herself, Heather claimed that she didn't want to tire him. He needed the rest. Although not pleased with her answer, Cynthia didn't press. But the very next day Cynthia relayed a message from her father. Quinn asked to see Heather. She was so upset she didn't notice the speculative gleam in the teen's eyes.

Heather concentrated on her driving, refusing to panic. It didn't matter why he wanted to see her. All that was significant was that he was the one who had ended their relationship. It was Quinn who didn't have room in his heart for her, not the other way around. But she was the one looking forward not backward. He had lost the best thing that ever happened to him.

So why did she have to bite her lip to keep from crying? So what if she loved him with all her heart. So what that she was thrilled he'd be able to go home within a matter of days? Her emotions were no longer open for his inspection.

She still thought of him late into the night. She'd gotten to the point where she dreamed about him almost nightly . . . sweet, wickedly sensuous dreams . . . memories of their lovemaking. Damn! His was buried so deep in her heart that Heather wasn't certain she could visit him without making a fool of herself.

Despite her misgivings Heather arrived a mere half-hour before visiting hours ended the next evening. Quinn was alone in his room.

"Hi," he smiled, gingerly easing himself up a bit straighter in bed. The television was on, but he hadn't been watching. He clicked it off. "It's good to see you."

Heather sent his senses soaring in spite of the pain in his gut and the medication in his bloodstream. Her fire-engine red coat-dress was piped in a thick black braid and accented with a double row of jet buttons trimmed in gold. She carried a small black leather bag. Heather was stunning. Her soft golden frame was a bit slimmer than the last time he'd seen her. But she was every bit as beautiful. Dear God, he had missed her.

"I'd hoped you'd stop in," he said hesitantly, his dark gaze lingering on her full plump lips.

"I saw you the night of your surgery. How are you feeling?"

He chuckled, holding his stitches. "No wonder I don't remember. I'm better." His medical condition wasn't uppermost in his mind. If his conscience hadn't been kicking his behind, they would still be together. He was responsible for the shadows under her eyes. And he hated it.

"Where's Cynthia?" Heather stood with her arms crossed beneath her breasts, black three-inch heels tapping.

"She went to the cafeteria for a soft drink. She'll be back in a minute. Please sit down." He motioned toward the chair beside the bed.

"No, it's late. Quinn, I'm glad you're feeling better."

Quinn nodded. "You've been very kind to Cindy. Heather, I want you to know—"

Heather had never been particularly interested in his gratitude. She interjected, "I love Cynthia." And she loves me back, unlike you, she thought angrily. "Take care of yourself, Quinn. Oh, tell Cynthia I'll meet her in the lobby. Good night."

"Hea—"

Heather hurried out, telling herself how glad she was she hadn't stayed in a relationship with him. She'd learned from the experience. Unfortunately, she hadn't gotten over it or him. She shouldn't have come at all. It was over between them.

Quinn couldn't see the tears running down her face or hear the bitter sob she choked down. But he felt an ache in his chest that had nothing to do with his medical condition.

Twenty-three

"Just look at them!" Gwendolyn Carmichael said as she and Heather watched their parents dance the anniversary waltz. The sisters were forced to wipe tears from their eyes. Forty-five years today, and the entire family had come together to celebrate.

What had started as a small family gathering had mushroomed into a formal dinner dance at a fashionable downtown restaurant, complete with indoor waterfall and a jazz band. Their family was large enough with all four Gregory brothers and their wives and children to fill the private ballroom. Friends of the family were also included, plus aunts, uncles, and cousins. The restaurant had provided an elaborate spread with a distinctly New Orleans flare.

As the celebrating couple slowly circled the floor, their deep love for each other and appreciation for all that had been done to honor that love was easy to discern.

Once the dance floor began filling with other couples, Gwen tugged Heather's arm. "Come on, sis. You can keep me company while I repair the damage."

"Ericia and Angela look so grown up tonight in their evening gowns." She smiled warmly. "Do you know what those two are up to? They want to fix Cynthia up with cousin Sammy." Heather laughed, not waiting for an answer as they threaded their way through the crowd. "Cynthia looks so pretty in that frothy blue gown we found at Jacobson's, doesn't she? I'm glad the girls are still such good friends. It means so much to her." Heather sat on one of the vanity stools in front of the long makeup mirror.

"Uh-huh," Gwen murmured absently, retrieving a compact and tissue from her purse. Her eyes were on the blue pumps in the stall behind them. This was one conversation she didn't want overheard.

"I'm so glad we did this. Mom and Dad are on top of the world." When her sister failed to comment, Heather questioned, "Gwen?"

"I'll tell you in a minute," she said in a whisper. "That's a lovely dress, Aunt Naomi." She winked at their great-aunt slowly making her way to the sinks.

"Thanks, child," she beamed, every bit as petite and lovely as her two grandnieces. "You girls sure know how to put on the dog. Can't wait to get a piece of that bread puddin' they got out there."

Heather laughed. "Thanks, sweetheart." Giving her a hug, she said, "My, you sure look cute tonight. Great-uncle Jeff is gonna have to watch you."

The older woman giggled like a schoolgirl. "Shame on ya! Your mama and daddy sure look happy. Sweet girls, the both of ya." She kissed them both. "Now you two hurry. The dancing has started."

Once they were alone, Gwen burst out with, "No point in prolonging this. You're going be furious anyway."

Heather teased her. "Can't be that bad. You didn't tell Mama and Daddy about their surprise, did you?"

"I invited both the Montgomerys," she blurted out.

"Quinn?" Heather's eyes widened.

"That's the one," she said, biting her bottom lip as she waited for her baby sister to explode. She didn't have long to wait.

"Gwen! You didn't!"

"I couldn't help myself. Honey, I'm tired of seeing you so unhappy. You love that man."

"That's my problem, not yours! Why can't you mind your own business?"

"You're my business. Now sit down and listen to me."

Heather was fuming, but she complied.

"How are you going to work something out if you won't talk to him?"

"I don't have to listen to this! Gwen, you had no right!"

"I have every right. You're my baby sister—and I love you."

Heather glared ungraciously at her. "Gwendolyn Gregory Carmichael, don't start that baby sister and I love you stuff." But she didn't make an effort to leave. She couldn't, she was on the verge of tears. All because of her meddling sister. "I have nothing to say to him. And not much to say to you, either."

"You haven't talked to Quinn since he was in the hospital. That was two months ago. It's about time you stopped running from your feelings for him. Besides, I'm sick of that man calling me asking about you."

"You've discussed me with him?"

"Well, not exactly. Sis, he cares about you."

"It's over."

Gwen was right. Heather hadn't seen or spoken to him since she'd visited him in the hospital. Thoughts of Quinn were still so painful that Heather forced her mind toward other safer channels. Yet at the most unexpected moments, his image would flood her senses to the point that she couldn't stop herself from remembering. And with those memories inevitably came bittersweet longings.

The cruelest part of it all was that her love for him hadn't stopped. She actually worried about him, wondered if he was taking better care of himself. But her hopes and dreams of a future together were gone. She no longer believed he would conquer the demons that haunted him. In her estimation, Quinn didn't want to let go of the past.

All they ever really shared was Cynthia's love. She was a wonderful girl, and Heather truly appreciated the time he allowed her to spend with his daughter.

Why had she ever confided in her softhearted sister? Stupid! Stupid! Gwen couldn't stand to see anyone she loved in pain. Little Miss Fix-it!

"Heather, please don't be mad. John told me to stay out of it, but I wanted to help. I hate knowing you're miserable."

"Who's miserable? I'm getting my doctorate next month. I'm happy!"

"Like hell."

"I refuse to even think about this, especially tonight of all nights. Gwen, you knew I wouldn't want him here."

"Heather, you love that man. And I honestly believe he cares for you. Why should you both be alone? The anniversary party seemed as good an excuse as any. Besides, you would have killed me if I invited the two of you over for dinner. At least here there are so many people no one will notice."

"If he has nerve enough to show up and spoil Mama and Daddy's party, I won't ever forgive you!" Heather picked up her purse and stormed out of the ladies' room. She bit hard on her bottom lip to keep the tears burning her eyes from falling. Her own sister . . . She and Gwen had worked so hard to make this night unforgettable for their folks. Nothing must spoil this tribute to their parents' love, not even thoughts of what couldn't be.

"You girls sure did a great job. This is some sha-bang, kid. And the music is perfect. The folks love this "muddy water blues." Mark, Heather's eldest brother, swung her around the dance floor.

"Thanks, I'm just so pleased that everyone made it. Even out-of-town folks like you. Isn't that band something? No Hammer time tonight," she laughed.

"Yeah. Mama's been crying nonstop all night. And Daddy is booming with cheer. Great idea." He smiled down proudly at his baby sister as they danced.

Having the family together was a major accomplishment. The siblings threw themselves into sharing their parents' joy, as well as catching up on everyone's news.

"We don't get to see nearly enough of you, Dr. Gregory, big-time professor," she teased.

"Look out—come December and we'll have another Dr. Gregory in the family." They both laughed.

"I can't get over how tall the boys are. You and Janice

seem especially pleased with this latest pregnancy. Trying to get it, right this time?"

Mark chuckled. "We're praying for a little girl, that's for sure. This family could always do with another caramel-eyed midget." He gave Heather an affectionate squeeze.

She laughed, not the least bit put out by his teasing. "I miss you, big brother."

"Ditto! It's great to be back home, even if it's only for a weekend. Gwen's girls are even prettier than they were last Christmas. They look more like Mama each time I see them. Who's that dancing with Sammy?"

"Cynthia Montgomery," Heather said with a smile. Her eyes strayed to the door, and suddenly the air rushed from her lungs.

Standing not five feet away was the last man in the world she wanted to see. And the one she ached to be with. The white dinner jacket set the deep brown tones of his skin into stark relief. He was as good to look at as she remembered. Quinn's eyes slowly swept the room until they reached her. Heather quickly looked away.

"Heather?"

"What did you say?"

"Nothing, just trying to place that name. Montgomery? Is she any relation to the guy Gwen told me about?" Mark frowned when he realized what he'd let slip.

But Heather never heard Mark's question. Her large troubled eyes repeatedly traveled across the room. Why had he come? She wanted to shout at him that he didn't even know her parents. And who was that woman talking to him? That dress looked as if she had been poured into it.

"Are you angry with me?" Mark said, finally intruding into Heather's thoughts.

"No, of course not. Gwen has never been one to keep her mouth shut. Even as a kid she was a known blabbermouth."

They shared an understood laugh.

"Is Montgomery responsible for the shadows under your eyes?"

"Mark . . . it's a long complicated story. Let's talk about something else . . . please."

Heather watched as her sister greeted Quinn, then took his arm and walked him over to the head table where their parents were seated. To Heather's dismay Gwen introduced him to everyone, even all the aunts and uncles. In a few minutes she would no doubt be introducing him to the brothers.

"Would you like me and the boys to take him outside into the alley? No trouble."

Heather laughed in spite of herself as she looked up at her tall, handsome brother. The men in the family were all tall and lean, with skin the color of crushed walnuts, just like their father, while Heather and her sister favored their petite mother.

"I love you. But Mama would take a switch to all of us if you guys got into something here and spoiled their party. I just wish you didn't live so far away."

She refused to think of Quinn.

"I'm a telephone call away, whenever you need me, sis." Mark reminded. "Getting excited about graduation?"

An all too familiar deep baritone spoke from behind her. "May I cut in?"

"Quinn . . ."

"Heather?" Mark was clearly ready to refuse.

Heather reluctantly made the introduction. "Mark Gregory, Quinn Montgomery." The two men shook hands. The music had stopped, momentarily.

Quinn held out his hand as a sultry ballad filled the softly lit room. "Please . . ."

Irresistibly drawn by the mesmerizing warmth of his skin, Heather placed slim fingers into his palm. She managed to give her brother a reassuring nod before Quinn applied gentle pressure against the curve of her spine and eased her into his arms. He slid both hands around her waist, his large body moved with sensuous ease to the pulse of the music. His breath was a warm caress against her gleaming ebony braids. Neither spoke.

Four long desolate months since he'd held her in his arms. Four months since they'd made love. It was all he could do not to crush her to him. He was hungry . . . hungry for Heather. She couldn't help but feel his masculine response to their closeness.

She shivered, hoping to put some space between their bodies. He held her fast. "You shouldn't have come."

"You're beautiful. Is this a new dress? You do wonderful things to it. But I admit I'm prejudiced where you're concerned." He said huskily, "I've missed you, sugar," caressing her soft cheek with a fingertip.

It was hopeless. She just wasn't up to it. "I can't!" She pushed herself away from him and hurried toward the exit. She had to get away before she embarrassed herself and ruined her parents' anniversary party.

The door opened onto a stairwell. When Mark and Carl saw her leave, they started after her. Gwen managed to stop them. Quinn, she noted with satisfaction, was right behind her sister.

Heather leaned against the cool concrete wall near the stairs. She was angry, she was hurt, and she was resentful—all because of him. Despite Gwen's invitation, he had no right to be here! He'd gotten what he wanted . . . everything she had to give. There was nothing left. So why couldn't he leave her alone?

"Heather . . . are you alright?" Quinn was careful not to touch her, but he was close enough to appreciate the floral scent of her perfume.

She'd pulled her curled braids up into a cascading ponytail. Gold clips held it in place. He yearned to kiss the spot where her slender neck and smooth shoulder joined. His intense gaze moved over her bare shoulders and upper swells of her full breasts visible above the black silk strapless sheath. The bodice was embroidered with gold thread as was the wide belt that cinched her narrow waist. The floor-length gown was slit high on one side, tantalizing his senses as he caught an occasional glimpse of her lovely legs. He buried his hands in his pockets to keep from touching her.

"No! I'm not alright! I can't believe you could be so cruel as to come here tonight."

"Cruel?"

She finally lifted her tear-filled eyes to his. "You have no right to be here. And I don't care if you were invited by my meddling sister."

"Yes, damn it, my motives are selfish. I admit that. But I'm not here to hurt you. I needed to see you."

"Liar!" She pounded her fists into his chest, frustration and anger erupting inside of her. "Who asked you to stay away from me? Who? That was your idea!" Heather was past the point of even trying to conceal the bitterness she felt toward him.

He caressed her balled fists. "I had no choice."

"You walked out on me!" She fought to maintain her anger, her only real weapon against him.

Quinn's eyes were heavy with grief as he cupped her chin, his strong fingers prevented her from turning away. "Heather, you know why I left."

"Yes, I know. You're still in love with Cynthia's mother. And you have no room in your heart for me. That doesn't justify your being here. Your selfishness is unbelievable." Heather jerked away, unable to tolerate his touch. Her legs were so unsteady that she took advantage of the only means of support. She sat down on the bottom step, the silk dress forgotten. "Please . . . just go away. And leave me alone."

"Heather, please—just give me a chance. You've always been so generous, since the very beginning. Even after we broke up, you've been kind to my daughter. You didn't have to help her through that time while I was in the hospital. You didn't have to continue seeing her. She isn't even one of the kids you work with any longer. So please, baby, can't you be generous now? Listen to what I have to say."

"No, Quinn. You made your choice. And I've finally accepted that you don't want me. We have nothing to say to each other, Counselor."

Quinn was on shaky ground, and he knew it. She'd
spent too many months alone while he fought every feeling she aroused within him, fought them until he had no
choice but to accept them. He had no peace without her.
He had no life.

"You're wrong. I've never stopped wanting you, not
for one single second of the time we've been apart."

"You left me—" she choked out, hugging her arms
around herself, suddenly cold.

"I had to. Sweetheart, for years I've lived with a guilt
that consumed my every waking hour. Then you came
into my life and shook my foundation. I couldn't let go
of the past, yet I couldn't stop myself from reaching for
the sunshine . . . you."

Quinn slid out of his white dinner jacket. He dropped
it on her shoulders. When she tried to give it back, he
stepped out of her reach.

"Words . . . empty words. You're very good at them,
Quinn. I'll give you that."

Quinn almost laughed. Good with words? Professionally he was an expert at finding the right phrase that
would sway the jury into agreeing with him. His personal
thoughts, hopes, and dreams were left to languish inside
of him. No, he had no talent for expressing his emotions.
He hadn't ever told Peggy that he loved her, yet he had.

And now if he weren't careful, he might lose Heather
for good. His options were severely limited. He sat down
on the step beside her, careful to keep a distance between
them.

"I haven't done very well at reaching the one person
I need. I haven't been able to talk to you about my past.
This secret has been locked inside of me for years." He

sighed, nervously smoothing his mustache. "I've reached for the phone more times than I can count, hoping I could tell you all of it. I told myself that if you wound up hating me, so be it. You would know all of it."

He was afraid to look into her eyes . . . afraid of the possibility of condemnation. "I'm a coward where you're concerned, Heather. Like any man I wanted to impress you, and instead I've shown my weaknesses, my vulnerability, and an inability to cope with my personal problems." He wiped nervously at his damp brow with a handkerchief. "Sweetheart, after four months of torment, I couldn't take any more. I had to come."

"You hurt me," she whispered.

"I know. But I never meant to. When I think of how much you've helped me with Cynthia . . . how you've always been there for her—" His voice broke. "She needed you. But I also needed you. I was just too caught up in my own grief to realize it."

"You don't have to say these things."

"Yes, I do. I should have told you during the summer. I knew that I loved you then, but I still hadn't fully accepted it. I certainly hadn't come to terms with my part in Peggy's death. I was so torn inside." He sighed before saying, "I know I shouldn't have flown in for that barbecue. But Heather, you were such a temptation. I couldn't control my need for you. I know I did a lousy job of keeping my hands to myself and ended up hurting us both in the process."

Heather's heart started pounding when he said he loved her. Unable to keep quiet about her part in all of it, she said "It wasn't all your fault. I wanted you just as much as you wanted me."

"Thank you for that much," he whispered heavily.

"Nothing's changed, Quinn. I know nothing about you."

"What do you want to know?"

"Everything," she said, lifting her chin.

"My older brother Chad raised me after our parents had been killed in a car accident. I was twelve, Chad seventeen. Chad wouldn't stand for us being separated. He quit school and went to work to help support us. Chad did well." Quinn swallowed. "It wasn't until my high school graduation that I found out how my brother managed it. Chad was arrested for murder in a drug-related incident. He wasn't a bad kid, Heather. He got caught up with the wrong people."

"Quinn, I'm so sorry." She looked at him with wide troubled eyes.

"Heather, I've changed. I want to go on with my life. It's taken me close to six years, but I can finally say I have fully accepted Peggy's death."

"I'm glad for you," Heather said with genuine sincerity.

"I know you mean that," he said, taking her hand.

She allowed him to hold it, then she pulled free. She began pacing in front of him. Her black heels clicked against the concrete. Her voice was tight with bitterness when she said, "We were once on the brink of finding something very special together, then you pulled away. Now tonight you're here. I don't know what I think or feel."

"Just hear me out. Peggy and I were making love . . ." Quinn knew that he had startled Heather, but went on as matter-of-factly as he could manage. Hell, this must be worse than arguing a case before the Supreme Court. At least, his whole future wouldn't depend on the outcome.

". . . when I discovered the lumps in her breasts. She promised to see her doctor. And it wasn't much later that she finally did. Peggy was afraid of cancer. She couldn't forget that her mother had it when she was a child. In fact, Peggy's mother died of the disease. The poor woman had had a radical mastectomy and lost her husband because of it.

"Anyway, we had some terrible fights after we learned from the biopsy that her doctors recommended immediate surgery. To make a long story short, the next few weeks were pure hell for us. She refused to so much as consider the surgery, while I insisted on it."

He didn't look at Heather, he couldn't just then. "The truth is I badgered her into agreeing to the surgery. Peggy signed the consent forms only because she couldn't withstand the pressure I placed on her. If it had been left to her, she would have lived and died a whole woman."

To his horror his eyes filled with tears. Shit! Quinn was infuriated with himself. He dropped his head, struggling to regain control. He was unprepared for the soft hand Heather placed on his shoulder. He didn't look at her. He couldn't . . . not yet. But her warmth seeped through the layers of clothing separating them, providing support and understanding.

"The only reason she went through with it was to please me. Me! She died on the operating table. A perfectly healthy young woman died not from cancer, but of heart failure!"

He wanted to slam his fist into the wall. The rage was

just that keen. With difficulty he swallowed the harsh sob rising through his chest. When he was able to speak his voice was gravelly from turbulence. "For five years I've lived with grief and guilt. God knows she had a right to die the way she wanted. Surgery was never the answer for her. I understand that now. I should have listened. But I didn't."

"No. Don't you see, you fought for her the only way you knew how. There's no crime in doing what you believe to be right."

"All these years I kept thinking that if I'd just been able to convince her that I loved her, no matter what, then——" He stopped, unable to continue. After a time he said, "No matter how hard I tried, I couldn't get through to her. There was no earthly reason why she shouldn't have survived that surgery and had a complete recovery. The odds were in our favor!"

"Only one reason, Quinn. Peggy didn't want to live without her breasts."

"I know that now. It wasn't until recently that I was able to accept it. I've been living with the guilt for so long."

"But Quinn, it wasn't your fault. How long could she have lived without that surgery?"

"That's not the point. I didn't respect her last wishes." He scowled. "I had to either find a way to finally accept my part in Peggy's death, or spend the rest of my life regretting what it was too late to do a damn thing about." He paused, then cradling her cheek in his wide palm and with a finger beneath her chin, he turned her face so that he could look into her eyes. "Finally I can say I've worked my way through the self-pity and guilt. At last I can honestly say I feel I'll make it."

"I'm glad for you . . . so glad." Heather stood on tiptoe and lightly brushed her lips against his.

The simple gesture was impossible to resist. Quinn groaned deep in his throat. He pulled her into his arms and pressed his lips to hers. Her responsive kiss was not only unbelievably sweet, but also offered an underlying sense of comfort.

"I would have never made my way through this emotional maze without you, Heather. I love you. You've made the difference in my life. You've filled the empty spaces within me, sugar. Through you, I've come to realize that part of my life doesn't have to be over. Can we try again, baby? I know I've hurt you when I only meant to protect you . . . from me."

"Stop," she whispered, pressing her fingertips to his mouth. It was too much. And it was happening so fast. Feelings of disbelief and fear outweighed the hope fighting for survival inside of her. Slowly yet firmly she shook her head. "I don't see how—"

"Have your feelings changed for me?" He forced the words past the constriction in his throat.

"We're not discussing me." She took a deep breath before she said, "You say you love me—but Quinn, love involves sharing the bad as well as the good. What kind of relationship can we have if you can't talk to me? Unless you can be open with me, how am I going to know that you believe in me? How?"

For weeks she'd lived on nothing but hope that he would change his mind and give love a chance to grow. He was doing that now. And with a sinking heart, she recognized it wasn't enough. She needed to know he had absolute faith in her.

Quinn stared at her, not knowing what more she wanted from him.

"Oh, what's the use!" Heather cried in frustration. She scrambled to her feet.

Quinn was at the door ahead of her. His hand prevented her from opening it.

"No more. I can't take any more of this," she said raggedly, resting her forehead against the door's smooth surface.

"It's true, then," he whispered. "Cindy told me you were seeing some jerk who drives a Jag."

"So what? I haven't asked you who you're sleeping with these days, now have I?"

"I sleep alone. So who is he? Is he the reason you've stopped loving me?"

"His name is George Parker. He's a friend of my brother's, nothing more. Quinn, please. Let me pass. I've got to get back before the others start searching for me."

"It's not finished between us, Heather. Not by a long shot." Quinn bent his head and tasted the creaminess of her nape and bare line of her soft shoulders. His hands spanned her waist, easing her back into the cradle of his thighs. His lips traced the delicate shape of one earlobe. His voice was rough with anger, frustration, jealousy, and desire. "I won't give you up. I can't!"

Heather leaned against him. "Oh, Quinn . . ." She'd missed him desperately. Her body was sheltered, wrapped against his. "What do you want me to say?"

"Say you love me. Say that when it's time to leave tonight, we'll leave together."

"And what about Cynthia?"

"She already knows about us. In fact she's rooting for us. No more excuses. Tell me . . ."

Slowly turning and sliding her arms up his chest, she sighed. "I tried to stop, but I couldn't."

"Tell me."

"I love you."

His mouth was relentless as he claimed hers. His tongue plunged inside. It was the sweetness of her response to him that seemed to seep inside of him, warm him, ease his doubts and soothe his worries that he had taken too long too get his life back together. His mouth gentled over hers.

When he eventually lifted his head, he smiled that slow sexy smile that always made her heart pound wildly in her chest. It was no different now.

"My whole family is on the other side of that door, Quinn. What about them?"

"First we dance. Later we talk and talk and talk. Afterward I plan to make some slow, sweet love to you until the sun comes up."

Heather laughed at the sheer arrogance of the man. "You're awfully sure of yourself, aren't you?"

"Mmmm, come on, we have an anniversary to celebrate."

As Quinn escorted her back onto the dance floor, he felt lucky. She was giving him an opportunity to salvage what had begun that day in his office. That was why he'd come. Pride hadn't eased the loneliness he'd endured since their separation. Nor had pride filled his arms as perfectly as she was doing now. His blasted pride had provided no comfort in his empty bed. He'd laid night after night aching for her. He couldn't lose her!

Twenty-four

Quinn had trailed Heather home. He quickly crossed to her car. It was too dark for Heather to see him clearly, but she felt his tension.

Quinn longed to press his lips against hers. Instead he asked, "All set?"

She nodded, suppressing a quiver of excitement. The past few hours had whirled by in an exciting blur. Everyone had a wonderful time, especially her folks. Quinn being near had heightened her own pleasure. She pushed her worries aside, focusing on only one point: Quinn loved her.

But as he walked with her to the front door, he was deep in thought. He was still very much the private, self-contained man she had come to love . . . and detest. Heather never knew what he was thinking or feeling. It amazed her that he had revealed so much of himself tonight. The things he had said about Peggy, his family . . . she still couldn't believe his candor.

"I hope Cynthia doesn't feel neglected by the change in plans. She'd expected to stay with me tonight." Heather was chattering but couldn't seem to help it. Her nerves were somewhere in her throat.

Quinn surprised her when he laughed softly. "Hardly. She was tickled that we've made up. And as much as she loves you, she was thrilled by the chance to sleep over at Ericia and Angela's. I can't let her go over there every time she asks, or Gwen would end up suing me for child support."

Heather smiled, realizing she'd been holding her breath. Butterflies licked at her stomach as she wondered if he'd changed his mind. Maybe he did love—

Quinn stayed her hand as she reached for the light switch in the foyer. A low lamp had been left on in the living room. It was more than enough light . . . too much in fact. "We don't need that."

Her nerves slowly began to dissipate, replaced by a rapid jolt of sexual tension. It had been too long. Tilting her head toward him, her voice was husky with feminine longing. "Something to drink?"

He shook his head. "Can you tell how much I've missed you, sugar?"

Shivers of sweet yearning ran down her spine. "I missed you, too. The difficult time was when you were ill. Oh, Quinn, I couldn't stand not knowing how you were after you left the hospital." She caressed his cheek with a fingertip. "I hung on to Cynthia's every word, afraid you would go back to work too soon or you wouldn't follow the doctor's orders by staying on your diet. Oh, honey . . ." She traced the shape of his mouth.

He eyed the sexy little mole at the corner of her rose-tinted lips. "Marry me, Heather," he whispered.

Startled caramel eyes met dark gray eyes. "Are you sure?"

"Yes . . . I love you. I want you."

She wanted to laugh . . . to cry. She did neither. She'd been so afraid of his quietness. She'd been thinking . . . She wasn't even sure what she'd been thinking.

"Quinn . . ." She breathed the sound into his mouth, her soft lips and warm tongue welcoming him. Quinn drank deeply. Her mouth was hot and sweet as honey, her fleshy lips so soft, so lush. But he'd been without for too damn long. He had to have Heather . . . now.

"Make love to me, Quinn," she moaned breathlessly, inhaling his masculine scent. She laced her arms around his neck, loving the hard male feel of his body. "I need you . . . now."

He felt as if his entire body was pulsating with a primitive force too powerful to be ignored. He shuddered with anticipation as he swung Heather up into his arms. He felt like an ageless African warrior—proud, strong, invincible—with his woman in his arms.

He didn't let her down until they'd reached her bedroom. He realized his hands were trembling as her body slid down against his.

When she went to turn off the bedside lamp, he said, "Leave it on." His voice was gravelly with desire. "I want to look at you. I want to see your face when I'm inside of you." He chuckled at her blush, thrilled by it. He kissed her smooth cheeks.

She watched in fascination as he removed his clothes. His eyes smoldered with unrestrained passion as he watched her watching him. By the time Quinn moved to Heather, his sex was full and high.

"Pretty girl." He kissed her over and over again. "It's been too long . . . too long." His large warm hands quickly removed her clothes. He felt as if he were unwrapping a priceless treasure, each layer bringing him closer to his heaven on earth.

Heather was weak with need by the time he held her in his arms, her soft breasts pillowed against his bare chest. She could feel the rhythm of his heart from where her cheek rested over the swell of his breastbone.

"I'm sorry, baby," he whispered, lowering his head. "I never meant to put you through the kind of hell I've put you through these last few months. I never meant to hurt you." He placed a series of kisses along her collarbone and soft shoulders. "Forgive me—"

"Yes—" Her lips were crushed beneath his. Heather forgot what she was about to say. She concentrated on loving her man. Nothing mattered but him.

When she rubbed the throbbing tips of her breasts against him, Quinn groaned, thrusting his tongue into the honeyed depths of her mouth. His boldness was richly rewarded as she returned the caress, suckling on his tongue.

Soft, husky sounds poured from deep inside her throat as she responded to his urgency. He was right. It had been too long since they had loved each other. This time there could be no doubt about the loving. With her need every bit as acute as his, Heather buried her small oval nails into his muscular shoulders, raking them down his spine.

Quinn loved it, just as he loved her. He couldn't move from her lips. He feasted within the warmth of her mouth, stroking then savoring her tongue. When he raised his head to look at her, he marveled at her beauty. Her warmth and generosity floored him. Words suddenly failed him. His eyes told her everything she needed to know about his love for her.

With a flick of a strong wrist, comforter, blankets, top sheet, and pillows went tumbling to the floor. Soon his heated dark brown flesh glided against her soft molten-gold flesh. He kissed skin smoother and softer than the finest satin. His mouth loved her from the hollow at the base of her delicately boned throat down to the petal softness of her inner thighs and slender feet.

Heather moaned in delight, deciding wildly that her whole body was one huge erogenous zone. When Quinn warmed Heather with the wet rough velvet of his tongue, she stopped thinking altogether. Every curvy centimeter of her petite length was privy to the brush of his thick black mustache and the heat of his mouth. She never felt more loved or cherished.

"It's been so damn long . . ." he grumbled into the sensitive valley between her breasts as he licked their fleshy underside. "Touch me, please."

"Yes . . . oh, yes," she managed in a soft voice filled with passion.

She caressed his smooth chest, focusing on tantalizing his ebony nipples with her fingertips. Quinn quivered in reaction as she worried the nipple, quaking from the pleasure as she laved him with her wet, wonderfully hot mouth. Heather ever so slowly drew circles around his nipple with her tongue, further inflaming his senses. He was gasping for breath when she kissed the scar on his stomach, then licked it. When her lips neared dense black hair, he grabbed her, pulling her up to him.

"I can't take much more." His mouth devoured hers. But Heather had a mind of her own. She intended to give him all he could take and then some. While he kissed her, her hands caressed his manhood. She moved her hands up and down his erection, caressing the broad tip repeatedly.

Quinn groaned hotly. Knowing he was fast approaching his limit and having no intentions of cheating either of them, he lifted her hands to his mouth. He placed a kiss in each soft palm. Then his mouth settled on hers as he covered her body with his.

He chuckled with pure masculine arrogance when she lifted her damp heat against his erection. "You're ready, aren't you, sweetheart."

There was no need for confirmation. The heaviness of her lids, the elongated tips of her breasts, all spoke of her readiness. He didn't tease her . . . he couldn't. His lean fingers played briefly in the dewy curls between her soft thighs. He wanted her so badly, he hurt from the wanting. His control was practically nonexistent as his blood pounded feverishly inside his veins.

But this wasn't about sexual gratification. What they shared was much much more. He loved her the way only a man in love could love his woman . . . thoroughly. He fingered her slick feminine folds, circling the highly sensitive nub that seemed to be waiting for his caress. Quinn gave Heather the firm pressure she craved.

She cried out, "Quinn . . . now. I can't wait."

"Take me," he grunted against her neck, his body a mass of barely contained desire.

Heather guided him to her moist heat. She wrapped her limbs around him and sobbed his name over and over again.

"Yes . . ." he said with a ragged sigh. His eyes were

tightly closed as he slowly absorbed the absolute pleasure of being inside Heather. "I love you."

Her heart overflowed with the joy. But she knew he was holding back a vital part of himself and she wouldn't tolerate it. "Please . . ." She instinctively tightened inner, muscles. "I want all of you."

Busy tonguing that delicately scented place behind her ear, he answered, "I don't want to hurt you, baby. You're so small. It's been a while since we've been together."

But Heather couldn't think of denying either of them full pleasure. She moved sensuously beneath him. Quinn was powerless to resist her. She was so deliciously hot that he couldn't fight her and his own need to possess every sweet inch of her. He clenched his jaw as he slowly filled her. She sighed her pleasure and rewarded him with wet kisses along his jawline and the thick cord of his neck—any and every part of him that she could reach.

He sipped from her mouth, then licked each of her nipples in turn before he began thrusting deeply within her. She gasped his name until his name was an indistinguishable breathless moan. She welcomed the hard, long, sweep of his manhood . . . tantalizing her . . . mesmerizing her. Over and over again she matched him thrust for sizzling hot thrust. Passion flared out of control.

"Tell me," he demanded through his teeth, his body drenched in perspiration.

"I love you." She gasped aloud as she gave everything that was within her power to give and accepted no less from him. They came together . . . shuddering and convulsing in an earth-shattering climax. Finally they were able to savor the wonder that was their love.

Neither was able to speak for some time. Heather lay across him, her head tucked under his chin, her full breasts filling the concave hardness of his stomach, her legs resting between his muscular thighs.

"I love you."

Quinn quirked a black brow. "It's about time! I've been waiting all night to hear you say it."

"But I did—"

"Not without prompting. You were so far gone you don't know what you said."

Heather laughed, snuggling closer.

"Are you still sorry you ever met me?"

"No!" she denied, caressing him. "I should never have said it."

"You were upset—and with good reason."

"This time will be different, won't it, Quinn?"

"Yes, I promise you." Resting his chin on her head, his voice was filled with disgust as he said, "I've wasted so much time. It wasn't until I thought I had lost you that I sought outside help."

"Outside help?"

"Mmmm, I made an appointment with Greg Martin, Peggy's doctor. He went over her case with me. I also had a long talk with Elaine. It's taken me a while, but I've come to accept my role in all of this."

"It wasn't your fault. You weren't responsible for Peggy's death."

"Heather, I think I'll always feel some responsibility for it. But at least now I know what really happened. Peggy knew about those lumps in her breasts long before I found them. She told Elaine, but she didn't tell me.

Nor did she see her doctor. She made her choice before I knew there was even a problem."

"Peggy told Elaine? But why didn't Elaine tell you?" Heather said in disbelief. "How could Elaine keep this from you?"

Quinn smiled. "You have to admit I haven't been exactly open to any kind of discussions about Peggy. Elaine was Peggy's best friend. She promised Peggy that she'd never tell me about the lumps. But she told me when I asked. And she seemed relieved."

"I see."

"Problem was with me. I pushed everyone close to me away. But it was my daughter who suffered the most. If it weren't for you, I would have lost her."

"No, Quinn. That's not true. Cynthia is thrilled to have her father back." Heather pressed her mouth to the hollow at the base of his throat. "The pain of keeping it locked inside for so long must have been horrible."

Quinn shivered from the brief contact, automatically tightening his hold on her, his right hand caressing the graceful lines of her back.

"I was so lost in guilt and self-pity that not even my child could reach me. You made me realize just what I was doing."

"It's behind you, sweetheart. You and Cynthia are closer now than you've ever been before. You didn't lose her."

His gaze settled on Heather's soft mouth.

"Have you been able to talk to her about her mother?"

"Yes. I'm surprised she hasn't told you about it. She seems to tell you everything these days," he said, humor sparkling his eyes.

"And how did she take it?"

"What you want to know is how much does she know, and does she blame me, as I've blamed myself, all these years." Quinn hesitated, tracing her soft mouth with a fingertip. "Heather, I got so tired of the secrets. I told her everything," he admitted, before saying, "and she took it much better than I'd hoped."

"She's a great kid."

Quinn couldn't agree more. His fingers threaded through Heather's braided hair. When he spoke his voice wasn't quite as carefree as he would have liked. "So when are you going to make an honest man out of me?"

"That depends . . ." she whispered, her eyes downcast.

He frowned. "On what?"

"On you," she said. "I love you, but I think we should wait. Give ourselves a little time."

"Time for what? We haven't been together in months. I've already spent too many nights without you. I should think you would be fed up with waiting for me to get my head together."

"Quinn, we don't need to rush into marriage."

"And how long do you think we need to decide if we're right for each other?"

"Maybe six months, possibly a year."

"No!" Quinn exploded, setting her away from him. "You can't be serious! Wait an entire year to be together?" He stared at her for a time before he got up. He paced in front of the bed, oblivious to his nudity. "Why, baby?" he demanded, trying not to show the hurt he was feeling.

She dropped her head, thoughtful. She wasn't trying to make him angry, but she had to be sure. "It's not as if we can't be together." She propped herself up against the headboard, her legs tucked under her.

"I know being a stepmother won't be easy, especially to a teenager who has had some serious problems," he said, half to himself, as he pushed a trembling hand over his short natural.

"You know as well as I do that Cynthia isn't the problem. Quinn, it's too soon."

"For whom, Heather? Me or you?"

"I think you need more time to come to terms with all your feelings about Peggy. I know how much you loved her. It's difficult to let go. I think you need to say goodbye without me interfering. Later we can make a fresh start together."

He swore bitterly. "No, Heather. I've been in hell for over five years!" He paced. He finally stopped, sitting on the window seat. His brown length was dark and appealing against the pale peach cushions.

Finally he said with difficulty, "After we broke up last summer, I knew I needed help in order to put the past behind me. So I started working with Dr. Johnson on getting through the grief." He watched her closely when he said. "I loved Peggy, Heather. She mothered my child. But she's dead. I'm ready to go on with my life. Maybe you'll be taking a risk if you accept . . ."

Heather went to him and put her arms around his waist, squeezing him tight. "I'm so glad you told me."

"Me, too. From now on everything is out in the open between us," he promised, lifting her chin so he could see her face. "Life is a gamble, sweetheart. Heather, I want you to be my wife."

"I want that, too. But I couldn't stand it if we married and later you came to regret it. I couldn't! I want for always, Quinn."

"You've got it with me, Pretty girl. I'm ready to make a total commitment to you. And I want the same from you. In my book that means marriage and pretty brown babies."

Whatever she had been about to say was smothered beneath the onslaught of his mouth.

"Marry me now," he said with a moan, "I need you so badly." His mouth moved insistently over hers, his tongue boldly staking his claim. He sighed with pleasure as she bit his bottom lip, sharp sweet little bites that aroused him.

"I should never have kissed you." He ran his stubbled cheek against the valley between her breasts. He gave each plump nipple a soft licking. "I can't get enough of you."

She smiled, her soft mouth swollen from his kisses. It was foolish to let the risk involved overshadow the love she felt for him and Cynthia.

Her eyes shimmered like semiprecious stones. Quinn waited, his mouth a hairsbreadth away from hers. Their fingers were laced.

"Heather . . ."

"Is next month too soon?" she laughed. She quivered from the force of her emotions and his scalding kisses as they rained over her face, her neck and throat, then came to pay homage at her sweet lips.

"Heather . . ." Quinn said, his voice thick with a mixture of joy, love, and relief.

Her eyes locked with his. "I love you with all my heart."

His full mouth lifted in a confident grin. "December wedding . . . a small family affair." He brushed aside the damp braids clinging to her neck as he kissed her throat.

"How did you know?"

"That it's important to you to have Cynthia and your entire family at our wedding?"

Heather nodded, eyes brimming with tears, too choked up with happiness to speak.

"Gwen told me about your dream."

Heather's eyes went wide.

"Don't be angry. She felt sorry for me."

Heather giggled, deciding then and there that she was going to have to thank her meddling sister for interfering.

"Interested in honeymooning in Egypt? Cruising the Nile?"

"Oh, Quinn . . ."

"I'll make you happy, my precious love. I promise. And I intend to show you just how much you mean to me each day of our lives together. Each day . . ." Quinn's voice trailed off as his kisses began.

About the Author

Bette grew up in Saginaw, Michigan. She graduated from Central State University in Wilberforce, Ohio. She began her teaching career in Detroit and completed her Master's degree from Wayne State University. She is currently teaching in the HeadStart program for the Detroit Public Schools. She is thrilled about the release of her first novel, FOR ALWAYS, and looking forward to hearing from readers. You may write her at P.O. Box 625, Warren, MI 48090-0625.

PUT SOME FANTASY IN YOUR LIFE—
FANTASTIC ROMANCES FROM PINNACLE

TIME STORM   (728, $4.99)
by Rosalyn Alsobrook
Modern-day Pennsylvanian physician JoAnn Griffin only believed
what she could feel with her five senses. But when, during a freak
storm, a blinding flash of lightning sent her back in time to 1889,
JoAnn realized she had somehow crossed the threshold into another century and was now gazing into the smoldering eyes of a
startlingly handsome stranger. JoAnn had stumbled through a rip
in time . . . and into a love affair so intense, it carried her to a point
of no return!

SEA TREASURE   (790, $4.50)
by Johanna Hailey
When Michael, a dashing sea captain, is rescued from drowning by
a beautiful sea siren—he does not know yet that she's actually a
mermaid. But her breathtaking beauty stirred irresistible yearnings
in Michael. And soon fate would drive them across the treacherous
Caribbean, tossing them on surging tides of passion that tran-
scended two worlds!

ONCE UPON FOREVER   (883, $4.99)
by Becky Lee Weyrich
A moonstone necklace and a mysterious diary written over a century ago were Clair Summerland's only clues to her true identity.
Two men loved her—one, a dashing civil war hero . . . the other, a
daring jet pilot. Now Clair must risk her past and future for a passion that spans two worlds—and a love that is stronger than time
itself.

SHADOWS IN TIME   (892, $4.50)
by Cherlyn Jac
Driving through the sultry New Orleans night, one moment Tori's
car spins out of control; the next she is in a horse-drawn carriage
with the handsomest man she has ever seen—who calls her wife—-
but whose eyes blaze with fury. Sent back in time one hundred
years, Tori is falling in love with the man she is apparently trying to
kill. Now she must race against time to change the tragic past and
claim her future with the man she will love through all eternity!

*Available wherever paperbacks are sold, or order direct from the
Publisher. Send cover price plus 50¢ per copy for mailing and handling to Penguin USA, P.O. Box 999, c/o Dept. 17109, Bergenfield, NJ 07621. Residents of New York and Tennessee must
include sales tax. DO NOT SEND CASH.*